The Entailed Hat

The Entailed Hat

or
Patty Cannon's Times

George Alfred Townsend

"Gath"

Edited and Illustrated by

Hal Roth

Nanticoke Books
Vienna, Maryland

Copyright © 2000 by Nanticoke Books

Printed and bound in the United States of America by Victor Graphics

ISBN 0-9647694-3-3

Published by Nanticoke Books, Vienna, Maryland 21869

First Printing—March, 2000

Books by Hal Roth:

Conversations in a Country Store
Reminiscing on Maryland's Eastern Shore (1995)
Second Printing (1997)

You Can't Never Get to Puckum
Folks and Tales from Delmarva (1997)

The Monster's Handsome Face
Patty Cannon in Fiction and Fact (1998)

You Still Can't Get to Puckum
More Folks and Tales from Delmarva (2000)

This edition of *The Entailed Hat* is dedicated to the memory of Dr. Jerry Shields—scholar, writer, friend—who is pictured reading from a first edition in "Cowgill House," now Woodburn, home of Delaware's governor.

Contents

vii .... Dedication
viii .... Contents
x .... Illustrations
xiii .... Acknowledgments
xv .... Foreword
xix .... Introduction
xxiii .... Original Dedication
1 .... Chapter 1–Two Hat Wearers
6 .... Chapter 2–Judge and Daughter
13 .... Chapter 3–The Foresters
17 .... Chapter 4–Discovery of the Heirloom
22 .... Chapter 5–The Bog Ore Tract
28 .... Chapter 6–The Custises Ruined
34 .... Chapter 7–Jack-o'-lantern Iron
38 .... Chapter 8–The Hat Finds a Rack
55 .... Chapter 9–Ha! Ha! The Wooing On't
65 .... Chapter 10–Master in the Kitchen
70 .... Chapter 11–Dying Pride
79 .... Chapter 12–Princess Anne Folks
97 .... Chapter 13–Shadow of the Tile
103 .... Chapter 14–Meshach's Home
122 .... Chapter 15–The Kidnapper
131 .... Chapter 16–Bell-crown Man
142 .... Chapter 17–Sabbath and Canoe
153 .... Chapter 18–Under an Old Bonnet
166 .... Chapter 19–The Dusky Levels
172 .... Chapter 20–Caste Without Tone
188 .... Chapter 21–Long Separations
206 .... Chapter 22–Nanticoke People
212 .... Chapter 23–Twiford's Island
224 .... Chapter 24–Old Chimneys
233 .... Chapter 25–Patty Cannon's
248 .... Chapter 26–Van Dorn

261............ Chapter 27–Cannon's Ferry
277............ Chapter 28–Pacification
280............ Chapter 29–Beginning of the Raid
285............ Chapter 30–Africa
292............ Chapter 31–Peach Blush
307............ Chapter 32–Garter Snakes
318............ Chapter 33–Honeymoon
323............ Chapter 34–The Ordeal
333............ Chapter 35–Cowgill House
342............ Chapter 36–Two Whigs
349............ Chapter 37–Spirits of the Past
361............ Chapter 38–Virgie's Flight
371............ Chapter 39–Virgie's Flight, Cont.
386............ Chapter 40–Hulda Beleaguered
394............ Chapter 41–Aunt Patty's Last Trick
404............ Chapter 42–Beaks
408............ Chapter 43–Pleasure Drained
415............ Chapter 44–The Death of Patty Cannon
429............ Chapter 45–The Judge Remarried
438............ Chapter 46–The Curse of the Hat
441............ Chapter 47–Failure and Restitution

Illustrations

Front Cover—Nassawango Iron Furnace
Back Cover—Teackle Hall

vii	Dr. Jerry Shields
xxi	George Alfred Townsend
5	Somerset County Courthouse
16	Nassawango Iron Furnace
27	Bog Ore Carts at Nassawango Furnace
78	Washington Tavern
82	Teackle Hall
83	St. Andrew's Episcopal Church
84	Teackle Graves
109	View across the Manokin River Bridge
123	Manokin Presbyterian Church
125	Manokin River
144	Deal Island Beach
147	Joshua Thomas Chapel
199	St. Paul's (Spring Hill) Episcopal Church
201	Mason Dixon Cornerstone
203	Mardela (Barren Creek) Mineral Springs
205	Vienna on the Nanticoke River
216	Site of Twiford's Wharf
234	Site of Joe Johnson's Tavern
254	Site of Patty Cannon's House
273	Woodland (Cannon's) Ferry and Cannon Hall
286	View from Federalsburg River Crossing
295	Barratt's Chapel
297	Delaware State Capitol
298	State Offices on Dover Square
303	Tavern on Dover Square
334	Woodburn (Cowgill House)
339	Rear View of Woodburn (Cowgill House)

340 . . . . . . The Chancellor's House
345 . . . . . . Chesapeake and Delaware Canal
347 . . . . . . Chesapeake and Delaware Canal
354 . . . . . . Kingston Hall
355 . . . . . . Rehoboth Presbyterian Church
357 . . . . . . Ruins of Coventry Episcopal Church
362 . . . . . . Makemie Memorial Presbyterian Church
363 . . . . . . All Hallows Episcopal Church
374 . . . . . . Cape Henlopen Breakwater
427 . . . . . . Sussex County Courthouse
428 . . . . . . The Chancellor's Grave
442 . . . . . . The Cannon Graves

With the exception of the photographs of the author, George Alfred Townsend, and Dr. Jerry Shields, all illustrations show sites mentioned in the novel as they appeared in 1999 or 2000, nearly two centuries after the incidents portrayed.

The photograph of George Alfred Townsend appears through the courtesy of the Maryland Department of Natural Resources.

All other photographs were taken by Hal Roth.

Acknowledgments

Elsie Smith and I once worked together in the often rewarding, often frustrating business of public education. When I heard that Elsie had retired, I said, "Well now, I can't let her get too comfortable too quickly," and called to ask if she would proofread and comment on my edited edition of *The Entailed Hat.* She agreed to do so, and I thank her for her many hours of reading and telephone conferencing which have made the product you hold in your hand better than it otherwise would have been. If you find errors or rough spots, it is probably because I did not listen to her advice.

The print of the Entailed Hat which appears on the title page and with each chapter heading has been borrowed from the 1954 edition by Tidewater Publishers.

                                                                Hal Roth

Foreword

For over a century now, those who inquire as to the best source of information about Patty Cannon and her gang are often directed to *The Entailed Hat* by "Gath."

That peculiar pen name was apparently suggested by a verse in Samuel: "Tell it not to Gath," a term which includes the initials of the author, George Alfred Townsend. When asked one evening in the lobby of the old Purnell Hotel in Snow Hill on Maryland's Eastern Shore to explain the *nom de plume*, Townsend replied, "'G' is for George, 'A' is for Alfred, 'T' is for Townsend, and 'H' is where I'm going when I die."

Townsend was born in Georgetown, Delaware, on January 30, 1841, almost twelve years after Patty Cannon died in that town's jail and the same year in which the *Narrative and Confessions of Lucretia Cannon*, a melodramatic and mostly fictitious account of Patty's life, was published. His father was a carpenter and itinerant Methodist preacher, who later in life practiced medicine. As a result of his father's various callings, Townsend lived in a dozen towns on Delmarva and traveled the peninsula extensively in his early years. Later, preparing to write his first novel, he visited the town of Reliance, saw the tavern and Patty's home before the buildings were remodeled or razed, had personal contact with individuals who had known Patty Cannon and the gang of cutthroats, and was able to collect, among other information, accurate physical descriptions of the participants. As far as can be determined, names of mob members used throughout the story are those of actual individuals.

Townsend became a reporter for the *Inquirer* in Philadelphia and then for the *Herald* and *World* in New York. His coverage of the last battles of the Civil War and the assassination of President Lincoln brought him national recognition. After reporting the Austro-Prussian War, he settled in Washington, DC, where he became a syndicated columnist and began to sign his articles "Gath."

Gathland Park, near Burkittsville, Maryland, contains one of the five homes Townsend built there for his family and guests as well as a huge stone arch he erected as a tribute to both Union and Confederate writers and artists who reported the Civil War. It is the only monument dedicated to war correspondents in the world.

In 1891, in an interview published in *Lippincott's Monthly Magazine*, Townsend explained that he had planned early in life to write a series of American historical novels. "I found my fortieth birthday approaching," he related, "and nothing achieved. Nearly in despair, I sat down and wrote *The Entailed Hat*, which consumed a considerable part of two years."

In his pamphlet, *The Infamous Patty Cannon in History and Legend* (1990), Jerry Shields reported having been told that Harper & Brothers had quickly withdrawn the first edition because of objections from some prominent families in Maryland and Delaware and then, after modifications were made, republished it later in 1884 in the form we know. If such an edition existed, it would be a valuable collectors' item today. I contacted several rare book dealers and experts and asked if they had ever heard of such an issue. None had, and all considered the possibility to be remote.

When I questioned Shields about the rumor, he said he had been told of someone in possession of such a volume, "But I borrowed the book, checked it thoroughly against the edition I had, and found there was no difference. What I have learned," Shields told me, "is that Townsend made cuts himself and obviously avoided calling certain key names of prominent families, but gave enough evidence so that if you were really interested, you could find out who they were."

In the *Lippincott's* interview, Townsend is quoted as saying, "It [*The Entailed Hat*] had to be cut down by the publishers to get it within commercial paying space." Having to sacrifice portions of his work, the author complained, "affected me almost like the death of my children."

The Entailed Hat's popularity is evident in the fact that it has been reprinted several times over the years and has become a classic in the Chesapeake Bay region. More than anything else he wrote, Townsend's novel claimed for its author some of the literary immortality he had sought. Townsend died in 1914.

John A. Munroe once described *The Entailed Hat* as a "remarkable book" and called it "Delaware's expiation for the sins that accompanied slavery." Some might disagree with the latter evaluation, but few have ever challenged Gath's literary achievement.

I have recognized that Townsend had access to whatever records existed in his lifetime and also to people who actually knew Patty

Cannon and her associates. As a scrupulous and respected reporter who was fortified with an abundance of experience, we can be certain of his interest in truth and accuracy. What we cannot always know is where in *The Entailed Hat* its creator crossed the line between fact and invention.

To alter another artist's work will always border on arrogance, and some will consider it nothing less than blasphemy that I have dared to tinker with an icon such as *The Entailed Hat*. Indeed, the kindest of several critics used the terms "audacious" and "imprudent" to describe the project even before the printer and binder had completed their labors. Others, however, have encouraged an edition containing a text which is more acceptable to the modern reader. I understand both views.

While modifying spelling, punctuation, and often the structure of sentences and paragraphs to hopefully make them more appealing and smooth flowing, I have striven to retain as much as possible of the flavor of Townsend's writing style. I hope I am not being overly presumptuous to believe that he would make most of the changes himself if he were writing the book today.

As I believe *The Entailed Hat*'s dialogue accurately reflects the language of the period and thereby contributes immeasurably to our understanding and the reading experience, it has essentially been retained intact. Some will complain about having to interpret what may, in places, be unfamiliar dialect, but that is the very essence of the people as they were, and I believe that Townsend, in addition to presenting much historical truth and tradition here, has also attentively employed the regional vernacular of the early nineteenth century.

Hal Roth
Vienna, Maryland
January, 2000

Introduction

Once the author awoke to a painful reflection that he knew no place well, though his occupation had taken him to many, and that, after twenty-five years of describing localities and society, he would be identified with none.

"Where shall I begin to rove within confines?" he asked, feeling the vacant spaces in his nature: the want of all those birds, forest trees, household habits, weeds, instincts of the brooks, and tints and tones of the local species which lie in some neighborhood's compass and complete the pastoral mind.

Numerous districts rose up and contended together, each attractive from some striking scene or bold contrast or lovely face, and wiser policy might have led his inclinations to one of these, redundant, perhaps, in wealth or literary appreciation. Yet the heart began to turn, as in first love or vagrancy almost as sweet, to the little, lowly region where his short childhood was lived and where the unknown generations of his people darkened the sand—the peninsula between the Chesapeake and the Delaware.

Far down this peninsula lies the old town of Snow Hill on the border of Virginia. There the pilgrim entered the courthouse and asked to see an early book of wills. In it he turned to the name of a maternal ancestor of whom grand tales had been told him by an aged relative. His breath was almost taken by finding the following provisions, dated February 12, 1800.

> I give and bequeath to my son, Ralph Milbourn, my BEST HAT, TO HIM AND HIS ASSIGNEES FOREVER, and no more of my estate.
>
> I give to Thomas Milbourn my small iron kettle, my brandy still, all my hand-irons, my pot-rack, and fifteen pounds bond that he gave to my daughter, Grace Milbourn.

The next day a doctor took the author on his rounds through "the Forest," as a neighboring tract was almost too invidiously called, and through a deserted iron-furnace village almost of the date of these wills.

Everywhere he went, the Entailed Hat seemed to the stranger in the land of his forefathers to appear in the vistas, as if some odd, reverend, avoided being was wearing it down the defiles of time. Now like Hester Prynne wearing her Scarlet Letter, and now like Gaston in his Iron Mask, this being took both sexes and different characters as the author weighed the probabilities of its existence. At last he began to know it and started to portray it in a little tale.

The story broke from its confines as his own family generation had broken from that forest and sought a larger hemisphere. Yet, wherever the mystic Hat proceeded, his truant fancy had also been led by his mother's hand.

Often she had told him of old Patty Cannon and her kidnapper's den and her death in the jail of his native town. He found the legend of that dreaded woman had strengthened instead of having faded with time, her haunts preserved, and eyewitnesses of her deeds to be still living.

Hence this romance has much local truth in it. It is not only the narration of an episode but the story of a large region comprehending three state jurisdictions and also of that period when modern life arose upon the ruins of old colonial caste.

George Alfred Townsend at Gathland,
his mountain-top estate in Maryland

To

Judge George P. Fisher
of Delaware

and

Hon. John A. J. Creswell
of Maryland

Lovers of Old Times

Welcomers of the New Era

∞

"Friends! Trust not the heart of that man for whom
Old Clothes are not venerable."

—Carlyle: *Sartor Resartus*

Two Hat Wearers

Chapter 1

Princess Anne, as its royal name implies, is an old seat of justice and gentle-minded town on the Eastern Shore. The ancient county of Somerset had been divided many years before the Revolutionary War and its courts separated. The original courthouse faded from the world, and the forest pines have concealed its site.

Two new towns arose and still flourish around the original records gathered into their plain brick offices, and he would be a forgetful visitor in Princess Anne who would not say it had the better society.

He would get assurances of this from the best people living there, and yet more solemn assurances from the two venerable churches, Presbyterian and Episcopalian, whose gravestones, upright, recumbent, or in family rows, in epitaphs Latinized, poetical, or pious say, "*We* belonged to the society of Princess Anne." That, at least, is the impression left on the visitor as he wanders amid their myrtle and creeper or receives the bows of the lawyers and their clients on the wide, loamy streets.

There were but two eccentric men living in Princess Anne in the early half of our century, and both of them were identified by their hats. The first of these was Jack Wonnell, a poor fellow of some remote origin who had once attended an auction and bought a quarter gross of beaver hats. Although that happened years before our story opens, and the fashions had changed, Jack produced a new hat from the stock no oftener than when he had well worn its predecessor. At the rate of two hats a year, he was very slowly extinguishing the store. Like most people who frequent auctions, he was not provident, except in hats, and presented a startling appearance in his patched and shrunken raiment whenever he mounted a bright new tile and took to the sidewalk. His name in all grades of society had become "Bell-crown."

The other eccentric citizen was the subject of a real mystery and even more burlesque. He wore a hat which was more than a century old with a tall, steeple crown and stiff, wavy brim, nearly twice as high as the high hats of these days. It had been rubbed and recovered and cleaned and straightened until its grotesque appearance was infinitely increased. If the wearer had walked out of the court of King James I directly into our times and presence, he could not have produced a more singular effect.

He did not wear this hat on every occasion, nor every day, but always on Sabbaths and holidays, funeral or corporate celebrations, certain English church days, and whenever he wore the remainder of his extra suit, which was likewise of the genteel, shabby kind and terminated by greenish gaiters, the counterpart in color of the hat.

Meshach Milburn, or "Steeple-top," was a penurious, grasping, hardly social man of neighborhood origin. His family was generally unsuccessful and undistinguished and said to be dying out for so many years that it seemed to be always a remnant, yet never quite gone.

He alone of the Milburns had lifted himself out of the forest region of Somerset and settled in the town. By silence, frugality, hard bargaining, and, finally, by money lending, he had become a person of unknown means—himself almost unknown.

He was ostensibly a merchant or storekeeper and did deal in various kinds of things, keeping no clerk or attendant but a Negro named Samson, who knew as little about his mind and affections as the rest of the town. Samson's business was to clean and produce the mysterious hat, which he knew to be required every time he saw his master shave.

As soon as the lather cup and hone were agitated, Samson went, without inquiry, into a big green chest in the bedroom over the old wooden store and drew the steeple-crown out of a leather hatbox, where Meshach Milburn always sacredly replaced it himself. Then "Samson Hat," as the boys called him, exercised his brush vigorously and put the queer old headgear in as formal shape as possible. Periodically he attended to its rehabilitation through the medium of the village hatter, never leaving the shop until the tile had been repaired and suffering none whatever to handle it except the mechanic. In addition to this, Samson cooked his master's food and performed rough work around the store, but had no other known qualification for a confidential servant except his bodily power.

He was now old, probably sixty, but still a most formidable pugilist, and he had caught, running afoot, the last wild deer in the county. Though not a drinking man, Samson Hat never let a year pass without having a personal battle with some young, willing, and powerful Negro. His physical and mental system seemed to require some such periodical indulgence, and he measured every Negro who came to town solely in the light of his prowess. At the appearance of some Herculean or clean-chested athlete, Samson's eye would kindle, his smile start up, and his friendly salutation would be: "You're a *good* man! 'Most as good as me!" He was never whipped, rumor said, but by an inoffensive black class leader whom he challenged and compelled to fight.

"Befo' God, man, I never see you befo'. I'se jined de church. I kint fight. I never didn't do it!"

"Can't help it, brother," answered Samson. "You're too good a man to go froo Somerset County. Square off or you'll ketch it!"

"Den if I must, I must! May de Lord forgive me!" And after a tremendous battle the class leader came off nearly conqueror.

Whenever Samson indulged his gladiatorial propensities, he disappeared into the forest whence he came. Being a free man of mental independence equal to his nerve, he merely waited in his lonely cabin until Meshach Milburn sent him word to return. Then silently the old Negro resumed his place, looked contrition, took the few bitter, overbearing words of his master, and brushed the ancient hat.

Meshach kept him respectably dressed but paid him no wages. The Negro had what he wanted, but wanted little. On more than one occasion the court had imposed penalties on Samson's breaches of the peace, and he lay in jail, unsolicitous and proud, until Meshach Milburn paid the fine, which he did grudgingly, for money was Meshach's sole pursuit, and he spent nothing upon himself.

Without a vice, Meshach Milburn appeared to have no emotion and hardly a virtue. He had neither pity nor curiosity, visitors nor friends, professions nor apologies. Two or three times he had been summoned on a jury. Each time he put on his best suit and his steeple-crown and formally went through the task. Wearing the ancient tile, he attended the Episcopal worship every Sunday and great holiday, often drawing more audience than the sermon. He gave a small sum of money and took a cheap pew, and from his prayer book read many admonitions he did not follow.

He was not litigious, but there was no evading the perfectness of his contracts. His large, searching, hazel eyes, almost proud and quite unkindly, and his Indian-like hair were the leading elements of a face not large, but appearing so, as if the buried will of some long frivolous family had been restored and concentrated in this man and had given a bilious power to his brows and jaws and glances.

The boys hooted his hat, and the little girls often joined in, crying, "Steeple-top! He's got it on! Meshach's loose!"

He paid no attention to anybody until once some carousing fellows hired Jack Wonnell to walk up to him and ask to swap a new bell-crown for the old, decrepit steeple-top. Looking Wonnell sternly in the face, Meshach hissed, "You miserable vagrant! Nature meant you to go bareheaded. Beware when you speak to me again."

"I was afraid of him," Jack said afterwards. "He seemed to have a loaded pistol in each eye."

No incident beyond indiscriminate ridicule was recorded of this hat except once, when a group of little children in front of Judge Custis's house began to whisper and titter. One, the judge's daughter and bolder than the rest, gravely walked up to the unsocial man. It was the first of May, and he was in his best suit.

"Sir," she said, "may I put a rose in your old hat?"

The harsh man looked down at the queenly child, standing straight and slender with an expression of composure and courtesy on her face. He then looked up and over the judge's residence to see if any mischievous or presuming person had prompted this act. No one was in sight, and the other children had run away.

"Why do you offer me a flower?" he said, but with no tenderness.

"Because I thought such a very old hat might improve with a rose."

He hesitated a minute. The little girl, as if wellborn, received his strong stare steadily. He took off the venerable old head gear and put it in the pretty maid's hand. She fixed a white rose to it, and he placed the hat again on his head and took a small piece of gold from his pocket.

"Will you take this?"

"My father will not let me, sir."

Meshach Milburn replaced the coin and said nothing else, but walked down the street amid more than the usual simpering and closed the weather-beaten door of the rickety little storehouse behind him.

Somerset County Courthouse in Princess Anne

Judge and Daughter

Chapter 2

Judge Custis was the most important man in the county. He belonged to the oldest colonial family of distinction, the Custises of Northampton, whose fortune, beginning with King Charles II and his tavern credits in Rotterdam, ended in endowing Colonel George Washington with a widow's mite. The judge at Princess Anne was the most handsome man, the father of the finest family of sons and daughters, the best in estate, most various in knowledge, and the most convivial of the Custises.

In that region of the Eastern Shore where there is so little diversity of productions, Judge Custis had an exaggerated reputation as a mineralogist. He had begun to manufacture iron out of the bog ores found in the swamps and hummocks of a neighboring district, and with the tastes of a land-holding and slave-holding family had erected a considerable town around his furnace, his own residence as proprietor conspicuous in the midst. There he spent a large part of the time, not always in the company of his family, entertaining friends, enjoying the luxuries of terrapin, duck, wines, and, as rumor said in the forest, all the pleasures of a Russian or German nobleman on a secluded estate.

He could lie down on the ground with the barefooted foresters, equal and familiar with them, and carry off their suffrages for the state senate or the assembly. In Princess Anne he was more discriminating, rising in that society to his family stature and surrounded by alliances which demanded what is called *bearing*. In short he was the head of the community, and his wealth, originally considerable, had been augmented by marriage, while his credit extended to Philadelphia and Baltimore.

Not long after his young daughter Vesta placed the rose in Meshach Milburn's mysterious hat, Judge Custis said to his lady at the breakfast table, "That man has been allowed to shut himself in like a dog too long. He owes something to this community. I'll go down to his kennel under pretense of wanting a loan—and I do need some money for the furnace."

After breakfast he took his cane and passed out of his large mansion and down the sidewalk of the level street. As usual there were some Negroes around Milburn's small, weather-stained store, and Samson Hat, among them, shook hands with the judge, not a particle disturbed at the latter's condescension.

"Judge," said Samson, looking the large, portly gentleman over, "you's a good man yet, but de flesh is a little soft in yo' muscle, Judge."

"Ah, Samson," answered Custis, "there's one old fellow that is wrastling you."

"Time?" said the Negro. "We can't fight him, sho. Dat's a fack. But I'm good as any man in Somerset now."

"Except my daughter's boy, the class leader from Talbot."

"Is dat boy in yo' family?" exclaimed Samson, kindling up. "I'll walk dar if he'll give me another throw."

The judge passed into the wide-open door of Milburn's store. A few Negroes and poor whites were at the counter, and the proprietor was measuring whiskey out to them by the cheap dram in exchange for coonskins and eggs. He looked up, a trifle surprised at the principal man's advent, and merely said, "Morning."

Judge Custis never flinched from anybody, but his intelligence recognized in Meshach's eyes a kind of nature he had not yet met, though he was of universal acquaintance. It was not hostility nor welcome nor indifference. It was not exactly spirit. As nearly as the judge could formulate it, the expression was habitual self-reliance, and if not habitual suspicion, the feeling most near it, which comes from conscious unpopularity.

"Mr. Milburn," Judge Custis said, "when you are at leisure, let me have a few words with you."

The storekeeper turned to the poor folks and remarked bluntly, "You can come back in ten minutes."

They all left without further command, and Milburn closed the door. The judge moved a chair and sat down.

"Milburn," he said, "they tell me you lend money and that you charge well for it. I am a borrower sometimes, and I believe in keeping interest at home in our own community. Will you discount my note at legal interest?"

"Never," replied Meshach.

"Then," said the judge, smiling, "you'll put me to some inconvenience."

"That's more than legal interest," answered Milburn sturdily. "You'll pay the legal interest where you go, and the inconvenience of going will cost something too. If you add your expenses as liberally as you incur them, you are always paying a good shave."

"Where you have risks," suggested the judge, "there is some reason for a heavy discount, but my property will enrich this county and all the land you hold mortgages on."

"Bog ore," muttered the money lender. "I never lent money on that kind of risk; I must read upon it. They say manufacturing requires mechanical talent. How much do you want?"

"Three thousand."

"Secured upon the furnace?"

"Yes."

Meshach computed on a piece of paper, while the judge studied his singular face and figure with easy curiosity. He was rather short and chunky, not weighing more than one hundred and thirty pounds, with long, fine fingers of such tracery and separate action that every finger seemed to have a mind and function of its own. Looking only at his hands, one might say, "There is a pianist, a penman, a woman of skill or a man of peculiar delicacy." All the fingers were well produced, as if the hand instead of the face was meant to be the mind's exponent and reveal its portrait there.

The face of Meshach Milburn was uncommon. The effects of one diet and one climate, low, uninvigorating, and invariable from generation to generation, had brought his features to nearly aboriginal form and lines. From the cheek bones up he looked like an Indian and expressed a stolid power and swarthiness. His lower face was large in proportion and his nose so straight and its nostrils so sensitive that it was the only feature upon his face which seemed good company for his hands. When he confronted someone with his head thrown back a little, the effect was that of a hostile savage just burst from the woods.

"Look at him in the eyes," said the townsmen. "He's all forester!"

"But look at his hands," added an observant one. Ah, who had ever shaken his hand?

It was now extended to the judge, and he took from its womanly fingers the terms of the loan. Judge Custis was surprised at the moderation of Meshach, and he looked up cheerfully into that ever sentinel face.

"It is not the goodness of the security," said Meshach. "I make it low to you socially."

The Custis pride started with a flush to have this ostracized and hooted Shylock intimate that their relations could be more than a prince's to a pawnbroker. But the judge was a politician with an adaptable mind and address. "Speaking of social things, Milburn," he said carelessly, "our town is not so large that we don't all see each other sometimes. Why do you wear that forlorn, unsightly hat?"

"Why do you wear the name Custis?"

"Oh, I inherited that."

"And I inherited my hat."

There was a pause for a minute, but before the judge could tell whether it was an angry or an awkward pause, the storekeeper said, "Judge Custis, I concede that you are the best bred man in Princess Anne. Where did you get authority to question another person about any decent article of his attire?"

"I stand corrected, Milburn," said the judge. "Good feeling for you more than curiosity made me suggest it. And I may also remark to you, sir, that when you lend me money, you will always do it commercially and not socially."

"Very well," replied Meshach Milburn, "and if I ever enter your door, I will then take off my hat."

∞

The next morning Meshach Milburn surprised Samson Hat by saying, "Boy, when you have another fight and make yourself a barbarian again, remember to bring about a peck of the bog ores back from Nassawango Furnace."

∞

The years moved on without much change in Princess Anne. The little Manokin River brought up oysters from the bay and carried off the corn and produce. The great brick academy at neighboring Lower Trappe boarded and educated the brightest youths of the best families on the peninsula, and these, as the annual summers brought their fullness, perceived what portion of their beauty remained with Vesta Custis. Like Helen of Troy she became a woman almost imperceptibly. Sent to Baltimore to be educated, her return was followed by suitors, and the young men of the peninsula remarked with chagrin, "None of us have a chance. Some great city nabob will get her."

But the academy boys, visitors, and townspeople had one common opportunity to see and hear her—when she sang every Sabbath and church day in the Episcopal church. Her voice was the natural expression of her beauty—sweet, powerful, free, and easily trained. A divine bird seemed hidden in the old church when this noble yet tender voice broke forth, but those who turned to see the singer who had made such paradise looked almost on Eve herself.

She was rather slight, tall, and growing fuller slowly every year, like one in whom growth was early, yet long, and who would not wholly mature until near middle life. Her head, however, was perfection even in girlhood, not less by its proportions than its carriage. Her graceful figure bore it like the first splendor of the peach. As she seemed ever to be ripening, so she seemed never to have been a child.

Judge Custis made her his reliance and pride. She never reproved his errors nor treated them familiarly, but settled the household by a consent which all paid to her character alone. More than once she had appeared at the furnace mansion when the judge's long absence had awakened some jealousy or distrust.

"Father, please come home with me. I want you to drive me back."

The easy, self-indulgent judge would look a slight protest, but at the soft, spirited command, "Come, sir! You can't stay here any more," dismissed his companions and took his place at the head of Princess Anne society.

Vesta was almost a brunette with the rich colors of her type. She had eyebrows like the raven's wing, ripe, red lips, and hair whose darkness and length, released from the crown into which she wound it, might have spun her garments. Her eyes were steel blue, in which lights had the effect of black. She was dark, with sky breaking through like the rich dusk and twilights over the Chesapeake.

Since she possessed such beauty and accomplishments, people wondered that she was not proud. But her pride was too ethereal to be seen. It was not the vain consciousness of gifts and endowments but the serene sense of worthiness, of unimpaired health, honor, and descent, which made her kind and thoughtful to a degree only less than piety. Grateful for her social rank and parentage, she adorned but did not forget them. The suitors who came for her were weighed in this scale of perfect dessert. Not one had survived the test, yet none knew where he failed.

"Vesta is too good for any of them," exclaimed the judge on more than one occasion. "When I get the furnace in such shape that it will run itself, I will take my daughter to Europe and give her a musical education."

In truth, the judge had expectations of his daughter, for the reputation he had attained as a manufacturer was not without its drawbacks. He maintained two establishments. He supported a large body of laborers and dependents, some of whom he had brought from distant places under contract. The experiment in which he had embarked was still an experiment, and he was subject to the knowledge and judgment of his manager, being himself rather the patron than the manufacturer at the works. On many days, when he was supposed to be testing the percentage and mixture of his ores, he went gunning on the ocean bars, crabbing on Whollop's Beach, or hunting up questionable company among the forest girls or around the oystermen's and wrecker's cabins. He had plenty of property and family endorsers, however, and seldom failed to have a satisfactory interview with Meshach Milburn, who was now assisting him at least once a quarter to keep both principal and interest at home.

The judge had grown thicker with Meshach, but the storekeeper merely listened and assented and took no pains to incur another criticism on his motives. As ever, Meshach wore his great hat to church and on festive days, and it was still derided and held to be the town wonder. Vesta Custis often saw the odd little man come into church while she was singing, and she fancied that his large, coarse ears were turned to receive the music she was making. She faintly remembered that once she had held that wonderful hat. More than that she knew nothing, except that the wearer was a humble-born, grasping creature—a forester without social propensities or, indeed, any human attachments. Compared to his sordid master, the Negro who lived under his roof was beloved, and all testimony concurred that Meshach Milburn deserved neither commiseration, friendship, nor recognition. The judge, however, indulgent in all things, said the money lender had a good mind and was no serf.

Milburn had ceased to deal with Negroes or dispense drams. His wealth was now known to be more than considerable. He had ceased, also, to lend money on the surrounding farms, and rumors came across the bay that he was a holder of stocks and mortgages on the Western Shore and in Baltimore and Pennsylvania. The little town of Princess Anne was full of speculations about him, and even his age was uncertain.

Jack Wonnell measured it by hats. Said Jack, "I bought my bell-crowns the year Milburn's daddy and mammy died. They died of the bilious within a few days of each other out in Nassawango. I wear two bell-crowns a year; I come out every Fourth of July and Christmas. T'other day I counted what was left, and I reckoned that Meshach couldn't be forty-five at the wust."

Vesta Custis was only twenty years old when the townsfolk thought she must be twenty-five, so long had she been the beauty of Somerset. Her mother had always looked with apprehension on the possible time when her daughter would marry and leave her, for Judge Custis had long ceased to have the full confidence of his lady, whose fortune he had embarked without return on ventures still in doubt.

The Foresters

Chapter 3

One Saturday afternoon in October Meshach Milburn drew out his razor, cup, and hone and prepared to shave, albeit his beard was never more than harmless down. By a sort of capillary attraction, Samson divined his purpose and brought out the mysterious hat from the big green chest.

"Put it down," commanded the money lender. "Go out and hire me a carriage with two horses—two horses, do you mind."

Samson dropped the hat in wonderment.

"Make yourself decent," added Meshach. "I want you to drive; go with me and keep with me. Do you understand?"

"Yes, marster."

When the Negro departed, Meshach himself took up the tall, green, buckled hat with the stiff, broad, piratical brim. He looked it over long and hard.

"Vanity, vanity," he murmured. "Vanity and habit. I dare not disown thee now because they give thee ridicule. Without thee they would give me nothing but hate."

With surprise too great for jeering, the people around the tavern and courthouse saw the note shaver go past in a carriage driven by his Negro, and with two horses. Jack Wonnell took off his shining beaver to cheer. As the phenomenal team receded, however, the old cry ran down the stilly street: "Steeple-top! He's got it on! Meshach's loose!"

The carriage proceeded out the forest road and soon entered upon the sandy, pine-slashed region called Hardscrabble or Hardship. Here the roads were sandy as the hummocks and hills in the rear of a sea beach, and low, lean pines covered the swells and ridges. In occasional level basins, where stiff clay was exposed, some forester's unpainted hut sat black and smoking on the slope, without a windowpane, an ornament, or anything to relieve life from its monotony and isolation.

But where the rills ran off to the continuous swamps, leafage appeared in splendrous versatility. The maple stood revealed in all its fair, light harmonies. The magnolia drooped its ivory tassels and scented the forest with perfume. The kalmia and the alder gave undergrowth and brilliancy to the foliage. Hoary and green with precipitate old age, cypress trees stood in moisture and drooped their venerable beards from angular branches, and, overhanging its evergreen kinsmen, the bald cypress looked down upon the autumn swamp woods like some hermit artist on the rich pigments on his palette.

But nothing looked so noble as the sweet gum, which rose like a giant plume of yellow and orange, a chief in joyous finery, where the cypress was only a faded philosopher. Beside such a tall gum tree, where a wellspring shone at the bottom of a hollow cypress, Samson Hat reined in and borrowed a bucket from the hut across the road to water the horses.

"Marster," ventured the Negro, "dey say your gran'daddy sot dis spring."

"Yes," said Milburn, "and built the cabin. Yonder he lies on the knoll by that stump, up in the field—he and more of our wasted race."

"An' yon woman is a Milburn," added the Negro socially. "I know her by de hands."

The barefoot woman, living in one room and a loft, and the floor but a few inches above the ground, cried out impudently, "If I could have two horses, I'd buy a better hat!"

Milburn did not answer her, but marked the small, ungathered ears on the fodderless corn stalks, the shrubs of peach trees—the largest of which grew on his ancestors' graves, the little cart for one horse or ox, which was at once family carriage and farm wagon, and the few pigs and chickens of stunted breeds around the woman's feet.

"Drive on, boy," he exclaimed. "The worst of all is that these people are happy."

"Dat's a fack, marster," laughed Samson. "Dey wouldn't speak to you in Princess Anne. Dey think everybody's proud an' rich dar."

"Here the sea once dashed its billows on a bar," said Milburn reflectively. "That geology book relates it. From the North the hummocks recede in waves, where successive beaches were formed as the sea slowly retreated. They strike water below the sand and gravel, hardly deeper than a human grave, and below the water they drink, there is nothing but black mud. No lime is in the soil. Except for the wonderful bog ores, not a mineral exists in all this low, wave-made peninsula, where my people were shipwrecked."

"Dat must be in de Bible," Samson observed in his genial, wondering nature. "De Milburns been heah so long dey must hab got shipwrecked wid ole Noah."

"All families are shipwrecked," Meshach replied absently, "who cast their lot upon an unrewarding land, and, growing poorer and down from generation to generation, can never leave it, and at last can never desire to go."

"Marster, dar is one who got to go some ob dese days. It's me—pore ole Samson."

"Ha! Has someone set you on to demand your wages?"

"No, marster, I am old. It's you dat I'm troubled about. Dar's none to mend for you, cook for you, cure yo' sickness, or lay you in de grave."

No more was said until they passed the settled part of the forest and entered one of the many straight aisles of sky and sand among the pines, which had been opened on the great furnace tract of Judge Custis. He had several thousand acres here, and for miles the roadways were cleft towards the horizon.

The moon rose behind them as they entered the furnace village. Lights twinkled through the open doors of many cottages, and the furnace flames darted over the forbidding millpond, where iron ore grew in the depths like a vegetable creation.

Above the pond's surface, between steep banks of dark pines, hundreds of strong cypress trees towered from the water on splayed and conical roots, taller than the forest growth. The furnace lake lay black or white or crimson red, as the shadows or moon or flames struck upon it, and the stained water foamed through the dam breast, where an ancient road crossed.

Tawny, chilly, and solemn, the pond repeated the forms of the groves it submerged. Shaggy shadows added depth and dread to the effect. Some strange birds hooted as they dipped their wings in the surface, and, flying upward, seemed also to be sinking down. As Meshach felt the pond's chill, he drew down his hat and buttoned his coat.

"The earliest fools who turned up the bog ores for wealth," he said, "released the miasmas, which slew all the people roundabout. They killed all my family but set me free."

Nassawango Iron Furnace

Discovery of the Heirloom

Chapter 4

Judge Custis was in his bedroom in the mansion at the middle of the village and was recovering from the effects of a long wassail. In his nervous condition he started at the sound of wheels and, drawing his curtains, looked out upon the long shadow of an advancing figure crowned with a steeple hat.

This human shadow strengthened and faded in the alternating light until it was defined against his storehouse, his warehouse, his cabins, and the plain, and it seemed also against the wall of dense forest pines. Then footsteps ascended the stairs. His door opened, and Meshach Milburn, his holiday hat on his head, stood on the threshold, his eyes vigilant and bold and all his Indian nature to the front.

"My God, Milburn!" exclaimed the judge. "Odd as it is to see you here, I am relieved. I thought Old Nick was coming."

"Shall I come in?" asked Milburn.

"Yes. I'm sleeping off a little care and business. Let your man stay outside on the porch. Draw up a chair. It's money, I suppose, that brings you here?"

The money lender carefully put his formidable hat upon a table, took a distant chair, pushed his gaitered feet out in front of him, and laid a large pocket book on his lap. Then, addressing his whole attention to the host, he appeared never to wink while he remained.

"Judge Custis," he said straightforwardly, "the first time you came to borrow money from me, you said that Nassawango Furnace would enrich this county and raise the value of my land."

"Yes, Milburn. It was a slow enterprise, but it's coming all right. I shipped a thousand tons last year."

"Judge Custis," continued the money lender, "I told you when you made the first loan that I would investigate this ore. I did so years ago. Specimens were sent by me to Baltimore and tested there. Not content with that, I have studied the manufacture of iron for myself—the society of Princess Anne not grudging me plenty of solitude—and I know that every ton of iron you make costs more than you get for it. The bog ore is easy to smelt but is corrupted by phosphate of iron and is barely marketable."

The judge sat with eyes wide open and paler than before.

"You have found that out?" he whispered. "I did not know it myself until within this year—so help me God!"

"I knew it before I made you the second loan."

"Why did you not tell me?"

"Because you forbade our relations to be anything but commercial. I was not bound to betray my knowledge."

"Why did you, then, from a commercial view, lend me large sums of money again and again?"

"Because," said the money lender coolly, "you had other security. You have a daughter."

Judge Custis broke from the bedcovers and rushed upon Meshach Milburn. "Heathen and devil!" he shouted, taking the money lender by the throat, "do you dare to mention her as part of your mortgage?"

They struggled together until a powerful pair of hands pinioned the judge and bore him back to his bed. Samson Hat was the man.

"Judge!" he exclaimed, gentle but firm, 'you is a good man, but not as good as me. Cool off, Judge."

"I expected this scene," said Meshach Milburn. "It could not have been avoided. I was bound in conscience and in common sense to make you the only proposition which could save you from ruin, for, Judge Custis, you are a ruined man."

Overcome with excitement and suspended stimulation, the old judge fell back on his pillow and began to sob.

"Give him brandy," said Meshach Milburn. "Here is the bottle. He needs it now."

The wretched gentleman eagerly drank the proffered draught from the Negro's hands. His fury did not revive, and he covered his face with his palms and moaned piteously.

"Judge Custis," remarked Meshach Milburn, "if the apparent social distance between us could be lessened by any argument, I might make one, for the difference is in appearance only. The healthy flesh which gives you and yours stature and beauty is a matter of food alone. My stock has survived five generations of such diet as has bent the spines of the forest pigs and stunted the oxen. Money and family joy will give me comely children again. My life has been hard but pure."

The old judge felt the last unconscious reflection. "Yes," he uttered solemnly, "no doubt heaven marked me for some such degradation as this when I yielded to low propensities and sought my pleasure and companions in the huts of the forest."

"You claim descent from the Stuart Restoration; I know the tale. A creditor of the two exiled royal brothers, for sundry tavern loans and tipples, drew for his obligation an office in far-off Virginia. Seizures, confiscations, slave trade, marriages—in short, the long game of advantage—built up the fortunes of the Custises until they expired in a certain judge, whose notes of hand a hard man, forest born, held over the judge's head on what seemed hard conditions, but conditions in which was every quality of mercy except consideration for your pride."

The judge made a laugh like a howl. "Mercy?" he exclaimed. "You do not know what it is! To ensnare my innocent daughter in the damned meshes of your principal and interest! Call it malignity—the visitation of your unsocial wrath on man and an angel—but not mercy!"

"Then we'll call it compensation," continued Meshach Milburn. "For twenty years I have denied myself everything. You denied yourself nothing. Your substance is wasted. Renew it from the abundance of my thrift. It was not with an evil design that I made myself your creditor, although, as the years have rolled onward and solitude chilled my heart that has always pined for human friendship, I could not but see the kindling glory of your daughter's beauty. Like the schoolboys, the married husbands—yes, like the slaves—I had to admire her. Then, unknowing how deeply you were involved, I found offered to me for sale the paper you had negotiated in Baltimore—paper, Judge Custis, dishonorably negotiated."

The money lender rose, walked to the sad man's bed, and held the handful of notes boldly over him.

"It was despair, Milburn," moaned the judge.

"And so was my resolution. Said I, 'This lofty gentleman would cheat me, his neighbor, who has suffered all the contumely of this *good society*, and on starveling opportunity has slowly recovered independence.

Now he shall take my place in the forest, or I will wear my hat at the head of his family table.'"

"A dreadful revenge," whispered Custis with a shudder. "Such a hat is worse than a cloven foot. In God's name, whence came that ominous hat?"

Milburn took up the hat and held it before the lamplight, so that its shadow stood gigantic against the wall.

"Who would think," he said sarcastically, "that a mere headcovering, elegant in its day, could make more hostility than an idle head? I will tell you the silly secret of it. When I came from the obscurity of the forest, sensitive and anxious to make my way, and slowly gathered capital and knowledge, a person in New York directed a letter of inquiry to me. It told how a certain Milburn, a Puritan or English Commonwealth man, had risen to great distinction in that province, had revolutionized its government, and suffered the penalty of high treason."

"True enough," said Judge Custis, pouring a second glass of brandy. "Milburn and Leisler were executed in New York during the lifetime of the first Custis. They anticipated the expulsion of James II and were entrapped by their provincial enemies and made political martyrs."

"The inquirer," said Meshach, "who had obtained my address in the course of business, related that after Milburn's death his brethren and their families had sailed to the Chesapeake, where the Protestants had successfully revolutionized for King William, and making choice of poor lands, they had become obscure. He asked me if the courthouse records made any registry of their wills."

"Of course you found them?"

"Yes. It was a revelation to me and gave me the honorable sense of some origin and quality. I traced myself back to the earliest folios at the close of the seventeenth century."

"Any property, Milburn?" asked the judge, voluptuous and reanimated again.

"My great-grandfather had left his son nothing but a hat."

"Not uncommon," exclaimed Judge Custis. "Our early wills contain little but legacies of wearing apparel, household articles, bedding, pots and kettles, and the elements of civilization."

"The will on record said, '*I give to my eldest son, Meshach Milburn, my best Hat, and no more of my estate.*'"

"Ha, ha, ha!" laughed the judge loudly. "Genteel to the last! A hat of fashion, no doubt, made in London. Quite too ceremonious and topgallant for these colonies. He left it to his eldest son, en*tiled* it, we may say. Ho! ho!"

"When my indignation was over, I took the same view you do, Judge Custis, that it was a bequest of dignity, not of burlesque, and I made some inquiries for that 'best Hat.' It was a legend among my forest kin, had been seen by very old people, was celebrated in its day and worn by my grandfather thankfully. He left it to my father, still a hat of reputation."

"Still en*tiled* to the oldest son! Ha, ha, Milburn."

"My father sold the hat to Charles Wilson Peale, a native to our peninsula, who knew the ancient things existing here that would help him to form Peale's Museum. I found the hat in that museum, covering the mock figure of Guy Fawkes."

"Conspirator's hat—bravo!" exclaimed the judge.

"It had been used for the heads of George Calvert and Shakespeare, but in time of religious excitements was proclaimed to be the true hat of Guy Fawkes. I reclaimed it and brought it to Princess Anne. In a vain moment I put it on my head and walked into the street. It was assailed with halloos and ribaldry."

"It was another Shirt of Nessus, Milburn; it poisoned your life, eh?"

"Perhaps so," replied Milburn with intensity. "They say what is one man's drink is another man's poison. You will accept that hat on the head of your son-in-law or no more drink out of the Custis property!"

The Bog-ore Tract

Chapter 5

Resolution of character and executive power had been trifled away by Judge Custis. The trader had concluded the interview with a decision and fierceness that left the gentleman's mind paralyzed. He saw in sad fancy the execution served upon his furniture, the amazement of his wife, the pallor of his daughter, and the indignation of his sons.

He also shrank before the impending failure of his furnace, on which he had raised so much state and local fame. People would say, "Custis was a fool and deceived himself, while old Steeple-top Milburn played upon the Custises' vanity and turned them into the street."

"No doubt," thought the judge, "that fellow Milburn can get anything when he gets my house. He may command the poor folks' vote because he is of their class. He is a lender to many of the rich. Who could have suspected his intelligence and address? He handled me as if I were a forester and he a judge. A very remarkable man."

He was interrupted by the entrance of Sampson Hat.

"Where's your master, boy?" asked the judge.

"He's gone up to de ole house, Judge, where his daddy and mammy died. It's de place where I hides after my fights."

"May the ague strike him there! Let the bilious sweat from the mill-pond be strong tonight, that like Judas of old his bowels may drop out. But no," the irresolute man hesitated, "I have no right to hate him."

"Judge," the old Negro said softly, "my marster is a sick man. He ain't happy like you an' me; he's 'bitious an' lonely. Dat's enough to spile angels. He's proud as Lucifer and full of hate at Princess Anne an' de people, but a gooder man I never knowed. Your darter might git a better man, but not a pyor one."

"Purity goes a very little way on the male side of marriage contracts," exclaimed the judge. "It's always assumed and never expected. You need not remember, Samson, that I expressed any anger at your master."

"My whole heart, Judge, is to see him happy. Hard as he is, dat man has power to make him loved."

The Negro said a humble good-night, and the judge lay down upon his bed to think of the dread alternatives of the coming week. Voluptuous even in despair, he slept before he had come to any conclusion.

Samson Hat walked up the side of the millpond on a sandy road divided from the water by a dense growth of pines. Bullfrogs and insects serenaded the forest, and the furnace chimney smoked lurid on the midnight. At the distance of half a mile or more an old cabin stood in decay in a sandy field near the road. It had no door in the hollow doorway and no sash in the one gaping window. The step leading to the sill was broken, and some of the weather boarding had rotted from the skeleton. The old end chimney bore it toughly up, however, and the low brick props under the corners stood plumb. Within lay a single room with open beams. A sort of cupboard stairway projected over the fireplace, and another door and window were in the rear. Meshach Milburn sat on an old chair before the fireplace, revealed by the light of burning weather boards he had thrown upon the hearth. A little heap of bog-iron ore and a bottle sat in front of him.

"Come in, Samson," he called. "Don't think me turned drunkard because I am taking this whiskey. I drink it to keep out the malaria and partly as a communion cup, for tonight the barefooted ghosts who have drooped and withered here are with me in spirit."

"Dey was all good Milburns who lived heah, marster," the Negro said. "Dey had hard times but did no sin. Dey shook wid chills and fevers, not wid conscience."

"I shall shake with neither," said the money lender. "Go up into the loft and sleep till you are called."

The Negro obeyed without remark and disappeared behind the cupboard-like door. Milburn sat before the fire and looked into it long, while a procession of thoughts and phantoms passed before it.

He saw a poor family of independent Puritans setting sail at different dates from English seaports. Some were indentured servants hoping for a career. Some were avoiding the civil wars. Others were small political malefactors, noisy against the oppressions of Cromwell and conspirators against his power. Thrown into English jails, they were delivered to be sold into slavery, driven through the streets of market towns, placed on troop ships between the decks among the horses, and set up like the blacks at auction in Barbados. In time they continued westward. One—the fortunate possessor of some competence—sailed his own ship across the Atlantic and delivered to Massachusetts her governor and gentry. Another—incapable of being suppressed, although a servant—seized the destinies of an aristocratic colony and held them for a while, until accumulating enemies bore him down, and wedlock and the gibbet followed close together. Poverty would not relinquish its grip upon the race. They struggled up like clods upon the plowshare and fell back again into the furrow.

As Meshach Milburn thought of these things, he took up a portion of the bog ore from the hearth.

"Here is iron," he said thoughtfully, "true iron, which makes the blood red, molds into infinite forms, nails houses together, binds wheels, and casts into cannon and ball. But this iron ran into a bog, formed low combinations, and had no other mold than twigs and leaves afforded. Its volcanic origin was forgotten when it ran with sand and gravel along the low, alluvial bar, away from the mountain vein and upland ore. Like an oyster it is dredged from the stagnant pool, impure, inefficacious, corrupted. So it is with man, whose magnetic spirit follows the dull declivity to the barren sandbars of the world and lodges there. I am of the bog ores, but that exists which will flux with me, clean me of rust, and transmit my better quality to posterity. Oh, youth, beauty, and station—lovely Vesta. For thee I will be iron!"

Milburn looked around the single room inquiringly. He placed his finger upon the crevices in the weather boarding. He opened the little closet below the stairs, and a weasel dashed out and shot through the door. He ascended the steep, short stairs and examined the black shingles with a torch. Nothing was there except a litter of young owls, whose parents had gone poaching. Returning then, he searched on every open beam and rotting board, as if for writing.

"They could not write," he thought. "Nothing is left to me down a century and a half to tell that I had parents—not even a sign."

As he spoke, he felt an object move behind him, and looking back, the shadow of the Entailed Hat was dancing on the wall. As he threw his head back, so did it. As he retired from it, the hat enlarged until the little room could hardly hold its shadow. Retiring again, he lifted it from his head with bitter courtesy, and the shadow did the same. The man and the shadow each looked at a peaked hat and stroked it.

"This is everything," exclaimed Milburn. "The humble, hundred heads are at rest in the sand. One gravestone would mock them all. But once the family brain expanded to a hat, and that survived the race. I am the Quaker who respects his hat, the cardinal who is crowned with it, and yes, the dunce who must wear it in his corner."

Then the picture of his parents arose upon his sight: a cheerful father with two or three old slaves, plowing in the deep sand to drop some shriveled grains of corn, or tinkering a disordered mill wheel that moved a blacksmith's saw. Ever full of confidence in nothing which could increase, credulous and sanguine, tender and laborious, Milburn's sire nursed his forest patches as if they were presently to be rich plantations and was ever pricing Negroes, mules, tools, and implements in expectation of buying them. Nothing could diminish his confidence but disease and old age. He heard of the great improvement on the furnace tract and took his obedient wife and brood there. As laborers pulled out the tussocks and roots encrusted with iron from the swamp and creek, fever and ague came forth and smote them both.

How wretched that scene, when father and mother in this one bare room where Meshach sat, groaning amid their many offspring, almost too haggard to move, saw death creep upon each other—death without priest or doctor, without residue or cleanliness—the death the million die in lowly huts, yet oh, how hard.

"Haste, Sonny, *good* boy," the frightened father had said in his dependence on his wife, not knowing how ill he was. "Take the horse and ride into Snow Hill for the doctor. Poor mother is dreadful sick."

Bareheaded, barefooted, and almost crazy with excitement, Meshach leaped upon the lean old horse and pushed through the deep sand till he entered the shining streets of the white-hilled town. Rushing into the doctor's office, he cried, "Daddy and Mammy is sick at the furnace!" told his name, and fled.

As the boy rode home past the river full of splutterdocks, the yellow masts of vessels rising above the woods, the flat, forest-bounded fields of corn, and the small, white houses of the better farmers—at last entering the murmurous, complaining woods—he saw but one thing: his mother.

Was she to disappear from the lonely clearing and leave only the hut and its orphans, she who kept heaven here below and was the saints, the arts, the all-sufficient for her child? With her there could be no poverty. Without her, riches would be only more sand. With a little molasses she made Christmas kingly with a cake. She could name a little chicken "Meshach," and every egg it laid was a new toy. A mockingbird caught in the swamp became one of the family by her kindness. Would it ever sing again? The religion they knew was of her. The poor slaves saw no difference in mistresses while she was theirs. In sickness she was in her sphere—health itself had come. And once, when his father and she had quarreled, and the light of love being out made the darkness of poverty visible for the only time, Meshach saw her weeping and could not comfort her.

Then, blinded by tears, he lashed his nag along and entered the low door. She was dead!

"Sonny, Mammy's gone," the wretched father groaned. The little children huddling about the form lifted their wail, but the mockingbird could find no note for this and was hushed.

Milburn arose. The fire was low. He walked to the door, and there was a sign of day. The all-surrounding woods of pine were still dark, but on the sandy road and hummock field some light was shining like hopefulness against hope. The farm was plowed no more. The ungrateful centuries were left behind and abandoned like old wilderness battlefields, so sterile that their great events remain ever unvisited.

"Ho! Samson! Boy! It is time."

"Yes, marster," Samson answered from the loft.

As the Negro gathered himself and passed down the stairs, he saw Meshach Milburn before the fire, stirring the coals. Passing out, Samson stood a moment at the gate, then walked slowly up the road so as not to lose his master.

As he turned once to look back, flames burst out of the old hut and glistened on the evergreen forest, lighting the tops of mossy cypress trees in the millpond and revealing the forms of sandy fields. Before he could start back, Samson saw his master walk around the house, lighting the weather boarding from place to place with a torch. Then the low figure capped by the long hat came up the road as if with mighty strides, so lengthened by the fire.

"No need of alarm, boy," Milburn said, and holding the ancient tile up in the light of the blaze, the filial incendiary exclaimed, "Henceforth my only ancestral hall is *here*."

"Ah, marster," said the Negro, "fine as de hat may be and mean as de roof, yo' hat will never give comfort like a home. De hat will never hold two heads, and dat makes happiness."

"At least," answered Milburn bitterly, "the hat will cover me where I go. Rotted roofs such as that was make captives of bright souls."

They looked on the fire in silence for a few minutes.

"You have burnt me out, boss," old Samson finally said. "I ain't got no place to go an' hide when I fights now. It makes me feel solemn."

"Peace," replied Meshach Milburn. "Now for the horses and Princess Anne."

Bog-ore Carts at Nassawango Furnace

The Custises Ruined

Chapter 6

Vesta Custis heard early wheels upon the morning air and, looking through the blinds, saw a double team coming up the road from Hardship.

"Mother," she said, "is that Father coming yonder? No, it is not his driver."

"Why, Vesta," exclaimed Mrs. Custis, "that is old Milburn's man."

"Samson Hat? So it is. What is he doing with two horses?"

Here Vesta laughed aloud and began to skip about in her long, slender slippers, whose insteps would spare a mouse that darted under.

"Why, Mamma, it is Milburn himself in a hack and span. See the steeple-top hat, copper buckle and all. Isn't he too funny for anything. Dear me, he is staring right up at this window. Let us duck!"

Vesta's slender, ivory-grained arms, divided from her beautiful shoulders only by a spray of lace, pulled her mother down.

"Don't be afraid, dear. He can see nothing but the blinds. Perhaps he is looking for the judge."

Vesta rose again in her white morning gown, like a stag rising from a snowdrift, and said, "He sits there like an Indian riding past in a show, Mamma. Did you ever see such a hat?"

"I think it must be buggy by this time," the mother said, and both of them shook with laughter again. "Unless," added Mrs. Custis, "the bugs are starved out."

"Poor, lonely creature," Vesta observed. "He can only wear such a hat from want of understanding."

"His understanding is good enough, dear. He has the green gaiters on."

They laughed again, and Vesta's hair, shaken down by her merriment, fell nearly to her slippers, like the skin of some coal-black beast that had sprung down a poplar's trunk.

"Ah well," exclaimed Vesta, as her maid entered and proceeded to wind up the satin cordage on her crown, "can a woman know what men are in their minds? Old ladies frequently wear their coal-scuttle bonnets long past the fashion, but it is from want. This man is his own master and not poor. His companion is a Negro, and his taste is a moldy hat, old as America. We should be happy that it is not necessary to pry into such minds. A little refinement is the next blessing to religion."

"Your father's mind is a puzzle, too, Vesta He has everything these foresters lack: education, society, standing, and comforts. Yet the moment your eye is off him, he returns to the forest like an opossum. He can't be traced up by his hat, like this man. I think it's a shame on you, particularly. If he doesn't come home this day, I shall send for my brother and force an account of my property from him."

"I'll take the carriage after breakfast, Mamma, and seek him at the furnace or wherever he may be. Those bog ores have given him a great deal of trouble."

"I wish I had never heard of bog ore," exclaimed Mrs. Custis. "He goes to the forest looking like a magistrate and gentleman and comes back looking like a bog trotter and drunkard. There must be women in it!"

In an impulse of weak rage the lady got up, walked to her mirror, and looked at her face. Apparently satisfied that such charms were trampled upon, she dried her tears and resumed: "Vesta, my dear, I would not cast a stain upon you for the world, but flesh and blood *will* cry out. If your father doesn't do better, I will separate from him and leave Princess Anne."

"Why, Mother!"

The daughter's bright eyes were large and startled now, and their steel-blue tint grew plainer under her rich black eyebrows.

"Unless he reforms, I will do it, if I die!"

Vesta stood, her lips parted and her teeth just lacing the coral of her lip. With her head thrown back and a pallor in her cheeks, she looked like Eve first bearing the Creator's rebuke.

"A separation in this family," she whispered, "would scandalize all Maryland. It would break my heart."

"Darling daughter, *my* heart must be considered sometimes. I was something before I was a Custis. I am a woman, too."

Still pale, Vesta crossed to her mother's side and kissed her.

"Don't, Mamma, ever harbor a thought like that again. You who have been so brave and patient longer than I have lived."

"Ah, Vesta, it is the length of injury that wears us out. What if something should happen to us? None are so unfit to bear poverty as we."

"We cannot be poor," said the daughter soothingly. "Don't you remember where it says, Mother, 'As thy day, so shall thy strength be?'"

"My child," Mrs. Custis replied, "your day is young. Life looks hopeful to you. I am growing old, and where is the arm on which I should be leaning? What are we but two women left? There is another passage on which I think when we sit so often alone: 'Two women shall be grinding at the mill. One shall be taken and the other left.' Is that you, or is it I? Listen, my child. It is time that you should feel the melancholy truth. Your father's habits have mastered him. He is beyond reclamation."

Vesta was kneeling, and she slowly raised her head and looked at her mother with her nostrils dilated.

"Don't look at me so," the poor lady pleaded. "I thought you ought to know it."

"How dare you say that of my father—of Judge Custis?"

In that tense moment, wheels were heard. The daughter went to the window and looked down. "Hush, Mother," she said. "It is Papa. Wash your eyes at the toilet, and let us meet him cheerfully. Never say he is beyond reclamation while we can try."

A kiss smoothed Mrs. Custis's countenance. Vesta was dressed for breakfast in a few moments and descended to the library to be received in her father's arms. He held her close for a long while and by little fits renewed his embrace. She felt that his breath was feverish, and his arms trembled. Looking up at him, she saw that he was flushed and haggard.

"Vessy," he said with a feeble attempt to smile, "I want a glass of brandy. Mine gave out at the furnace, and the morning ride has weakened me. Where is the key?"

She looked at him as if to measure his need of stimulant. Then, without a word, she led the way to the dining room and unlocked the liquor closet, turning her back lest he might not drink his need.

"Naughty man," Vesta said, standing off and looking at him when he was done. "I was going down to the furnace for you after breakfast. We will have no more of this truancy. Mamma and I have set our feet down. Like other businessmen, you must come back from the furnace every night and go again in the morning. Be kind to Mamma this morning, sir. She feels your neglect."

Vesta had already rung for the judge's valet, who now drew off his boots, supplied slippers and dressing gown, and led him to his bath. In a quarter of an hour the judge reappeared, smiling suggestively at Vesta, and turned again towards the dining room.

"Not that way," she said. "Here is Mamma, and we are ready for prayers. Here is the place in the Bible."

They all went to the family room, where the dressing maids of Vesta and her mother were waiting for the morning prayers. Vesta placed the open Bible on her father's knee, and he began absently and stumblingly to read. It was in the book of Samuel and seemed to be some old Jewish mythology. He suddenly came to a verse which arrested his sensibilities by its pathos: "And David sent messengers to Ishbosheth, Saul's son, saying, 'Deliver me my wife Michal.' And Ishbosheth sent and took her from her husband, even from Phaltiel, the son of Laish. And her husband went with her along, weeping behind her. Then said Abner unto him: 'Go, return.' And he returned."

Judge Custis saw at once the picture this compact history aroused. The inexorable David, perhaps, had married another's love. Occasion had arisen to embitter her kin, and they took her back and gave her in happiness to her pining lover. But again, the man of correct habits triumphed over the sons of the king and dispatched Abner to tear his wife from her true husband's arms. Poor Phaltiel followed her weeping until ordered to go back. And back he went, forever desolate.

The scene recalled the brutal demand of his creditor. The judge's eyes silently overflowed, and he could not see.

Vesta had watched him closely and detected a great anxiety or illness in her father. Lest her mother might also notice it, she interposed in the lesson by reading the Episcopal form of prayer, in which they all bent their heads. Once or twice, as she went on, she detected a suppressed sob, especially at the paragraph: "Thou who knowest the weakness and corruption of our nature and the manifold temptations which we daily meet with, we humbly beseech thee to have compassion on our infirmities and to give us the constant assistance of thy Holy Spirit, that we may be effectually restrained from sin and excited to our duty."

The Custises Ruined

At the breakfast table the judge bit off some toast and filled his mouth with tea, but could not swallow. A hand softly touched his elbow, and a wine glass full of brandy glided within his reach. He looked up into the rich, yearning face of his dark-eyed daughter, and his heart burst forth. He leaned his head upon the table and cried in his grief, "Darling, we are ruined!"

Mrs. Custis arose and looked fearfully at the judge, and Vesta turned to the servants and motioned them to go.

"No," Judge Custis said, perceiving the motion, "let them hear it. They must be sold, faithful servants. Perhaps it may warn them to escape in time."

The servants, bred like ladies, quietly left the room.

Growing paler, Mrs. Custis exclaimed, "Daniel Custis, have you lost everything in that furnace?"

"Everything!"

"And my money, too?"

"Yes."

"Merciful God!"

Before the weak lady could fall, Vesta's arm was around her, and her finger on the table bell. Servants entered, and Mrs. Custis was carried out, her daughter following.

When Vesta returned, her father was walking up and down the floor with his long silk handkerchief in both hands, weeping bitterly. She looked at him with all the might of a daughter first called upon to act alone in a great crisis. Her feeling of perfect pride towards him had received a blow by her mother's statement: "Your father's habits have mastered him beyond reclamation." Could it be true, that the grand, kind gentleman was beneath the diver's reach, where light could not pierce nor hope overtake? Was her father, the first gentleman of Somerset, a drunkard, and no ray of heaven to beam upon his grave?

She saw his danger now, written on his face. His hair was thinner and very gray, and his rich, dark eyes intimidated, as if his manly confidence was gone. His skin was faded and spotted with alcohol, and on his nose and lips were signs of coarser sensuality. This father had been Vesta's angel until this moment. Now, there might not be an angel in the universe to fly to his rescue. A dreadful humility descended into the daughter's spirit.

"God forgive me," she thought. "How blind and how proud and sinful I have been."

She walked to her father and tenderly kissed him, then led him to a sofa, placed a pillow for him, and made him stretch his once proud form there. Procuring a bowl of water, she washed his face free of tears and bathed it in cologne. The voluptuous nature of the judge yielded to the perfume and the easy position, and he sobbed himself to sleep like an exhausted child.

Sitting by the sleeping bankrupt, watching his breast rise and fall and hearing his coarse snoring, the wish arose, often repeated in a woman's life, to have been born a man and know how to help her father. That suggested she had brothers who ought to be summoned, but it occurred to her that every one of them had leaned upon him. Though conscious that it was wicked, Vesta felt her pride rise against the thought that any being outside that house, even a brother, should know of its disgrace.

What could she do? She thought of her jewels, her riding mare, her watch, her father's own gifts, and then the thought perished that these could help him.

Could she not earn something by her voice, which had sung to such praises? Alas, that voice had lost the ingredient of hope, and she feared to unclose her lips lest it might come forth in agony, crying, "God, have mercy!"

"I have nothing," said Vesta to herself, "except love for my father and mother. Nothing can be done until he awakens and tells me the worst. Meantime, it would be wicked for me to increase the agitation already here, where I must be the comforter."

Jack-o'-lantern Iron

Chapter 7

As a sick headache seized her, and she kept to her room, Mrs. Custis was in no condition to give annoyance that day. Infirm of will, purely social in her marriage relations, and never aiming higher than respectability, she missed the coarse mark of her husband, who, with all his moral defections, probably was her moral equal. Mrs. Custis had no insight into charity. Her mind was bounded by the municipality of Baltimore, which, particularly among its mercantile aristocracy, esteemed itself the world.

The Baltimore that ruled the Chesapeake had no more perfected product than Mrs. Custis—amiable, social, afraid of new ideas, frugal of money, seldom intellectual, but possessing a beauty that powerfully attracts until, by the limited sympathies supporting it, the husband from the outer world discerns how hopelessly slavery and caste sink into an old shipping society.

Her modesty and virtue were as natural as her prejudices. She believed that marriage was the close of female ambition, and marrying her children was the only innovation to be permitted. She thought certain accomplishments due woman, but none of them must be masculine in prosecution. She shrank from a professional woman as from an infidel or an abolitionist. Reading was meritorious up to an orthodox point, but a passion for new books was dangerous, probably irreligious. To lose one's money was a crime; to lose another's money the unforgivable sin. That was Baltimore public opinion, which she thought was the only opinion entitled to consideration.

The old Scotch and Irish merchants there had made it the law that enterprise was only excusable by success, and that success only branded an innovator. A good standard of society, therefore, had barely permitted Judge Custis to take up the bog ore manufacture, and, failing in it, his wife thought he was no better than a Jacobean.

On the Eastern Shore, where society was formed before Glasgow and Belfast and their precise formulas of life had colonized the Chesapeake, a gentler community arose. Religion and benevolence were depositions rather than dogmas there. Moderate poverty was the not unwelcome expectation, wealth a subject of apprehensive scruples, kindness the law, pride the exception, and grinding avarice like Meshach Milburn's was the mark of the devil entering into the neighbor and the fellow man.

Except in his Virginia voluptuousness, Judge Custis was representative of his neighbors. His neighbors were neither prudes nor hypocrites, and he respected them more than the arrogant race in the land of Accomack and the Virginia peninsulas, whose traits he had almost lost. Sometimes it seemed to him that the last of the cavalier stock was his daughter Vesta. From him it had nearly departed, and his sense of moral shortcomings expanded his heart and made him tenderly pious to his kind, if not to God. He admired newcomers, new business modes, northern intruders, and ideas, feeling that perhaps the last evidence of his aristocracy from nature was a chivalric resignation. The pine trees said to him, "Ye shall go like the Indian, but be not inhospitable to your successors. Leave them your benediction, that the great bay and its rivers may be splendid with ships and men, though ye are perished forever." A perception of the energy of his countrymen and a pride in it, though it might involve his personal humiliation, was Judge Custis's only remaining claim to heaven's magnanimity. Still, rich in human nature, he was beloved by his daughter with all her soul.

He awoke refreshed, long after noon. A glass of milk and a plover broiled on toast, with sprigs of new celery from the garden, were ready for him to eat. He made this small meal silently.

As the tray was removed, Vesta said, "Now, Papa, before we leave this room, you are to tell me the whole injury you have suffered and what all of us can do to assist you. If you had succeeded, the reward would have been ours, and we must divide the pains of your misfortune with you without any regret. Courage, Papa, and let me understand it."

The judge looked feebly at Vesta and finally said, "My child, I am the victim of good intentions and self-enjoyment. I am less than a scoundrel and worse than a fool. I am a fraud, and you must be made to see it, for I fear you have been proud of me."

"Oh father, I have," said Vesta. "You were my God."

"Let us throw away idolatry, my darling. It is the first of all the sins. How loud the first commandment speaks to us this moment: 'Thou shalt have no other gods before me!'"

"I have broken it," sobbed Vesta. "I loved you more than my Creator."

"Vesta," said the judge, "you are the only thing of value in all my house. The work of nature in you is all that survives the long edifice of our pride. The treasure of your beauty and love still makes me rich to thieves, who lie in ambush all around us. We are in danger. We are pursued. Oh, God, pity the pure in heart."

As the judge, with an earnestness so rare in him of late, threw wide his arms and raised his brow in agony, Vesta felt her idolatry return. He was so grand, standing there in his unaffected pain and helplessness, that he seemed to her some manly Prometheus, who had worked with fire and iron to the exasperation of the jealous gods. Admiration dried her tears, and she forgot her father's references to herself.

"What is iron?" she asked. "Tell me why you wanted to make iron. If I can enter into your mind and sympathize with the hopes you have had, it will lift my soul from the ground. I should have asked for this lesson long ago."

The judge strode up and down till she repeated the question and brought him to his seat. He collected his thoughts and resumed his worldly tone as he proceeded to tell the tale of iron.

"I have duplicated loans on the same properties," he said at last, "incurring, I fear, a stigma upon my family and character, as well as the ruin of our fortune."

Vesta arose with pale lips and a sinking heart. "Oh, Father," she whispered in a frightened tone, "who knows this terrible secret?"

"Only one man," said the judge, cowering down to the carpet, his courage and volatility immediately gone. "Old Meshach Milburn knows it all. He has purchased the duplicate notes and holds them with his own. He has me in his power and hates me. He will expose me unless I submit to an awful condition."

"What is it, Father?"

The judge looked up in terror, and meeting Vesta's pale but steady gaze, hid his face and groaned, "Oh, it is too disgraceful to tell. It will break your mother's heart."

"Tell me at once," exclaimed Vesta in a low and hollow tone. "What further disgrace can this monster inflict upon us than to expose our dishonor? Can he kill us more than that?"

"I know not how to tell you, Vessy. Spare me, my darling. I hide my face for shame."

Vesta paused, her mind expanded to touch every point of suggestion. She looked down at her father, who did not move, then stooped and raised his face to find some solution to his mysterious evasion. He shut his eyes, as if she burned him with her wondering look.

"Papa, look at me this instant! You shall not be a coward to me."

He broke from her hands and retreated to a window, looking at her with a timorous countenance.

"I wish you to go this moment, find Mr. Milburn, and bring him to me," Vesta said. "You must obey me, sir!"

The judge raised his hands in protest, but before he could speak, a shadow fell upon the window, and the figure of a small, swarthy man covered with a steeple-crowned hat advanced up the front steps.

"Savior, have mercy!" murmured Judge Custis. "The wolf is at the door."

Vesta took her father in her arms, kissed him assuringly, and said, "Papa, send a servant to open the door. Have Mr. Milburn shown into this room to await me. Go and engage my mother affectionately, and both of you remain in your chamber till I am ready to call you."

The proximity of the dreadful creditor had almost paralyzed Judge Custis, and he glided out like a ghost.

The Hat Finds A Rack

Chapter 8

After writing several letters, Meshach Milburn had locked the store and had taken the broad street for Judge Custis's gate. The news of his disappearance towards the furnace with an extravagant livery team had spread among all the circle around the principal tavern, and they were discussing the motive and probabilities of the act with that deep inner ignorance so characteristic of an instinctive society. Jimmy Phoebus, a huge man with a broad face and small forehead, was called upon for his view.

"It's nothin' but a splurge," said Jimmy. "Sooner or later everybody splurges. Meshach's jest spilin' with money an' must have a splurge—two hosses an' a nigger. If it ain't a splurge, I can't tell what ails him to save my life."

A general chorus went up of, "Dogged if I kin tell to save my life!"

Levin Dennis, the terrapin buyer, made a wild guess: "I reckon Meschach is a-goin' in the hoss business. He's a-ben in ever'thin' else an' has tuk to hosses. If it tain't hosses, I can't tell to save my life!"

All the lesser intellects of the party executed a low chuckle, spun halfway around on their boot heels and back again, and muttered, "Not to save my life!"

Jack Wonnell, wearing one of the new bell-crowns and looking like a vagrant who had tried on a militia grenadier's bear-skin hat, added his opinion: "Ole Milbun's gwyn to see a gal. Fust time a man changes his regler course wilently, it's a gal. I went into my bell-crowns to git a gal. Milbun's gwyn get a gal out yonda in the forest. If that ain't it, I can't tell to save m'life!"

The smaller fry, not being trained to suggestion, grinned, held their mouths agape, executed the revolution upon one heel, and echoed, "Dogged ef I kin tell t' save m' life!"

"He's a-comin', boys," exclaimed Jimmy Phoebus. "Now we'll take off our hats an' do it polite. By smoke, thar's goin' to be hokey-pokey of some kind or nuther in Prencess Anne."

The smallish man in the Guy Fawkes hat and the old, ultra-genteel, greenish gaiters walked towards them with his resinous, bold eyes to the front and his nose, like any silken terrier's, informing him of what was in the air. His skin had the pallor of a sick persons, and he seemed to display less than his usual expression of hostility to Princess Anne.

"He's got the ager," remarked Levin Dennis. "Them's the shakes comin' on him by tomorrey, ef I know tarrapin bubbles."

The nearest approach to profanity current in that land was again heard fluttering around: "To *save* my life."

Jimmy Phoebus had the name of being descended from a Greek pirate or patriot who had settled on the Eastern Shore, and with his rich, brown complexion, broad head, and Mediterranean eyes, Phoebus looked it yet.

"Good afternoon, Mr. Milburn," Jimmy said loudly and carelessly.

"Good afternoon, Mr. Phoebus. Gentlemen, good afternoon."

As he responded with a voice hardly genial but placating, Milburn lifted his ancient hat, and in an instant seemed to come a century nearer to his neighbors. His stature was reduced, and his unsociableness seemed modified. He now looked to be a smallish, friendless person, as if some ownerless dog had darted through the street and heard a kind chirp at the tavern door, where his reception before had been stones. His voice, with a little tremor in it, emboldened Levin Dennis to speak also: "Look out for fevernager this month, Mr. Milburn."

Meshach bowed his bead, gliding along as if bashfully anxious to pass.

"Nice weather for drivin'," added Jack Wonnell, having also taken off his own tile of frivolity to feel the effect.

But this remark was regarded by the group as too forward, and a low chorus ran round of "Jack Wonnell can't help bein' a fool to save his life!"

Passing on, Milburn said to himself, "Are those voices kinder than usual, or am I more timid? What is it in the air that makes everything so acute and my cheeks to tingle? Am I sick, or is it love?"

The word frightened him, and the sand under his feet seemed to crack. A woodpecker in an old tree tapped as if it was the tree's old heart quickened by something. The houses all around looked like live objects with their windows fixed upon his walk like married folks' eyes.

As he came in sight of Judge Custis's residence, so expressive of old respect and long intentions, the money lender almost stopped, so mild and peacefully it looked at him—so undisturbed while he was palpitating.

"Why this pain?" thought Milburn. "Am I afraid? The house is mine, and yet it does not fear me. It has been here so long that it has no fears, and every window in it faces me kindly. The three gables survey yonder forest landscape like three old magistrates on their benches, administering justice to a county where never till now was there a ravisher."

The thought produced a moment's pride in him. "It is the forest these gentles have to fear today," he thought resentfully. Then another image stopped him: "What has that forest ever felt of injury or hate, with every cabin door unlatched, and no robber feared by any there. The blossoms on the Negro's peach tree, the ripe persimmons on the roadside, plenteous to every forester's child, and humility and affection making all richer without a dollar in the world. And I, the richest upstart of the forest, compelled to buy affection like an indifferent slave."

Seeing him walk so slowly, a large dog at Custis's home came down the path to the gate, also walking slowly, and showed neither animosity nor interest, except mechanically to walk behind him towards the door.

"The dog knows me," thought Meshach, "from life-long seeing of me, but never wagged his tail in all that time. Could I acquire the heart even of this dog, though I might buy him?"

Milburn walked up the steps and sounded the substantial brass knocker. It struck four times, loud and deep, and the stillness that followed was louder yet, like the unknown thing after sentence has been passed. He seemed to be there a very long time with his heart quite vacant, as if the debtor's knocker had scared every chatter out of it, and yet his temples and ears were ringing. He was thinking of sounding the knocker again, when a lady's servant rolled back the bolt and bowed to his question whether the judge was in.

He entered the broad hall of that distinguished residence, and taking the Entailed Hat from his head, hung it up at last on a carved mahogany rack of colonial times, where better head coverings had been wont to keep equal society. The venerable object, once there, gave a common look to everything, Meshach thought, and deepened his personal sense of unworthiness. He tried to feel angry, but his apprehension was too strong.

"Oh, discriminating God," he thought, "is it not enough to create us so unequal, that we must also cringe in spirit and acknowledge it. I expected to feel triumphant when I lodged my despised hat in this man's house, but I feel meaner than before."

The room opened by the lady's maid was the library, containing three cumbrous cases of books, several oil portraits with deep, gilded frames, and a map of Virginia and its northeastern environs, including all the peninsula south of the Choptank River and Cape Henlopen. Near the door was a clock, tall enough for a giant to stand in, solemnly cogging and waving time, lending a sense of evening to the place, which was increased by a wood fire flickering on tall, brass fire irons. And before the fire several wide, comfortable, leather chairs were drawn, all worn to luxurious attitudes.

A woman's rocking chair was disposed among them as though every other chair deferred to it. This was the first article to arrest Milburn's attention. It was so different, so suggestive, almost a thing of superstition, poised like a woman's instinct and will upon nothing firm, yet, like the sphere it moved upon, traversing a greater arc than a giant's seat would fill. Purity and conquest, power and welcome seemed to abide within it, like the empty throne in Parliament.

Milburn touched the fairy rocker with his foot. It started easily and gracefully, and when it died away, he pressed his lips to the top of it, nearest where her neck would be, and whispered, "God knows that kiss, at least, was pure."

He then looked at the portraits, and though they were not inscribed, he guessed at them from the insight of local lore or envious interpretation.

"Yon saucy, greedy, superserviceable rogue," thought Meshach, "with wine and beef in his cheeks and silver and harlotry in his eye, was the Irish tavern keeper of Rotterdam, who kept a heavy score against the banished princes whom Cromwell's name ever made to swear and shiver. They paid him in a distant office in Accomack, where they might never see him and his bills again. There, they let him steal most of the revenue, and his loyalty, of course, was in proportion to his booty. Many a time, no doubt, he was procurer for both royal brothers, Charles and

James, making his tavern their stew with Betty Killigrew or Lucy Walters or Katy Peg, or even Anne Hyde, the mother of a queen—of her who was the Princess Anne, godmother of our worshipful town here. I have not read in vain," concluded Meshach, "because my noble townsmen drove me to my cell."

The figure in the next portrait was clothed in military uniform—a higher type of manhood, shrewd and vigilant, but magisterial. "That should be Major General John Custis," thought Milburn, "son of John the Tapster, a shifty, marrying fellow who first began greatness as a salt boiler on the ocean islands until his father's friend, Charles II, made Henry Bennet, the king's bastard son's father-in-law, Earl of Arlington and lessee of Virginia. All the province for forty shillings a year rent! Those were pure, economical times around the court. So the salt boiler John flunkeyed to Arlington's overseers, named his farm 'Arlington,' hunted and informed upon the followers of the Puritan rebel Bacon, then turned and fawned upon King William, too. His grandchildren, all well provided for, spread around this bay. So much for politics in a merchant's hands."

The tone of Meshach's comment had somewhat raised his courage, and a sense of pleasurable interest in the warm room and genial surroundings led him to pass the time quite contentedly till Judge Custis would be ready.

∞

Meanwhile, the steeple-top hat was giving silent astonishment to the house servants, who assembled to gaze upon it from the foot of the hall. The chamber servant, Virgie, had carried the information to the colonnade that the dreadful creditor had come, and Roxy, the table waiter, had carried it from the colonnade to the kitchen, where the common calamity immediately produced a revolution against good manners.

"Hab he got dat debbil hat on he head chile?" inquired Aunt Hominy, laying down the club with which she was beating biscuit dough on the block.

"Yes, aunty, he's left it on the hatrack. I'm afraid to go past it to the do'."

Aunt Hominy threw the club on the blistered bulk of dough and retreated towards the big, black fireplace, her face expressing so much

The Hat Finds A Rack   43

fright and cunning humor together that it seemed about to turn white.

"De Lord a-massy, chillen," exclaimed Aunt Hominy, "le's burn dat hat in de fire! Maybe it'll liff de trouble off o' dis yer house. We got de hat jess wha' we want it, chillen. Roxy, gal, you go fetch it to Aunt Hominy."

The girl started as if she had been asked to take up a snake. "Deed, Aunt Hominy, I wouldn't touch it to save my life. Nobody but ole Samson ever did that."

"Go 'long, gal!" cried Aunt Hominy. "Didn't Miss Vessy hole dat ar' hat one time an' pin a white rose in it? Didn't dat drefful Meshach Milburn offer Miss Vessy a gole dollar, an' she wouldn' have none ob his gole? Dat she did. You git dat hat, chile. Poke it off de rack wid my pot hook heah. 'Twon't hurt you, gal. I'll sprinkle ye fust wid camomile an' witch hazel dat I keep up on de chimney jamb."

Aunt Hominy turned towards the broadly notched chimney sides, where fifty articles of Negro pharmacy were kept—bunches of herbs, dried peppers, bladders of seeds, and bottles of every mystic potency.

"Aunty," answered Virgie, "if I wasn't afraid of the bad man, I would be afraid to move that hat because Miss Vessy would be mortified. Think of her seeing me treating a visitor's things like that. Why, I'd rather be sold."

"Dat hat," persisted Aunt Hominy, "is de ruin ob dis family. Dat hat, gals, de debbil giv' ole Meshach an' made him wear it fo' de gift ob gittin' all de gole in Somerset County. Don't I know when he wore it fust? Dat was when he begun to git all de gole. Fo' dat he been po' as a lizzer, sellin' to niggers, cookin' fo' heseff, an' no 'count, nohow. He sot up in de loft ob he ole sto' readin' de Bible upside down to git de debbil's frenship. De debbil come in one night an' says to ole Meshach, 'Yer's my hat. Go, take it, honey, an' measure land wid it, an' all de land you measure is yo's, honey.' An' Meshach's measured mos' all dis county in. Jedge Custis's land is de last."

The relation affected both girls considerably and still more the group of little colored boys and girls who came up to listen, almost chilled with terror. But it produced the greatest effect on Aunt Hominy herself, whose imagination, widened in the effort, excited all her own fears and gave irresistible vividness to her legend.

"How can his hat measure people's lands in, Aunty?" Virgie asked, drawing Roxy to her by the waist for their mutual protection.

"Why, chile, he measures land in by de great long shadows dat debbil's hat frows. Meshach sots his eyes on a good farm. Says he, 'I'll measure dat in.' So he gits out dar some sunup or sundown, when de sun jest sots a'mos' on de groun, an' ebery tree an' fencepos' an' standin' thing goes a-way over de land, frowin' long, crooked shadows. Dat's de time Meshach stans up wid dat hat de debbil gib him to make him longer, jest a-layin' on de fields like de shadow ob a big church steeple. He walks along de road befo' de farm, an' wherever dat hat make a mark on de ground, all 'tween it an' whar he walks is ole Meshach's land. Dat's what he call his mortgage."

The children had their mouths wide open, and the maids heard with faith only less than fear.

"But Aunt Hominy," said Roxy, "he never measured in Judge Custis's house and all of us in it."

"Didn't I see him a-doin' ob it?" whispered Aunt Hominy, stooping in the contraction of her own fears and looking up into their faces with her fists clinched. "He's a-ben comin' along de fence on de darkest, cloudiest nights dis long a time, like a man dat was goin' to rob somethin', an' peepin' up at Miss Vessy's window. He took de dark nights when de streets ob Prencess Anne was clar ob folks, an' de dogs was in deir cribs, an' nuffin' goin' round but him an' wind an' cold an' rain. One night, while he was watchin' Miss Vessy's window like a black crow from de shadow ob de tree, I was a-watchin' ob him from de kitchen window. De moon dat had been all hid come right from behin' de rain clouds all at once, gals, an' scared him like. De moon was low on de woods, chillen, an' as ole Meshach turned an' walked away, his debbil's shadow swept dis house in. He measured it in dat night. It's ben his ever since."

"Well," exclaimed Roxy after a pause, "I know I wouldn't take hold of that hat now."

"I am almost afraid to look at it," said Virgie, "but if Miss Vessy told me to go bring it to her, I would do it."

"Le's us all go together," ventured Aunt Hominy, "an' take a peep at it. Maybe it won't hurt us if we all go."

Aware that Judge Custis and his wife were not near, the little circle of servants filed softly from the kitchen through the covered colonnade and thence along the back passage to the end of the hall. Here they made a group, gazing with believing wonder at the King James tile.

∞

The Hat Finds A Rack   45

Vesta Custis, after changing her morning robe for a walking suit and kneeing speechless awhile to receive the unknown will of heaven, came down the stairs in time to catch a glimpse of the servants staring at the strange old hat on the hall rack. They hastily fled at her appearance, and she looked up at the queer, faded article hanging among its betters. Remembering that she once held it in her hand, there descended along the years the odor of a rose and the impression of a pair of bold, startled eyes gazing into hers. She opened the library door, and the same eyes were looking up from her father's easy chair.

"Mr. Milburn, I believe?" said Vesta, walking to the visitor and extending her hand.

He arose, bowed, and hardly saw the hand in the earnest look he gave her. She did not withdraw her hand till he took it, and then he did not let it go. His look continuing, she dropped her eyes to the hand that held her own and observed that it was a gentleman's. Its fingers were long and almost delicate, the texture white, the palm warm, and it seemed to hold her with something like a brotherly pressure, respectful, and gentle too.

As he did not speak immediately, Vesta returned to his far less inviting face with its straight, black hair and high cheek bones. Its shape was broad and powerful, the chops long, the yellowish-brown eyes wide open and intense, and there was no real beard upon him anywhere. His complexion was dark and forester-like, showing a diet lacking in nutrition. His teeth were good and the mouth rather small. Hardly taller than Vesta, he seemed uncertain or confused, and Vesta came to his rescue by withdrawing her hand naturally.

"I have seen you many times, Mr. Milburn, but never here, I think."

"No, miss, I have never been here, nor anywhere in Princess Anne. You are the first lady here to speak to me."

"Will you sit, Mr. Milburn? You owe this visit so long that you will not be in haste today. I hope you have not felt that we were inhospitable. Little towns often encourage narrow circles and make people more selfish than they intend."

"You could never be selfish, miss," said Milburn, still with a wild, regarding gaze, like the eyes of a startled ox.

It was slightly embarrassing to Vesta to meet that uninterpretable look of inquiry and homage, but she made allowance for her visitor's want of sophistication. He was like an Indian before a mirror in the excitement of apprehension and delight. The most beautiful thing he had ever seen was within the compass of his full sight at last, and whether to detain it by force or persuasion, he did not know.

Her dark hair, silky as the cleanest tassels of corn, fell naturally from her perfect head, and her teeth, white as the milky cornrows, moved in the May cherries of her lips. The delicate arches of her brows, shaded by blackbird's wings, enriched the clear sky of her harmonious eyes, where mercy and nobility kept company, as in heaven.

"How could you know I was unselfish, Mr. Milburn?"

"Because I have heard you sing."

"Oh, yes, you hear me in our church; I remember."

"I have heard you every Sunday that you sung there," said Meshach, with hardly a change of expression.

"Are you fond of music, Mr. Milburn?"

"I like all I have ever heard—birds and you."

"I will sing for you, then," said Vesta, taking the relief the talk directed her to. A piano was in another room, but to avoid changing the scene as well as to use a simpler accompaniment for an ignorant man's ears, she brought her guitar, and placing it in her lap, struck the strings and the key to these tender words:

> Oh, for some sadly dying note,
> Upon this silent hour to float,
> Where, from the bustling world remote,
>   The lyre might wake its melody.
> One feeble strain is all can swell,
> From mine almost deserted shell,
> In mournful accents yet to tell
>   That slumbers not its minstrelsy.

> "There is an hour of deep repose,
> That yet upon my heart shall close,
> When all that nature dreads and knows
>   Shall burst upon me wondrously;
> Oh, may I then awake, forever,
> My harp to rapture's high endeavor;
> And, as from earth's vain scene I sever,
>   Be lost in immortality.

The Hat Finds A Rack   47

When Vesta ended, she remarked with emotion, "Those lines were written by a young clergyman from New York, Rev. James Eastburn, at my grandfather's house in Accomack County. He was only twenty-two years old when he died at sea of consumption. His is the only poetry I know of, Mr. Milburn, which has been written in our beautiful old country here."

"I wondered if I should ever hear you sing for me," said Milburn. "Now that it is realized, I feel skeptical about it. You are there, Miss Custis, are you not?"

Vesta was puzzled. Under other circumstances she would have been amused, since her humor could flow as freely as her music. It seemed to her that the odd little man might be cracked in the head.

"Yes, indeed, Mr. Milburn. If it were a dream, I should have no expression all this day but song. I think I never felt so sad to sing as just now. Father is ill, and Mamma is ill also. I have become the business agent of the family, and I have heard within this hour that Papa is deeply involved. You are his creditor, are you not?"

Meshach Milburn bowed.

"What is the sum of Papa's notes and mortgages? Is it more than he can pay by the sacrifice of everything?"

"Yes. He has nothing to sell at forced sale which will bring anything, except the household servants. You would not like to sell them?"

"Sell Virgie! She was brought up with me. What right have I to sell her any more than she has to sell me?"

"None," said Milburn, "but there is law for it."

"To sell Roxy and old Aunt Hominy and the young children—how could I ever pray again if they were sold? Oh, Mr. Milburn, where was your heart to let Papa waste his plentiful substance in such a hopeless experiment? If my singing in the church has given you happiness, why could it not move you to mercy? Think of the despair of this family, my father's helpless generosity, my mother's marriage settlement gone, too, and every other son and daughter parted from them."

"I never encouraged Judge Custis's expenditure for a moment," Meshach said, "though I lent him money. The first time he came to borrow, my mind was in a liberal disposition, for you had just entered it with your innocent attentions. I supposed he wanted a temporary accommodation, and I gave it to him at the lowest rate one Christian would charge another."

"You say I influenced you to lend my father money? Why, sir, I was a child. He has been borrowing from you since my earliest recollections."

The creditor took a leather wallet from his breast pocket and, arising, laid its contents on the table. He opened a piece of folded paper and drew two objects from it: one a lock of blue-black hair like his own, and the other a pressed and faded rose.

"This flower," said Milburn with reverence, "Judge Custis's daughter fastened in my derided hat. I kept it till it was dead and laid it away with my mother's hair—the two religious objects of my life. That faded rose made me your father's creditor, Miss Custis."

Vesta took the rose and looked at him with surprise and inquiry. "Why did not this flower speak for us," she asked, "to open your lips after that to save my father? You informed yourself and knew that he was hurrying to destruction, but still you gave him money at higher interest."

Milburn looked at her with diminished courage, but sincerely, and replied, "Your voice sang between us, Miss Custis, every time he came. I did not admit what it was, but the feeling that I was being drawn near you still opened my purse to your father until he has drained me of the profits of years. I did know that he probably could not repay me, but every Sabbath you sang at the church, and that seemed some compensation. I was bewitched. Indistinct visions of gratitude and recognition from you filled the preaching with concourses of angels, all bearing your image and hovering above me. The price I paid for that unuttered hope has been princely, but never grudged. It has been pure, I believe, or heaven would have punished me. The more I ruined myself for your father, the more successful my ventures were in all other places. If you were my temptation, it had the favor or forgiveness of the God in whose temple it was born."

Vesta arose with a frightened spirit. "Do I understand you?" she said, her rich, gray eyes wide under startled lashes. "My father has spoken of a degrading condition? Is it to love you?"

For the first time Meshach Milburn dropped his eyes. "I never supposed it possible for you to love me," he said bitterly. "I thought God might permit me someday to love you."

"Do you know what love is?" asked Vesta with astonishment.

"No."

"How came you, then, to be interpreting my good acts so basely, carrying even my childhood about in your evil imagination and cursing my father's sorrow with the threat of his daughter's slavery?"

Milburn heard these hard imputations with perfect humility.

The Hat Finds A Rack   49

"I think you have not loved, Miss Custis," he said with a slight flush. "I have believed you never did."

"I loved my father above everything," Vesta faltered. "I saw no man besides."

"Then I displaced no man's right by coveting your image. Sometimes it seemed you were being kept free so long to reward my silent worship. I do not know what love is, but I know the gifts of God as they bloom in nature repel no man's devotion. The flowers, the birds, and the forest delighted my childhood. My youth was spent in the study of myself and man. At last a beautiful child appeared to me, spoke her way to my soul, and it could never expel her glorious presence. All things became subordinate to her, even avarice and success. She kept me a Christian, or I should have become utterly selfish. She kept me humble, for what was my wealth when I could not enter her father's house. I am here by a destiny now. The power that called you to this room, so unexpectedly to me, has borne us onward to the secret I dreaded to speak to you. Dare I go further?"

She tried to repress her insulted feelings and not say something that would exasperate her father's creditor, but the possibility of marrying him was too tremendous to reply.

"This moment is a great one," Milburn continued, "for I feel it is to terminate my visions of happiness and kindness as well. You have expressed yourself so indignantly that I see no thought of me has ever lodged in your mind. Why should it have done so, though I almost dreamed it had because you filled my life so many years with your rich image. I thought you might have felt me, like some apparition, often stealing around this dwelling in the dark and rain, content with the ray of light your window threw upon the deserted street. Now I see that I was a weak dunce. Better for me that I had hugged the debasing reality of my gold and lost my eyes to everything but its comfort."

He looked towards the door, but Vesta sat down in the fairy rocker and detained him.

"You have told me the feeling you think you had, Mr. Milburn. Poor as we Custises are now, it will not do to be proud. How did you ever think that feeling could be returned by me? My youth, my connections, everything would forbid me—without haughtiness—to see a suitor in you. You took no means to turn my attention towards you. You could have been neighborly. You did not even wear the commonest emblems of a lover."

"I have had reasons, also proud, Miss Custis. Since I see that I am not likely to make myself otherwise attractive, I will put the substantial merits of my case to you. This house is already mine. In a few weeks the law will put me in possession of your father's entire property. I shall change outward circumstances with him in Princess Anne. He is too old to adopt my sacrifices and recover his situation. He may find some shifting refuge with his sons and daughters, but, even if his spirit could brook that dependence, it would be very unnecessary, when, by marrying his creditor, you can retain everything he now has to make his family respectable. I offer you his estate as your marriage portion."

He took up from the table the notes her father had negotiated and laid them in her lap.

Vesta sat, rocking slowly and deeply agitated. She had in her mouth the comfort and honor of her parents and could confer them in a single word. It was a responsibility so mighty that it made her tremble.

"Oh, what shall I say?" she thought. "It will be a sin to say yes. To say no would be a crime."

"You shall retain every feature of your home: your servants, your mother, her undiminished portion, and your liberty in the fullest sense. I will contribute to send your father to the legislature or to congress to sustain his pride and keep him well occupied. He may appear to have sold the furnace to me, and I will accept the unpopularity of closing it. I ask only to serve you and inhabit your daily life like one of these Negroes you are kind to, and if I am ever harsh to you, Miss Vesta, I swear to surrender you to your family and depart forever."

Vesta shook her head. "When heaven has been called down to the marriage solemnity, there is no separation but one," she said. "It is before that act we must consider everything. How could I make you happy? I will dismiss my own happiness. Yours must then comprehend mine. Kindness might make me grateful, but gratitude will not satisfy your love."

"Yes," exclaimed Milburn, chasing up his advantage with tremulous ardor, "the long famine of my heart will be thankful for a dry crust and a cup of ice. Here at the fireside let me sit and warm and hear the rustle of your dress, and grow in heavenly sensibility. You will redeem a savage. You will save a soul."

"It is not the price I must pay to do this, I would have you consider, sir," Vesta replied, her attention somewhat arrested by his intensity; "it is the price you are paying—your self-respect, perhaps—by the terms on which you obtain me. It may never be known out of this family that I married you for the sake of my father and mother, but how am I to prevent you from remembering it, especially when you say that I am the sum of your purest wishes? If your interest would consume after you obtained me, we might, at least, be indifferent, but if it grew into real love, would you not often accuse yourself?"

Meshach Milburn sat down, cast his large brown eyes upon the floor, and listened in painful reflection. "You cannot conceive that I have had any real love for you?" he exclaimed dubiously.

"You have seen me and desired me for your wife; that is all," said Vesta. "That I can imagine. Lawless power could do that anywhere. To be an obedient wife is the lot of woman. Love, such as you have some glimmering of, is a mystic instinct so mutual, so gladdening, yet so free, that the captivity you set me in to make me sing to you will divide us like the wires of a cage."

"There is no bird I ever caught," said Milburn, "that did not learn to trust me. Your comparison does not, therefore, discourage me. And you have already sung for me, the saddest day of your life."

A slight touch of nature in this revelation of her strange suitor called Vesta's attention to the study of him again. With her intelligence and sense of higher worth coming to her rescue, she thought, "Let me see all there is of this Tartar. Perhaps there may be another way to his mercy."

As she recovered composure, however, she grew more beautiful in his sight, her dark, peerless charms filling the room, her kindling eyes conveying love, her skin like the wild plum's, and raven brows and crown of luxuriant hair rising upon a queenly presence worthy of an empress's throne. Such beauty almost made Milburn afraid.

"Who *are* you?" she asked with a calm, searching look. "Have you any relations or connections fit to bring to this house—to me?"

"Not one that I know," said the forester. "I am nothing but myself and what you will make of me."

"Where were you born and reared?"

"The house does not stand which witnessed that misery," said Milburn with a flush of pride. "It was burned last night, not far from the furnace which swallowed your father's substance."

"Why, I would be afraid of you, Mr. Milburn, if your errand here was not so practical. Omens and wonders surround you. Birds forget their natural life for you. Iron ceases to be occult when you take it up. Your birthplace in this world disappears by fire the night before you foreclose a mortgage upon a gentleman's daughter. Is all this sorcery inseparable from that necromancer's hat you wear in Princess Anne?"

She had touched the sensitive topic by a skillful approach, yet he changed color as if the allusion piqued him.

"Nature never rebuked my hat, Miss Vesta, and you are so like nature it will not occupy your thoughts. I recollect the day you decorated my old hat. Said I, 'Perhaps this vagrant head covering, after all its injuries and wanderings, may some day find a peg beneath my own roof and the kind welcome of a lady like that little miss.' That was several years ago, and today, for the first time, my hat is on the rack of your hall. The long wish of the heart is not often denied. We are not responsible for it. The only conspiracy I have plotted here was that I did not oppose most natural occurrences, all drawing towards this scene. My magic was hope and humility. I dared to wear my ancestor's hat in the face of a contemptuous and impertinent provincial public, and it gave me the pride to persevere till I should bring it home to honors and to noble shelter. If you despise my hat, you will despise me."

"No, Mr. Milburn, I try never to despise anything. If you wore your family hat from some filial respect, it was, in part, piety. But was that your motive in being so eccentric?"

Milburn felt uneasy again. He hesitated, then said, "In perfect truth, I fear not. There may have been something of revenge in my mind. I had been grossly insulted."

"Is it not something of revenge which instigates you here, even in this profession of love?" exclaimed Vesta judicially.

Meshach looked up, and the shadows cleared from his face. "I can answer that truthfully, lady. Towards you, not an indignant thought has ever harbored in my brain. It has been the opposite: protection, worship, tender sensibility."

"Has that exceptional charity extended to my father?"

"No."

Vesta would have been exasperated but for his candor.

"My father never insulted you, sir."

"No, he patronized me. He meant no harm, but that old hat has worn a deep place in my brain through carrying it so long, and it is a subject that galls me to mention it. Yet I must be consistent with my only eccentricity. Wherever I may go, there goes my hat. It makes my identity, my inflexibility. It achieves my promise to myself, that men shall respect my hat before I die."

"Pardon me," said Vesta, not uninterested in his character, "I can understand an eccentricity founded on family respect. We were Virginians, and that is next to religion there. The Negroes of our family share it with us. You had a family, then?"

Milburn shook his head. "No, not a family in the sense you mean. Generations of obscurity. A parentage only virtuous. No tombstone anywhere. No crest nor motto. Not even a self-deluding lie of some former gentility, shaped from hand to hand till it commits a larceny on history and is brazen on a carriage panel. We were foresters. We came forth and existed and perished like the families of ants upon the ant hills of sand. We migrated no more than the woodpeckers in your sycamore trees and made no sound in events more than their insectivorous tapping. Out yonder, beyond Dividing Creek, in the thickets of small oak and low pines, many a little farm scratched from the devouring forest, speckling the plains and wastes with huts and with little barns of logs, once bore the name of Milburn. Through all the localities of the Pocomoke, to and beyond the great Cypress Swamp, they are dying but never dead. The few who live expect no recognition from me and envy me nothing I have accumulated. My name has grown hard to them. My hat is the subject of their superstitions. My ambition and success have lost me their sympathy without giving me any other compensation. You behold a desperate man, a merciless creditor, a tussock of ore from the bogs of Nassawango, yet one whose only crimes have been to adore you and to wear his forefathers' hat."

"Is this pride, then, sir, wholly insulted sensibility?"

"I cannot say, Miss Custis. You may smile, but I think it is aristocracy."

"I think so too," Vesta exclaimed reflectively. "You are a proud man. My father, who has had reason to be proud, is less an aristocrat, sir, than you."

Milburn's flush came and stayed a considerable while. He was not displeased at Vesta's compliment, though it bore the nature of an accusation.

"You are aristocratic," explained Vesta, "because you adopted the obsolete hat of your people. Whatever vanity led you to do it, it was the satisfaction of some origin, I think."

She checked herself, seeing that she was entering into his affairs with too much freedom.

"I suppose that somewhere, sometime," the strange visitor said, "some person of my race has been influential and prosperous. Indeed, I have been told so. He was elevated to both the magistracy and the scaffold, but my hat had even an older origin."

"Tell me about that ancestor," said Vesta, the heartache from his greater errand instigating her to defer it, while she was yet barely conscious that the man was original, if not interesting.

Before he began, Milburn drew up his compact little figure and opened the door to the hall. The wind from some of the large, cold apartments of the house gave almost a shriek and scattered the fire in the chimney.

Vesta felt her blood chill as her visitor reentered with the antediluvian hat and placed it upon the table beneath the lamp.

It had that look of gentility victorious over decay, which suggested the mummy of some Pharaoh brought into a drawing room on a learned society's night. Rising through her pain, Vesta repressed a smile at the gravity of the forester guest who was about to demonstrate his aristocracy through this old hat. It also seemed to her that the portraits of the Custises on the wall carried indignant noses in the air, as if sensing the presence of some unburied pretender as the effigies of the Norman kings in Westminster Abbey might become aroused to feel Oliver Cromwell lying among them in state.

The hat, Vesta perceived, was Flemish, such as was popular in England when the Netherlands was her ally against the house of Spain. She attempted to exert her liberality and perceive some beauty in this hat, but the utmost she could admit was the tyranny of fashion over the mind—over the soul, it seemed—for this old hat, inoffensive as it was, weighed down her spirits like a diving bell.

The man without his hat had somewhat redeemed himself from low conversation and ideas, but now that he brought this hat in and associated his person with it, she shrank from him as if he had been a triple-hatted Jew peddling around the premises.

The obnoxious hat also exercised an exciting influence over Meshach Milburn. He resumed his strong, wild-man's stare, deepened and lowered his voice, and told the tale, tracing his hat to Raleigh's times and through Sir Henry Vane to America till it became the property of Jacob Milborne, the popular martyr who was executed in New York, and his brethren, driven into Maryland, brought with them the harmless hat as their only patrimony.

Ha! Ha! The Wooing On't

Chapter 9

It was twilight when Meshach Milburn closed his story, and silence and pallid eve drew together in the Custis sitting room, resembling the two people there thinking on matrimony, the one grave as conscious serpenthood could make him, the other fluttering like the charmed bird.

Vesta spoke first: "How intense must be your head to create so many objects around it within the world of a hat. You have only brought the story down a little way towards our times."

"I began the tale of Raleigh out of proportion," said Milburn, "and it grew upon the same scale, like the passion I conceived for you so intensely, that in the climax of this night I am scarcely begun."

"Yet, like Raleigh, I see the scaffold," said Vesta with an attempt at humor that for the first time broke her down, and she raised her hands to her face to hush the burst of anguish. It would not be repressed, and one low cry, deep with the sense of desertion and captivity, sounded through the deepening room and smote Milburn's innermost heart.

He obeyed an impulse he had not felt since his mother died. He threw his arms around Vesta, drew her to his breast, kissed her like a child, and whispered, "Honey, honey, don't cry now. It will break my heart."

The act of nature seldom is misinterpreted. Vesta, having labored alone so long with this obdurate man, her young faculties strained by the first encounter beyond her strength, accepted the friendship of his sympathy and contrition as if he had been her father. In a few moments the paroxysm of grief was past, and she disengaged his arms.

"You are not merciless," said Vesta. "Tell me what I must do. You have broken my father down, and he cannot come to my help. Take pity on my inequality and advise me."

"Alas, child," said Milburn, "my advice must be in my own interest, though I wish I could find your confidence. I am a poor creature and do not know how. It is you who must encourage the faith I feel starting somewhere in this room, like a chimney swallow that would fain fly out. Chirrup, chirrup to it, and it may come."

Standing a moment, trying to collect her thoughts and wholly failing, Vesta accepted the confidence he held out to her with open arms. Blushing as she had never blushed in her life—though he could not know it in the evening dark—she kissed him once.

"Will that encourage you to advise me like a friend?" she said.

"Alas, no," sighed Milburn fervently. "It makes me the more your unjust lover. I cannot advise you away from me. Let me plead for myself. I love you!"

"Then what shall I do," exclaimed Vesta, "if you are unable to rise to the height of my friend, and my father is your slave? Do you think God can bless your prosperity when you are so hard with your debtor? The full sacrifice falls on me, though I never was in your debt consciously and have never wished injury to anyone."

"Would you accept your father's independence at the expense of the most despised man in Princess Anne?" Milburn spoke without changing his kind tone. "Would you let me give him the fruit of many years of hard toil and careful saving in order that I shall be disappointed in the only motive of assisting him—the honorable wooing of his daughter?"

Vesta felt her pride rising.

"Your father's debts to me are tens of thousands of dollars," continued Milburn. "Do you ask me to present that sum to you and retire to my loneliness out of this bright light of home and family, warmth and music that you have made? That is the test you put my love to—banishment from you. Will you ask it?"

"I have not asked for your money, sir," said Vesta. "Yet I have heard of love doing as much as that, relieving the anguish of its object and finding sufficient joy in the self-denying deed."

"I do not think you personally know of any such case, though you may have read it in a novel. Men have died and left a fortune they could no longer keep to some cherished lady or have made a sacrifice for a beautiful and noble woman, but where did you ever hear, Miss Vesta, of a famished lover surrendering every endowment that might win the peerless one, to be himself returned to his sorrow, tortured still by love and by his neighbors ridiculed? What would Princess Anne say of me? That I had been made a fool of, and hurl new epithets after my hat?"

Vesta searched her mind, thinking she must alight upon some such example there, but none suited the case.

Meshach took advantage of her silence. "As I have understood, the gifts of a lover are everywhere steps to love. He makes his impression with them. They are expected. Nothing creates happiness like a gift, and it is an old saying that blessings await him who gives and also her who takes, and that to seek and ask and knock are praiseworthy."

"Oh," said Vesta, "but to be *bought*, Mr. Milburn? To be weighed against a father's debts. Is it not degrading?"

"Not where such respect and cherishing as mine will be. Rather exalt yourself as more valuable to a miser than his whole lendings and greater than all your father's losses as an equivalent, and even then putting your husband in debt, being so much richer than his account."

"Where will be my share of love, married so?" asked Vesta. "To love is the globe itself to a woman, her youth the mere atmosphere thereof, her widowhood the perfume of that extinguished star. And all my mind has been alert to discover the image I shall serve, the bright youth ready for me, looking on one after another to see if it might be he, and suddenly you hold between me and my faith a paper with my father's obligations and say, 'Here is your fate. This is your whole romance. You are foreclosed upon!' How are you to take a withered heart like that and find glad companionship in it? You will be disappointed. It will recoil upon me that I sold myself."

"The image you waited for may have come," said Milburn undauntedly, "even in me. Love often springs from an ambush, and you cannot prepare the heart for it like a field. I recollect a fable I read of a god loving a woman, and he burst upon her in a shower of gold. What was that but a rich man's wooing? We get gold to equalize nobility in women. Beauty is luxurious and demands adornment and rich setting. The richest man in Princess Ann is not good enough for you, and the mere boys your mind has been filled with are more unworthy of being your husband than the humble creditor of your father. Such a creation as Miss Vesta required a special sacrifice and success in the character of her husband. The annual life of this peninsula could not match you, and a monster had to be raised to carry you away."

"You are not exactly a monster," Vesta remarked with natural compassion, "and you compliment me so warmly that it relieves the strain of this encounter a little. Do not draw a woman's attention to your defects, as she might otherwise be charmed by your voice."

"That also is a part of my sacrifice," said Meshach, "like the money which I have accumulated. Without a teacher but love and hope, I have educated myself to be fit to talk to you. It is all crude now, like a crow that I have taught to speak, but encouragement will make me confident and saucy, and you will forget my sable raiment—even my hat."

A chilliness seemed to attend this conclusion, and Vesta touched her bell. Virgie entered and took her mistress's instructions: "Bring a tray and tea and lights, and place Mr. Milburn's hat upon the rack."

The girl glanced at the antique hat with a timid light in her eye, but her mistress's head was turned as if to intimate that she must take it, though it might be red hot. Virgie obeyed and soon brought in the tea.

"It is good tea," said Milburn, drinking not from the cup but the saucer. "It is chill this evening; let me start your fire."

He walked across the room, shivering a little, and poked the charred logs into a flame. As he set on more wood, the walls sprang into yellow flashes, between which Vesta saw her forefathers in their gilt frames dart cold glances at her. Yet with all their respectability, how helpless they were to take her body or her father's honor out of pawn. For the first time she felt the hollowness of family power and made a long, careful survey of her suitor to see if there was any apology for him as a husband.

His figure was short, but with strength and elasticity. Better clothes might fit him daintily, and Vesta dressed him in fancy with lavender kids upon his small hands, a ring upon his little finger, a carnelian seal and ribbon at his fob pocket, and ruffles in his shirt bosom. In place of his dull suit she would give him a buff vest with pearl buttons and white gaiters instead of those shabby green things over his feet, and put upon his head a neat silk hat with narrow brim to raise his height slenderly. A coat of olive or dark blue and trousers of the same color would relieve his ornaments. Thus transformed, Vesta could conceive a passable man whom a lady might grow considerate towards by much praying and striving, and she wondered, now, how this man had managed to soothe her already to that degree that she had voluntarily kissed him. She would be afraid to do it again, but it was as clearly on record as that she had once put a flower in his hat.

Vesta said to herself, "He has power of some kind. That story, little as I heard of it, was told with an opinionated confidence I wish my poor father had something of. Could I ever be happy with this man? By study and piety God might open the way, but it seems closed to me now."

"The night wears on, Miss Custis," said Meshach. "Its rewards are already great to me. When may I return?"

"I think we must determine what to do this night, Mr. Milburn," Vesta said with rising determination. "We have not come one point nearer to a solution of this obligation of my father. Up to now we have considered it as my obligation, and that may have unduly encouraged you. I can work for my living, Sir."

"You *work*?" repeated Milburn.

"Why not? Other women who are left poor work for their children or a sick husband. I love my father; why should I not work for him. Poverty has no terrors but the loss of pride."

"You hazard that, whatever happens," said her suitor, "but you will not lose it by evading the lesser evil for the greater. I have heard of women who fled to poverty from dissatisfaction with a husband, but pride survived and made poverty dreadful. Pride in either case increased the discontent. You should take the step which will let pride be absorbed in duty, if not in love."

"Duty? That is a reposeful word, Mr. Milburn. How is it my duty to do what you ask?"

"I think I perceive that you have a loyal heart, a conscientiousness that deceit cannot even approach. Something has already made you slow to marriage, else I would not have had the chance to be now rejected by you. Marriage has become too formidable to you, perhaps, by the purity of your heart, more so because you looked upon it to be your destiny. It *is* your fate, but you contend against it. Look upon it, then, as a duty such as you expect in others—in your slave maid, for instance."

"Alas," Vesta said, "she may marry freely. I am the slave."

"No, Miss Vesta, she has been free. But if sold among strangers with your father's effects, she will feel so perishing for sympathy and protection that love, in whatever ugly form it comes, will be God's blessing to her poor heart. What you repel in the revulsion of fortune—the yoke of a husband—millions of women have bent to as if it was the very rainbow of promise set in heaven."

"How do you know so much of women's trials, Mr. Milburn? Have you had sisters or other ladies to woo?"

"I have seen human nature in my little shop, not like your rare nature, refined by happy fortune and descent, but of moderate kind and struggling downward like a wounded eagle. At first they have come to me for cheaper articles of necessity or smaller portions than other stores would sell, looking on me with contempt. In the end they have sacrificed their last slave, their last pair of shoes, and when it was too late, their false pride has surrendered to shelter in a Negro's hut or to dance barefooted in my store for a cup of whiskey."

"Sir," exclaimed Vesta indignantly, rising from her rocker, "do you set this warning for me?"

As she rose, Meshach Milburn thought his wealth was merely pebbles and shells to her perfection, now animated with a queen's spirit. "Miss Vesta," he said, "pardon me, but I have just issued from many generations of forest poverty, and, knowing how hard it is to break that thralldom, I would stop you from taking the first step towards it. The bloom on your cheek, the mold you are the product of—without flaw—the chaste lady's tastes and thoughts and inborn strength and joy are the work of God's favor to your family for generations. He continues that favor in laying those family burdens on another's shoulders, to spare you the toil and care, the anxiety and slow decay that this violent change of circumstances means. It would be a sin to relapse from this perfection to that penury."

"I cannot see that honorable poverty would make me less a woman," exclaimed Vesta.

"You do not dread poverty because you do not know it," Milburn continued. "It grows in this region like the old field pines and little oaks over a neglected farm. Once there was a courthouse settlement on Dividing Creek, where justice, eloquence, talent, wit, and heroism made the social center of two counties. But they moved the courthouse, and the forest speedily choked the spot. Not an echo lingers now of that former glory. You can save your house from being swallowed up in the forest."

"By marrying the forest hero?" Vesta said, though she immediately regretted it.

"Yes," Milburn said stubbornly. "I have met the house of Custis halfway. I am coming out of the woods as they are going in unless the sacrifice be mutual."

"Let us not be personal," Vesta pleaded with her grace of sorrow. "I feel that you are a kind man, at least to me, but a poor girl must make a struggle for herself."

She saw the tears stand instantly in his eyes and pressed her advantage.

"Your tears are like the springs we find here, so close under the flinty sand that nobody would suspect them, but I have seen them trickle out. Tell me if I would not be happier to take up the burden of my father and mother, and let us diminish and be frugal instead of cowardly flying into the protection of our creditor by a union which the world, at least, would pronounce mercenary. My father might come up again, in some way."

"No, Miss Vesta, your father can hold no property while any portion of his debts remains unpaid. The easier way is to show the world that our union is not mercenary by trying to love each other. Throughout the earth, marriage is the reparation of ruined families—the short path and the most natural one, too. Ruth was poor kin, but she turned from the harvest stubble that made her beautiful feet bleed to crawl to the feet of old Boaz and find wifely rest, and her wisdom of choice we sing in the psalms of King David and hear in the proverbs of King Solomon, sons of her sons."

"I am not thinking of myself, God knows," said Vesta. "Gladly could I teach a little school or be a governess somewhere or, like our connection, the mother of Washington, ride afield in my sunbonnet and straw hat and oversee the laborers."

"That never made General Washington, Miss Vesta. It was marriage that lent him to the world—first, his half-brother's marriage with the Fairfaxes, and next, his own with Custis's rich widow. Had they been looking for natural parts only, some Daniel Morgan or Ethan Allen would have been Washington's commander."

"Why do you draw me to you by awakening the motive of my self-love?" asked Vesta. "That is not the way to preserve my heart as you would have it."

"In every way I can draw you to me," said Milburn, trembling with earnestness, "I feel desperate to try. If it is wrong, it arises from my sense of self-preservation. Without you I am a dismal failure, and my labor in life is thrown away."

"Do you really believe you love me? Is it not ambition of some kind, perhaps a social ambition?"

"To marry a Custis?" Milburn exclaimed. "No, it is to marry *you*. I would rather you were not a Custis."

"Ah, I see, sir," Vesta's face flushed with some admiration for the man. "You think your family name is quite as good. So you ought to. Then you love me from a passion?"

"Partly that," answered Milburn. "I love you from my whole temperament, whatever it is. From the glow of youth and the reflection of manhood. From appreciation of you and also from worship. From the eye and the mind. I love you in the vision of domestic settlement, in the companionship of thought, in the partition of my ambition, in my instinct for cultivation. I love you, too, with the ardor of a lover stronger than all because I must possess you to possess myself, because you kindle flame in me, and my humanity of pity is trampled down by my humanity of desire. I cannot hear your appeal to escape. I am deaf to sentiments of honor and courtesy if they let you slip me. Give yourself to me, and these better angels may prevail, being perhaps accessory to the mighty instinct I obey at the command of the Creator."

As he proceeded, Vesta saw the very ecstasy of love shine in Meshach Milburn's face. His dark, resinous eyes were like forest ponds flashing at night under the torches of Negro 'coon hunters. His long lady's hands trembled as he stretched them towards her to clasp her, and she saw upon his brow and in his open nostril and firm mouth the presence of a will that seldom fails, when exerted mightily, to reduce a woman's and make her recognize her lord.

Yet with this strong excitement of mental and animal love, which generally animates man to eloquence if not to beauty, a weary something, nearly like pain, marked the bold intruder, and a quiver not like will and courage went through his frame. It was this which touched Vesta with the sense that perhaps she was not the only sufferer there, and pity, which saves many a lover when his merits could not win, brought the judge's daughter to an impulsive determination.

"Mr. Milburn," she said at last, pressing her hands to her head, "this day's trials have been too much for my brain. Never in all my life together have I had realities like these to contend with. I am worn out. Nay, sir, do not touch me now (he had tried to repeat his sympathetic overture and pet her in his arms). Let us end this conflict at once. You say you will marry me; when?"

"It is yours to say, Miss Custis. I am ready any day."

"And you will give me every obligation of my father, so that my mother's portion shall be returned to her in full, and this house, servants, and demesnes be mine in my own right?"

"Yes," said Milburn. "I have such confidence in your truth and virtue that you shall keep these papers from this moment until the marriage day."

"It will not be long, then," Vesta said, looking at Milburn with a will and authority fully equal to his own. "Will you take me tonight?"

"Tonight?" he repeated. "Not tonight, surely?"

"Tonight, or probably never."

He drew nearer to look into her countenance by the strong firelight. Calm courage, like Joan of Arc in the flames, met his inquiry.

"At your command," said Milburn, "I will take you tonight, though it is a surprise to me."

He flinched a little, nevertheless, his conscience being uneasy, and the same trembling Vesta had already observed went through his frame again.

"What will the world say to your marriage after a single day's acquaintance with me?"

"Nothing," Vesta answered, "except that I am your wife. That will at least silence advice and prevent intrusion. If I delay, these forebodings may prevail, if not with me, with my family, some of whom are to be feared."

"It is you, dear child, I am thinking of—whether this haste will not be repented or become a subject of reproach to yourself. To me it cannot be, having no world but myself and you."

Vesta came forward and lifted his hand, which was cold.

"I believe you love me," she said. "I believe this hand has the lines of a gentleman. I will trust to you a family confidence. The troubles of this house are like a fire which there is no other way of treating than to put it out at once. My father will not be disturbed beyond his secret pain at the step I am to take, for he appreciates your talents and success. It is for him I shall take this step, if I take it at all, and I have yet an hour to reflect. But my mother will be resentful, and her brothers and kindred in Baltimore will express a savage rage, in the first place at my father's losing her portion. Next to that, and I hope less bitterly, they will resent my marriage to you. Exposed to their interference, I might be restrained from going to my father's assistance. They might even force me away and break our family up, leaving father alone to encounter his miseries."

"I see," said Milburn. "You would give me the legal right to meet your mother's excited people."

"Not that merely. I would put it out of her power and theirs to prevent the sacrifice I meditate making. My father's immediate dread is my mother's upbraiding—that he has risked and lost her money. It has sent her to bed already, sick and almost violent. I might as well save the poor gentleman his whole distress if I am to save him a part."

"Brave girl!" exclaimed Meshach Milburn in admiration. "It is true, then, that blood will tell. You intend to give your mother the money which has been lost and silence her complaint before she makes it?"

"Just that, Mr. Milburn, and to say, 'It is my husband's gift and a peace offering from us all.'"

"Is it not your intention, honey," asked the creditor, "to take Mrs. Custis into your confidence before this marriage?"

She looked at him with the entreaty of one in doubt, who would be resolved. "Advise me," she said. "I want to do the best for all and spare all bitter words. Is it necessary to tell her?"

"No. You are a free woman. I know your age—though I shall forget it by and by." This first gleam of humor rather became his strange face. "If you tell your father, it is enough."

"I hope I am doing right," Vesta said, "and now I shall take my hour to my soul and my Savior. Do you ever pray, sir?"

Milburn recoiled a little. "I do not pray like you," He replied. "My prayers are dry things. I do say a little rhyme that my mother taught me in the forest."

"Try to pray for me to do right," said Vesta, "that I may not make this sacrifice and leave a wounded conscience. And now, sir, farewell. At nine o'clock, go to our church and wait. If I resolve to come, there you will find the rector and the arrangements made. If I do not come, I think you will see me no more."

"Oh, beautiful spirit," exclaimed her lover, "oppress me not with that fear."

"If another way is made plain to me," Vesta said, "I shall go that way. If my duty leads me to you again, you will be my master. Though your errand here was a severe one, I thank you for your sincerity and the kind consideration you seem to have had for me so long. Farewell."

"Angel! Vesta! Honey!" Milburn cried. "May I kiss you?"

"Not now," she answered, interposing her hand.

The door stood wide open and Virgie in it, holding the Entailed Hat. Milburn took it with a shudder, covered himself, and departed.

Master in the Kitchen

Chapter 10

The kitchen had been a scene of anything but culinary peace and savor during the long visit of the hat's owner. Aunt Hominy and the little darkeys had made three stolen visits to the hall to peep at the dreadful thing hanging there, as if it were a trap of some kind, liable to drop a spring and catch somebody or explode like a mortar or torpedo. As hour after hour wore on, and Miss Vesta did not reappear, Aunt Hominy was beside herself with superstition.

"Honey," she exclaimed to Virgie, "jess you take in dis yer dried lizzer an' cammermile. You drap de lizzer in dat ole hat, an' you sprinkle de flo' whar ole Meshach sots wi' de cammermile, an' you say 'Shoo!' Maybe it'll spile his measurin' of Miss Vessy in."

"No, Aunty. If old Meshach measured *me* in, I wouldn't make the family ashamed before him. Miss Vessy is powerful wise, and maybe she'll get the better of that wicked hat."

"Yes," added Roxy, "she's good, Aunt Hominy, an' says her prayers every night an' mornin'. I've heard tell that witches can't hear the Lord's name an' stay, nohow. Maybe Miss Vessy will say in Meshach's old hat, 'Matthew, Mark, Luke, an' John, bless the bed that I lie on.' That'll make the old devil jess fly up an' away."

"No, gals," insisted Aunt Hominy, "cammermile is all dat'll keep him from a-measurin' of us in. Don't ole Meshach go to church an' hab a prayer book an'—listen dar, honey, ef she ain't a-singin' to him!"

As Virgie answered the bell, Aunt Hominy took down her cherished chamomile, sprinkled the little children, and gave them each a glass of sassafras beer to bless their insides.

"Lord a-bless 'em!" exclaimed the old lady. "Ef de slave buyer comes, Aunt Hominy'll take 'em to de woods an' jess git los', an' live on teaberries, slippery ellum, haws, an' chincapins. We don't gwyn stay an' let ole Meshach starve us like a lizzer."

"Aunt Hominy," said Roxy, "maybe ef you bake a nice loaf of federal bread, or a game pie, or persimmon custard, an' send it to ole Meshach, he won't sell us to the slave buyers. He never gets nothin' good to eat an' don't know what it is. A little taste of it'll make him want mo'."

"Roxy, gal," said Aunt Hominy, "I'd jess like to make a dumplin' bag out o' dat steeple hat he got. When I skinned de dumplin', de hat would be bad spiled, chillen, an' den de judge would git his lan' back dat Meshach's measured in. De judge would say, 'Meshach, ye hain't measured me fair. Wha's yer yardstick, ole debbil?'

"Den Meshach he say, 'De hat I tuk it in wid done gone an' burnt by dat ole Hominy, makin' of her puddin's.'

"'Den,' says de judge, 'ye ain't measured me squar. I won't play. Take it all back!'

"Chillen, we must git dat ar ole hat, or de slave buyers done took us all."

They started to take another peep at the storied hat, when Virgie emerged from the parlor door with the dreaded article in her hand, and, hanging it on the peg, came with superstitious fear and relief into the colonnade. Aunt Hominy hurried her to the kitchen, strewed her with herb dust, waved a rattle of snake's teeth in a pig's weazen over her head, and ended by pushing a sweet piece of preserved watermelon rind down her throat.

"Did it hurt ye, honey?" inquired Aunt Hominy, her eyes full of excitement.

"'Deed I don't know, Aunty," Virgie answered. "All I saw was Miss Vessy looking away from me as if she might be going to be ashamed of me, and I picked the thing up and took it to the rack. All I know is it smelled old, like some of the old clothes chests up in the garret, when we lift the lid and peep in, and it seems as if they were dead people's clothes."

The little Negroes, Ned, Vince, and Phillis, heard this with shining eyes and dived their heads under Aunt Hominy's skirts and apron while the old woman exclaimed, "De Lord a-massy!" and began to blow what she called "pow-pow" on the girl's profaned fingers.

"I don't believe it's anything but an ugly, old, nasty, dead folks' hat," exclaimed Virgie. "He just wears it to plague people. He was drinking tea just like Miss Vessy, but I thought his teeth chattered a little, as if he had smelt of the old hat and it give him a chill."

"Where did he get that hat, Aunt Hominy?" Roxy asked. "Did he dig it up somewhere?"

The question seemed to spur the old cook's easy invention, and after a cunning yet credulous look up and down the large kitchen, where the pale light at the windows was invisible in the stronger fire beneath the great stack chimney, Aunt Hominy whispered, "He dug dat hat up in ole Rehoboff ruined church yard. He foun' it in de grave."

"But you said this afternoon, Aunty, that the bad man gave it to him."

"De debbil met him right dar," insisted Aunt Hominy, "in dat ole obergrown churchyard, whar de hymns ob God used to be raised befo' de debbil got it. He says to Meshach, 'I make you de sexton hyar. Go git de spade out yonder, whar de dead house used to be, an' dig among de graves under de myrtle vines an' fin' my hat. As long as ye keep de Lord an' de singin' away from dis yer big forsaken church, you may keep dat hat to measure in eberybody's lan'. So nobody now kin sing or pray in dat church. Nobody but Meshach Milburn ever prays dar. He goes dar sometimes wid his Chrismas giff on he head an' prays to de debbil."

Thus does an unwonted fashion arouse unwonted visions, as if it brought to the present day the phantoms which were laid at rest with itself, and they walked into simple minds and produced superstition there.

Aunt Hominy was never stimulated to inventions of this kind, but she immediately absorbed them, and they became religious beliefs with her. Her manner, highly animated by her terror and belief, produced more and more superstition in the minds of the girls and children, and the conversation fell off.

The little Negroes wandered hither and thither, unable to sleep, yet unable to attract sufficient attention from anyone till Judge Custis, who had been waiting for hours for his creditor to go, slipped down the back stairs in his old slippers and came to the kitchen for company's sake.

His fine presence and familiar address put a new complexion at once on the African end of the house. He picked up the children by twos or threes, woolled them, chased them, tossed them, and drove the lurid images of Aunt Hominy's mind out of their spirits. He set Roxy on his shoulder and caught Virgie by the waist. Finally he piled them on Aunt Hominy, who ran behind her biscuit block.

"De Lord a-massy, Judge!" exclaimed Aunt Hominy, delighted and showing her white teeth. "Go 'long, Judge, Missy Custis ketch you! Miss Vessy's a-comin' befor' de Lawd!"

The children were screaming, getting into the riot more while pretending to try to get out, invading the judge's back and rubbing their clean wool into his whiskers. And the two neat servants, brought up like white children in his family, were not unaccustomed to jovial handling and petting from their master, which he commonly concluded by a present.

"Old woman," the judge said to Aunt Hominy, "can you give me a bit of broiled something for my stomach? I want to eat it right here."

"Don't got nothin' but a young chicken, marster. Mebbe I kin git ye a squab outen de pigeon house in de gable yend."

"That's it," exclaimed Judge Custis. "A tender squab, a little toast in cream, a glass of morning milk, and a bunch of fresh celery will just raise my pulse and put courage into me. Get it, my faithful old girl; it's the last I may ask of you. Old Samson Hat is going to own you next."

"No, sah! I'll run away from Prencess Anne fust. De man dat cleans ole Meshach Milburn's debbil hat shan't nebber hab me."

"Well, it'll be one of you. If you don't take Samson, Roxy must, or Virgie. The old fellow will be very influential with our new master, and we're all depending on you, Hominy, to make him so comfortable that he will just keep the family together."

Sobriety came in on this attempted witticism, and the old cook saw a film grow into the judge's smiling eyes.

"Old marster," she exclaimed, raising her hands, "you's jess a-sottin' dar an' breakin' your poor heart. Don't I know when you is a-makin' believe? Mebbe dis night is de las' we'll ever see you in your own warm, nice kitchen, an' never mo', dear ole marster, kin Hominy brile you a bird or season de soup you like. Bless God, dis time we'll git de squab an' de celery an' de toast befo' ole Meshach Milburn measures all we got in."

While the children crawled around the judge's knees, setting up a dismal wail to see him sob, the two neat house girls, forgetting every contingency to themselves, also sobbed like his own daughters to see him unmanned. But Aunt Hominy only felt desperately energetic at the chance to cook the last supper of the Custis household.

She lighted a brand of pine in the fire and started one of the stable boys up a ladder by its light to ransack the pigeon cote. In a little while both a chicken and a bird were broiled and set upon the kitchen table upon a spotless cloth, and a plume of lily-white celery and smoking toast in velvet cream warmed the judge's nostrils and dried his tears.

Roxy stood behind him to wait on his wishes. Virgie subdued every expression of grief and comforted the children and poor Aunt Hominy. With silent tears streaming down her cheeks to see him suffer, she kept up a chatter of Epicurean talk, lest he might turn and see her miserable.

As he finished his meal and took out his gold toothpick, feeling a comfortable joy of such misery and sympathy, Vesta opened the door and said, "Papa!"

"My child?"

"Let me speak with you, Papa."

Judge Custis rose and raised his hands to Aunt Hominy in speechless recognition of her service, but not till the door closed behind him did the old cook's cry burst through her quivering lips, "Oh, chillen, chillen, he'll never eat no mo' like dat again. Ole Meshach's measured him in!"

Dying Pride

Chapter 11

At the termination of Milburn's long visit, Vesta retired to her room, read a passage in the Bible, said a prayer, and tried to think. She began to see her duty loom up like a prodigious thing, crowding out every consideration but one—her modesty. She would cease to be a maid within the circuit of the clock or forsake her family and drive that great bloodhound of duty over the threshold of her ruined home.

In the one case lay outward devastation—the red eyes of parents and servants, the prying constables lodged upon the premises to see that nothing was smuggled out, the ring of the auctioneer's bell, and the fingering of boors and old gossips over the cherished things of the family. With this done, the vast old house would be a hollow barn, and she and her mother visitors at the jail where her poor father looked through the bars and bent his head in shame.

Then the servants, one after another, mounted upon the courthouse block, the old gray servitors mocked, the little children parted like calves by the butcher, and the young girls feeling the desperate apprehensions of abuse and violation.

Vesta glanced in her mirror by the light that flamed in her brazen grate and saw the blushes climb like flying virgins at the sack of towns, up the white ramparts of her neck and temples.

The form which had altered so little from childhood, supple and straight and molded to perfection, was to fall like the young hickory tree in the August hurricane. She had felt the breath of the man she would yield her life to, irresistible and hot as that storm, when he held her for a moment in the transport of passion and made his fearless avowal of desire.

To marry any man now seemed hard. To marry this one was inexpressible shame, and at the thought of it she could not shed a tear, such paralysis came over her. She had read of the recent Greek revolution, where elegant ladies of Scio and other isles of the Aegean Sea, educated in the best seminaries of Europe, had been sold by the thousands as common slaves in the markets of Constantinople and carried to their estates by brutal Turks with all the gloating anticipation of lust and tyranny.

Her mind wandered over the procession of women who had been the sport of conquest since Eve lost Paradise by her simplicity: the Jewish maidens carried to Babylon, the Gothic virgins dragged at the horse tails of the Moors, the daughters of Palestine and Byzantium consigned to Arab sensualists and made to follow their nomadic tents, and the almond-eyed damsels of China, surrendered by their parents to the wild Kalmucks, to be beaten and starved on every cold plain of Asia till life was laid down with neither hope nor fear.

"I am happier than millions of my sex," Vesta said. "My captor does not despise me, at least. Perhaps he will treat me kinder than I think and give me time to draw towards him without this deadly pain and shame."

Then she almost repented of her hasty decision to marry this night instead of after longer acquaintance, which Mr. Milburn, no doubt, would have granted. His words were remembered with accusation: "What will the world say to your marriage after a single day's acquaintance with me? Will this haste not be repented or become a subject of reproach to you?" Was it too late to recall her words and ask for delay?

"No," Vesta thought, "I will not let him begin to think me weak and changeful already."

To see if there was the least glimmer of relief from this marriage, Vesta crossed to her mother's room and found Mrs. Custis with her head wrapped in handkerchiefs steeped in cologne. She had a vial of laudanum in her hand and was in a condition bordering on hysteria.

"Mamma," Vesta said, "are you in pain?"

"Oh!" screamed Mrs. Custis, "I am just dying here of cruelty and brutality. Your father is a villain. I'll have that rascal Milburn killed. Go get me ink and paper, daughter, and sit here and write me a letter to my brother Allan McLane. He shall settle with Judge Custis for this robbery and take you and me back to Baltimore, leaving your father to go to the almshouse or the jail, I don't care which."

"Mother," exclaimed Vesta, "what a sin to abuse poor father now in all his trouble."

"Trouble!" echoed Mrs. Custis mockingly. "What trouble has he had, I would like to know? Living in the woods like a Turk among his barefooted forest concubines. Spending my money, raked and scraped by my poor father in the sugar importation. The family is broken up. We are paupers, and now it is save yourself. I'll take care of you if I can, but your father may starve for any aid I will give him."

"Then he shall have the only aid in my power, Mother," said Vesta decisively.

"Your aid!" Mrs. Custis exclaimed. "What have you got? Your jewels, I suppose. How long will they keep him? You had better keep your jewels for your wedding and have it come quickly, for marriage is now your only salvation."

"My last jewel shall go, then," Vesta said with a pale resolution that darted through her veins like ice.

"Save your jewels," Mrs. Custis continued, "and choose a husband before this thing is noised abroad. You have a large list to select from. There is your cousin Chase McLane with an estate in Kent and crazy for you. There is that young fool Carroll with thousands of acres on the western shore and the widower Hynson of King George, Virginia, with eighty slaves and stables full of race horses. You can marry any of these Dennis boys or take Captain Ringgold of Frederick, who lives in elegance at West Point, or be mistress of Tench Purvience's mansion on Monument Square in Baltimore. All you have to do is write a letter. Or better, take tomorrow's steamer for Baltimore and use your Uncle Allan's house. Become engaged and married there."

"Mamma," Vesta said without rebuke, "if I could so heartlessly leave my father, I could be capable of deceiving any of those gentlemen."

"Deceiving?" Mrs. Custis remarked, filling her palm and brow with cologne. "What is man's whole work with a woman but deceit? To court her for her money. To kiss her into taking her money out of good mortgages and putting it into bog iron ore. To tell her, when past middle life, that she has nothing to live upon except the charity of the public or reluctant friends. All this for an experiment! The Custis family are all knaves or fools. Your father is a monster."

Vesta went to her mother's side and bathed her forehead.

"Dear Mamma," she said, "let you and I do something for ourselves, while Papa looks around and finds something to do. We can rent a house in Princess Anne and open a seminary. I can teach French and music. You can be the matron and do the correspondence and business. And if Papa is at a loss for larger occupation, he can lecture on history and science. Our friends will send their children to us, and we shall never be separated. I will give up the thought of marriage and live for you two."

Mrs. Custis made a gesture of impatience. "And be an old maid!" she blurted. "That is insufferable. What are all these accomplishments and charms for but a husband, and what is he for but to provide bread and clothes? Don't be as crazy as your unprincipled father. Try no experiments. Drop philanthropy. Money is the foundation of all respectability."

"Can it be so?" Vesta thought to herself. "Does it not, then, justify the man who solicits me in his means of getting money?"

"Mother," Vesta said, "you would have me marry, then?"

"There is no would about it; you *must* marry!"

"Marry immediately?"

"Yes, the sooner the better—to a rich man."

"Give me your blessing, and I will try," Vesta said. "I think I know such a one."

Mrs. Custis kissed her daughter and moaned about her poor head and lost marriage portion, and Vesta set out to look for her father.

She found him as described in the luxury of tears and squab, as comfortable among his Negro servants as in the state legislature or at the head of society, and they wrapped up in his condescension and misfortunes.

As Vesta witnessed the scene of such patriarchal democracy in the old kitchen, she wondered if that voluptuous endowment of her father was not the happy provision to make marriage unions tolerable and social revulsion philosophical. Wherever her father went, he made welcome and warmth.

"Roxy," Vesta said as she left the kitchen, "do go up to my mother and stay with her all this night. Make your spread there beside her bed. Virgie, put on your hood and carry a letter for me."

She sat before her father. He was too undecided to speak and saw by her expression that it was no time for loquacity. She sealed the letter, and her father heard the direction she gave to Virgie with curiosity greater than his embarrassment.

"Take this to Rev. William Tilghman, Virgie. Give it to him only and see that he reads it before you leave. If he asks you any questions, tell him please to do precisely what this note says and, as he is my friend, not to disappoint me."

The girl's steps were hardly out of hearing when Vesta opened the drawer of the library table and took out a package of papers tied with a string. She unloosed it, and her father recognized from where he sat his notes of hand and mortgages.

"Gracious God, my darling," exclaimed Judge Custis, "how came you by those papers?"

"They are to be mine tonight, Father, in one hour. The moment they become mine, they will be yours."

"Why Vessy," said the judge, "if they are yours even to keep a minute, the shortest way with them is up the chimney!"

He made a stride forward to take them from her hand. She laid them in her lap and looked at him so calmly that he stopped.

"You may burn the house, Papa," she said. "It is still your own. But these papers you could only burn by a crime. It would be cheating an honorable man."

"Honorable! Who?" the judge exclaimed.

"He who is to be my husband."

"Marry Meshach Milburn!" the judge shouted. "Oh, curse of God—not him!"

"Yes, this night," answered Vesta. "I respect him. I hold these obligations by his trust in me. They are my engagement ring."

Judge Custis raised a howl like a man into whom a nail is driven and fell at his daughter's feet and clasped her knees.

"This is to torture me," he cried. "He has not dared to ask you?"

"Yes, and my word is passed, Father. Shall that word—the word of a Custis—be less than a Milburn's faith. By the love he bore me, Mr. Milburn gave me these debts for my dower—a rare faith in one so prudent. If I do not marry him, they will be given back to him this night."

"Then give them back, child, and save your soul and your purity, lest I live to be cursed with the sight of my noble daughter's shame. This marriage will be unholy, and the censure to follow it will be the bankruptcy of more than our estate—of our simple fame and old family respect. We have friends left who would help us. If you marry Milburn, they will all despise and repudiate us."

"I do not believe it," said Vesta. "The sense and courage of that gentleman—and he is a gentleman of many gifts—will compel respect even where false pride and family pretension appear to put him down. Who that underrates him will make any considerable sacrifice to assist us? Will your sons do it? Then by what right do they decide my marriage choice? No, Father, I only do my part to support our house in its extremity, as these gentlemen and others have done before."

She pointed to the portraits of Custises on the wall. If any looked dissatisfied, he met a countenance haughty as his own.

"Vesta," her father said, "you know you do not love this man."

Looking at the longing in his face, which now wore the solicitude of personal affection, she melted under it.

"No, Father," she said with a burst of tears, "I love you."

She threw her arms around him and kissed him long and fondly, both weeping together. He went into a fit of grief that admitted no conversation till it was partly spent. At last he lay with his gray hairs folded to her heaving bosom, where the compensation of his love made her sacrifice more precious.

"I feel I am doing right, Father," she said tenderly. "Till now I have had my doubts. No other young heart is wronged by my taking this step. I have never been engaged, and it now seems providential, as I could not then have gone to your assistance without injuring myself and another. Your debts are too great for any but this man to settle. Your life has been one long sacrifice for me, and till this day not a cloud has darkened above to give me the first shower of sorrow. I trust this will refresh my soul and make its humility grow. It would rejoice me so much, Father, if you could respond to my sacrifice with a better life."

"God help me, I will," he sobbed.

"That is very comforting to me. I will not enumerate your omissions, Father, but if this important step in my life does not arrest some sad tendencies I see in you, the disappointment may break me down. Intemperance in you—a judge, a gentleman, a husband, and a father—is a deformity worse than Mr. Milburn's honest, unfashionable hat. Do you not feel happier that my husband is not to be a drunkard?"

"He has not that vice, thank God," admitted the judge.

"Be his better example, Father, for I hope to see you influence him to be kind to me, and the sight of you walking downward in his view will degrade me more than bearing his name or sharing his eccentricities. If you love me, let not your dear soul slide out of the knowledge of God."

"Pray for me, dear child. My feet are slippery and my knees are weak."

"Begin from this moment to lean on heaven," Vesta said. "It is far better than this world's consideration. What would strengthen me now but God's approval, though I go into a captivity I dreamed not of. Even there I can take my harp beneath the willows, like them in Babylon, and praise my Maker."

She sat at her piano and sang the hymn the young Rev. Eastburn composed in her grandfather's house, taking it from the Episcopal collection:

> Oh holy, holy, holy Lord!
> > Bright in Thy deeds and in Thy name,
> Forever be Thy name adored,
> > Thy glories let the world proclaim!
> Oh Jesus, Lamb once crucified
> > To take our load of sins away,
> Thine be the hymn that rolls its tide
> > Along the realms of upper day!
>
> O Holy Spirit from above,
> > In streams of light and glory given,
> Thou source of ecstasy and love,
> > Thy praises ring through earth and heaven!

As her voice filled the two large rooms in almost supernatural clearness and sweetness, then died away in melody, she rose, kissed her father again, and said, "Courage, love. We shall be happy still."

A knock at the door, and there entered the young clergyman she had sent for, a sandy-haired, blue-eyed, boyish person with easily-freckled, fair skin and a look of youthful chivalry under his sincere Christian humility.

"Good evening, William," Vesta said. "I did not expect to see you till we reached the church, but sit, and I will answer your questions. Father, you are to go with me to the church, you and Virgie. Mr. Tilghman is to marry us."

"Now, Vesta," said the young man as her father left the room, "whom are you going to marry in such haste as this?"

"Did you have the church made ready as I requested?"

"I did. The sexton is there now, lighting the fire."

"I thought you were loyal as ever, William, and depended upon you. Thanks, dear friend. I am to marry Mr. Meshach Milburn at nine o'clock."

A cloud came over the young man's serene face, though his features retained their habitual sweetness.

"I can marry you, cousin, even to Meshach Milburn," he said, "if that is your wish. Why do you marry him?"

"It is not loyal of you to ask, William, but I will give you this answer: He has asked me. He is also devoted and rich. To avoid excitement and possibly opposition—though it would be vain—we are to be married without further notice, and Papa is to give me away."

After a moment's silence the young rector exclaimed, "Cousin Vesta, have I lived to see you a mercenary woman? Has this man's asserted wealth found you cold enough to want it, when love has been so generously offered you by almost every young man of station in this region and from abroad—even by me? The scar is on my heart yet. No, I will not believe such a thing of you. There is a reason back of the fact."

"William, if you respected me like your sister, as you once said you ever would, you would not add the weight of your doubt to my other burdens this night, but take my hand with all the strength of yours and lift me onward."

"I will," the rector said, swallowing a dry spot in his throat. "Though it was a bitter time I had when you refused me, cousin, the pain led me to my vows at the altar where I minister, and I have had the assistance of your beautiful music there. I know that on your part this marriage is as pure as my sister's. I will inquire no further as to what penalty you are paying for another, what mystery I cannot pierce."

He raised his hands above her head. "The peace of God that passeth understanding abide with you, dear sister, forever."

He went out with his eyes filled with tears, but hers were full of heavenly light, feeling his benediction to be righteous.

The Washington Tavern

Princess Anne Folks

Chapter 12

The Washington Tavern, or rather the brick sidewalk which came up to its doors and was the lounging place for all the grown loiterers in Princess Anne, had been in the greatest activity all that Saturday afternoon, since Jack Wonnell reported that the steeple hat had disappeared into the broad mansion of Judge Daniel Custis.

Jack Wonnell had a worn bell-crown on his head, which had been exposed to all kinds of weather, as he was in the habit of fishing in these beaver hats and never owned an umbrella in his life. He lived near Meshach in the old part of Princess Anne and was the subject of the money lender's scorn and contempt for tending to make a mutual eccentricity ridiculous. Milburn had been willing to be hated for his hat, but Jack Wonnell made all unseasonable hats laughable. Although he had no reasons of reverence and stern consistency, as did his rich neighbor, in his own mind and in plain people's he seemed to have a better defense for violating the standard taste of dress. The people said that Jack Wonnell, being a poor man, could not buy all the fashions and was merely wearing out a bargain, and that he knew he was ridiculous and set no such conceit on his absurdity as that grim Milburn. They rather enjoyed his playing the Dromio to that Antipholus and turning the comedy of Meshach's error into farce.

Jack Wonnell was a frivolous, unambitious, incontinent, inoffensive, childish fellow who spent his time amusing and obliging people: running errands, driving stage, gardening, fishing, playing with the lads, and courting poor, white, bound girls. He had partly embraced his bargain by Meshach's example, having been impelled to bid on his lot of old hats by Jimmy Phoebus.

"Dirt cheap, Jack," Jimmy had said. "They'll last you all your life, and they're better hats than old Meshach Milburn's."

To his infinite amusement and dignity, Wonnell's appearance in the bell-crown hats attracted the severe regard of Milburn and set the little town on a grin. The joke went on till Jimmy Phoebus and some others prompted Jack, with the promise of a gallon of whiskey, to ask Meshach to trade the steeple-top for the bell-crown. The intense look of outrage, hate, and the accompanying menace his townsman returned really frightened Jack, and he had prudently avoided Milburn ever since, keeping a close eye on his whereabouts so as not to be surprised by him.

In this way Jack Wonnell had followed Meshach to the courthouse corner. From the open space between it and the courthouse he peeped after Milburn up the main cross street, called Prince William, which stopped right at Judge Custis's gate. There, in the quiet of early afternoon, he heard the knocker sound, saw the door open, and beheld the Entailed Hat disappear into the great doorway.

Scarcely believing himself, Wonnell ran back to the tavern and exclaimed, "May I be struck stone dead ef ole Meshach ain't gwyn into the jedge's!"

"You're a liar!" said Jimmy Phoebus, catching Jack by the back of the neck and pushing his bell-crown down till it mashed over his nose and eyes. "What do you mean by telling a splurge like that?"

"I seen him, Jimmy," was the bell-crowned hero's smothered cry. "If I didn't, hope I may die!"

"What did he go there for?"

"I can't tell, Jimmy, to save my life."

"Whoooop!" cried Phoebus, waving his old straw hat, itself nearly out of season. "If it's a lie, Jack Wonnell, I'll make you eat a raw fish."

"Levin, you slip by Custis's and see if ole Meshach hain't passed around the fence or dropped along Church Street and hid in the graveyard, where he sometimes goes. I'll stay yer and make Jack Wonnell account for sech lyin'."

Levin Dennis, a boyish, curly-haired, graceful-going orphan, walked up the cross street past Church Lane and the back alley and slowly turned the long front of Teackle Hall. He then traversed the parallel street towards the lower bridge on the Deil's Island road till he could turn and see the three great-chimneyed buildings of Teackle Hall lifting their gables and lightning rods from the back. The partly stripped trees allowed that manorial pile to stand forth in much of its length and imposing proportions. To avoid being suspected of curiosity, Levin continued to the bridge at Manokin Landing and counted the geese on a lawn there, as they took to water like a fleet of white schooners, then ascended the rise beyond the bridge and looked over to see if Meshach might have taken a walk down the road.

Returning, he swept the back view of Princess Anne from the low bluff of cedars, which bordered the Manokin marshes to the vale of the little river as it descended between Meshach's storehouse and the ancient Presbyterian church. Nothing was visible of the owner of the distinguishing hat. Returning to Teackle Hall and passing around the north wing, Levin looked at every window as if Meshach might be there, but he saw nothing except the dog, which to Levin's eye appeared uneasy and ran out of the gate to make friends with him.

"So, Turk," Dennis muttered, patting the dog's head, "no wonder you're scared, boy, to see old Meshach Milburn come in."

According to rumor, Teackle Hall was built at the close of the Revolutionary War by an uncle or grand-uncle of Judge Custis. He had come from Virginia, somewhere between Accomack and Northampton counties, and went into shipbuilding on the Manokin, adding some privateering and banking. Going abroad once, he brought back from some ducal residence the plan of Teackle Hall.

It was nearly two hundred feet in length and would have made three respectable churches standing in line with their sharp gables to the front. The bold wings connected with the bolder center by colonnades, in which panels of slate or grained stone made an attic story above the lines of windows. Lintels and sills of the same stone capped every window in the many-sided surface of the whole stately block. It was built of brick brought over in vessels from the western shore or possibly from the North or Europe and painted a gray stone color.

Its central gable had deeply carved eaves and a pediment base to shed rain, with a large circular window in that pediment. The two mighty chimneys were parallel with the ridge of the roof and rose nearly from the middle of the two opposite slopes, bespeaking four great fireplaces below. A flat, low-galleried observatory upon the roof gave views of portions of the bay on clear days.

The wings of Teackle Hall had similar but lower chimneys straddling their roofs. Trees of oak, gum, holly, and pine, along with a great

Above: Main Entrance of Teackle Hall

Below: Teackle Hall from the Garden

willow, some tawny cedars, and bushes of rose and lilac dotted the grassy lawn. The Virginia creeper and wild ivy climbed here and there to the upper windows. A tall, broad, paneled doorway opened on a low portico platform with steps and seemed to say, "Men of port and consideration come in this way. Inferiors enter by some of the smaller doors."

Levin Dennis, who had never sounded that knocker, though had often taken his terrapins to the kitchen, stared in concern at the door where it was reported Meshach Milburn had gone in. He would hardly have been surprised if that intruder had now appeared at one of the three deep windows over the door with a firebrand in his hand.

Levin muttered to himself, "Rich folks, I reckon, must make a trade. Maybe it's hosses; maybe not. I know it ain't hats."

He then turned down to the Episcopal Church, only a square from Teackle Hall and on a street between it and the main street. Its front turned from the town and looked over the fields and farms like a good pastor who is warming at the fire with his hands behind him.

St. Andrew's Episcopal Church

The church was a single-storied, long edifice of British bricks with its semicircular choir next to the street. Adjoining the choir was a spire of more modern brickwork built up to an open bell cupola and open ribbed dome, also of brick and tipped with a gilded cross. The ivy was greenly matted around the choir and ran along the side of the church. Levin Dennis walked under four tall, round-topped windows of stained and wired glass till he came to the end gable or front of the church, which stood in unworldly contemplation of the graveyard and the back fields.

There, since the Stamp Act Congress, when Princess Anne was not half a century old, the church had taken its stand, backed up to the town, recluse from its gossip. Between its tall, rounded doors and little windowpanes set into panels like spectacles, the ivy vines arose in form like the print of The Crucified, reaching out to the one glorified window in the gable, in whose red dyes glimmered the triumph of a bloody countenance. The mossy, often-scraped walls, the mossified pavement, and the greenish tombs of marble under the maples and firs showed the effect of shade, solitude, and humidity upon all things of brick in this climate.

The Teackle Graves in the Episcopal Churchyard

No sign of the unpopular townsman was to be seen anywhere, but as Levin Dennis peeked around the foliage in the yard, he beheld a man he had never observed before, of a tall, bearded, suspicious, and ruffianly exterior, lying flat on the top of a memorial vault and with his head and feet half concealed in some cedar brambles.

"Hallo!" Dennis shouted.

"What do you hallo for?" said the man. "Don't you never come to a churchyard to git yer sins forgive?"

"No," said the terrapin finder, "not till I knows I has some sins."

"What air you prowlin' about the church then fur?" demanded the stranger, standing up in his boots, into which his trousers were tucked. He stood such a straight, long-limbed, lithe giant of a man that Levin saw he could never run away, even if the intruder meant to chew him up right there.

"I ain't a-prowlin', friend," answered Levin Dennis; "I was jess a-lookin'."

"Lookin' fur what, fur which, fur who?" asked the man, taking a step towards Dennis, who felt himself to be no bigger than one of the other's long, ditch-leaping, good-for-wading legs.

"Why I was jess a-follerin' a man—that is, friend, not 'zackly a man, but a hat."

"A hat?" The man walked up to Dennis and stood over him like a pine tree over a sucker. "Yer's yer hat," pulling an old, straw, over-worn article from Dennis's head. "No wind's a-blowin' to blow hats into graveyards. Or did you set yer hat under a hen in yere, by a stiffy?"

Dennis looked up, laughing, though not all at ease. His amiable want of either intelligence or fear made his most natural reply to the pertinacious intruder.

"No, man," Dennis said, "it was a hat on a man's head—ole Meshach Milburn's steeple-top. I was a-follerin' of him."

The man clapped the hat back on Levin's head. "Stow your wid! You're a poor hobb, anyhow. Is thair any niggers to sell hereby?"

"Oh, that's your trade—nigger buyin'. Well, there's mighty few niggers to sell in Prencess Anne, unless (here a flash of intelligence shone in Levin's eyes) that's what's took ole Meshach Milburn to Jedge Custis's. He goes nowhar 'less there's trouble or money for him."

"And where is Judge Custis's, you rum chub?"

"Yander," pointing to Teackle Hall.

"Ha! That's a judge's? And niggers? Well, it's no hank for a napper bloke. So bingavast! Git! Whar's the tavern?"

"I'm a-goin' right thair," answered Levin, much relieved. "You must be a Yankee or some other furriner, sir."

"No, hobb, I'm workin' my way back to Delaware from Norfolk, by pungy to Somers's cove. Show me to the tavern, an' I'll sluice your gob. I'll treat you to swig."

At the prospect of a drink, of which he was too fond, Levin led the way to the Washington Tavern, where there was a material addition to the attendance since Jimmy Phoebus had called to every passerby that Meshach Milburn, on the testimony of Jack Wonnell, had disappeared through Judge Custis's doorway.

Nearly a dozen townsfolks were discussing the why and wherefore, when Levin Dennis suddenly came out of Church Street with a man over six feet high, of a prodigious pair of legs, arms nearly as long, a cold, challenging, yet restless pair of blue eyes, and with coarse and stringy, reddish-brown beard and hair.

The free Negro Samson Hat, being a little way off, was observed to cast a beaming glance of admiration at the athletic proportions of the stranger, who looked as if he might shoulder an ox or outrun a horse.

"Hallo!" exclaimed Jimmy Phoebus, looking the stranger over boldly, yet with indifference. "You're cuttin' a splurge too, Levin. Where's Meshach?"

"Can't see no sign of him, Jimmy. Guess Jack Wonnell hit it, an' he's gone in the jedge's. Mebbe he's buyin' of Jedge Custis's niggers. That's this gentleman's business."

Jimmy Phoebus, himself no slight specimen of a man, gave another glance at the stranger from the black cherries of his eyes but made no sign of acquaintance.

"Whoever ain't too nice to drink with a nigger buyer," said the man, "can come in an' set up his drink with my redge, for I'm rhino fat an' just rotten with flush."

There was a pause for somebody to take the initiative, but Jimmy Phoebus, turning his big, broad, Greekish face and small forehead on the stranger, remarked, "I never tuk a drink with a nigger buyer yit, an', by smoke, I reckon I'm too old to begin."

The man stopped and measured Jimmy up. "Humph!" he said with a sneer, "you look to be a little more than half nigger yourself. If I was dead broke, I'd run you to market an' git my price for you."

"No doubt of it whatever, as fur as you're concerned," said Jimmy, while the man pushed Levin Dennis towards the bar.

Either the new movement of Meshach Milburn or the example of the strange man set Princess Anne in a tipsy condition that day. The stranger was full of money and treating indiscriminately. The pavement before the hotel was continually beset with loiterers, and the bar took money and spread mischief.

So when, an hour after dark, the unpopular townsman passed by on the opposite side of the street to avoid the crowd, one of the loudest and most unanimous yells he had ever heard in his experience rang out from the Washington Tavern: "Steeple-top! Steeple-top! Old Meshach's loose! Whooop!"

"Laugh on," thought Meshach. "Till now I never knew the meaning of 'let them laugh who win.'"

He felt confirmed in his idea to be married in the Raleigh tile, and when he saw Samson Hat, Milburn said, "Boy, brush all my clothing well. Then go back to the livery stable and order a buggy to be ready for you at ten o'clock. At that hour set out for Berlin and bring Rhody Holland back with you in the morning."

"It's more dan thirty mile, marster, an' a sandy road."

"Take it slow. I will write you a letter to carry. I am going to be married tonight, Samson, to the rose of Princess Anne."

"Dar's on'y one," said Samson. "Not Miss Vesty Custis?"

"Yes, Samson. Princess Anne may now have something to howl at. The poor girl may be lonesome, as no doubt she will be dropped everywhere on my account. I cannot think of a soul to be my young lady's maid, unless it is Rhody."

"Yes, Marster, wid all your money you're pore in friends. In women friends you is starved."

"You may go with me to the church," said Meshach. "I suppose you want to see me married."

"Yes, sir. Dat I do! Wouldn't miss dat fo' my Christmas gift. I 'spect dat gal Virgie will come wid Miss Vesty to de cer'mony."

"Perhaps so. You are not thinking of love, too, Samson?"

"Well, don't know, marster. Virgie's a fine gal, sho'. I am a little old, Marster Milburn, but I'll have to look out for myself, I 'spec, now you done burnt down my spreein' place. Dar's a wife comin' in yar now, so if you don't speak a good word fur me wid some o' Miss Vesty's gals, I'm aboot done."

"Well boy," Meshach said, "you have got the same chance I had: the upper hand. I owe you a nice little sum in wages. You may be able to buy one of the Custis housemaids and set her free—marry her or be her owner. You are a free man."

Samson shook his head gravely. "Dat won't do among niggers. Niggers never kin play de upper hand in love like white people. Dey has to do it by love itseff—by kindness, marster."

Observing his employer to shake a trifle, Samson Hat asked him if a dram of whiskey would not be proper.

"No, boy, this is a wedding without wine. I shall need all my wits to find my manners."

Milburn and his Negro left the old store by the town bridge and, passing by the river lane called Front Street into Church Street, walked back of the hotel, avoiding its triflers. They reached the church in a few minutes, unobserved.

They entered and found it warmed, and the minister was already present in his surplice, kneeling alone at the altar. Mr. Tilghman arose with his youthful face pale and tears upon his cheeks. Seeing his neglected parishioner and the serving man, he came down the aisle.

"Mr. Milburn," he said, extending his hand, "after this ceremony I hope to congratulate a Christian-hearted bridegroom and one who will take the rare charge which has fallen to him in tender keeping. My endeavor shall be to love you, sir, if you will let me. Miss Vesta is the priestess of Princess Anne, and if you take her from our sight and hearing, even God's ministrations in this church will seem hollow, I fear."

"To me they would," said Milburn, "though from no disrespect to our pastor."

Tilghman continued, "You have been a faithful parishioner during my brief labor here, as you were in my boyhood, when I little dreamed I should fill that desk. You know, perhaps, that it was from the hopeless love of my cousin Custis I fled to God for consolation, and he made me his humble minister."

"I have heard so," said Milburn, "or, rather, I have seen so."

"Pardon my mentioning a subject so irrelevant to you, sir, but though I have surrendered every vain emotion for my cousin, her happiness is a part of my religion, and this sudden conclusion of her marriage, about which I have asked only one question, has urged me to throw myself upon your sympathy."

"What do you ask, William Tilghman? No matter! Your request is granted."

"How have I won your favor?" the young rector asked, somewhat surprised.

Milburn mechanically picked his hat from a pew and held it a little way up. "You were the only boy in this village who never cried after this hat."

"Then it was probably overlooked by me. Before my spirits had been depressed by unhappy love, I was mischievous like the other boys. I did not know I was any exception to their habits."

"It was grateful to see that exception," said Milburn. "Hooted people make fine distinctions."

"Oh, Mr. Milburn, forgive the boys. They are made for laughter, and little causes excite it, like dogs to bark from health and exercise. It was scarcely more than that.

"The request I make is to let me be your friend because I have been your wife's. Frankness becomes my calling, and I think you need friendly, cordial surroundings to bring out your usefulness and give you the freedom that will take constraint out of your family life and, without diminishing your good sensibilities, dispel any morbid ones. This will open a way for Vesta to see her domestic career, which otherwise might become so rapidly contracted as to disappoint you both. You have seen her the idol of her wide circle, free as a bird, indulged by her kind and by providence also till joy and grace, beauty and health, faith and hope live abundant in her, and you are the beneficiary of it all. You must control her society hereafter. May I become your friend and let my love for your wife recommend me to your confidence, as you to mine and to my prayers?"

"Have I another friend already?" exclaimed Milburn, his voice quivering. "What wealth she brings me was never known before. William, you will be ever welcome to me."

They clasped hands, and old Samson Hat, sitting back, was heard to chuckle aloud such a warning laugh that Meshach's response to it, in a sudden pallid shivering, seemed slightly out of keeping. He was recalled, however, by the entrance of Judge Custis with his daughter and her maid, Virgie.

Vesta was very pale but neither shrinking nor negative. On the contrary, she supported her father rather than received his support, and Milburn saw the judge's worn, helpless face, the pride faded from it, and pity for his daughter absorbing every other feeling of depression.

Judge Custis wore his best suit with the coat tails falling to his knees behind, the body cut square to the hips and the collar raised high upon his stock of white, enameled English leather. His low-buttoned vest exposed his shirt buttons of crystal and gilt, and a ruffle, ironed with nimble touches by Roxy's slender hands, parted down the middle like sea foam. Similar ruffles at the wrists were clasped by chain buttons of pearl and silver. His vest was of figured Marseilles stuff, and gaiters of the same material partly covered his shoes. His heavy seal with his coat of arms upon it fell from a pale ribbon at his fob. Debtor though he was and answering at the bar of the church to a heavy personal and family judgment, his large and flowing lines of body, deeply cut chin, full eyes, and natural height and grace of stature made him a marked and noble presence anywhere.

Dropping off a mantle of blue velvet at the touch of her maid, Vesta Custis stood in a party dress of white silk, her neck, shoulders, and arms bare. As she halted a minute in the aisle, Virgie struck the cloth sandals from her mistress's white, silk slippers, and when she removed her hood of home embroidered cloth, a veil of white fell to her train.

The dingy light from the whale oil lamps gathered around the pair of diamonds in her delicately molded ears like the marveling eyes of poor folks' children. Her fine gold watch chain, twice dependent from her neck, disappeared in the snowy mold of her bosom, on whose heaving drift swam a magnolia bud and blossom, each with a leaf. Her father's picture, in a careful miniature set in pearls, lay higher on her breast, fastened by a pearl necklace. Her hands were covered with white gloves, and her arms were without ornament. Dropping in dark ringlets around her forehead and temples, her hair was combed upward farther back, then gathered around a pearl comb in high braids, and the plentiful loops drooped to her shoulder.

Milburn glanced at the treasures of her peerless charms, never till now revealed to his sight, and their splendor almost made him afraid.

Never had he attended a theater, a ball, or anywhere from which he could have foreseen a swan-like neck and bosom sculptured like these, and arms as white as the limbs of the silver maple, warmed with bridal life and modesty.

Her lips, parted and red, her great rich eyes with their brows of raven black, like entrances to the caves of the Cumaean sibyl, her small head borne as easily upon her neck as a dove upon a sprig—all flashed upon Milburn's thrilled yet flinching soul as the revelation of a divinity.

As she stepped forward, he spoke to her with that bold instinct or ecstasy she had observed when she first addressed him in her father's house, ten hours before.

"You have dressed yourself for me?" he said.

"Sir, such as I could command upon this necessity, I thought to do you honor with."

"For *me*, to look so beautiful. What can I say? You are very lovely."

"It is gracious of you to praise me. Shall we wait, or are you ready?"

Unable to speak again, he gave her his hand, and she was calm enough to notice that it was hot, as if he had fever. Her father reached out also and took the bridegroom's other hand.

"Milburn," he said huskily, "this is no work of mine. My daughter has my consent only because it is her will."

"The nobler to me for that," Milburn said, his countenance strangely flushed. "What shall we do, my lady?"

"Give me your arm. Have you brought a ring, sir?"

He drew from his vest pocket a lean, little gold ring, worth hardly half a dollar. "It was my poor mother's," he said.

Without another word she walked forward, her arm drawing him on. Virgie followed, and her father brought up the rear. Samson Hat, feeling uneasy at being awarded no part in the ceremony, slipped up the aisle as far as the big, stiff-aproned stove in the middle of the church. Ducking his body behind it, he kept his head and faculties in the center of the events.

Mr. Tilghman had preceded them in his surplice, and taking his place at the altar, his countenance pale as death, he read the exordium in an altered voice: "Dearly beloved, we are gathered together here, and in the face of this company, to join together this man and this woman in holy matrimony."

"What 'company' is here?" thought Vesta. "Not alone these Negroes and my father. No, I feel behind me the generations of our pride and helpless ease, the worthy younger suitors I have been too exacting and particular to see the consideration and merits of, the golden hours in which I might have improved my mind, brilliant opportunities I was not jealous of and which will be mine no more because I had not trimmed my virgin lamp. So I slept away my girlhood, till now I awaken at the cry, 'The bridegroom cometh,' and I behold. Yes, I have been a foolish virgin and am surprised when my fate is here. Perhaps my guardian angel also stands behind me, the cross advanced that I must take, my crown concealed. But somewhere, midway of this journey of life, she may give it to me and say, 'Well done!'"

"This 'company,'" thought Milburn, his head swimming, "gathered to see me marry. What company? Besides these Negroes, my sole spectators, I seem to feel the populous forest peering on: the barefoot generations, the illiterate broods, the instinctive parents, the sandy graves. They give forth my lost tribe, and all cry at me, 'Go! Leave us, proud one! Despiser, go!' Yet there is one I see, pure as my bride, white as my captive's bosom, her soul all in her believing eyes and saying, 'Oh, my son, it is a woman like me that has come into your life, and her heart is very tender. By your mother's dying love, be kind to the poor stranger you have bought.'"

He answered, "I will," aloud. It seemed almost a miraculous coincidence that it was a response to the minister's question.

He heard the corresponding inquiry put to his bride in the clergyman's gentlest tones: "Wilt thou obey him and serve him, love, honor, and keep him, in sickness and in health, and forsaking all others, keep thee only unto him, so long as ye both shall live?"

"I will," said the judge's daughter, clear as music, and the judge drew a long, deep sigh, saturated with tears as if from the deepest wells of grief.

Joining Vesta's hand to the bridegroom's, the minister lost his office and speech for a moment. The slave girl burst into a wail she could not control. Only the bride stood calm.

When both had made the solemn promise, Vesta reached for the ring and gave it to her old lover, the minister, and Virgie loosened her glove. Mr. Tilghman, his tears silently falling upon his book, passed the ring to Meshach and saw its tiny circle hoop her white finger round. It was no bigger than a straw, yet formidable as a martyr's chain. His prayers were said with deep feeling, and he pronounced them man and wife. Then, with his boyish countenance as bright as faith could make it, the minister shook Meshach's hand and said, "My friend, may I take my kiss?"

Meshach nodded, but his face was like a ball of fire, and he hardly knew what was asked.

Mr. Tilghman kissed Vesta, saying, "Cousin, your husband is my friend, so love and friendship both surround you now. May your happiness be, like your goodness, securest when you surmount difficulties, like those birds that cannot float at perfect grace till they have struggled above the clouds."

"May I kiss you now?" Milburn asked, gazing with a wild look upon her rich eyes.

As she obediently raised her lips, a strange, warm, husky breath, not natural nor even passionate, came from his nostrils. The judge, looking at this—no pleasing scene to him—exclaimed within his soul, "Is Meshach drinking? His eyes look fiery."

After also kissing his daughter and saying, "May God reward you with triumphs and compensation beyond our fears," the judge said to Milburn, "I suppose in the sudden conclusion of this union you have made no arrangements as to where you will go. So come to Teackle Hall and make it your home."

"Is that your wish, my dear one?"

"Yes," Vesta replied, "but it is yours to choose, sir."

"You have business with your father for an hour," Milburn said. "Meantime, I require something at my warehouse, and as it is yet early in the night, may I leave you a little while?"

She bowed her head again, and while they proceeded towards the church door, Samson took the opportunity to seize both of Virgie's hands.

"Virgie," he exclaimed, "is all dat kissin' a gwyin' on an' we black folks git none of it? Come hyeah, purty gal, an' kiss yer ole gran'fadder!"

Virgie consented without resistance until Samson continued, "Oh, what peach an' honey, Virgie. Gi me anoder one! I say, Virgie, sence my marster an your mistis have done gone an' leff us two orphans, sposen we git Mr. Tilghman to pernounce us man an' wife, too?"

Virgie drew away. "Samson Hat," she said, "what's that you are talking about? You ought to be ashamed of yourself. You are old enough to be my father!"

"'Deed I ain't, my love. I'm good as four o' dese new kine o' Somoset County beaux. I'm a free man. Maybe I'll sot you free too, Virgie—me an' my marster yonder. He says we better git married. 'Deed he does."

"You are just an impertinent old Negro," the girl replied. "Do you suppose any well-raised girl would have a man who got rich by cleaning the bad man's hat? You're nothing but the devil's serving man, sir."

"Look out dat debbil don't ketch you, den," said Samson, "you pore, foolish, believin' chile. Look out dem purty black eyes don't cry for ole Samson yit. He's done bound to marry some spring chicken, ole Samson is, an' I reckon you'll brile de tenderest, Virgie."

Indignant but flattered at her first real proposal, and from one of the richest men of her color in Princess Anne, Virgie hastened to tie on her young mistress's walking shoes.

As they stepped from the happy old church, where Vesta's voice had so often seemed to carry her soul like a lark to heaven's gate in flights of harmony, she saw fall upon the pavement of the churchyard the long, preposterous, moon-thrown hat of the bridegroom.

"Now that he has married me, what will he do with that hat?" Vesta thought. "Will he continue to afflict me with it?"

Her heart sank down, so that she felt relieved when he kissed her again at the gate and said, "I will come soon, darling," and went with his man into Princess Anne.

"Is your buggy harnessed, Samson?" his master asked when they turned the courthouse corner.

"Yes, marster."

At this moment a large crowd of men, comprising all the idle population in town as well as many Saturday-night bacchanalians from the country and coasts, some standing before the tavern, others on the opposite sidewalks or gathered on the courthouse corner, seeing the hatted figure of Meshach rise against the moonlight, raised the scattering cry: "Man with the hat loose! Steeple-top! Three cheers for old Meshach's hat!"

With a minute's irresolution, as if hesitating to go through the crowd, Milburn turned into the main street, crossed it, and continued down the opposite sidewalk on the same side with his domicile. The jeers and jests continued.

"Dar's rum a-workin' in dis town all arternoon, marster," his faithful Negro said, "eber sence dat long man come in from de churchyard wid Levin Dennis. Look out, marster!"

He had scarcely spoken, when three men were seen to bar the way—two of them drunk, the third ugly with drink—having emerged from a groggery that stood across the street from the tavern, where further beverage had been denied them. The first was Jack Wonnell. He hiccuped, cried "Steeple-top!" and slunk behind a mulberry tree. The second man was Levin Dennis, hardly able to stand, and he sat down on the groggery step, smiling up idiotically.

The third man, rising like a giant out of his boots, his arms swaying like loose grapevines, and his bearded face streaked with tobacco drippings, looking insolence and contempt, brought the flat of one hand fairly down on the crown of Milburn's tile with the words, "Halloo! Yer's Goosecap! Hocus that cady, old Gripefist!"

The hat, age being against it, wilted down on Meshach's eyes, and the heedless stroke, unconsciously powerful, staggered him.

Samson, who had drunk in the giant's qualifications with an instant's admiration, immediately drew off, seeing his master insulted, and struck the tall stranger a blow with his fist. The man reeled, rallied, and sought to grapple with Samson.

That skillful pugilist bent his knees, slid his shoulders back, and, avoiding the clutch, threw his trunk forward with the blow studied well, planting his knuckles in the white man's eyes. The tall ruffian went down as from a bolt of lightning.

Milburn saw this happen in a minute of time, and his eye, looking for something to defend himself, dropped on the brick pier under the groggery steps, where Levin Dennis sat stupefied by the scene. A brick in the pier was loose, and Milburn stepped towards it. In this small interval the stranger had recovered himself, staggered to his feet, and had drawn a dirk-knife.

"The ruffian cly you!" he bellowed. "Knocked down by a nigger, too! Hell have you then!"

As he darted forward, he described a rapid circle backward and downward, aiming to turn the knife through Samson's bowels, which he would have done had not Meshach, wresting the loose brick from the pier, aimed it at the exposed portion of the assassin's body and struck him full in the pit of the stomach. The man's eyes rolled, and he fell like one stone-dead, his dirk sticking in the sidewalk.

"Let him lie there," said Meshach contemptuously. "No danger of such a dog dying. If there is time, he shall mend in the jail. Take to your buggy, boy, and keep out of the way."

The Negro needed no warning, as the impiety of striking a white man was forbidden in a larger book than the Bible—the book of ignorance. He disappeared through the houses and was a mile out of Princess Anne, driving fast, before the new man had raised his head from the ground.

"Where's the nigger?" he gasped, his pale face painted by his bloodshot eyes. "What kind of coves are you to let a black bloke fight a white man? I'll cut his heart out before I tip the town."

He looked around on the crew which had crossed over from the tavern. Meshach had vanished into his store.

Jimmy Phoebus was the only one to speak. "Nigger buyer," he said, "if you are around this town from now till midnight, or after midnight tomorrer—Sunday night, ole Meshach Milburn will have you in that air jail till spring, by smoke! He'll find out yer aunty's cedents, whair you goin', whair you been, what's yer splurge, an' all yer hokey-pokey. You've struck the Ark of the Lord this time—ole Milburn's Entailed Hat! Take my advice an' travel!"

The man washed his face at the tavern pump, turned the bank corner, and disappeared in the night towards Teackle Hall.

Shadow of the Tile

Chapter 13

As Vesta and her father stepped over the sill of Teackle Hall, it seemed very dear yet somewhat dread to them, having been reclaimed at the penalty of a new member of the family, and he an intruder. Vesta and her father went to the library, and he threw some wood upon the low fire and lighted the lamp and candles. Turning, he took his daughter in his arms and bitterly sobbed, "What shall I do, oh, what shall I do!"

Vesta also yielded to the luxury of grief but was speechless till the judge said, "My darling, I have dreamed of your wedding day many a time, but it was not like this. Music and joy, free-heartedness, a handsome, youthful bridegroom, our whole connection gathered from the army and navy, from South, West, and North, and all happy except poor Daniel Custis, about to lose his child."

"Your child is not to go," Vesta whispered. "Is that not a comfort?"

"I do not know. Had I seen you waste with consumption like a dying lilac tree, its clusters fewer every year till it deadened to the root, I could have wept in heavenly sympathy and learned from you the way I have not walked, but to be a forester's plucking in your flower, stripped from my stem and trodden in the sand, your pride reduced, your tastes unheeded, your heart dragged into the wigwam of a savage and made to consult his maudlin will—oh, what shall I do!"

"I do not fear my husband like that," Vesta said, opening her father's arms. "I think he will rather raise my mind to serious things for which I have some desire though, I fear, no talent. Something tells me, Papa, that this life we have led—easy and happy, comfortable and independent—is passing away. Our family race must learn the new lessons of the age if we would not see it retired and obscure. Is that not so?"

"I fear it is God's truth, my darling. The life we have led is only a remnant of colonial or, rather, provincial dignity, to which the nature of this republican government is hostile. Tobacco, which was once our money, is disappearing from this shore, and we cannot grow wheat and corn like the rich young West. Money is becoming a thing and not merely a name, and it captures every other thing: land, distinction, talent, family, even beauty and purity. The man you married understands the art of money, and we do not."

"Then are we not impostors, Papa, if we assume to be better than our real superiors? Surely we must persevere in those things the age demands and excel in them to sustain our pride."

"Yes, if the breed is gamecock, it will accept any challenge, not only war and politics, but mechanics, shop keeping, cattle herding—anything."

"Papa, if you can see these things that are to be so clearly, why can you not take the wise steps to plant your family on the safe side?"

"Ah, we Virginians were always the best statesmen, but we died poor. Having no manual craft, slight bookkeeping, yet an unlimited capacity for office, we foresaw everything but the humiliation of ourselves, and that we hardly admitted when it had come, so much were we flattered by our philosophic intellects. Our newest amusement is to expound the constitution to them who are doing too well under it, although our fathers who made it, like Jefferson and Madison, died only yesterday, overwhelmed with debts. And poor Mr. Monroe is run away to New York, they say, to dodge the Virginia bailiffs."

"Well, Papa, I have saved you from that fear. Here are your notes to Mr. Milburn and others. Sit down and look them over carefully and see if they are all here."

He took them up with volatile relief, laughter on his tear-marked face, and said, "We'll burn them, Vessy."

"Nay, sir, not until you have seen them all. A single note missing would give you the same perplexity, and there is no daughter left to settle it."

He looked at her with a smile, yet annoyance. "You are not going to make a Meshach Milburn of me?"

"Stop, sir," Vesta said. "You might do worse than learn from my husband."

Something strange in her expression baffled the judge. "Ha!" he interjected, "have I a rival already, daughter? Is his conquest as complete as that?"

"I promised to honor him a few moments ago, and I believe I can, Papa. All that you tell me adds to my respect for a man who seems to be only what he is."

"Perhaps you can love him, too?" the judge said, watching her with an apprehension a little like wonder, a little like jealousy.

"Oh, I wish I could, Papa. That also I promised to do, and I will try. But my work will all be a failure if you do not become reconciled to Mr. Milburn. It was for you I married him, and to save your name, your peace, your independence, and the upbraiding we expected from Mamma at the loss of her dower. He is now your son-in-law, still in the prime of life, with the business training you lament that you do not possess. Begin this moment, Papa, and learn his habits. Count and identify those notes."

Judge Custis looked them over separately, ran the number of notes he had given over in his mind, and said, "Yes, he has made fair restitution. There are none missing."

"Restitution implies that he has robbed you, Papa. A just man did not speak there. Every penny in those debts is stamped with Mr. Milburn's injuries and coined by his sacrifices. Have you spent his money remembering that?"

"No, my child, I suppose not."

"Give me the notes, Papa."

She took them and sat silently thinking a few moments. "If I were a man, Papa," she said at length, "I would try to learn business sense. It must be so respectable to live with one's mind able to help one's security and one's friends and prepare for age or sickness while strong and healthy. Now, I think I will not let you burn these notes till you have paid the price of them. Please write a transfer of this house, servants, and your manor to me, Vesta—yes, Vesta Milburn!" She blushed as she spoke her new-worn name for the first time.

"Alas," sighed her father, "Vesta Custis no more. I begin to feel it. Well, Mrs. Milburn, I will give you the title. For what must I make over these old properties to you?"

"In consideration of my repayment of the sum of my mother's estate to you for her, for which you have given her no security whatever. It is not provided for by these notes. I have only Mr. Milburn's promise that he will pay her this money, very heedlessly risked and lost by you, Father. Is it also restitution for Mr. Milburn to pay your debts to mother?"

"No," said the judge guiltily, "that he pays on account of his passion for you. He may cheat you there."

"I do not believe it because he has been faithful to me so many years before I knew he loved me. A man who keeps himself pure for a woman he has no vows to will pay her father's debts of honor when he has promised."

Judge Custis found the issue quite too warm for his convenience, and, blushing as much as Vesta, he sat down and drew up a conveyance of his property to Vesta Milburn in her own right and in consideration of twenty-five thousand dollars paid to Mrs. Lucy Custis on account of judgment confessed to her by Daniel Custis.

"There, my dear," he said, passing it over. "What do you want with it? Are you not sure of a home here as long as you live, even with me as the proprietor?"

"No! The tragedy nearly finished here may be repeated, Papa, and all of us be homeless if you can go in debt again. I shall not do that—not even for my husband. Here Teackle Hall will stand to protect you all from the cold if bad times ever come again."

"You have paid a greater price for it, my child, than it is worth, and you are entitled to it."

"Besides, dear Father, if Mr. Milburn needs any reminder of his promise to repay Mamma's dowry, this will give it. He intended his gift to be my marriage dower, and were I to convey it to you, I should first ask his consent—not in law, perhaps, but in delicacy."

"Oh, yes," the judge said carelessly, "I am glad you have such good reasons. Yet, my beautiful, my last child—pride of my race—I hate to see you so ready for this business, this calculation and foresight. It is not like the Custises. I fear this man Milburn has thrown his net around your nature in a single day and annexed you to his sordid existence. At this moment the redeeming thing about you is that you cannot love him."

"Dear Father, thoughts like that beset me, too—the pride of aristocracy, the remembrance of what has been—but I want to be honest and not cheat my heart or any person. We have fallen from our height. He has raised himself from his condition, and there is no deception in my conduct. He knows I do not love him. Instead of standing upon an obdurate heart, I pray God to melt my nature and mold it to his affection."

Regarding her a moment with increasing interest, Judge Custis came forward and kissed her forehead. "Amen, then," he said. "May you love your husband. I will do all I can to love him, too."

"That is spoken like a true man," Vesta said. "And now, Father, good night. Be ready for Mr. Milburn's arrival. Ring for a decanter and some cake. After your fast it will not hurt you to drink a glass of sherry with the bridegroom."

He kissed her and felt her trembling in his arms. As she started to go, she returned and clung to him again. Her face was pale with fear.

"Oh, dreadful God," he muttered, "to visit my many sins upon this spotless angel. Where shall I fly?"

A step was upon the porch, and Vesta flashed up the stairway.

Judge Custis went to his door, apprehensive and in tears. A strange man stood there with his eye bruised and blood dripping down to his coarse, rope-like beard. He was in liquor and so pale that it was apparent by the starlight.

"Good evening," said the man. "You don't know me, Judge Custis. No matter. I'm Joe Johnson."

The judge, whose tears had taken him far from things of trivial memory, looked at the man and repeated, "*Joe* Johnson. Not Joe Johnson of Dorchester?"

"Yes, Judge, Joe Johnson the slave dealer. I've bought many a nigger from a Custis when it was impolite to sell 'em. So they let me run 'em off and cussed me for it to the public, an' that's made me onpopular, Judge Custis. That's my fix tonight."

"I think you have been fighting, Johnson," said the judge with suppressed dislike.

"I've been knocked down by a nigger," said the man with a glare of ferocity, removing his hand from the wounded eye as if it inflamed his recollection of the blow to see the drops of blood drip from his beard to the porch. "This town is too nice to abide a dealer in the constitutional article, so they set on me when I was a little jingle-brained with lush. While the nigger klemmed me in the peep, a little white villain with a steeple-bonnet hit me in the bread bag with a stone. I've come yer, Judge, to lie up in the kitchen an' sleep warm over Sunday, for the cops threaten to take me if they catch me before midnight."

"I suppose you know, Johnson, that I am a magistrate, and the proper harborage I give to breakers of the peace is the jail."

"I'm not afraid of that limbo, Judge Custis, when I come to you. Old Patty Cannon has done you many a good turn with Joe Johnson's gang about election times in the upper destreeks of Somerset. Patty always said Judge Custis was a game gentleman that returned a favor."

The judge's countenance lighted up with a vote-getter's smile, and he said, "Joe, you're a terrible fellow, but dear old Aunt Patty did always take my part. I suspect, Joe, that you have run afoul of Samson, who is a boxer and the hired man of Meshach Milburn, though I wonder that he could get away with your youth and size. You haven't been playing your tricks on anybody's Negroes, have you, Joe?"

"No, upon my word, Judge. I took a load of Egypt down the Nanticoke to Norfolk an' shipped 'em to Orleens. Says I, 'I'll go back Eastern Shore way an' see if there's any niggers to git.' I tramped from Somers's Cove to Princess Anne an' sluiced my gob at Kingston an' the Trappe till I felt noddy with booze. I lay down in the churchyard to snooze it off. Bein' awaked before my nod was out, I felt evil an' chiveyish. The tavern blokes an' the nigger an' the feller with the steeple-shap all checked me at once."

"Well, Joe, for Aunt Patty's sake I'll take care of you. Go to the kitchen door, and I'll step through the house and tell Aunt Hominy to give you supper and breakfast and a place to get some sleep. But you must keep out of the way and slip off quietly on Sunday, for we have had a wedding in the family today, Joe, and though I cannot understand your peculiar slang, I suspect the bridegroom to be the man who knocked the breath out of you."

The stranger lifted his hand from his bloody eye again and counted the red drops splashing down from his beard.

Judge Custis marked his scowl. "Tut, tut," said the judge, "you will never get your revenge of that man. He is too strong. I don't wonder that he disabled you. And don't you ever get into his clutches, Joe, for if he knows you are here, I shall be forced to send you to jail this very night. Keep out of the hands of Meshach Milburn. He has knocked the breath out of you, Mr. Johnson, but there are some whose hearts he has twisted out of their bodies."

"I'll meet him somewhere," Joe Johnson muttered, "but not in Princess Anne."

Pulling his slouched hat down to cover his eyes, he stalked away to find the kitchen.

"Oh, what a day can bring forth," Judge Custis thought, raising his hands to the October stars: "Meshach of the ominous hat the host in my parlor; Joe Johnson, the son-in-law of Patty Cannon, the guest of my kitchen."

Meshach's Home

Chapter 14

Vesta hardly knew how long she had slept, but it was day, and her eyes slowly turned towards the remainder of her bed to see if it was occupied.

The bridegroom was not there.

She reached her foot into her slipper at the bedside and in one swift step passed before her mirror, whispering, "I have dreamed it all."

The fresh, flushing skin and radiant contrasts of hair and eyes seemed so welcome to her in their perfect assurance of health that she whispered again, "Have I dreamed it? He is not here. Oh, am I free?"

Then a feeling of reproval came over her, as the memory of yesterday rose to her mind, and the vow she had made to honor and obey seemed to have been too easily repented. She looked upon her hand, and the thin, pathetic thread of gold reaffirmed her memory of the wedding.

At the next suggestion a blush coursed through her like a redbird in the apple blossoms: perhaps he had stolen from her chamber as stealthily as he came, while she was drowned in deep slumber.

A glance into the mirror again revealed those blushes repeating each other like the aurora in the northern dawn till, with a searching consciousness and her voice raised above the whisper, she said, "Be still, silly girl!"

Opening the door, she found Virgie lying on the rug without, warmly wrapped in her mistress's blanket shawl but wide awake.

"Virgie, no one has passed?" asked Vesta.

"No, Miss Vessy. Nobody could have stepped over me. My mind has been too awake, if I did sleep a little. Maybe he ain't a-coming, Miss Vessy. Maybe he's ashamed."

"Hush, Virgie," Vesta said, "you are speaking of your master."

Throwing a morning robe around her shoulders, the maiden bride tripped noiselessly to her mother's apartment. The door was open, the night taper floating in its vase, and Mrs. Custis lay asleep with her bank book under her pillow.

"Shall I wake her?" Vesta thought. "Yes. If I do not need her experience, I do want her confidence, and not to give her mine would seem deceit now."

Vesta kissed her mother softly and placed her cheek beside that lady's thin, respectable profile, as Mrs. Custis awoke and said, "Daughter, mercy! Why what has become of you? It seems to me I have seen nobody for days, and I wanted to express my indignation even in my dreams. Where have you been?"

"Oh, Mamma," Vesta said, taking Mrs. Custis's head in her arms, "I have been finding your lost fortune, which troubled us all so much. It is to be given back to you, dearest. My husband has promised to do so."

"Your husband? Whom have you selected that he is so free with his money? How could you hear from Baltimore so soon? Now don't tell me a parcel of stuff, thinking to comfort me. Your father is a villain, and my connections shall know it."

Mrs. Custis drew her bank book from under her head and began to cry as she looked at its former total.

"Darling Mamma," Vesta said, "seeing you so miserable yesterday on account of Papa's failure, and your portion gone with it, I accepted an offer of marriage and have a rich man's promise that, first of all, your part shall be paid to you. This house and our manor with everything as it is—the servants, the stable, and the movables—belong to me in my own name, paid for in Papa's notes and by him transferred to me to be our home forever, so that a revulsion like yesterday may not again cross the sill of our door. Does not that deserve a kiss, Mamma?"

"I don't believe a word of it," said Mrs. Custis. "This is another trick to deceive me. I don't accuse you of it, Vesta, but you are the victim of somebody and your father. Who can this man be, so free with his ready money? It's not the style in Baltimore to promise so liberally as all that. Have you accepted young Carroll?"

"No, nor thought of him, Mamma."

"Then it must be that widower fool, Hynson, ready to sell his Negroes for a second wife like you."

"He has neither been here in body nor mind," Vesta said. "Never in my mind."

"That would be a marriage to make a talk. It wouldn't be like you to bestow so much beauty on a widower. I think there is a certain vulgarity about an elegant girl marrying a widower. She is so refined, and he is generally so sleek and sensual. Did you hear from Charles McLane?"

"Nothing Mamma. Let me ease your mind by telling you that my husband lives here in Princess Anne. He was father's creditor, Mr. Meshach Milburn. He has loved me unknown for years. I saw a way to stop all scandal and recrimination by marrying him at once, that the society we know would have but one rather than two subjects of curiosity. Papa saw me married to Mr. Milburn last night, and I bear his name this Sabbath day."

"His wife? Meshach Milburn? The vulgarian in the play-actor's hat? That man! Daughter, you play with my poor head. It is going again. Ohhh!"

"Mother, it is true; I am Mrs. Milburn. My husband is your benefactor."

It was unnecessary to say more, for Mrs. Custis had really fainted.

"Poor Mother," thought Vesta, "I am confirmed in my fear that if she had been told of my purpose, she would have opposed it bitterly."

Roxy was summoned to assist Vesta, and after Mrs. Custis had become conscious and sighed and cried hysterically, her daughter spoke plainly: "Mother, I appreciate your disappointment in my marriage, though I should be the one to make complaint and receive sympathy. But I do not desire it. Indeed, I will not permit any person to disparage my husband or draw odious comparisons between my poverty and his exertions. If there are any merits to please a man in my body or in my society, they have fallen to him under the law of providence. "I pity your illness, dear Mamma, but I fear that Mr. Milburn is ill, too, for he has not been here all night, though he left me at the church gate."

"I hope the viper is dead!" Mrs. Custis said with great clearness, and energized it by sitting up in bed.

Roxy left the room.

"I hope he has been murdered," continued Mrs. Custis, "and that the murderer will never be discovered. If there is any spirit of the McLanes left in my brothers and nephews, they will wipe out in blood the insult of this marriage between my daughter and the man who set a trap upon the honor of a respectable family."

Vesta arose with a pale, troubled face, yet with some of her mother's prejudice flashing back. "He can defend himself, Mamma. I shall go to seek him now, since he is so much hated for me."

She returned to her room and put on a walking suit.

Vesta found her father in the library, dozing in a large chair. His feet were upon a leather sofa, and a silk handkerchief was drawn across his crown, under which were the dry beds of tears that had coursed down his cheeks.

With a touch of joy she saw that the sherry in the decanter was untouched and the two glasses still clean. Even while making an all-night vigil to wait for the unwelcome son-in-law, he had not relapsed into his habits. He started as she entered, then stared at her between his dazed wits and a mute inquiry that she could understand.

"He has not come, Papa, and Mamma—oh, she is severe."

Trembling at the throat for a moment, Vesta rushed into her father's wide-open arms and buried the sob in his breast.

"Poor soul. Poor lamb. Poor thing," he said over and over, while his temper slowly rose. Vesta felt his tones change as he petted her and at last heard him hoarsely say, "By God!"

"Shh," she whispered, raising her hand to his mouth.

"I will kill somebody," he went on, finishing his sentence.

As she drew away, he strode across the room and back again, a noble exhibition of passion that had a noble origin in fatherly pity.

"Don't lose your true pride, Papa, after you have persevered so long," Vesta said. "It is Sunday. Do you think he will come? What can have happened?"

"He will either come or fight me," Judge Custis remarked. "I have tried to be a peaceable man and Christian magistrate, albeit a poor hypocrite in some things, but I am pushed too far. My wife's smallness is worse than insanity and wickedness put together. Between her and this money-broking fiend and my neglected child entrapped into such a marriage, by God, I will clean my old dueling arms and appeal to injustice itself to set me even."

If he had been fine looking in his grief, he was thrice more attractive in his sincere high spirit. Admiring him in spite of her cares, Vesta did not like to see him in this unnatural recklessness.

"Dear Father," she said soothingly, "you have no cause for quarrel."

"I have every cause," he cried. "The proposal to marry you was an insult for which I should have challenged him and shot him if he declined. Now he has married you and absconded, using you and the Custis honor with contempt. In my day I was the best shot in eastern Virginia. I can kill a man in this cause as easily as I have broken either of a man's arms, at choice, in my courting days. Public opinion will clear me under this provocation. Abhorrent as dueling is to me, I can acquit my own conscience. My sons-in-law would leap to take the quarrel up and rid the world of Meshach Milburn."

"That is Mamma's idea, to kill the debtor who has been especially kind to her. She says she will send for Uncle Allan McLane and is more unreasonable than ever. Your feelings, Papa, are unjust. Something we do not know of has happened to Mr. Milburn. He was not himself all the while at the church. Now that I recollect, he was not ardent for the marriage to be so soon. It was I who hastened the hour. Having progressed so far with the recovery of our fortunes, let us be right in everything, and let us await the fulfillment of events hopefully."

"Milburn was drunk at the ceremony; I saw that," Judge Custis said, "but it was no excuse. In fact, what good can come of this violent alliance? It seems to me that we have leaped from the frying pan into the fire. I feel ugly, my daughter, and there is no concealing it."

"Then you are in the mood to talk to Mother this morning," Vesta said, "while you have some unusual will and spirit. I fear this resentful sullenness she is showing more than your passing emotion, Papa. Be firm, yet kind with her, and I will go to find my husband. He may be more justly complaining of my absence than we of his neglect."

"You don't mean that you are going to visit him at his den?"

"I shall go there first. It would have been my home last night had he required it. To tell the truth," Vesta said, blushing, "the poor man was so kind to me yesterday, in spite of his object, and so quaint and so seemingly dependent on me, that my charity is enlisted for him. I could almost have married him from pity."

The judge's temper fell a little in the study of his daughter's blushing. "Wonderful," he thought to himself. "That poor corn-bred fellow has already made more impression on this girl's pride than a hundred cavalier gallants."

"We truly are a republic, Vesta," he said. "You lay down the Custis character as easily as our old connection, Lord Fairfax, accepted the democracy of his hired surveyor, Mr. Washington, before he died."

"I laid down the Custis name yesterday," Vesta said, "though not their better character, I hope. There is only one law of marriage, Papa. It is where the wife follows the husband."

She looked a little archly at him, and though she may not have meant it, he was reminded of his own fear of his wife.

Aunt Hominy now came in, having been told by Virgie to prepare coffee. The old cook had a strange look, as of one who had been up all night at a fire or a protracted meeting. She poked her head in as if afraid to come farther.

Vesta went out and kissed her kindly. "Poor Aunty Hominy, did you think I was sold or abused because I had been married? Dear old aunty, I shall never leave you."

Aunt Hominy's countenance bore a profound melancholy mixed with fear that the judge remarked he had seen on the faces of niggers that had stolen something.

"Miss Vessy," she stammered at last, "is you measured in by ole Meshach? Is he got you, honey? Dat he has, chile. He's gwyn to bury you under dat pizen hat. Po' little girl! Po' Miss Vessy!"

"Oh, Aunt Hominy," Vesta said, "he will be a kind master in spite of his queer hat and take good care of you and all the children. He is my husband and will love you all for me."

A dumb, terrified look adhered to the old black woman's face. "No, he won't be kind to nobody," she rasped. "You has gwyn been lost, Miss Vessy. You is measured in. De good Lord try an' bress you. Hominy ain't measured in yit. Hominy's kivered herself wid cammermile an' drunk biled lizzer tea. Hominy's gone an' got Quaker."

"What's *Quaker*, Aunt Hominy?"

"Quaker," the old woman repeated, backing out and looking down, "Quaker's what keeps him from a-measurin' of me in."

Having taken her coffee and toast, Vesta drew on her bonnet and shawl, as the old servant glided back into the depths of Teackle Hall.

The tears rained upon Hominy's cheeks, as her wringing hands and up-flung arms and shape convulsed. She raised a wild African croon, as over the dead, giving her voice a musical inflection like the jingle of Juba rhyme: "Good-bye, Miss Vessy! Good-bye, Aunt Hominy's baby!

Good-bye, dear young missis! Good-bye, my darlin' chile, furever, furever, an' oh, furever! Little Vessy Custis, oh, chile, farewell!"

As she left Teackle Hall with Virgie, Vesta thought that some African superstition had, by the aid of dreams, drawn the faithful servant's brain into a passing excitement.

At the corner of old Front Street, extending almost out upon the little Manokin bridge, Meshach Milburn's two-story house and store stood with a door upon both streets. Though planted low in a hollow, it stood forward like Milburn's challenging countenance, unsupported by any neighbors.

The View Across the Manokin River Bridge from Meshach Milburn's toward the Presbyterian Church

"Don't it look like a witch's, Missy?" Virgie said, as Vesta took in its not unpicturesque outlines, its crude plank carpentry, weather-rotted tile roof, decrepit chimney at the far end, one garret window in the sharp gable, scant little windows above stairs, and the doors low to the sand.

"It may have been the pride of the town fifty years ago, Virgie. I have passed it many a day, looking with mischievous curiosity to show the steeple-hat to some city friend, little thinking I must ever enter the house. But hear that willful bird singing so loud. Where is it?"

"I can't tell to save my life. It ain't in the tree yonder. It's the first bird up this mornin', Miss Vessy, sho'."

"Is not the larger door standing ajar, the one with the four panels in it?" Vesta asked. "Yes, it is unfastened and partly open."

The blood left Vesta's heart a moment as the thought ran through her mind: "He has been watched, followed home, and murdered." The idea seemed to explain his absence on his marriage night.

Like flame upon a burning ship, lighting up the wide ocean with its bright terrors, Vesta saw the infinite relations of such a crime. Her almost secret marriage, her custody of her father's notes, the record of them upon her husband's books, his last word at the church gate: "I will come soon, darling," and now this silent abode with its door ajar on Sunday dawn before the town was up—all might bear the suspicion of a dreadful crime by the ruined house of Custis against their friendless creditor.

This thought, personal to her father, was immediately dismissed. If the idea touched her that her tremendous sacrifice had been arrested by heaven and her purity saved between the altar and the nuptials by her purchaser's bloodshed at the hands of some meaner avenger, it never passed beyond the portal of her mind. She repulsed it, thinking instead of the easy prey her husband might have been—hated by many; defended by none; known to be very rich; no loss to the community, as it might think in its financial ignorance; and his only guard a stalwart Negro notorious for fighting.

Believing Milburn to deserve better than his present fame, Vesta advanced towards the door of the old store with a spirit of commiseration and awe, and still the wild bird from somewhere poured out a shriek, a chuckle, a hurrah, enough to turn her blood to ice.

As Vesta pushed open the old, seasoned door, it dragged along the floor, and the loose iron bar and padlock, as it dropped down, made a ring that brought an echo like a tomb's from the hollow interior.

"'Deed, Miss Vessy, I'm 'fraid to go in there," Virgie said.

"You are not to come in till I call you, but hear that bird rioting in song. Does Mr. Milburn keep birds?"

"I can't tell, Miss Vessy. That bird's a mocker. It must be in there somewhere. Oh, don't go in, Miss Vessy. Something will catch you, sho'."

But Vesta was already gone, following the piercing sound of the native bird that seemed to be in the loft.

She saw a little counter of pine and a pine desk built into it, bundles of skins, some cord wood, a pile of lumber and boxes, a few barrels of oil or spirits, and dust and cobwebs thick on everything. A little way in from the door, the light and darkness had weird effects upon each other, increasing the apparent distances and changing forms. The sun, now risen, made turning cylinders of gold dust at certain knotholes in the eastern gable, across whose film she observed two lean mice stand upon the floor, unalarmed and tamely watching her come.

The screaming of the bird was conveyed through the thin floor from above with loud distinctness. Every note of singing things from the hawk's gloating cry to the swallow's twittering alarm seemed to be imitated by it with the most rapid versatility and even hurry, as if the creature was trying every bird language with the hope of finding one which mankind could understand.

It was idle to expect to be heard amid such clamor. Having pounded on the floor a few times, Vesta made her way to a cupboard that she thought might turn out to be a stairway. Sure enough, a door opened on its dark side, and light flickered down from above.

At this moment the bird's notes abruptly ceased, and a voice, unlike anything Vesta had ever heard in her life, yet human, spoke in response to a more natural human voice, both issuing from above.

The second voice seemed to be Milburn's. The first was something like it, yet unlike anything from the throat of man. The superstition she had been rebuking in her servant came with a thrilling influence upon her entire nature. She was about to fly, but called out one word as she arrested herself: "Gentlemen!"

The loud, unclassifiable voice immediately answered, "Gent gent-gent-gent-en! T-chee, t-chee! Gents, tss-tss-tss! Ha! Gentle-men!"

"May I come up?" Vesta cried.

"Come, p-chee! Come chee! Come tsee! See me! See me! See me! Come p-chee! Come see! Come see me!"

The last accentuation, in spite of the bird's interference, was sufficiently distinct to amount to an invitation. Raising her eyelids dependently to heaven, Vesta went up the stairs.

She put her head into a large, long room, which took up the whole contents of the second story and was lighted on three sides by the small windows she had seen without. It had no carpet nor floor covering of any kind. The fire had gone out upon the hearth, but the chill atmosphere was melting before the sunshine, which streamed in at both sides of the fireplace, clearly revealing every object in the apartment. There were clothes pegs, a wooden table with a blue plate, blue cup and saucer, saucepan, and a coarse knife and fork upon it. There was a large green chest, a leather hatbox, and a fifty-year-old hair trunk nearly falling to pieces. Black silhouettes of a woman and a man in little, round, ebony frames hung over the mantel, and between them a silhouette of a face she had no difficulty in recognizing to be intended for her own.

Stretched upon a low, child's trundle bed, the bridegroom lay in his wedding dress and gaitered shoes with his steeple-crowned hat on the faded quilt beside him. His face was as red as burning fever could make it.

Vesta went forward, put her hand upon the motionless form of her husband, and said, "Mr. Milburn."

"Milburn!" echoed a voice of piercing strength, though ill articulated.

Vesta looked around in astonishment and saw nobody. "Husband!" she said louder, stooping over him.

"S'band! S'band! See! See!" shouted the wanton voice, almost at her elbow.

With one hand on the helpless man's brow, Vesta turned again, almost indignantly, for the tone seemed to address some sense of neglect or shame in her. Still, nothing was to be seen.

The voice now seemed to come from the chimney at the opposite end of the room and was accompanied by a fluttering and scratching, as if some spirit of evil with the talons of a rat or a bat was trying to break in where the prostrate man lay on the bed of oblivion.

"Meshach! Meshach!" rang the half-human cry. "Hoo! Hoo! Vesty! Vesty! Sweet! Sweet! Sweet! Ha, ha! See me! See me! Meshach, he! Vesty, she! She! She! She! Hoot! Hoot! Ha!"

Her ears and heart tingling at the use of her own name, Vesta looked again and saw a common bird of a gray color on the dusty wooden mantel. It had dashes of brown and black on its wings, a whitish breast, and it was greatly agitated, as if it meant to fly upon her or some other intruder she could not see.

The bird's black pupils sparkled with nervous activity. Its upper bill was beaked like a hawk's, its lower as sharp as a lance, and between them issued an infuriated melody and epithet. It flung itself into the air above her head, uttering sounds of such mellow richness and such infinite variety of modulation that the old hovel almost burst with intoxicated song, combining gladness, welcome, fear, defiance, superstition, and horror together, like Orpheus gone mad and losing the continuity of his golden notes.

Suddenly it flung itself upon the bed of the sick man and, with a twitching hop and rapid opening and shutting of the tail, like the fan of a disturbed beauty, perched upon Milburn's peaked hat. With a convulsive struggle of its throat and body, as if it were in superhuman labor, the bird brought out as distinctly as man could speak the words, "'Sband! 'Sband! Vesty! Vesty! Sweet! Sweet! Come see! Come see!"

By a quick, expert movement, Vesta grasped the bird and smoothed it against her bosom, soothing its excitement.

She had just heard what Audubon had avowed and recently published in the beautiful edition of his works, to which her father was a subscriber, that some claim the American mockingbird to be capable of imitating the human voice, though the naturalist remarked that he himself had never heard the bird do it.

The present verification of the mockingbird's power, Vesta thought, might have issued from its excitement at the silent and helpless condition of its master—that master who had told Vesta that no bird in the woods ever resisted his seductions and mystic influence.

"If that be true," Vesta said to herself, "there is no danger of this vociferous pet making his escape if I put him out the window till I can see if his master speaks or lives."

She raised the window and flung the mockingbird into the air. It came down and dropped into the old willow tree beneath, there setting up a concert of which the Sabbath morning might have been proud, when in the cornfields the free-footed Savior went plucking the milky ears. Vesta could but stop a minute and listen.

The liquid notes chased each other around in circles of dizzy harmony, as if angels were at hide-and-seek on the blue branches of the air, eluding each other in pure-heartedness, chasing each other with eager love, sighing praise and happiness as their supernal hearts emitted music in the glow of ecstasy, and carrying upward the loveliest emotions of the earth in yearning sympathy for nature. No language that Vesta could identify was woven into that maze of morning song, which challenged the floods of sunshine with its fullness and golden weight, matching light with sound, spontaneous both, and rivals for the favors of the soft atmosphere.

Singing with all its heart, outdoing all it knew, forgetting imitation in wild improvisation, watching her window as it danced upon the twigs and fluttered into the air, conscious of her listening as it purled and warbled towards her, sounding every pipe and trumpet in the orchestra of its rustic bosom—virginal and clarion. hautboy and castanets—the mockingbird seemed almost supernatural to Vesta.

She thought to herself, "Oh, what wedding music in the cathedral at Baltimore could equal that? And this poor man receives it for his epithalamium without cost, as truly as if nature were greeting my coming to him in the old poet's spirit:

> Now all is done; bring home the bride againe;
> Bring home the triumph of our victory;
> Bring home with you the glory of her gaine,
> With joyance bring her and with jollity:
> Sing, ye sweet angels, Alleluia sing.
> That all the woods may answer, and your echo ring.

Relieved from the agitation of the mockingbird, Vesta now gave her whole attention to her husband. The high heat of his brain and circulation and his muttering, like delirium, seemed to indicate that he had an intense attack of intermittent fever.

She heard him repeat the words several times: "I will come soon, darling," and the simplicity of his devotion to her, unloved as he was, had such flavor of pathos in it that the tears started to Vesta's eyes.

"Poor soul," she said, "it will be long before I can love him. *There*, his hunger must be enduring. But my duty is not the less clear to stay by his side and nurse him as his wife."

At this conclusion she looked Milburn over carefully to see if any wound or sign of violence appeared upon him. Finding none, and he all the time wandering in his sleep, she climbed the ladder and peeped into the garret to see if his servant might be there. Samson's bed, as she supposed it was, had not been disturbed. Descending, she raised the window over the door she had entered and beckoned Virgie to come up.

"Take this cup," she said to the quadroon. "Go to the spring near here and bring it to me full of water."

As the girl tripped away, Vesta found a piece of paper and wrote her father a note, telling him to come to her.

When the girl returned, her mistress said, "I want you to get a roll of new rag carpet at Teackle Hall and have it brought here to spread upon this floor. Send me, too, a pair of our brass andirons and pack some glass, tableware, and linen in a basket. Tell Papa to bring one of his own nightshirts. And tell him to take down my picture in the sewing room and wrap it up and send it. I must have Mamma's medicine box and a wheelbarrow of ice. Let Hominy make some strong tea and hot water toast. Do not forget, Virgie, that this sick gentleman is my husband and a part of our own family."

The girl's face preserved its respect with difficulty as she heard the last part of the sentence, but she replied to what she understood to be a warning by saying, "Miss Vessy, I never tell anybody tales."

"No, dear, you do not. I only feared you might forget the very different view we must take of Mr. Milburn from his former life here."

Being again left alone, Vesta took the cup of spring water, raised the disturbed man's head, and gave him a drink.

As he opened his eyes to see whom it was, she heard him say with an articulate sigh, "Heaven."

With the remainder of the water and her handkerchief she washed his hot skin and kept it moist. Fitful murmurs such as "Darling, angel, beautiful lady," came from his roving brain as perception and poison contended for his mind.

Woman's inborn sense of happiness after doing good offices and being appreciated was attended with a certain intellectual elation and even amusement at having witnessed what was altogether new to her— the life of the meaner class of white people. She looked at the dexterous silhouette of herself, probably cut long ago from memory by the man who never knew her until yesterday.

Guessing the companion profiles to be his mother and father, Vesta mentally exclaimed, "I can see nothing insincere about this man's statement to me. Here are all the proofs of his deep attachment to me long before he forced my name upon Papa with such apparent insolence. If Papa could see these with a woman's interest, he would have a full apology in them. Here, too, is the bird that sings my name. What strength of prepossession the master must have had to make the feathered pupil repeat the sound of 'Vesta' and to call me 'sweet.' What resources, too, without the use of money or social aids. He knows the story of our English beginning, while we make it an idle boast. To him Cromwell and Milton, Raleigh and Vane are men of today. I think I see one of those Puritans, whom I have heard as sprinkled through Virginia, in my husband. We are the Cavaliers, and here is the Roundhead, even to the King James hat."

As she was led onward in these probabilities, Vesta took up the demure old hat and looked it over without superstition and reflected, "Do we not exaggerate trifles? Why should this man be derided because he covers his head with an old hat? What of it? Suppose it shows some vanity or eccentricity. Why is there more merit in covering that than by expressing it in the dress? The styles we wear are the derision even of the current journals, and what will be thought of them fifty years hence, when the fashion magazines show me as I look—the envy of my moment, the fright of my grandchildren?"

With rising color she put the hat in the leather hatbox and shut it up.

In a little while Judge Custis made his way up the stairs and exclaimed as soon as he looked at Milburn, "Curses come home to roost. It was only night before last that I said in the presence of Meshach's Negro, 'May the ague strike him, and the bilious sweat from Nassawango millpond.' He slept by it that night, while I was tossing in misery. The next night it was his turn. He has the bilious intermittent fever, the legacy of all his fathers. He exposed himself extraordinarily that night, I suppose, and I hear that he burned the old cabin in the morning. Now he will burn in memory of it for the next ten weeks. He has, I suspect, what is called the double quotidian type of the fever, with two attacks in twenty-four hours."

"Poor man!" exclaimed Vesta.

"Now I can account for his appearance at the marriage ceremony last night. The fever was on him, but he went through it by hard grit. Probably returning here to get some relief, he just fell over on that bed, and his head left him for some hours. The paroxysm goes away during sleep and returns in the morning. So before he could get abroad today to report himself at Teackle Hall, another fever came, and a furious one. He will have good luck to survive forty days of fever with probably eighty sweats in that time."

"He must be doctored at once, Papa."

"Well, I am a good enough doctor for the bilious fever. He will want cold lemonade, cold sponging, and ice to suck when the fever is on him. When the chills intervene, he will want blanketing, hot bottles at his feet, and hot tea or something stronger. In the rest between attacks of fever and chill, he will want calomel and Peruvian bark, and if these delirious spells go on, he may want both bleeding and opium."

"Here are some of the things he immediately needs," Vesta said, as a tall white man she had never seen before came up the stairs with Virgie, bringing Susquehanna ice in a blanket, a roll of carpet, and other articles she had sent for. The man's face wore a large bruise that heightened his savage appearance.

"Judge," exclaimed the stranger, "I'm doin' a little work to pay fur my board. Who's your whiffler? He'll know me when he sees me next time."

Following the stranger's eyes, Vesta and her father saw Meshach Milburn half raise up from the low trundle bed, as if trying to get at Joe Johnson. His lips moved, and he partly articulated, "Catch the—scoundrel—*him!*"

"Joe," said the judge, "slip away. He recognizes you as the assailant yesterday. Don't hesitate; see how he glares at you."

"Oh, it's the billy-noodle with the steeple-nab cheat, him that settled me with the brick," Johnson said in a low voice." So I have piped him. Ah, that's plumby."

As the tall man started to go, Milburn's countenance relaxed. He wandered again in his head and fell back upon the bed.

"I told you he was a hard hater, Mr. Johnson," the judge remarked.

"Them shakes is the equivvy for the bruise he give me, that is, till we both heal up. He's painted the ensigns of all nations on my stummick, judge, but a blow is cured by a blow."

With an admiring look at Virgie, Joe Johnson drew his long figure down the stairs like a pole.

"What a brutal giant," Vesta said. "And how came he to be doing our errands?"

"Aunt Hominy hadn't nobody to bring the wheelbarrow load, and this man said he'd come, Miss Vesty, so I couldn't say anything."

"He's a man of a good deal of influence in the upper part of our county and in Delaware," said the judge uneasily. "After the wedding last night he slapped Meshach's hat, and old Samson knocked him down for it. He would have killed Samson, I hear, but for your bridegroom, who felled him with a timely brick. It's a hard team to pass on a narrow road—Meshach and Samson—hey, Virgie?"

"I'm glad old Samson beat him," the pretty quadroon said.

"Oh, what troubles will not that hat bring upon us?" Vesta thought, and then said, "If Mr. Milburn was strong, I think he would hardly let that man get out of the county before night."

"Well, daughter, what are you going to do with these articles he has brought?"

"They are to make this room comfortable. See, he has my picture here, cut by his own hands. I want to put a better one before him. Help me hang it, Papa."

In a few minutes the bright oil portrait, recently painted by Mr. Rembrandt Peale, was taking the sunlight upon its warm brunette cheeks in full sight of the bridegroom, and the thick rag carpet warmed the floor. Virgie had made a second errand to Teackle Hall and brought back the lady's rocking chair that Milburn so much affected, and toilet articles and dark cloth to hide the bare boards in places. The old loft soon wore a reasonable appearance of habitable life. Virgie made up the fire, and the brass andirons took the cheerful flame upon them. After her father had cut and squeezed the lemons, Vesta sweetened the lemonade and added some magnesia to make the drink foam.

"Really," said Judge Custis, "this miserable den takes the rudimentary form of a home. I suppose there are now more comforts in his sight than Meshach's whole race ever collected. What is your next move, Vesta?"

"To stay right here, darling Papa, till it is safe and convenient to carry Mr. Milburn home."

"Oh, folly. It will excite scandal and be repulsive to my feelings. This loft over a former groggery is no place for you. The news will spread from Chincoteague to Arlington. Every Custis that lives will censure me and outlaw you."

"I think you had best see Mr. Tilghman before the service, Papa, and have the marriage announced this morning. That will settle the excitement before night. As for staying here, my home is where he needs me. At his will I should have to stay here altogether. But I wish to do this, Father. It is of the greatest necessity to improve my intercourse with my husband while he is sick, that the hasty marriage we made may still have its period of acquaintance and good understanding. I want to sound the possibilities of my happiness. He will be less my master now than in his strength and possession. Perhaps . . .," Vesta's voice fell, and she turned to gaze upon the bridegroom, whose fever still consumed his wits. "Perhaps," she continued, "I can influence his dress—his appearance."

"You mean the steeple-top," Judge Custis exclaimed petulantly.

At the loud sound of this familiar word, the feverish man's ears were pierced as through some ever-open ventricle, like an old wound.

"Steeple-top! Who cried 'steeple-top'?" he muttered. "Can't you see I'm married. *She* hears it. Oh, spare and pity her."

He wandered into the miasmatic world again, leaving them all touched, yet oppressed.

"How the very flintstone will wear away before the waterdrop," Judge Custis finally said. "His obdurate heart has been bruised by that nickname. In public he never appeared to flinch before it, but you see it inflicted a never-healing wound. Who has not his vulture?"

"And how unjust to pursue this man with such frivolous inhospitality so many years," Vesta exclaimed, her splendid eyes flashing. "No account has been made of his private reasons, his family piety, or of his stern taste, perhaps. He must have a reason for his wardrobe, that being, it would seem, the only thing there can be no independence about. Did you hear, Papa, his feeling for me? Strangely enough, my own mind was thinking of that hat. It seems bigger than the steeples of the churches. It rises between the people and worship, between us and charity and faith—I almost said hope, too."

"The colored people say he has to wear that hat because the devil makes him," the trim, fawn-footed Virgie said. "Aunt Hominy says the bad man wouldn't let him make no mo' money if he didn't go to church in that hat. Some of the white people says so, too."

"You don't believe such foolish tales, Virgie?" Vesta said.

"Deed, I don't believe anything you say is a story, Miss Vessy. Aunt Hominy believes it. She's 'most scared out of her life about Mr. Milburn coming to the house, an' she's got the little ones a'most crazy with fear."

"Poor, dark, ignorant soul," Vesta said. "She is, however, more excusable than grown men whose prejudices against an article of dress are as heathen in character as her fetish superstition."

"If he is good to you, Miss Vessy," the slave girl said, "I'll think the bad man hasn't got anything to do with him. If he treats you bad, I'll think the bad man has."

"Sometimes I feel as if men ought to have been left wild like the animals," the judge said, rinsing out Milburn's mouth with a piece of ice, "for the obstacles to liberty raised by fashion and civilization are Asiatic in their despotism. Think of the taxes we pay to fashion, when we refused less to kings. Think of the aristocracy based upon dress after we have formally extirpated it by statute. Think of the influence the boot makers and mantua makers of Europe exert upon our presidents and senators, and through the women of this country upon all the men in the land. A million women who do not know that there are two houses of Congress know what bonnet the Duchess d'Angouleme is wearing and how Charles X ties his cravat in Paris. So the devil always gets a worm in every apple. The French Revolution abolished feudality, titles, great landed property, and only omitted to abolish fashion. That worm—a silkworm it is—is devastating republican government everywhere, using the women to infect us."

"Yet," said Vesta, "love of dress in the nature of woman is no stronger than the love of woman is in man. Some righteous purpose is in it, Papa, to ornament ourselves like the birds and let art be born."

"God knows his own mysteries," Judge Custis said. "But Vesta, go home with me to your own comfortable home and let Virgie stay here to keep watch."

"Master, I'm afraid to stay here," the girl exclaimed, sidling towards her young mistress.

"Then I will stay and be nurse," the judge said. "Fear not. I will give him only wholesome medicine, whatever poison he has given me and mine. You stay in Teackle Hall, my precious child. Indeed, I must command it."

Vesta smiled sadly and pointed to her husband. "He commands me now, Papa. You were too indulgent a master and spoiled me. Virgie and I will both remain, and you conciliate Mamma. All is going well. Really, I am happy and grateful to my Heavenly Father that he is smoothing the way so gently that I thought would be so hard."

"The conditions of this disease are repulsive, my child. You are a lady."

"No, I am a woman," said Vesta. "That man and I must see one or the other die. You do not know how easy it is for a woman to nurse a man. Though love might make the task more grateful, yet gratitude will do much to sweeten it. He has loved me and taken the shadow from your old age. Shall I leave him here to feel that I despise him? No!"

She kissed her father and gave him his cane. "Come back this afternoon, my love," she said to him.

"Nothing on earth is like you," exclaimed the old man. "I fear you are not mine."

"Wherever you may have strayed, you are full of good," Vesta said."

As the sound of the judge's feet passed from the doorway below, the sick man, with a sigh as from burning fire, opened his eyes and looked around. They fell upon her picture.

"What is that?" he murmured. "I dreamed nothing like that just now."

"It is my picture. I am here," Vesta said, bending over him. "Don't you know me?"

"Who are you, dear lady?" he breathed with fever-weakened eyes and struggling mind. "Do I know you?"

"Yes, I am Vesta. I was Vesta Custis; I am now your wife."

His eyes opened wide, as if hearing some wonderful news. "Wife? What is that? My wife? No."

"Yes, I am Vesta Milburn, your wife."

He seemed to remember, and with compassion for him she stooped and kissed him.

"God bless you," he sighed and passed away into the Upas shades again.

At that minute the mockingbird flew in the open window and fluttered above the lowly bed. Perched upon the headboard, it began to sing: "'Sband! 'Sband! See! See! Vesty, sweet! Vesty, sweet! Ha, ha! Hurrah!"

The Kidnapper

Chapter 15

As he walked abroad into the Sunday sunshine, it seemed to Judge Daniel Custis that he had never seen a more perfect day. The leaves were turning on the great sycamore trees, the maples along the rise in the road wore their most delicate garments of nankeen, and young hickories and a high gum tree, splendid in finery, beckoned him across the Manokin bridge to the opposite hill, where the Presbyterian church overlooked the town.

The judge, whose eyes were filled with happy tears, partly at the relief to his circumstances accomplished by Vesta's great sacrifice and partly by the scene of her natural honor and fidelity to the man who had forced her wedding vows, took the northern course and crossed the little bridge. As he went up the hill, the town spread out behind him in the stillness of the Sabbath. Quail and fall birds piped and cackled in the corn and grain stubble. Some wild geese in the south flew over the low, gray woods towards the bay. A pack of hounds bayed somewhere like distant music, and he heard turkeys gobble at an adjacent farm, where abundance showed in the fat poultry that roosted in the trees like living fruit.

While he drank in the wine of autumn, with its taste of frost like the first acid in sweet cider, he saw a carriage or two come over the level roads towards Princess Anne. The church bell told their errand as it dropped its fruity twang into the serenity. So easily, so musically, so regularly it rang, like the voice of something pure and steady even in its joys. The judge took off his broad, white fur hat and listened with something between courtesy and piety.

Manokin Presbyterian Church

As the bell continued, other carriages came towards town, and some passed him, their inmates bowing and often stealing a look back to see Judge Custis again, the first man in the county.

They looked upon a gladdened soul and humbled heart, which the sharp band of affliction had made to bleed, while an unforeseen providence in his darling child had kissed the wound to sleep and sucked the poison from it.

Raising his brow towards the bright blue sky, as if he could not raise it high enough to feel more of that heavenly rest encinctured there, the judge sighed a happy wish, like the kiss of love after a quarrel, when doubt is dispelled or wrong forgiven: "Oh, make me as a little child. Wash out my stains. Lead me in the path my child has walked, or I shall never see her in the life to come."

His lips trembled, and his breast heaved convulsively in the idea of being unfit to enter where his child would go in the more abundant life beyond the present. He received from within, clearer than Holy

Scriptures, a distinct sermon from the long-empty pulpit of conscience and revelations. He felt the justice of the final separation of the impure from the pure, of the faith of perseverance in good to draw onward towards holiness itself, and of perseverance in sensuality and selfishness to detain the spirit in its husk of swine.

His agony increased.

"Where shall I drift if I go on," he said, "playing the sleek magistrate and family head and loving to slip away in the dark like Negroes hunting coons by night? What is escaping discovery to the increasing degradation of my own sanctuary, my created spirit? Can I find the way I have wandered down and retrace my steps? There is little of life left me to do it in, but by God's help I will try. Yes, this golden Sabbath I will do something to begin. What shall it be?"

He put on his hat and said to himself, "I will go to the Methodist meeting house. They work directly upon the conscience, deepen the sense of sin, and preach a quick cleansing as by light shining in. There I may grovel in the sight of men and women and arise redeemed. But no," he thought, "it is the Sabbath my daughter's marriage is to be announced in our own church, and it would be cowardly, not to say unseemly, to fly from one worship to another now. If I go to church this morning, it must be to our own. Is there any excuse but cowardice for not going?"

He looked into his debtor nature to see what he owed to anybody that might be settled this day.

Slowly, and almost to his dislike, there arose an obligation to his wife—the obligation of love he was defrauding her of, if, indeed, he loved her at all with the ardor of old times.

She had fretted his passion away in sticklings for little proprieties, narrowing understanding, and subservience to effeminate social traditions. She jarred upon the health of his intellect with her unsympathetic refinements, pitiful uncharities, and fear of all catholicity. She was gentility itself without the spark of nature. Believing that she inhabited the castle towers of exclusiveness and social righteousness, she had made his home the donjon of his knighthood, at once the loftiest domestic apartment and the prison.

Nevertheless, she was his wife, and something of her nature must be in Vesta, though the judge had not found it. He reflected that his waywardness might have sharpened her peculiarities and spread the distance between their minds, till deprived of a husband's guidance, her fluttered woman's nature had quit the pasturage of the fields and air and perched upon her nest and vegetated there.

"I have gone away from her," he said, "and complain that she has not grown. I have myself abounded in village dignity and pretension and set her the example of respecting nothing else. I have been a fraud and wonder that she is not worldly wise."

He found his infirm will very obdurate against making love to his wife again, but the request he had just made of heaven, to lead him into the right steps, prevailed upon him to make his worship at home this morning.

"Yes," he said, "I will start right. She is sick and alone and Vesta taken from her. I will send a note to the rector to announce the marriage and do my worship at Teackle Hall this day."

The Manokin, spreading wider as it flowed farther from the town, till it moistened fringes of marsh and cut low bluffs into the fields, never seemed to invite him so much to wander along its sluices as this morn.

The Manokin River West of Princess Anne

"If my wife would only walk with me into the country," he said restlessly, "how more companionable we would have been to each other. But she cannot walk at all. Masculine intercourse ceased between us years ago, and the dull, small range of household talk and the dynastic gossip of the good families wear down my spirits. But I have been a truant husband, and my tongue is parched by dusty rovings in prodigal ways. Let me woo her again with all my might."

He walked through Princess Anne, worship now having commenced in all the churches, and saw nobody upon the street except a divided group before the tavern. There he heard Jimmy Phoebus speak to Levin Dennis sharply: "Levin, what you doin' with that nigger buyer? Ain't you got no pride left in you?"

The judge saw that Joe Johnson, safe from civil process on Sunday, even if his enemy had not been helpless in bed, was washing Levin Dennis's brandy-sickened head under the street pump, plying the pump handle and shampooing him with alternate hands.

"Jimmy," Levin answered, when he was free from the spout, "this gentleman's give me a job. I'm goin' to take him out for tarrapin on the sound. He's goin' to pay me for it."

"Tarrapin catchin' on a Sunday ain't no respectable job for a Dennis, nohow," cried Jimmy Phoebus bluntly, "an' doin' it with a nigger buyer is a fine splurge fur you, by smoke! I can't see where your pride is, Levin, to save my life."

Jack Wonnell, wearing a bell-crown, looked on with timid enjoyment of this plain talk, opening his mouth to grin, shutting it to shudder.

Dropping Levin Dennis, the big stranger strode in his long jack boots, into which his coarse trousers were stuffed, right to the front of Jimmy Phoebus and glared at him through his inflamed and unsightly eye. Jimmy met his scowl with a mildness amounting almost to contempt.

"Hark ye!" said the stranger, "you have been a-picking a quarrel with me all yisterday, an' today air a beginnin' of it again. Do you want to fight?"

"No," said Jimmy, whittling a stick, "I ain't fond of fightin', an' I never do it of a Sunday. I wouldn't be guilty of fightn' you, by smoke!"

"I have tuk a bigger nug than you an' nicked his kicks into the bottom of his gizzard till his liver lights fell into my mauleys. So it's nish or knife betwixt us, my bene cove," said Johnson, putting his hand upon his hip, where he carried a sheath knife.

"Raise that hand," said Jimmy Phoebus with a quick pass of his whittling knife to the giant's throat. "Raise it, or yer goes yer jugler, by smoke."

As Phoebus spoke, he lifted one foot of a prodigious size as deftly as an elephant hoisting his trunk and, without moving either his own body or countenance, kicked the man's hand from his hip pocket. It was done so automatically that the other turned fiercely to see who kicked him, and his knife, partly raised, was flung by the force of the kick several yards away.

"Pick up his knife, Levin," Jimmy said, "or he'll hurt hisself with it."

At this moment Judge Custis came up and pushed the two powerful men apart.

"Fighting on Sunday in our public street," he exclaimed. "Phoebus, I wouldn't have thought it of you."

"This yer bully, Judge," Jimmy said coolly, "started to take Prencess Anne the fust day, an' ole Meshach's Samson knocked him a-sprawlin', an' Meshach hisself finished him. Today, he starts in to lead off yon poor imbecile Levin Dennis, an' as I expresses my opinion of it, he draws his knife on me. So I takes my foot, Judge, that you have seen me untie a knot with, an' I spiles his wrist with it. Take care of his knife, Levin—he's a pore creetur without it."

"We'll have this out, nope for nope, or may I take the mornin' drop!" growled the strange man.

"That kind of language ain't understood in honest company," Jimmy Phoebus said. "I s'pose it's thieves' lingo used among your friends, or maybe big words you bully strangers with when you want to cut a splurge. Now, as you've been licked by a nigger an' kicked by a white man, maybe you can understand my language. Hark you, too, nigger buyer! Do you know where I saw you first?"

For the first time a flash of fire came from the pungy captain's black cherries of eyes, and his huge, broad, swarthy face expressed its full oriental character.

"The last time I saw you, Joe Johnson, was not a-lurkin' in Judge Custis's kitchen fur no good, nor a-insultin' of the judge's t'other visitor, Milburn of the steeple-top, it was a-huggin' the whippin' post on the public green of Georgetown, State of Delaware, an' the sheriff a-layin' of it over your back. An' after he sot you up in the pillory, I took the rottenest egg I could git an' bust it right on the eye where that nigger bruised you yisterday!"

As Joe Johnson slunk back, desperate with rage yet unable to deny, the oppressive silence was broken by Jack Wonnell's unthinking interjection: "Whoop, Jimmy! Hooraw for Prencess Anne!"

"An' why did I git that egg an' make you smell it, Joe Johnson? Because, by smoke, you was a stinkin' kidnapper, robbin' of the pore free niggers of their liberty, knowin' that they didn't carry no arms an' couldn't make no good defense. That's your trade, an' it's the meanest an' most cowardly in the world. It's doin' what the Algerynes does in fair fighting. You're a fine American citizen, ain't you? I know your gang, an' a bloody one it is, but you can't look a white man in the eye because you're a thief and a coward!"

The Hellenic nature of the bay captain had never displayed itself to the judge with this fullness, and he felt some natural admiration as he took Phoebus by the arm.

"Well, well," said the judge, "let him go now, Phoebus. Mr. Johnson, don't let me see you in Princess Anne again today. Continue your journey and disturb us no more, or I shall put criminal process upon you, and you see we have stout constables in Somerset."

As he led Phoebus around the corner of the bank, the judge said, "James, my wife is so sick that I must keep house with her this morning, and I want a little note left at the church for Mr. Tilghman. Will you take it?"

"Why, with pleasure, Judge," the nonchalant villager replied. "I don't look very handsome in the 'Piscopal church, but I'll do a arrand."

As the judge wrote the note with his gold pencil on a leaf of his memorandum book, he said, "James, did you identify that man yesterday?"

"Yes, I knowed him as soon as he come to the tavern. This mornin', seein' of him around town, I was afear'd Samson Hat would stumble on him, an' the nigger buyer would kill him for yisterday's blow. Thinks I, 'Samson is too white a nigger to be killed that way, by smoke,' but the prejudice agin a nigger hittin' a white man is sich in this state that Joe Johnson, bloody as he is, would never have stretched hemp for Samson Hat. So I picked a quarrel with the nigger buyer to take the fight out of him before Samson should come. He won't fight nobody now in this town. His hokey-pokey is done yer."

"You took a great risk, Phoebus. He is such an evil fellow in his resentments that I let him hide and eat in my quarters for fear of some ill requital if I refused. That gang of Patty Cannon's is the curse of the Eastern Shore."

"An' if you'll pardon a younger an' a poorer man, Judge, it's jest sich gentlemen as you that lets it go on. You politicians give them people 'munity an' let 'em alone because they fight fur you in 'lection times an' air popular with foresters an' pore trash because they persecutes niggers an' treats to liquor. You know the law is agin their actions on both sides of the Delaware line, but in Maryland they're a dead letter."

"You speak plain truth, James Phoebus, brave as your conduct, but the poor men must make a sentiment against these kidnappers because among the ignorant poor they find their defenders and equals."

"Judge," the pungy captain said, "they's a-makin' a Pangymonum of all the destreak about Patty Cannon's. It's a shame to liberty, by smoke. In open day they lead free niggers—men, wimmin, an' little children who's free as my mommy and your daughter—to be sold. Now yer, we're raising hokey-pokey about the Algerynes and the Trypollytins capturin' of a few Christian people an' sellin' of 'em to Turkey, an' about the Turkey people makin' slaves of the Christian Greek folks. Henry Clay is cuttin' a big splurge about it, an' money is bein' raised all over the country to send it to 'em. Commodo' Decatur was a big man for a-breakin' of it up. By smoke, they're sellin' more free people to death an' hell along Mason and Dixon's line than up the whole buzzum of the Mediterranean Sea."

The brown-skinned speaker was more excited now than he had been during all the collision with Joe Johnson.

"Indeed, Phoebus, they have kidnapped several thousand people, the Philadelphia abolitionists say, but the reports must be exaggerated. The demand for Negroes is so great since the cotton gin and the foreign markets have made cotton a great staple and the direct importation of slaves from Africa has been stopped, that there is a great run for border state Negroes, and free colored people seldom are righted when they have been pulled across the line."

"They never are righted, Judge. I'm ashamed of my native state. Only a few years ago, when I was a boy, people around yer was a-freein' of their niggers, an' it was understood that slavery would a-die out, an' everybody said, 'Let the evil thing go.' But niggers began to go up high. They got to be wuth eight hunderd dollars, whair they wasn't wuth two hunderd, an' all the politicians begun to say, 'Niggers is not fit to be free. Niggers is the bulrush or the bulwork or the bull somethin' of our nation.' An' then kidnappin' of free niggers started, an' the next thing, they'll kidnap free American citizens!"

"Tut, tut, James, it will never go that far."

"Won't it? What did Joe Johnson say to me last night before the Washington Tavern? He said, 'I've sold whiter niggers than you. I kin run you to market an' git my price for you.'"

The bay sailor took off his hat and continued: "Look on my brown skin an' black eyes an' coal black hair. Whair did they come from? They come from Greece, whair Leonidas an' Marky Bozarris an' all them fellers came from. That's what my daddy said, an' he know'd better than me. I'm nothin' but a pore Eastern Shore man sailing my little vessel, but I'm a free-born man, an' I tell you, Judge, it's a dangerous time when nothin' but his shade of color protects a free man."

"James Phoebus," the judge said gravely, "I hope you believe me when I say that I think all these things outrages, and they grow out of the greater outrage of slavery itself. We are being governed by new states, hatched in the Southwest from the alligator eggs of old slavery that had grown into political and moral disrepute with us in Maryland and Virginia."

"There's no nigger in me," Phoebus said, putting on his hat, "but I have taken these hints about my looking like a nigger to heart, an' I'll take a nigger's part when he is imposed on, as if he was some of the body an' blood of my Lord Jesus. Now you hear it!"

"And brave enough you are to mean it, my honest fellow. So do my errand, and good morning, James."

Bell-crown Man

Chapter 16

As the judge and Phoebus turned the corner of the bank, Samson Hat appeared, driving a young white girl down Princess Anne's broad main street.

"There's the nigger that set my peep in limbo," muttered the Negro dealer, "but even he shall go past today. This accursed town is packed agin me."

He took a long look at Samson, however, who mildly returned it in the most respectful manner, as if he had never seen the strange gentleman before.

"And now, my pals," Joe Johnson said, turning to Levin Dennis and Jack Wonnell, "we will all three go down to the bay. I'll pervide the lush and pay the soap, while you ketch the tarrapin an' let me sleep my nazy off."

"I'll go an' no mistake!" cried Jack Wonnell, who had been taking a drink of pump water out of his bell-crown. "So will you, Levin."

Levin Dennis hesitated. "I want to tell my mother first," he said. "Maybe she won't like me to go of a Sunday. She'll send Jimmy Phoebus after me."

Joe Johnson took a bag of gold from inside his waistband and held up a piece of five before the boy's bright eyes. "Yer! It's yourn if you don't have no mother about it. Pike away with me, pig widgeon, and I pay you this pash at sundown."

Levin's credulous eyes shone, and, with one reluctant look towards his mother's cottage, he led the way into the country.

Little was said as they walked an hour or more towards the west, the stranger apparently brooding upon his indignities and twice passing around the jug of brandy, which Jack Wonnell was made to carry. Before noon they came to a considerable creek, out in which was anchored a small vessel bearing on her stern in illiterate, often inverted letters, the name *Ellenora Dennis*.

"What's that glibe on yonder?" asked Johnson.

"That's his mother's name, boss," Jack Wonnell said. "She's a widder an' purty as a peach."

"Ain't you got no daddy, paplap?" Johnson asked coarsely.

"He's gone sence I was a baby," Levin answered. "He went on Judge Custis's uncle's privateer, that never was heard of no mo'. We don't know if the British tuk him an' hanged him, or if the *Idy* sunk somewhair an' drowned him, or if she's a-sailin' away off. I has to take care of mother."

"Humph," growled Johnson. "Son of a gander and a gilflirt. Got the ole families into him. No better loll for me."

Drawing a punt concealed under some marsh brush, young Levin pushed off to his vessel, made her tidy by a few changes, pulled up the jib, and brought her in to the bank.

"I never ketched tarrapin of a Sunday befo', Mr. Johnson, but I reckon tain't no harm."

"Harm? What's that?" Joe Johnson sneered. "Hark ye, boy, no funkin' with me now! When I begin with a kinchin cove, I starts squar. If ye think it's wicked to ketch tarrapin, why, I want 'em caught. If you don't keer, you kin jest stick up yer sail an' pint for Deil's Island, an' we'll make it a woyige."

Not quite clear as to his instructions, Levin took the tiller, and Jack Wonnell stood in the bow with the terrapin tongs, while the catboat skimmed down Monie Creek before a good breeze and a lee tide. The chain dredge for terrapin was thrown over the side, but the boat made too much sail for Wonnell to take more than one or two tardy animals, as they hovered around the transparent bottoms, making ready for their winter descent into the mud.

"Take up yer dredge," Johnson commanded in a few minutes; "it makes us go slow."

Jack Wonnell obediently made a few turns on the windlass, and as the bag came up, two terrapin of the common diamondback variety rolled onto the deck, and a skilpot.

"That's enough tarrapins," Johnson said. "Say, spooney, is it wicked now?"

The boy laughed, a little pale of face, and Johnson closed his remark with, "Nawthin' ain't wicked! Sunday is dustman's day to be broke by heroes. D'ye s'pose yer daddy on the privateer wouldn't lick the British of a Sunday? The way to git rich, sonny, is to break all the commandments at the post an' pick 'em up agin at the score."

"That's the way, sho' as you're born, Johnson," chuckled Jack Wonnell, not clear as to what was said.

Levin felt a little shudder pass through him. By Wonnell's aid they raised the main sheet, and the light boat went winging across Monie Bay, starting waterfowl as it tacked through them.

"Here's another swig all round," Joe Johnson exclaimed, "an' then I'll go below to lollop an hour, for I'm bloody lush."

Levin drank, and it took the shuddering instinct out of him.

As he disappeared into the little cabin, Joe Johnson cried, "Pint her for Deil's Island thoroughfare an' wake me at the old campground fur to dine."

The two neighbors felt relieved of the long man's company, and Jack Wonnell lay on his back astern and grinned at Levin as if there was a great unknown joke between them, finally whispering, "Where does he git all his gold?"

Levin shook his head. "Can't tell, Jack, to save my life. Nigger tradin', I reckon. It must be a payin' business."

"Best business in the world. Wish I had a little of his money, Levin. Huueoo! Then wouldn't I git my gal!"

"Who's yo' gal, Jack, for this winter?"

"You won't tell nobody, Levin?"

"No, hope I may die."

Jack put his bell-crown up to the side of his mouth, executed another grin, winked one eye knowingly, and whispered, "Purty yaller Roxy—Jedge Custis's gal."

"She won't have nothin' to do with you, Jack; she's too well raised."

"She ain't yit, Levin, but I'm follerin' of her aroun'. There ain't no white gal in Princess Anne purty as them two house gals of Jedge Custis's."

"What kin you do with a nigger, Jack? You never kin marry her."

"Maybe I kin buy her, Levin."

"She ain't fur sale, Jack. Jedge Custis never sells no niggers. When some of Jedge Custis's niggers in Accomack run away, he wouldn't let people hunt for 'em."

Jack put his bell-crown to the side of his mouth again, grinned hideously, and whispered, "Kin you keep a secret?"

Levin nodded yes.

"Hope a-may die?"

"Hope I may die, Jack."

"Judge Custis is gwyn to be sold out by Meshach Milburn."

"What a lie, Jack!"

Levin let the tiller go, and the *Ellenora Dennis* swung around and flapped her sails as if such news had driven all the wind out of them.

"Jack," Levin exclaimed, "Jimmy Phoebus says you've turned out a reg'lar liar. Now I believe it, too."

"Hope a-may die," Jack Wonnell protested. "I never does lie. Jimmy called me a liar fur sayin' Meshach Milburn was gone into the jedge's front do', but we saw him come out of it, didn't we?"

"Yes, that was so, but this yer one is an awful lie."

"Well, Levin, purty yaller Roxy told me, an' she's too purty to lie. I loves that gal like peach an' honey, Levin, an' I don't keer whether she's white or no. She's mos' as white as me an' a good deal better."

"So you do talk to Roxy some?"

"Levin, I'll tell you all about it, an you won't tell nobody. I picks magnoleys an' wild roses an' sich purty things fur Roxy to give her missis, an' Roxy gives me cake an' chicken an' coffee at the back door, knowin' I ain't got much to buy 'em with. Lord bless her, she's a white angel with a little coffee in her blood, but it's ole goverment javey an' more'n half cream."

Levin laughed and said that Jack must have learned that out of a book.

"Oh," said Jack, shutting one eye and joining in the grin, "sence I ben in love, I kin say lots o' smart things. I seen purty little Roxy grow up from a chile. As she begin to round up an' git tall, says I, 'Nigger or no nigger, she's a angel.' The white gals all throwed off on me caze I wasn't earnin' nothin', an' I sot my eyes on Roxy Custis. I says, 'What kin I do fur to make her shine to me?' So I kept a-follerin' of her everywhere, an' I see her one day comin' along the road a-pickin' the wild blossoms. I says, 'Roxy, what you doin' of with them flowers?'

"'They're fur my missis, Miss Vesty,' says she. 'She lives on wild flowers, an' they're all I has to give her. I want her to love me as much as Virgie.'

"Then I says, 'Roxy, I kin git you flowers for your missis. I know whair the magnoleys is bloomin' the whitest an' a-scentin' the whole day long.'

"'Do you?' says she. 'Oh, Mr. Wonnell, I would like to have a bunch of magnoleys to put on Miss Vesty's toilet every day.'

"'I'll git 'em fur you, Roxy,' says I, 'becaze I allus thought you was a little beauty.'

"Says she, 'I'd give most anything to surprise Miss Vesty with flowers every day—rale wild ones.'

"'Then,' says I, 'I'll git 'em fur you for a kiss.' An' she most a-blushed blood red an' ran away."

"That's what I told you, Jack, she's raised too well to be talkin' to white fellers."

"Nobody's raised too well," rejoined Jack Wonnell, "to be deaf to love an' kindness. Says I to myself, 'Jack, you skeert that gal. Now say nothin' mo' 'bout the kiss an' go git her the flowers every day, an' she'll think mo' of you.' So away I went to King's Creek an' pulled the magnoleys, an' I come to the do' an' asked ole Hominy to bring down Roxy for a minute. Roxy, she come, an' was gwyn to run away till she saw my flowers. She stopped a minute, an' says I, 'I jest got 'em for you, Roxy, becaze I see you when you was a little chile.'

"She tuk 'em an' says, 'It was very kind of you, sir,' an' kercheyed an' melted away.

"Next day I was thar agin, Levin, an' to make it seem like a trade, I says, 'Roxy, kin ye give me a cup of coffee?'

"'Law, yes,' she says, forgittin' her blushin' right away.

"So I kept shady on love an' put it on the groun's of coffee. An' Levin, I everlastin'ly fetched the wild flowers till that gal got to be a-lookin' fur me at the do' every day, an' I'd hide an' see her come to the window an' peep fur me.

"One day, as I was a-drinkin' of the coffee, she says, 'Mr. Wonnell, what do you put yourself at sech pains fur to 'blige a poor slave girl that ain't but half white?'

"I thought a minute, so as to say something that wouldn't skeer her off, an' I says, 'Roxy, it's becaze I'm sech a pore, worthless feller that the white gals won't look at me.'

"The tears come right to her eyes, an' she says, 'Mr. Wonnell, if I was white, I would look at you.'

"'I believe you would, Roxy.' says I, 'becaze you've got a white heart.'"

"Jack, you're a doggone smart lover." said Levin. "I didn't think you had no kind of sense."

"Love makin' is the best sense of all," said Jack. "It's that sense that keeps the woods a-full of music, where the birds an' bees is twitterin' an' hummin' an' matin'. Love is the last sense to come after you can see an' hear an' feel, an' they're give to people to find out somethin' purty to love. Love was the whole day's work in the Garden of Eden befo' man got too industrious. It's all the work I do, an' I hope I do it well."

"Now what did Roxy tell you about Judge Custis and Meshach Milburn?"

"You see, Levin, as I kept up the flower givin', I could see a little love start up in purty Roxy, but she didn't understand it, an' I was as keerful not to skeer it as if it had been a snowbird hoppin' to a crumb of bread. She would talk to me about her little troubles, an' I listened keerful as her mammy becaze little things is what wimmin lives on, an' a lady's man is only a feller patient with their little talk. The more I listened, the more she liked to tell me, an' I saw that Roxy was a-thinkin' a great deal of me without she or me lettin' of it on.

"This mornin' she came to the door with her eyes jest wiped from a-cryin'. Says I, 'Roxy, little dear, what ails you?'

"'Oh, nothin',' says she. 'I can't tell you if thair is.'

"'Here's your wild flowers for Miss Vesty,' says I, 'beautiful to see.'

"'Oh,' says Roxy, 'Miss Vesty won't need 'em now.'

"Says I, 'Roxy, air you goin' to have all that trouble on your mind an' not let me carry some of it?'

"'Oh,' she says, 'I must tell you, fur you have been so kind to me. Don't whisper it, but my master is in debt to Meshach Milburn, an' he's married Miss Vesty, an' we think we're all gwyn to be sold or made to live with that man that wears the bad man's hat.'

"Says I, 'Roxy, darling, maybe I kin buy you.'

"'Oh, I wish you was my master,' Roxy said. An' jest at that minute, love bein' oncommon strong over me this mornin', I took the first kiss from Roxy's mouth, an' she didn't say nothin' agin it."

Here Jack Wonnell kissed the atmosphere several times with deep unction and ended by a low whoop and whistle, looking at Levin Dennis with one eye shut, as if to get Levin's opinion of all this.

"Well," Levin said, "I never ain't been in love yet. I 'spect I ought to be, but mother is all I kin take keer of, an' pore soul, she's in so much trouble over me that she can't love nobody else. I git drunk an' go off sailin' an' spend my money so keerless. If the Lord didn't look out for her, maybe she'd starve."

"Yes, Levin, you likes brandy as much as I likes the gals. You go off for tarrapin an' taters an' oysters, an' peddles 'em aroun' Prencess Anne. Then somebody pulls you in the grog shops, an' away goes your money, an' your mother ain't got no tea an' coffee."

"Jack," said Levin abruptly, "do you believe in ghosts?"

"I don't know, Levin. If I saw one, maybe I would, but I'm too trashy for ghosts to see me."

"Well now," Levin said, "there's a ghost or something that looks out for mother when I'm drunk or gone, an' it leaves tea an' coffee in the window for her."

"Sho'! Why Levin, that's Jimmy Phoebus. He's ben in love with your mother for years. He's your mother's ghost."

"No, Jack. I thought it was till Jimmy come an' asked me who I guessed it was. He was a little jealous, I reckon. I said, 'It's you, of course, Jimmy.'

"'No,' says he. 'By smoke, I don't do any hokey-pokey like that. What I give, I go an' give with no sneakin' about it or pryin' into Ellanory's poverty.'

"He was right down mad, but he couldn't find nothin' out. So I think it may be the ghost of father, drowned at sea, bringin' tea an' coffee an' sometimes a dress an' a pair of shoes to keep mother warm."

Standing against the tiller, Levin Dennis seemed to Jack Wonnell to be as fair and spiritual as a woman. His dark auburn hair, in short ringlets parted in the middle, gave his sunburnt countenance a likeness to some of the old, gentle families with which he was allied. His comely brow and large eyes grew serious with this relation of his father's mysterious fate.

His father, having been the son of a younger son in a date when primogeniture prevailed in all the bay region, possessed nothing. He went into the war against England as a sailor, and his family influence obtained for him the command of a new privateer launched on the Manokin, the *Ida*, which set sail with a good crew and superior armament amid the acclaims of all Somerset. Sailing past the capes into the ocean with all her bunting flying, she slid down the farther world to everlasting silence and the vapors of mystery.

His widow waited long and patiently with this only boy, Levin, and stories of every kind were current: that the captain had been captured and hanged by the enemy and the ship burned or condemned; that he had hoisted the black flag and become a pirate, quittin the western world for East India waters; and finally, that the Ida foundered off Guiana, and every soul was drowned.

The widow was neglected by her husband's connection, who were sullen at the loss of their investment and expected profits. She lived in the little house she had owned before her marriage and sank into the plainer tier of people, almost losing her identity with the ruling families to which her son was kin, but she was highly respected in her humbler class and solicited in marriage.

She was still young and fair, and Jimmy Phoebus had endeavored to marry her for years. Though she feared the absent lover might be alive and return to find her another's wife, he held on to his hope patiently, and though his means were limited and poor kin looked to him for help, he exercised many kind offices for her.

So her son grew up without a father's discipline. Supposed to be too respectable to put to a trade or be indentured, he lived by fugitive pursuits on land and water, hauling and peddling vegetables and provisions at times. And now, by the gift of Jimmy Phoebus, he sailed his little sloop, chiefly to carry terrapin to Baltimore. Rough sailor acquaintances, exposure, a credulous, easily led nature, and almost total neglect of school had made him wayward and often intemperate, but without developing any selfish or cruel characteristics. Being of an agreeable exterior and affable disposition, he fell prey to any strangers who might be in town—gunners, Negro buyers, idle planters, and spreeing overseers, many of whom hired his company and vessel to take their excursions. While loving his mother and being her only reliance, he was slipping further and further into manhood without steadiness, education, fixed principles, or any female influence to draw him to domestic constraints.

"Jack," said Levin Dennis, "what do you mean by gittin' money to buy Roxy Custis? You never git no money."

"Won't he give it to me?" Wonnell indicated the hatchway down which Joe Johnson had gone. "He's got bags of it."

"Him? Why, Jack, how much money do you s'pose a beautiful servant like Roxy will fetch?"

"Won't that piece he's gwyn to give you buy her?"

"Five dollars? Why, you poor fool, she will bring five hundred dollars—maybe thousands. This nigger trader, with all his gold, would be hard pushed, I 'spect, to buy Roxy."

Jack looked downcast and failed to wink or whistle.

"Gals like her," said Levin, "goes for mistresses to rich men, an' sometimes they eddicates 'em, I've hearn tell, to know music an' writin' an' grammar an' them things."

"An' a pore man who wouldn't abuse a gal most white like that, but would respect her an' marry her, too, they makes laws agin him. Maybe I kin steal Roxy."

Here Jack whistled low, shut one eye with deep knowingness, and grinned behind his bell-crown.

"You simpleton!" Levin said. "Where would you take her?"

"Pennsylvany, Cannydy, Turkey, or some of them abolition states up thar." Jack Wonnell indicated the North with his finger. "Ain't there no place where a white man kin treat a bright-skinned slave like that, as if they both was a Christian?"

"No," answered Levin, "not in this world."

The hero of the bell-crowns was much affected, and Levin thought he really was whimpering, though his vacant grin was a poor frame for grief.

"Jack," said Levin, "if what Roxy Custis told is true, the gal is the slave of your pertickler enemy, Meshach Milburn."

The wearer of the rival species of hat was badly sobered, as Levin mentally expressed it, at this dismal solution of his gentle dreams of love. He arose and walked to the bow of the boat and looked down into the flying waves over which the catboat skipped, as if he might seek the solution of his own disconnected yet harmless life in the bottom of the sound among the oyster rocks.

The water was now speckled with canoes and pirogues and little sailboats coming from Deil's Island preaching, and before them rose the low woody islands and capes which, with white straits between, enclose the scalloped aisle called Tangier Sound from the long blue nave of the Chesapeake. Like pigeons around a cathedral, the wildfowl flew in these complicated architectures of archipelago and peninsula.

Here, ospreys could be seen sailing in graceful pairs above the old wives' shoals. There, the canvasback duck, breaking the Sabbath to dive for wild celery that grows beneath the sound. In yonder tree the bald eagle, starting out upon his Algerine work of vehemence and piety to intercept the hawk and steal his cargo. The wild swan might be those faint, far birds flying so high over Kedge's Straits in the south, and the black loon, spreading his wings like a demon, disappearing close to the catboat and rising no more till memory has forgotten him.

Levin steered close to a point where he had been wont to scatter food for the black ducks and draw them to the gunner's ambush. Sheldrakes and goosanders, coots and gulls, whifflers and dippers made the best of Sunday, bathing and writing their winged penmanship on the white sheet of water.

Poor Jack Wonnell, returning with something on his face between a grin and a tear, said, "Levin, didn't I never harm nobody?"

"Not as I ever heard about, Jack. They say you ain't got no sense, but you never fight nobody. Everybody kin git along with you, Jack."

"No they can't, Levin. Meshach Milburn hates the ground I tread on. If he know'd I was in love with little Roxy, he'd marry her to a nigger."

"What makes him hate you so, Jack?"

"Becaze I wears my bell-crowns an' he wears the steeple-top hat, he thinks I'm a-mockin' of him. Levin, I ain't got no other kind o' hat to wear. Meshach Milburn needn't wear that air hat, but if I don't wear a bell-crown, I must go bareheaded. I bought the lot of hats with the only dollar or two I ever had. As they say, 'a fool an' his money is soon parted.' The boys said they was dirt cheap. There wouldn't be nothin' wrong to see in my bell-crowns ef all the people wasn't pintin' at ole Milburn's Entail Hat, as they call it. Why can't he, rich as a Jew, go buy a new hat, or buy me one? I don't want to mock him; I'm a-feard of him! He looks at me with them loaded pistols of eyes, an' it mos' makes me cry. I ain't done nothin'. I'm pore as them trash ducks," pointing to a brace of dippers, which were of no value in the market, "but I ain't got no malice."

"No, Jack, that trader could give you his bag of gold, an' it would be safe becaze it wasn't your own."

"I 'spect I will go to the porehouse someday, Levin. My ole aunt who takes keer of me can't live long, an' I ain't good fur nothin'. I can't git no jobs, an' I run arrands for everybody fur nothin', but the first money I git, I'm gwyn to buy a new hat with. Ever sence I wore these bell-crowns, Meshach hates me, an' I hope he's the only man that does hate me. I don't think Meshach kin be a bad man."

"How kin he be good, Jack?"

"Why, I have seen him in the woods when he didn't see me, callin' up the birds. Danged if they didn't come and git on him. Now birds ain't gwyn to hop on a man that's a devil. Do you believe he deals with the devil?"

"I do," said Levin. "I see sich quare things I believe in most anythin' quare. These yer tarrapins has got sense, and they're no more like it than a stone. One night when Mother and me hadn't nothin' to eat at home, an' she was a-sittin' there with tears in her eyes, wonderin' what we'd do next day, I recollected there was four tarrapins down in the cellar—black tarrapin—that was put there six months before. I said to Mother, 'I 'spect them ole tarrapins is dead an' starved, but I'll go see.'

"I found 'em under the woodpile. They didn't smell nor nothin', so I took 'em up to Mother an' put 'em on the kitchen table befo' the fire. I deviled 'em every way to wake up an' show some signs of life, but no, they was stone dead.

"'Well, Mother,' says I, 'put on your bilin' water, an' we'll see if dead tarrapin is fit fur to eat.' She smiled through her cryin' an' put the water on, an' when it began to bubble in the pot, I lifted up one of them tarrapins an' dropped him in the bilin' water. An', Jack, I'll be doggoned if them other three tarrapins didn't run right off the table an drop onto the flo' an' skeet for that cellar door.

"I caught 'em an' biled 'em, an' as we sat there eatin' stewed tarrapin without no salt or sherry wine or coffee or even cornbread, we heard somethin' scratchin' on the window. Mother fell back an' clasped her hands an' said, 'There, do you hear the ghost?'

"I rushed to the door an' hopped into the yard, an' not a livin' creature did I see. But there on the window shelf was packages of salt, coffee, tea, an' flour, an' a half a dollar in silver. I run back in the house, white as a ghost myself, an' I cried out, 'Mother, it's father's sperrit come again!'

"She made me git on my knees an' pray with her to give poor father's spirit comfort in his home or in heaven."

Sabbath and Canoe

Chapter 17

They now approached an island with low bluffs on which a considerable village appeared, shining whitely amid the straight brown trunks of a grove of pine trees. No people were moving about it, and there was but a single vessel at anchor in the thoroughfare into which they steered—a canoe, revealing on her bow a word neither Levin nor Jack could read except by hearsay: *The Methodist.*

"Jack," said Levin, "that was a big pine tree the parson hewed his canoe outen. She fell like cannon goin' off inter the swamp. She's a'most five fathom long, an' a man can lie down acrost her. She's to carry the Methodis' preachers out to the islands."

"Hadn't we better wake him up now?" said Jack Wonnell. "I 'spect you want a drink, Levin."

"Yes, I got a thirst on me like fire," Levin exclaimed. "I could do somethin' wicked now for a drink of that brandy, I 'spect."

Mooring against the shore, Levin went to his passenger, still stretched in deep sleep upon the bare floor of the cabin—a brawny, wiry man with strong chin and long jaws. His dark, reddish beard, matted with the blood that had spilled from his disfigured eye, disguised nearly half his face and gave him a wild, bandit look.

"Cap'n! Mister! Boss! Wake up! We have come to Deil's Island."

The long man, lying on his back, seemed unable to turn over upon his side, though he muttered in his stirred sleep such words as Levin could not understand: "The darbies, Patty! Make haste with them darbies! Put the nippers on her wrists an' twist 'em. Ha, the mort is dying.

Well, to the garden with her!"

At this he awoke, turned his cold eyes on Levin, and leaped to his feet.

"Did you hear me?" he cried. "It was only nums, kid, an' jabber of a nazy man. Some day this sleep talk will grow my neckweed. Don't mind me, Levin. Come, lush an' cock an organ with me, my bene cove."

"If you mean brandy," Levin said, "I must have some, or I'll jump out of my skin."

Joe Johnson gave him the jug and held it up, and the boy drank like one desperate.

"How the young jagger lushes his jockey," the tall man muttered. "He's in Job's dock today. I'll take no more. A bloody fool I was all yesterday, an' oaring with my picture frame. What place is this?"

"Deil's Island, sir."

"Ha, so it is. 'Twas Devil's Island once, till the Methodies changed it fur politeness. This is the camp meetin', then? Yer, Wonnell, take this piece of money an' go to some house an' fetch us a bite of dinner. We'll wait fur you."

Johnson led the way to the heart of the pine grove, where a deserted religious encampment of wooden huts in the shape of a horseshoe was located with a preaching stand elevated above empty benches at its open end. It seemed mysterious to observe this naked town and hollow pulpit, lying so suggestively under the long moan of the pine trees, which conferred together like dread angels in council and expressed impatience with the sins of men at every rising breeze.

At times the great branches paused, scarcely murmuring, as if brooding on some question propounded in their council or listening to human witnesses below. Then, as the zephyrs moved among them, they would converse gravely, only to pause again, as if almost dreading their own decision. At intervals a stern spirit within would rise and thunder and shake the shafts of the trees. Others would answer, then patience would have a season again. And so, with scarcely ever a silence that remained more than a moment, this council went on all day, continued all night, was resumed as the sun arose to comfort the world again, ceased not when the rainbow hung its assurance upon the storm. To trembling worshippers it typified the great synod of the Creator in everlasting session, ready to smite the world with fire, but suspending sentence in the evergreen pity of God.

In one of the deserted shells facing the preaching booth, Joe Johnson and Levin Dennis found benches, and at the tall man's example, Levin lighted a pipe and looked out between the escapes of smoke at Tangier Sound. He thought of his lonely mother in Princess Anne, wondering where he was, and of the days fast speeding by, bringing him to manhood with no change in their condition for the better. There was only penury and disappointment, a vague expectation of the dead to return, and deeper intemperance of the dead man's son and the widow's only hope. If the brandy had not begun to creep along his veins and shine bold in his large, girlish eyes, he might have cried out with a sense of misery, contagious from the music of the pines above him.

Deal Island Beach
The camp meeting ground stood in the woods to the rear.

"Levin," said Joe Johnson, "don't you like me?"

"Yes, Mr. Johnson, I think I does, 'cept when you use them quare words I can't understand."

"I'm dead struck with you, Levin," Joe Johnson said. "I want to fix you an' your mother comfortable. You're blood stock an' ought to be stabled on gold oats."

He drew the canvas bag of eagles and half eagles out of his trousers and held its mouth open for Levin to feast his eyes.

"Thar," he said. "I told you, Levin, I was a-goin' to give you one of them purties. I've changed my mind. I'm a-goin' to give you five of 'em."

"My Lord!" exclaimed Levin, "that's twenty-five dollars, ain't it, sir?"

"Correct, Levin. Five of them finniffs makes a quarter of a hundred dollars—more posh, Levin, I 'spect, than ever you see."

"I never had but ten at a time, an' that I put in this boat. Jimmy Phoebus put ten to it, an' that paid for her."

"What a stingy pam he was to give you only ten," Johnson exclaimed with disgust. "Ain't I a better friend to ye? Yer, take the money now!"

He pressed the gold pieces ostentatiously upon the boy, who looked at them with fear, yet fascination.

"What am I to do to earn all this, Mr. Johnson?"

"You comes with me fur a week—you an' yer boat. I charters you at that figger."

"But—mother?"

"Well, when we discharge pigwidgeon—your friend with the bell shap—all you got to do, Levin, is to send the hard cole to your mother by him, sayin', 'Bless you, Marm; my wages will excoos my face.'"

"Oh, yes, that will do. Mother will know by the money that I have got a long job and not be a-'spectin' of me. When do we sail, Cap'n?"

"How fur is it to Prencess Anne? What time tonight kin you make it?"

Levin stepped out of the shanty and looked at the wind and water, his pulses all a-flutter between the strong brandy and the wonderful gold in his pocket. As he watched the veering of the pine boughs to see which way they moved, their moaning seemed to be the voice of his widowed mother by her kitchen fire, saying, "Where is my son? Why stays he, oh, my Levin?"

"The tide's on the stand, Cap'n, an' will turn in half an hour. With this wind it will take us up the Manokin by dark, ef we git water enough in the thoroughfare without going aroun' by Little Deil's."

"I reckon it's eighteen mile to the head of deep water on Manokin," Johnson observed.

"Not quite, sir. Through the thoroughfare it's nigh eighteen. We've got four hours an' a half of daylight yet."

"Then stand for the head of Manokin an' obey all my orders like a 'listed man, an' I'll git ye and yer mother a plantation an' stock it with niggers," Johnson said. "Come, brace up!" offering the brandy jug and encouraging the boy to drink heartily.

While they stood in the shelter of the cottage going through this pastime, a voice from near at hand resounded through the woods and made their blood stop for an instant. It was a voice praying at high pitch, as if to be heard to the outermost bounds. The sincerity of the sound made Levin feel that the camp might still be inhabited by some spiritual congregation, which the eyes of profane visitors could not see.

The idea had scarcely seized upon him when a fluttering of wings was heard, and a flock of geese alighted on the old campground. They balanced their large, deacon-and-elder-like bodies upon the empty seats and set up as grave a squawking as if they were singing a hymn with that indifferent knowledge of harmony possessed by camp-meeting choristers.

The accident of their coming—no unusual thing on these exposed islands—might have made untroubled people only laugh, but it produced the contrary effect on both visitors. Levin was seized by a superstitious fear, and turning to Joe Johnson, he saw that person with a face so pale that it showed his blood-gathered eye yet darker and more hideous, and he was gazing upon the late empty preaching booth.

There, Levin observed a solitary man kneeling. He was of a plain appearance and dress with locks of womanly hair falling carelessly upon a large and almost noble forehead. His arms were raised to heaven, and his voice flowed out in a mellow stream of supplication.

"Who's he a-prayin' to?" Levin asked of Joe Johnson.

"Quemar!" muttered Johnson, as if he were terrified at something. "His potato trap is swallerin' ghosts. Curse on the swaddler. The kid will whindle directly. Come, boy, come!"

At this, seizing Levin's hand, partly in persuasion and partly as if he wanted the lad's protection, Johnson ran for the boat.

Levin was frightened, too, the more he saw the stronger man's fear. As they dashed across the campground, the wild geese took alarm, and, some running, some flying, they scudded towards the water.

A voice from the pulpit cried after the retreating men, but it only increased their fears. When they leaped on board the *Ellenora*, Joe Johnson was livid with terror. He ran partly down the companionway and stopped to look back.

"What did you run for?" Levin asked. "It was only Parson Thomas."

"You run first," the man replied, gasping for breath and a little ashamed. "What did he preach at me fur?"

"That's the parson of the islands," Levin said. "He started Deil's Island camp meetin' last year. He comes to the preachin' stand alone sometimes an' has a cry and a prayer. The geese scared me, Cap'n."

Joshua Thomas Chapel on Deal Island
Parson Thomas is buried at the near corner of the chapel.

"Push off!" ordered Joe Johnson. "My teeth are most a-chatterin' with the chill that mace cove give me."

Johnson pulled up the anchor, hoisted the jib, and showed such nervous apprehension that Levin subsided to managing the helm. He steered down the thoroughfare, which, for some distance wound around the camp meeting grove.

"Yer's Jack Wonnell comin' with the jug and the dinner. Shan't we wait fur him?"

"No! He's got the kingdom-come cove with him! Stop for nothin'!"

But the boat had to stop, as her keel scraped the mud in the almost dry thoroughfare.

A plain island man of benevolent, nearly credulous face hailed them, saying stutteringly, "Ne-ne-neighbors, d-d-don't be s-s-s-scared that a-way. We ain't h-h-heathens yer. B-B-Brother Wonnell's bringin' your taters and pone."

"Come on, an' be damned to you," Johnson cried to Wonnell. "What do we want with this tolabon sauce?"

"S-S-Swear not a-a-at all!" cried the parson of the islands. "'Twon't l-l-lift ye over l-l-low tide, brother. Stay an' eat, an' t-t-talk a little with us. Why, I have seen that f-f-face before."

"Never in a gospel ken," the slave dealer muttered with an oath.

"B-But it ca-can't be him," said the island parson with solemnity. "Ole E-be-be-nezer J-Johnson died s-s-several year ago."

"Who was he?" cried the slave dealer with a little interest.

"E-be-be-nezer Johnson," Parson Thomas replied, "was the wickedest man on the E-Eastern S-S-Sho' for twenty year. P-Pardon me, brother, fur a likin' ye to him, but somethin' in y-yur. . . (he passed his hand upon his skull) p-puts me in mind of him. It was h-hy-yur he was shot" (still keeping his hand upon his skull) through an' through, an' d-died the death of the sinner. I have p-p-put my f-finger through the two holes where the b-bullet come an' went an' rid this w-world of a d-d-demon."

The story appeared to have a fascination for the slave buyer, Levin thought, and Johnson exclaimed, "Well, hod, did he ever run afoul of you?"

"Oh, y-y-yes," answered the genial island exhorter with obliging loquacity. "It was t-t-twenty-s-s-seven year ago that I see ole E-be-be-nezer J-Johnson come on the campground of P-P-P-Pungoteague with a mob of p-p-pirates to break up the f-f-fust Methodies camp meetin' ever held about these sounds. He was en-c-c-couraged by ole K-King C-C-Custis, f-f-father of our Daniel Custis of Princess Anne, who was a b-big man fur the Establish Church an' d-despised the Methodies. It was a cowardly thing to do, but while K-King C-C-Custis laughed and talked a-durin' of the p-p-preachin', E-be-be-nezer J-Johnson started a fight. The p-preacher c-c-cut his eye and saw who was a-a-winkin' at the interference. He was a l-l-lion of the L-Lord and bore the c-c-commission of Immanuel. He knowed he was outen the s-state of Maryland and over in the V-V-Vergeenia county of A-Accomack, an' even if the l-laws was a little more t-t-tolerant sence the R-Revolutionary war, the a-ri-ri-stocracy there was b-bitter as ever t-t-towards the people of the Lord. He t-turned from his preachin' at last, right on King Custis, an' he pinted his f-f-finger at him straight. The p-preacher was L-L-Lorenzo Dow."

"Wheoo!" Jack Wonnell exclaimed with a grin. "I've hearn of him—a Yankee-faced teller, like a woman with long braids an' curls of hair fallin' around of his breast an' back, an' a ole straw hat, rain or shine."

"T-T-That was L-L-Lorenzo Dow," the parson of the islands said. "He t-turned on K-K-King Custis and screamed, 'W-Who art thou? The L-Lord shall smite thee, w-whited s-s-sepulcher, and m-mock thee in thy ch-ch-children's children, thou A-Ahab and thy J-J-Jezebel!' It was K-King Custis's wife he pinted at, the g-g-greatest lady and heiress in V-V-Virgeenia. Sh-She f-fainted in f-fear or r-rage to hear the prophecy and insult of her. Then, turning on E-be-be-nezer J-Johnson, L-Lorenzo Dow cried out, 'The dogs shall lie buried safer than his bones. Lay hold of him, b-b-brethren!'

"And s-something in L-Lorenzo Dow's t-trumpet blast made every M-M-Methodis' a giant. They s-swept on E-be-be-nezer J-Johnson, the bully of three states, an' beat him to the ground. They raced his band to their boats, an' they th-threw him into a l-l-little j-j-jail they had on the campground, f-for safe k-k-keepin'."

"What did King Custis do then, Pappy Thomas?" asked Levin.

"W-Why, brethren, w-what did he do but use his f-f-family in-f-f-fluence to g-git out a w-warrant for the preacher and his m-managers on the ground of f-false imprisonment and s-slander. Lorenzo Dow got over into Maryland s-s-safe from the w-w-warrant, but our p-p-presiding elder w-was p-put in jail till he could p-p-p-pay two thousand dollars fine. It almost b-beggared the poor Methodies of that day to raise so much money, but, g-g-glory be to G-God, we can raise it now any day in the year, and in the next g-g-generation we can buy our p-p-persecutors."

"So Ebenezer Johnson, accordin' to the autum bawlers patter, got popped in the mazzard, my brother of the surplice. But he didn't climb no ladder, did he?"

The stuttering host seemed not to comprehend this sneering exclamation, and Levin Dennis said, "King Custis wasn't killed, was he, Pappy Thomas?"

"It w-w-was his c-c-children's c-c-c-children his p-p-punishment was p-promised to," the island parson said, "and to the Lord a th-th-thousand y-y-years are but as d-d-days."

"The tide is fuller, Levin," Joe Johnson cried. "Your keel is clear. Now pint her for Manokin. So bingavast, my bene cove, an' may you chant all by yourself when I am gone!"

"G-G-God bless the b-boys!" the islander cried, "and k-keep them from the f-fire everlasting that is burning in your jug. And s-s-stranger, remember the end of E-be-be-nezer J-J-Johnson, and repent!"

The old man, barefooted, stoop shouldered, stuttering, yet with a chord of natural rhetoric in his high fiddle string of a windpipe, stood looking after them till they passed down the thoroughfare under the jib sail.

"That's a good man," Levin Dennis said, giving the tiller to Jack Wonnell and raising the sail. "He preached to the Britishers when they sailed from Tangier's Islands to take Baltimore an' told 'em they would be beat an' their gineral killed. He's made the oystermen all round yer jine the island churches an' keep Sunday. That stutterin' leaves him when he preaches. When he leads the shout in meetin', it's piercin' as a horn."

"He's a bloody Romany rogue," Joe Johnson muttered, "to tell me such a tale. But, kirjalis, he cursed not me.'

"What language is that, Mr. Johnson? Is it Dutch or Porteygee?"

"It's what we call the gypsy. Some calls it the Quaker. It's convenient, Levin, when you go to Philadelfey or Washinton or New York or some o' them big cities an' wants to talk to men of enterprise without the quails a-pipin' of you. Some day I'll larn it to you if you're a good boy."

They sailed out of the thoroughfare into the broad mouth of the Manokin, and a calm fell upon air and water for a little while. They could hear smothered music, as of drum fish beating beneath the water—"thum! thum!"—and crabs and alewives rose to the surface around them, chased by tailor fish. The catboat drifted into the mouth of a creek, where rock and perch were running on top of the water. In a few dips with the tongs Jack Wonnell raised half a bushel of oysters and opened them for the party. Along the shores, wild haws and plums still adhered to the bushes, and the stiff-branched persimmon trees bore thousands of their tomato-like fruit. Partridges were chirping in the corn, and crow blackbirds held a funeral feast around the fodder.

Some old, bayside mansions stretched their long sides and speckled Negro quarters along the inlets, half hidden by nut trees, and a turkey buzzard soared in the air like a voluptuary politician, taking beauty from nothing but his lofty station.

"The ole Eastern Sho'," Jack Wonnell said with his animated vacancy, "is jess stuffed with good things, Cap'n Johnson. You kin fall ovaboard most anywhair an' git a full meal. You kin catch a bucket o' crabs with a piece of a candle befo' breakfast an' shoot a wild duck mos' with your eyes shet."

"This country's good for nothin'," Joe Johnson said. "Floredey is the land. Wot kin a nigger earn for yer? Corn, taters, melons—faugh! Tobacco is a-givin' out, an' cotton won't live yer, but Floredey is the helldorader of the yearth."

"What's the helldorader?" asked Levin.

"That's Spanish or Porteygee for cheap niggers an' cotton," cried the trader. "Cotton's the bird!"

"I thought cotton was a wool," Levin said.

"No, boy, cotton is a plant, growin' like a raspberry on a bush, havin' pushed the blossoms off an' burst the pods below 'em, an' thar it is fur niggers to pick it. Thar's a Yankee in Georgey made a cotton gin to gin it clean, an' now all the world wants some of it."

"Some of the gin?" asked the irrelevant Wonnell.

"No, some of the cotton. They can't git enough of it. Eurip is crazy about it, but there ain't niggers enough to pick it all. So I'm in the nigger trade an' tryin' to be useful to my country, an' wot does I git fur it? I git looked down on, an' a nigger's pertected fur a-topperin' of me! But never mind, I'll be a big skull yet an' keep my kerrige—in Floredey."

"What's Floredey good fur?" Levin asked.

"It's full of nigger Injins—Simminoles—every one of 'em goin' to be caught an' branded an' put at cotton an' tobakker plantin' an' hog an' cow herdin'. More niggers will be run in from Cubey, an' all the free niggers in Delaware and up North will be sold. You an' me, Levin, is gwyn to own a drove of 'em, an' we'll have a orchard of oranges an' a thousand acres of cotton in bloom. We'll hold our heads up. Your mother shall be switched to a nabob. My wife will be a shakester in diamonds. We'll despise Cambridge an' Princess Anne, an' there sha'n't be a free nigger left on the face of the earth. We'll swig to it!"

The sick-headed yet fancy-ridden Levin drank again and listened to the dealer's tales of golden fruit on coasts of indigo, and palms that shelter parrots calling to the wild deer.

Jack Wonnell took the helm when Levin, still lulled by tales of wealth and lawless daring, lay down to sleep in the little cabin, and there he slept the deep sleep of the castaway when the vessel grounded at dusk in the sound of evening church bells at Princess Anne.

"Let him sleep," Joe Johnson said. "Yer, Wonnell, I give you tray of his strangers to take to his mommy," handing out three gold pieces. "Don't you forget it! Yer's a syebuck fur you," giving Jack a sixpence. "You an' me part company at Prencess Anne."

Under An Old Bonnet

Chapter 18

Vesta was sitting beside her unconscious husband, listening to his broken speech and thinking upon the rapidity of events, when she was attracted to the window by the sound of carriage wheels stopping at the door. Looking out, she saw Samson Hat step down, and there dropped from the carriage at a leap and a skip and without using the carriage step, a young female, whose head was invisible in an enormous coal-scuttle bonnet of figured blue chintz. Though she quickly executed the leap, Vesta observed that the arrival had forgotten to put on her stockings, and before Vesta could turn from the window, this singular object had darted up the dark stairs and thrown herself on the delirious man's bed.

"Uncle! Uncle Meshach! Air you dead, uncle? Wake up an' kiss your Rhudy!"

She kissed her uncle plentifully, while awaiting the same of him. The attack excited him a little without recalling his mind to any sustained remembrance, though Vesta heard the words "dear child" before he turned his head and chased the wild poppies again.

Wailing, "Lord sakes! Uncle don't know his Rhudy," the young female pulled her black apron over her head and had a silent cry—a little convulsion of the neck and not an audible sigh besides.

"She weeps with some refinement," Vesta thought.

The visitor was a tall, long-fingered, rather slight girl of probably seventeen, wearing clothing in which the fashion makers bore no guilt. Her bonnet was a remarkable object to Vesta, although she had seen some at a distance upon the heads of forest people coming in to the Methodist Church. It resembled the high-pooped ship of Columbus, which he had built so high on purpose, the girls at the seminary said, so as to have the advantage of spying the New World first. It also resembled the long, hollow, bow-shaped Conestoga wagons, which Vesta had seen going past her boarding school at Ellicott's Mills before the new railroad had reached there. As she had often peered into those vast, blue-bodied wagons to see what creatures might be passengers in their depths, so she took the first opportunity of the blue scuttle being jolted up to discern the face within.

It was a pretty face, containing a pair of feeling and mischievous brown eyes set in an attitude of wonder the moment they observed another woman in the room. The skin was pale, the mouth generous, the nose long, like Milburn's, but not so emphatic. The form of the face contained something fine amid the wild, cow-like stare the girl fixed on Vesta.

"Lord sakes," she exclaimed, "a lady's yer," then threw her apron over the bonnet again and held it there with long weather-stained fingers.

Vesta looked on with the first symptoms of amusement she had felt since the morning she and her mother, looking down from the windows of Teackle Hall, had laughed at the steeple-crown hat upon the man who was now her husband. It seemed a year ago. It was but yesterday.

"Old hats and bonnets," Vesta thought, "will be no novelties to me by and by. This family of the Milburns is full of them."

Addressing the new arrival, Vesta said, "This is your uncle, then? Where do you live?"

"I live at Nuark," answered the miss, taking down the black apron and looking from the depths of the bonnet like a guinea pig from his hole.

"Your uncle has a high fever," Vesta said kindly. "Though we think he is not in danger, it was right of you to come. Now take off your bonnet. What is your name?"

"Rhudy. I'm Rhudy Hullin, ma'am."

"Rhoda. Rhoda Holland, I think you say."

"Yes'm, Rhudy Hullin. I live crost the Pookamuke on the oushin side—out thar by Sinepuxin. I don't live in a great big town like Princess Anne; I live in Nuark."

At this the girl carefully extricated her head from the scuttle, looked it over with pride and anxiety, then carefully laid it on top of her uncle's hatbox.

"Uncle Meshach give it to me," she said with a sly inclination towards the sick bed. "Misc Somers draw'd it an' made it, but Uncle, he bought all the stuff. Did you ever see anything like it?"

"Never," said Vesta.

"Well, some folks out Sinepuxin said sech extravagins was a sin an' a shame, but Misc Somers, she said Uncle Meshach was rich an' hadn't but one Rhudy. It ain't quite as big as Misc Somers's bonnet, but it's draw'd mour."

Here Rhoda repeated what Vesta had observed twice before—an inaudible sniffle—and being caught in it, wiped her nose on her apron.

"You are cold. Take my handkerchief," Vesta said, and passed over her cambric with a lace border.

"What's it fur?" Rhoda asked, looking at it superstitiously. "You don't wipe your nuse on it, do you? Lord sakes, ain't it a piece of your neck fixin'?"

Vesta felt amused to see this weed of nature turn the handkerchief and hold it by the thumb and finger, as if she would become accountable for anything that might happen to it.

"I got two of these yer," Rhoda said. "Misc Somers made 'em outen a frock. They ain't got this starch on 'em. They're great big things. I always forgit 'em. My nuse wipes itself."

"Come near the fire and warm your feet," Vesta said. "Your ride from the oceanside through the Pocomoke forests this cold morning must have chilled you through. Take off your blanket shawl."

Rhoda laid the black and green shawl—which reached to her feet—on the chest and smoothed it with evident pride.

"Uncle Meshach bought that in Wilminton," she said. "Ain't it beautiful? I never wear it but when I come over yer or go to Snow Hill. Snow Hill's sech a proud place."

She had a way of laughing without a sound by merely indenting her cheeks, just as she expressed the sense of pain, the only difference being in the beaming of her eyes. Vesta thought it had something contagious in it. She would laugh broadly and in silence, as if she had been put on behavior in church and there had adopted a grimace to make the other girls laugh and save herself the suspicion.

As Rhoda pulled her skirts down to her feet, Vesta's observation was confirmed that she wore no stockings, and she could not help exclaiming, "My dear child, what possessed you to ride this October morning only half dressed? You might catch your death."

Rhoda caught her nose on the half sniffle, raised and dimpled her cheeks in a sly laugh, and cried, "Lord sakes, you mean my legs? Why, I ain't got but two pairs of stockings. Misc Somers is a-wearin' one of 'em, an' the ould pair's in the wash. It's so tejus to knit stockings an' sech fun to go barefoot that I don't wear 'em unless Misc Somers finds it out. Why, the boys can't see me."

She grimaced again so naturally and engagingly that Vesta had to laugh quite aloud and saw, meantime, that the young woman's oft-cobbled shoes covered a slender foot a lady might have envied.

"Now, Rhoda," Vesta said, almost indignantly, "why did you not ask your wealthy uncle for some good yarn stockings?"

"Him? Why, ma'am, he's got so many pore kin. If he begin to give 'em all stockin's, he'd go barefoot himself."

"Has he other nieces like you?"

"No," the girl quietly grimaced, her brown eyes full of laughter. "There's plenty of others but none like Rhudy. The woods is full of them others."

"So you are the favorite? Now, what was your uncle going to do with all his money?"

"Lord sakes," Rhoda said, "he was goin' to marry Miss Vesty with it. That's what Misc Somers said."

The mockingbird had been striking up once or twice in the conversation and now pealed his note loudly: "Vesta, she, she, she, she-ee-ee!"

A tingle she had felt more than once already in her brief knowledge of this forest family went through Vesta's veins and nerves, and she silently remarked, "How little a girl knows of men around her—what satyrs are taking her image to their arms. These people knew he loved me, when I knew not that he ever saw me."

She addressed the niece again. "Rhoda, did your uncle say he loved Miss Vesta?"

"No'm, he never said he luved nothin'. But I heard Tom shout, 'Vesty,' an' saw a lady's picture yonder between Grandpar an' Grandmem. I told Misc Somers, an' she says, 'Your Uncle Meshach's in luve.' Oh, I was right glad of it because he was so sad an' lonesome."

The fountain of sympathy burst again in Vesta's heart, and she felt that there were compensations which riches and station knew nothing of in humble alliances like hers.

"Rhoda," she said, going to the young girl and putting her hand upon her soft brown hair, "you have not noticed the new picture of a lady hanging up here, have you?"

"No'm, not yet. Everything is so quare in this room sence I saw it last. I hain't seen nothin' in it but you. Now I see the carpet an' the brass an'irons an' the chiney an'—Lord sakes, is that a picture? Why, I thought it was you."

"It is, Rhoda. I am Vesta. I am your new aunt."

The girl made one of her engaging, dimpled, silent laughs, as if by stealth again, then changed it to a silent cry by a revulsion as natural and rose to her feet and took Vesta in her arms. "I'm so glad, I will cry a little," Rhoda simpered, her eyes all dewy. "Oh, how Misc Somers will say I found it out first."

Vesta felt a chain of happy thoughts arise in her mind, which she expressed as frankly as the girl of forest product had spoken: "Yes, Rhoda, I am thankful to find a social life open to me where there seemed no way. You come here like a sunbeam. God bless you. I can hear you talk and teach you what little I know, and we will relieve each other watching him."

She felt a slight modification of her joy at this reminder, but the bird seemed to teach her patience as he suggested, hopping and flying in the air, "Come see! Come see! Come see!"

"Yes," thought Vesta, "Come and see. It is good counsel. I begin to feel the breaking of a new sense—curiosity about the poor and lowly. My education seems to have closed my observation on people of my own race who daily trod almost upon my skirts and whom I never saw —whom it was considered respectable not to see. My servants enjoyed my whole confidence because they were my slaves, yet I would have dropped in our misfortune to these plain white people. Then, Roxy and Virgie, sold to some temporary rich man, would have been above me, slaves as they would continue. How false and how fatal are both slavery and proud riches to the republicans we pretend to be. Compelled to see at last, I shall not close my eyes nor harden my heart."

The maid from Newark had meantime quietly inspected the rag carpet, the cloth hangings, the fairy rocker, and all the acquisitions of her uncle's abode.

Vesta showed her how to administer cool drink and sponging to the sufferer, and he saw them together with a look of inquiry, which the fever soon drove away.

"Are your parents living, Rhoda?"

"No'm, they're both dead. My mother was Uncle Meshach's sister, an' she married a rich man who biled salt an' had vessels an' kept tavern. Father Hullin died of the pulmonary. Mar died next. Misc Somers brought me up whar the tavern used to be. It ain't a-stand no more. Uncle Meshach owns it."

"Is it a nice place?"

"Now it ain't as nice as it use to be, Aunt Vesty, sence the shews don't stop thar no mour."

"The shoes? What is that?"

"The wax figgers an' glass blowers an' the strongis' man in the world. Did you ever see him?"

"No, dear." Vesta replied.

"I saw him," Rhoda said with a compression of her mouth and a gleam of her eyes. "He bruke a stone with his fist. Misc Somers kep the stone, an' what do you think it was?"

"Marble?"

"No'm; Chork! He jest washed the chork over with a little shell or varnish or something, an' of course it bruke right easy. So he wasn't the strongis' man in the world at all, an' if Misc Somers ever see him, she'll tell him so."

"Is it a little or a large house, Rhoda?"

"Oh, it's a magnificins house, twice as big as this, with the roof bent like a elefin's back an' three windows in it—rale dormant windows that looks like three eyes outen a crab, an' a gabil end three rows of windows high, an' four high chimneys. The rope walker said it was fit to be a rueyal palace. Then thar's the kitchen an' colonnade built onto it. It's the biggest house, I reckon, about Sinepuxin. That rope walker's a mountinbank."

"A mountain bank? You mean a mountebank—an impostor?"

"Yes'm. He allowed he'd break the rupe after he'd walked on it. He said it wasn't stretched tight enough an' went along a-feeling of it. Misc Somers found out that every time he teched of it he put on some bluestone water or somethin' to rot it, so it bruke easy. If he comes agin, Misc Somers's goin' to tell him he's a mountinbank. Lord sakes, she ain't afraid."

"So, since it has ceased to be a tavern, dear, you see no more jugglers?"

"The last shew there," Rhoda said, "was the canninbils an' the missionary. The missionary had converted of 'em, an' they didn't eat no more, but he tuld how they used to eat people. They stouled a pony outen the stables an' run to the Cypress Swamp, an' thar they turned out to be some shingle sawyers he'd just a-stained up. Misc Somers is a-waitin' for him."

"And so you were an orphan, brought up at the old roadside stage house at Newark? And who is Mrs. Somers?"

"Misc Somers, she's a aunt of Par Hullin. She an' me live together sence par an' mar died of the pilmonary. I have a passel of beaus takes me to the oushin on Sinepuxin beach, outen the way of skeeters, an' we wades an' sails an' biles salt an' roasts mammynoes. I can cut out most any girl from her beau, but I ain't found no man I love yet."

"I'm glad of that," said Vesta, "because then you will be satisfied with Princess Anne. They say your uncle will be sick here several weeks, and we can help each other to make him well. Now, he is waking."

Milburn opened his eyes and sighed. When he saw them together, he looked at Vesta with a bewildered doubt.

"I thought they said you had gone forever," he murmured.

"No, I am come forever, or until you wish me gone."

"I told them so," he sighed. "I said, 'She has high principle, though she cannot love me.'"

"Uncle Meshach, give Auntie time," cried Rhoda with a quick divination of something unsettled.

"You have a good niece," Vesta said, "and we shall love each other, I hope, and improve each other."

"Yes, that will be noble," he replied. "Teach her something. I have never had the time. Oh, I am very ill, and at a time like this, too."

"Be composed, Mr. Milburn," the bride said. "It is only nature taking the time you would not give her, and which she means for us to improve our almost violent acquaintance. I shall be happy sitting here and wish you would let your niece stay with me. I desire it."

He tried to smile, as the strong sweat broke upon him from his hands to his face.

"She is yours," he said, "the best of my poor kin. Do not despise us."

Vesta drew her arm around Rhoda and kissed her, that he might see it.

"What goodness," Milburn sighed with drowsy relief.

"Let us turn the covers under the edges, Rhoda," Vesta said, "and put your blanket shawl over him. He will get some sleep."

He turned, as if to see if she was there, and closed his eyes peacefully as a child.

"Now, Rhoda," said Vesta, "I hear Papa's carriage at the door. While he comes up, I shall ride back to see my mother and get a few things at home."

"Who is your poppy, Aunt Vesty?"

"Don't you know him? Judge Custis, who lives in Princess Anne."

"Jedge Custis! Why, Lord sakes, he ain't your par, is he, Aunt Vesty? He's one of my old beaus."

The judge brought Reverend Tilghman with him, and Vesta introduced Rhoda to them: "This is Miss Rhoda, Mr. Milburn's niece."

Judge Custis, a trifle blushing, took both of Rhoda's hands and said, "Ha, my pretty partner and dancing pupil. How are our friends at St. Martin's Bay and Sinepuxent? Many a sail and clambake we have had, Rhoda."

"You're a deceiver," Rhoda cried, somewhere between glee and accusation. "I'm goin' to plosecute you, Jedge, fur not tellin' of me you was a married man. My heart's bruke."

"Who could remember what he was, Rhoda, sitting all that evening beside you at—where was it?"

"The Blohemian glassblowers," Rhoda replied, "the only ones that ever visited the western himisfure. That little one, Jedge, with the copper rings in his years wasn't a Blohemian at all. He lived up at Cape Hinlupen, an' Misc Somers see him when she was a-buyin' of herring thar. She's goin' to tell him when she catches him at Nuark."

The young rector observed the flash of those bright eyes following the pleasing dimples, and the slips of orthography seemed never less culpable coming from such lips and teeth.

"William," said Vesta, "come around this afternoon and let us have our usual Sunday reading circle. Mr. Milburn will be awake and appreciate it, as he is one of your most regular parishioners. Rhoda, you can read?"

"Oh, yes'm. Misc Somers, she's a good reader. She reads the Old Testamins. The names thar is mos' too long for me, but I reads the Psalms an' the Ploverbs right well."

"Very well, then, we shall read verse about, so that Mr. Milburn can hear both our voices and his favorite minister's, too. You'll come, Papa?"

"Yes, if I can. We have had a love feast at Teackle Hall this morning. Your sister from Talbot is down, but I think I can get off."

"Lord sakes!" Rhoda said, looking at Mr. Tilghman candidly. "You ain't a minister now? Not a minister of the Gospil?"

"Unworthily so, Miss Rhoda."

"Well, I don't see how you was old enough to be convicted an' learn it all, unless you was a speretual merikle. Misc Somers see one at Jinkotig. They called him the enfant phrenomeny. He exhorted at five year old an' give his experyins at seven."

"Rare, Miss Rhoda," the rector said, hardly able to keep his reverence in amusement at her impetuosity.

"Oh, he made a wild excitemins, Aunt Vesty. The women give each other their babies to hold, while they tuk turns a-shouting.

"'Yer, Becky, hold my baby while I shout!' says one.

"'Now, Nancy, hold mine while I shout!'

"To see that little boy up thar tellin' of his experyins was meriklus, but that little phrenomeny was a dwarf, twenty year old, an' Misc Somers found it out an' told it."

"I'll be bound, Mrs. Somers knows," exclaimed the judge.

"That she do," continued Rhoda with a slight sniffle and a dimpling that suggested something to come. "Misc Somers says you held one of them babies, Jedge, to let its mother shout, an' pretended to be under a conviction, an' that you backslid right thar an' was a-whisperin' to the other mother. Lord sakes! Misc Somers finds it all out."

"Well," said the judge, finding the laugh against him, "I never did better electioneering than that day. By holding that baby five minutes, I made a vote, and the mother will hold it twenty years before she will make a vote."

"Misc Somers says, Jedge, you hold the women longer than thar babies, but I told her you was in sech conviction you didn't know one from the other. 'Oh,' she says, 'he's sly an' safe when he gits over yer on the Worcester side.' Misc Somers, she's dreadful plain."

During the continuation of this colloquy William Tilghman looked th interest on the two young ladies. Vesta, the elder by two or three ars, was richly endowed with the lights of both beauty and accomplishments. The maid from the ocean side was plainer, with no ornament within or without, but he could foresee a graceful woman with coquetry and fascination not wholly latent there. As his eyes met Rhoda's, he interpreted the look which almost every maiden casts on meeting a young man: "Is he single?" She shot this look so archly, yet so strongly, that the arrow wounded him a little as it glanced off. He smiled, but the consciousness was restored that he was still a young man as well as a priest. Love, which had closed a door like the portal of a tomb against him, began to come forth like a glow worm and wink its lamp athwart the dark. "She must come to Sunday school," he thought. "If she stays in Princess Anne, we will polish her."

Not satisfied with any lull in the conversation, the mockingbird pearted up as it saw Vesta withdraw and cried, "'Sband! 'Sband! Meeeshack! Meeee-shack! See me! See me! Gents! Gents! Gents! Genten! Sweet! Sweetie! Sweetie! Hoo! Hoo! See! See! Vesty, she! Ha! Ha!" It flew over its stirring master as if doubting that all was well since the strange lady was gone.

"That bird almost speaks," said William Tilghman. "I have spent many an hour teaching them but never could make one talk like that."

"Maybe you had too much to teach it," Rhoda Holland said. "It ain't often they can speak, an' they mustn't have much company to learn. Uncle Meshach hain't had no company but that bird for years. I reckon the bird got mad an' lonesome an' jest hooted words at him."

"What is it saying now?" Tilghman asked. "It is almost convulsive in its attempts to say something."

The gray bird, as impressive as a poor poet, seemed nearly in a state of epilepsy to bring up a burden of oppressive sound. As they watched it, almost tipsy with the intoxicant of speech, fluttering, driving, and striking in the air, it suddenly uttered a note liquid as gurgling snow: "L-L-Love! Love! Ha! Ha! L-L-Love!"

"Well done, old bachelor," Judge Custis remarked in spite of his fagged face, for good resolution and yesterday's unbracing had left him somewhat limp and haggard still. "He brings out 'love' as if he had made a vow against it, but the confession had to come. Many a monk would sing the same if instinct could find a daring word in his chorals. These mockers of Maryland were celebrated in the British magazines a hundred years ago, and I recall some lines about them:

> His breast whose plumes a cheerful white display,
> His quivering wings are dressed in sober gray,
> Sure all the Muses this their bird inspire,
> And he alone is equal to a choir.
> Oh, sweet musician, thou dost far excel

The soothing song of pleasing Philomel:
Sweet is her song, but in few notes confined.
But thine, thou mimic of the feathery kind,
Runs thro' all notes: thou only know'st them all,
At once the copy and th' original!"

"That's magnificins," Rhoda exclaimed with quiet delight. "Who is 'Fellow Mil,' Jedge?"

"Oh, that's the British nightingale. These American mockingbirds surpass them as one of our Eastern Shore clippers outsails all the naval powers of Europe."

"I've hearn the British Nightingale," Rhoda said with a flash of her eyes. "He was a blind man with green specticklers that sang 'Ome, Sweet 'Ome'—that's the way he plonounced it. He had to drink a whole tumbler of water, it affected of him so. Misc Somers, spying around to see if he was the rale nightin'gale, found out it was gin in that glass an' told about it."

Rhoda made even the minister laugh as she indented her cheeks and cast a sheep's glance at him and the judge.

Tilghman marveled that such forest English could be resented so little by his mind. It did not matter that she may have had no more lessons than the bird, whose difficulty he found even beautiful.

"But see, Mr. Milburn is wide awake. My friend, how do you feel?"

"Better," Milburn murmured. "I cannot lie here any longer. There is money, gentlemen, dependent on my getting about."

He started up with the greatest resolution and confidence and fell upon his head before he had left the coverlets.

"No, no," said the judge, as he and Tilghman picked Milburn up and arranged him as before. "Your will is matched this time, my brave son-in-law. You are back in the hut you have consumed, among the fires thereof, and the avenging blast of Nassawango furnace burns in your veins and cools you in the millpond alternately. Lie there and repent for the injury you have done a spotless one."

If Meshach heard this, it was not known, but the impulsive utterance strengthened the impression with Tilghman and Rhoda that Vesta's marriage was not altogether voluntary, and it produced on both a feeling of deeper sympathy for her.

"Judge," the young minister said, "do good for evil, if evil there has been. I have given him my hand sincerely. Perhaps you can relieve his mind of some business care."

"Mr. Milburn," the judge said, when he saw the resinous eyes roll towards him again out of that swarthy face, now pale with weakness, "I am out of a job now and can work cheap. Let me do any errand for you."

A look of petulance followed by one of inquiry came from Milburn's eyes, and he pressed his head between his wrists as if to bring back the blood that might propel his judgment. They heard him mutter, "No business prudence, yet plausible, persuasive. Might do it well."

The judge spoke now with some firmness: "Milburn, there is no use of your rebelling. Here you are and here you will lie till nature does her restoration, assisted by this medicine I have brought you. You must undergo calomel, and this quinine must set on its work of several weeks to break up the regularity of these chills. In the meantime, as your interests are also Vesta's, and Vesta's are mine, let me serve her, if not you."

The positive tone influenced the weakened system of the patient. He looked at all three of the observers and said to Tilghman, "William, I might send you but for your calling. Leave me with the judge a little while, both you and Rhoda."

Rhoda took the Conestoga bonnet from the top of the Entailed Hat box and, to the rector's exceeding wonder, arrayed herself in it.

"Let's you an' me take a walk," she said, putting her hand in Tilghman's arm with a quiet confidence. "I ain't afeared of Princess Anne people, if they are proud. Misc Somers says King Solomons was no better than a lily outen the pond an' said so himself."

Sincere as his humility was, the young man blushed a little at the idea of walking through his native town with that bonnet at his side. He belonged to one of the self-conscious and highviewing families of the old peninsula. His granduncle had been the staff officer of Washington and the messenger from Yorktown to Congress with the news, "Cornwallis has fallen." It was his chivalric sense, not his piety, which immediately dispelled the touch of coxcombry, when he felt that a lady had requested him.

"With happiness, Miss Holland," he replied.

He felt no shrinking thought again as he ran the gauntlet of the idle fellows of the town, many of them his former vagrant playmates. Rhoda was perfectly happy. He would have taken her to his grandmother's, with whom he kept house, but that aristocratic old dowager might say something to destroy Rhoda's confidence in her elegant appearance and easy vocabulary. As they walked past Teackle Hall, Vesta saw them and made them come in and eat a little.

At first Rhoda showed some uneasiness under this great pile of habitation, but Vesta was so gracious that the shyness quickly wore off. At a fitting moment the bride said, "My dear, there is a bonnet upstairs I expect to wear this winter, and I want to try it on you, whom I think it will particularly become."

Rhoda's quiet eyes flashed as she saw the new article and heard Vesta praise it upon her head. The old bonnet had received a cruel blow.

Tilghman accused himself that he felt a little relieved when he escorted Rhoda back to Meshach's in another bonnet. Vesta followed with her great shaggy dog Turk, not unconscious of people peering in wonder and excitement from every door and window of the town. From the servants in the kitchens to the aged people helped to their food with bib and spoon, the news was working in every household that the famed daughter of Daniel Custis was the prize of the junk dealer and usurer from Old Town by the bridge, who had enslaved a wife at last.

The Dusky Levels

Chapter 19

Left alone with Judge Custis, the new son-in-law asked to be propped up in bed, and nothing was visible that would support his pillow but the aged leather hatbox, which Custis, with a wry face, brought to do duty.

"My illness is unfortunate," Milburn gasped, "not only to me, but to the new ties I have formed. To the mutual interest my wife and I have in making up your losses on Nassawango Furnace, I have bought an interest in a great lawsuit."

"Then the day of reckoning of your enemies has come, Milburn."

"Not yet," said the sick man with a proud flash of his eyes, "unless I am no merchant and you are no lawyer, and the first I will not concede."

"Nor I the second," exclaimed the judge with some pride and temper.

"You were once a good lawyer, if a visionary," resumed the money lender with scant ceremony. "Had we been able to respect each other, we might have been confederated in things valuable to ourselves and to our time and place. But that is past, and you do not possess my confidence as my legal agent. I wish you to get another advocate for me."

"I am willing to be useful, even without your compliments," the judge said, remembering his Christian resolution. "We will not quarrel if I can serve you."

"I do not wish to hurt your feelings, but my strength is not great enough for unmeaning flattery. This marriage was so dear to my heart that I have put it before a very large interest about which I have no time to lose, and still I am helpless upon this bed. I will trust you to do my errand. Go to that chest, and you will find a package of papers in the cedar till at the end. Bring them here."

As the judge opened the old chest, a musty smell, as of mummies wrapped in herbs, ascended into his nose, and he saw some faded clothes, as those of poor people deceased, lying within. As he raised the lid of the till and saw the desired papers among a parcel of spotted and striped bird eggs, the mockingbird piped a noisy warning: "Come see! Come see! Meshach! He! He! Sweet!"

"Now, open the window yonder," said Milburn, taking the papers, "and let Tom fly out. He starts my nerves. Whoot, whit, Tom!"

Spreading its wings and tail, the mockingbird flew out the window and settled in the old willow below to have a Sunday afternoon concert, calling the passing dogs by name, whistling to them, and deceiving cats and chickens with invitations they familiarly heard: to eat, to shoo, to scat, and to roost.

"If he regulates his wife like that bird," the judge said to himself, "she will fly to heaven soon."

Milburn opened the papers, counted them, and handed them to his father-in-law.

"The papers will be plain to you, Judge Custis, after I have made a few words of explanation. You well know that the canal between the Delaware and Chesapeake is finished, and vessels are now passing through it from bay to bay. It is taking one hundred dollars a day in tolls, and twenty vessels already go past between sun and sun. It has been a cheap and quick work, costing something above two millions of dollars and taking only five years of time. And yet it has begun its mercantile life by a cheat upon a man to whom it is indebted as a promoter and contractor, and to whom I have advanced the means to compel justice and damages."

"Well, well, Milburn, I must pay tribute to your enterprise. The era of these great carrying corporations has barely begun, and you stake your little fortune against one of them that is backed by the great city of Philadelphia."

"The canal passes through the state of Delaware, in which is three quarters of its length of only fourteen miles, and there a suit will be free, to some extent, from the corruptions they might exercise in Pennsylvania. If successful there, we can more easily attach the tolls of the canal. I have no more faith in the Legislature of Delaware than of any other state. Kidnappers sit in its responsible seats, and it licenses lotteries to make prizes of its own honor. But we shall try our case before a simple jury, which will be flax in the hands of one lawyer in that state, if we can secure him. Hitherto, he has refused my contractor and will not take the case."

"Why, you must mean Clayton, the new senator," said the judge.

"That is the man," Milburn continued, pausing for strength and breath. "He is finely educated, I hear, and possesses a remarkable power over the agricultural and mixed races of that small state, whom he thoroughly understands by sympathy and acquaintance. I heard him in court at Georgetown, once, wither and confound the confederated kidnapping influences of the whole peninsula. Against the will and intention of the jury, he prevailed upon their fears and sensibilities to find a bold rogue guilty of stealing free men of color—a rogue who was in this room this very day, unless it is a delusion of my fever, and with whom I fancied I had been in collision somewhere."

"You only knocked him down with a brick after Samson had done it with his fist, and then the fellow came to me for shelter, afraid you would pursue him at law. I suppose he did an errand for my servants to this abode."

The judge looked around the room as if he had used the most respectable word he could possibly apply to it.

"I will compromise with such scoundrels as that one," Milburn said, "only when I am afraid of them. But to conclude my statement: For reasons of timidity, doubts of success, or political ambition—something I cannot fathom—Mr. Clayton will not hearken to my debtor, and I have not disclosed my own interest in the suit. He is at home from Washington, and an appointment has been made with him at his office in Dover tomorrow. You see I am unable to keep it, and I have no one else to send. Information reaches me that the canal company, discovering my money in the contractor's bank account, intends to retain Clayton forthwith. If you set out this afternoon, you can reach Laurel Town for bedtime. It is at least forty miles thence to Dover, and you might ride it tomorrow by noon, with push. In that case you have a chance to beat the Philadelphia emissary by several hours. I already have five thousand dollars at stake, and I believe I shall get damages of forty times five if I can retain that man.'

"I am ready to start at once," said the judge, rising up. "I can read these papers on the way. The saddle was my cradle, and I have a good horse. My valise can follow me on the stage tomorrow."

"Unless you see the best reasons for it, my name is not to be mentioned to anyone as a party to this suit. I am not popular with juries."

"Then good-bye, Milburn," said the judge. "As you treat my daughter, may God treat you."

"Amen," exclaimed the money lender, as the judge's feet passed over the door sill below, and he sank back to the bed, exhausted again.

∞

While the described proceedings occupied the white people, Roxy and Virgie loitered around the bridge behind the store, straying a little way up the Manokin brook.

"Virgie," said Samson Hat, meeting them under the willow tree, "when I carries you off an' marries you, I s'pect you'll be climbin' up in my loft, makin' it comf'able fo' me."

"You ought to be ashamed of yourself, you old, black, impertinent servant of darkness!" Virgie said. "Indeed, when I look at a man, he must be almost white—not all white, though, like Roxy's beau."

"Who's he, Roxy?" Samson asked.

Roxy blushed and said she had no beau and never wanted one.

"Roxy's beau," said Virgie, "is that poor, helpless Mr. Jack Wonnell. He comes to see her every day; he's devotion itself. Indeed, Samson, if you are going to marry me and Roxy marry all those bell-crown hats, we shall cure the town of its two greatest afflictions."

"Bad ole hats?" asked Samson.

"Roxy'll burn all the bell-crowns for her beau, and I'll bury the steeple-hat and you that cleans it, and the people will be so glad they'll set me free, and I can go north."

"Look out, Virgie; I'll put dat high-crown hat on you like Marster Milburn put de bell on de buzzard. He went up to dat buzzard one day wid a little tea bell in his hand an' says, 'Buzzard, how do ye like music?'

"Says de buzzard, tickled wid de compliment, 'I'm so larnid in dat music, I disdains to sing, an' I criticizes de birds dat does.'

"'Den,' says Marster Milburn, 'I needn't say to ye, P'ofessor Buzzard, dat dis little bell will be very pleasin' to yo' refine' taste.' Wid dat, he takes a little piece o' wire an' fastens de tea bell to de bird's foot an' says, 'Buzzard, let me hear ye play.'

"De buzzard flew, an' de bell tinkled, an' all de other buzzards hear some'in' like de cowbell on de dead cow dey picked yisterday, an' dey says, 'Who's dat a-flyin' heah? Maybe it's a cow's ghose!'

"So dey up, all scart, an' cross'd de bay, an' de buzzard wid a bell hain't had no company sence, becoz he stole a talent he didn't have, an' it made everybody oncomfitable."

"I've heard about Meshach bellin' a buzzard," said Roxy, "but they say he's got something on his foot, too, like a hoof—a clove foot. Did you ever see it, Samson?"

"He never tuk his foot off to let me see," said the Negro warily. "Dat bell on de buzzard, gals, is like white beauty in a colored skin. It draws white men an' black men like quare music in de air, but it makes de pale gal lonesome. She can't marry ary white man, an' she despises black ones."

The shrewd lover had touched a chord of young pain in the hearts of both those delicate quadroons. Both were so nearly white that the slight corruption increased their beauty, rounded their graceful limbs, plumpened their willowy figures, gave a softness like mild night to their expressive eyes, and blackened the silken tassels of their elegant long hair. No tutor had taught them how to walk—they who moved like skylarks on the air. Faithful, pure-minded, modest, natural, they were still slaves, and their place in matrimony, which nature would have set among the worthiest, was, by the freak of man's caste, as doubtful as the mermaid's.

Roxy was a little the shorter and fuller of shape, the milder and more pathetic. In Virgie the white race had left its leaner lines and greater unrelenting. She said to Samson, with the pique her reflections inspired, "I never thought the first man to make love to me would be as black as you."

"De white corn years—de rale sugar' corn," said Samson, "de blackbird gits. None o' dem white gulls an' pigeons gits dat corn. A white feller wouldn't suit you, Virgie."

"Why?" asked Roxy. "Virgie was raised among white children. So was I. We didn't know any difference till we grew up."

"Dat was what spiled ye," Samson said. "De colored man is de best husban'. He ain't thinkin' 'bout business while he makin' love, like Marster Milburn. The black man thinks his sweetheart is business enough. He works fur her to love her, not to be makin' a fool of her an' put his own head full of bambition, as dey calls it. You couldn't git along wid one o' dem pale, mutterin' white men, Virgie. Roxy's white man, he's most as keerless as a nigger. He kin't do nothin' but make love, nohow. Dat's what she likes him fur."

"He's as kind a hearted man as there is in Princess Anne," Roxy spoke up. "I never thought about him except as a friend. I know I shan't look down on him because he likes a yellow girl, for then I would be looking down on myself."

"Virgie," said Samson, "I reckon I'm a little ole, but you kin't fine out whar it is. Ye ought to seen me fetch dat white hickory of a feller in de eye yisterday, an' he jest outen his teens. I know it's kine of impedent to be a-courtin' of you, Virgie, dat's purtier dan Miss Vesty herself."

"Nobody is as pretty as Miss Vesta," Virgie cried, though delighted with the compliment. "She's perfection."

"As I was gwyn to say," Samson added dryly, "I never just knowed what I was a-lettin' Marster Milburn keep my wages fur till he married Miss Vesty. Den I sot my eyes on Miss Vesty's frien' an' maid, an' I says, 'Gracious goodness! Dat's de loveliest gal in de world. I'll git my money an' buy her an' set her free, an' maybe she'll hab me, ole as I am.'"

"She will, too, Samson, if you do that, I believe," Roxy cried. "See how she's a-smiling an' coloring about it."

Virgie's throat sent tremors to her long-lashed eyes, and a wild, speculative something throbbed in her slender wrists and beat in the little jacket that was molded to her swelling form: the first sight of freedom in the wild doe—freedom and a mate.

"My soul!" Roxy added. "If Mr. Wonnell could set me free, I think I might pity him enough to be his wife."

While she indulged the wild dream, Samson used the opportunity to stretch out his hand and take Virgie's. "Dis han' is too purty," he said, "to be worn by a slave. Let me make it free."

She turned away, but the Negro had been a wise lover and his plea pierced home. It struck the Caucasian fatherhood of the bright quadroon.

"Freedom is mos' all I got," the Negro continued. "It's wuth everything but love, Virgie. Dat you got. Maybe we kin swap 'em an' let me be yo' slave."

"Don't, don't," pleaded Virgie, pulling her hand very gently. "I'm a-feard of you. You clean the bad man's hat."

Caste Without Tone

Chapter 20

Judge Custis was well out of town, riding to the north, when the little reading circle assembled over the old store without his patronage. In the warm afternoon the windows were raised, and they could hear the mockingbird in its tree, tantalizing the great shaggy dog Turk by whistling to him: "Wsht! Wsht! Come, sir! Come, sir! Sic' em! Sic 'em, Turk! Wsht! Sirrah! Ha! Ha!"

Turk would run a little way, run back, see nobody, watch all the windows of the store, and finally he seemed to think the spot haunted or unreliable in some way. He would next run to the open store door and bark, run back, and from a distance watch the hollow dark within, as if a vague enemy lived there, mocking his obedient nature and keeping his mistress captive. Turk was a setter with mastiff mixing, worth a little for the hunt and more for the watch, but as an ornament and friend worth more than all. He was so impartial in his favors as to like Aunt Hominy and Vesta about equally and often slept in the kitchen before the great chimney fire.

"Do we worry you by reading here?" Vesta asked her husband.

"No, my darling. It is kind of you to bring music to my poor loft."

William Tilghman opened his Bible at a place marked by a little ribbon-backed Bristol card, inscribed "Watch with me" in Vesta's childhood by her learning fingers. He thought of his cousin, now fluttering between her betrayal to this Pilate and her crucifixion, and caught her eyes looking at the marker, as if saying to him and to the forest maiden, "Watch with me."

Tilghman started the reading, and Vesta followed. Rhoda did her part, also, but she had to labor hard to keep up, as the chapter was in the Acts, descriptive of Paul's voyage towards Rome, and had plenty of hard words and geography in it.

At one verse Rhoda's reading was like this: "'An'. . . when. . . we. . . had. . . sailed. . . slow. . . ly. . . many. . . days. . . an'. . . scare. . . skurse'—I declar', Aunt Vesty, this print is blombinable! 'Scace'—Oh, yes, 'scacely. . . were. . . come. . . over. . . again. . . Snid'—Mr. Tilghman, what is this crab kine of word?"

"'Cnidus.'"

"Well, I declar', a dog couldn't spell that. It looks like Snyder spelled by his hired man. 'Agains Cnidus. . . the. . . wind. . . not. . . snuffers'—No, 'snuffering.' Didn't I say 'snuffering?' I mean. . . ."

"'Sailed under Crete,' dear," assisted Vesta.

"'Suffering. . . us. . . we. . . sa. . . sailed. . . under'—I can't spell it nohow; nobody kin! 'Sailed under. . . Crety. . . over. . . again. . . Sal. . . Salm'—Oh, yes, 'psalms!'—No, 'Sal. . . money.'"

"'Salmone,'" explained the rector, not daring to look up. "'We sailed under Crete over against Salmone, and, hardly passing it, came unto a place which is called the Fair Havens, nigh whereunto was the city of Lasea.'"

"Lord sakes," exclaimed Rhoda, putting out a foot on which she wore Vesta's stocking, "did they have Fair Havens in them days? Was it this one over yer on the Wes'n Shu?"

"No," answered Tilghman, "Fair Havens was always a ready name for sailors finding a good port in trouble."

"Thar ain't no good port out thar on the oushin side now but Monroe's Inlet outen Jinkotig. The rest of 'em gits filled up, an' kadgin's the on'y way to kadge through of 'em, Misc Somers says."

"She means warping or pulling over a shoal inlet by a rope to an anchor," explained the pastor.

"Oh, yes, you know, Mr. Tilghman; that's kadgin'—pullin' over the bar by the anchor line. You're all a-groun' an' can't git nowhar, air a-bumpin' on the bar, an' the breakers is comin' dreadful in your side. You'll break all up if you stay thar. So you git the little anchor—the little one's better than ary too big a one—an' put it in the yawl an' paddle acrost the bar an' sot her, an' them aboard pulls as the billers lifts ye, an' so they keep her headed in, kadgin', kadgin', bumpety-bump. At las' you go clar of the bar an' come home to smooth haven in Sinepuxin."

"Yes, my sisters," appended the young minister, "we need often to kedge home, to warp over the bars of life, and hope in ever so small an anchor helps if we do not lose the line. Small hopes are often better than great ones, for o'er-great hopes swamp little vessels. Even hope must be artfully shaped and skillfully dropped to take hold of the unseen bottoms of opportunity. All of us have entertained burdensome hopes—heavy anchors—and they would not hold us against the breakers, but there may be little hopes, carried in advance of us, that will draw us into pleasant sounds and bays."

"We owe to you, Rhoda, this comforting hope," said Vesta, "and while you are with us, we shall teach you to read more confidently."

Vesta then sang Charles Wesley's hymn:

> Jesus, in us thyself reveal!
> The winds are hushed, the sea is still,
>   If in the ship Thou art.
> Oh, manifest Thy power divine;
> Enter this sinking church of Thine,
>   And dwell in every heart.

The sounds of her singing reached the people rambling curiously around on Sunday afternoon to see the principals in the surprising marriage.

As Vesta ended, Mr. Milburn called her, saying, "It is time for you to leave me till tomorrow."

"Is that your desire?"

"It is, kind lady. I have a servant man used to all my work, and you can hear of my condition through your slave girls going and coming. I want you to feel free as ever, though my wife at last. I did not seek you to cloud your morning, but to share your sunshine. Go to Teackle Hall, and there I will come when I am stronger. At no time do I ever wish you to sleep in this old stable."

"May I come and sit with you tomorrow, sir?"

"Oh, do so. I must see you a little, day by day."

"May I take Rhoda with me?"

"Yes, if you will do it. She is a poor girl, but that is not her fault."

Vesta bent and touched his forehead with her lips, and as she drew back, he raised his cold hand and put a piece of paper in hers.

"Present my love to your mother," he said in a chill, "and return to her the losses Judge Custis has named to me as her portion in Nassawango Furnace. The amount is in this check."

"You are an honorable man," Vesta said. "I have cost you dearly."

"It is the bumping of a few years on the bar," Meshach answered, trying to smile. "Be you my anchor out in calm water, and I will try to draw to you some day. It is not the price I pay that troubles me; it is the price you are paying."

"I am deeply interested in you," Vesta said. "If I should say more than that, it would not now be true."

"Thank you for that much," Milburn said. "Even your pity is a treasure, and I thank God that I have made so much progress. Before you go, let my bird come in, and then shut the window to keep the nighthawks and owls from finding him."

In spite of the rising violence of his chill, he managed to whistle a note or two, and Tom flew in the window, fluttered viciously around his head as if to be revenged for exile, then leaped on the old hatbox and set up a performance in which were all the menagerie of town and field.

∞

Mrs. Custis was found in her bedroom, much improved in spirits, but highly nervous.

"Oh, my poor, martyred, murdered idol!" she screamed, as Vesta came in. "Are you alive? Is the beast dead? Don't tell me he dares to live!"

"Yes, Mamma, here are his teeth," Vesta said, when she had kissed her mother warmly. "He has sent you a check for all your lost money, and his love, and me to live here with you in Teackle Hall. Liberty, restitution, as you name it, and his affection to both of us. Is he not a gentleman now?"

Mrs. Custis eagerly took the check.

"Do you believe it is good? Maybe he sent it to deceive me, while he takes advantage of your gratitude. Oh, these foresters are devils! I wish I had the money for it."

"It is good for everything he has, Mamma. Not to pay it would make him a bankrupt. He gave it to me almost with gallantry. Indeed, he is the most singular man I ever knew."

"That is the case with all pirates," said Mrs. Custis. "Something in the female nature attracts us to lawless men who take what they want —ourselves included. We were, I suppose, originally just seized and are looking out for the appropriator to this day. But you, Vesta, with the Baltimore blood in you, do not expect to play the Sabine bride tamely—to defend your spoiler and reconcile him to your brethren."

"I was thinking it was the Baltimore blood that made me appreciate Mr. Milburn, Mamma. The Custises were not traders."

"Pshaw, the Custises were libertines, unless history belies them. They had else no popularity in the scamp court of Charley-over-the-water. He thought the daughter of any gentleman in his following was made for his mistress, and a large percentage of the said damsels thought he was right."

"Mr. Milburn is no Cavalier; I can see that," Vesta said. "I am attracted to him by elements of such strength and simplicity that I fancy he is a Puritan."

"Puritan, fiddlestick!" Mrs. Custis said, putting the check in her bosom and pinning it there, and looking vigilantly at the pin afterwards. "Do not idealize this forester as of any beginning whatsoever. It is all wrong. Thousands of convicts were exported to Chesapeake Bay from the slums of London, Bristol, Glasgow, and other places, and propagated here like the pokeweed. With instincts of larceny and possibly a little rebellion in it, your man has robbed this house of your person. If he should also take your heart, the shame would be upon us."

"Oh, Mother, you are unforgiving."

"Of course I am; I am Scotch."

"You have not one son-in-law but this who would give you back the large amount your husband has misspent—not one who could do it but at a sacrifice you would not permit. For you and Papa to restore your faith in each other, I married our creditor, forcing him to the altar rather than he me, and he has already proved himself of more delicacy than you, if I am to believe you are in your right mind. No, I am no McLane."

"You are not if you do not use their Scotch-Irish perseverance to get the better of Meshach Milburn. You have obtained a marriage settlement with him; now have it confirmed and sue out your divorce before the legislature, publicly, as you have been profaned. Ask the State of Maryland for reparation. The McLanes and the Custises and their connections from the Christine River to the James will storm Annapolis, make your cause, if necessary, a political issue, and the courts will give you damages out of this beast's unpopular wealth."

Vesta looked at her mother with astonishment.

"What would become of my self-respect, my maiden name, if I made that show of my private grieving, mother?"

"You would be a heroine. Every old lover, of whom there are so many eligible ones, would feel his zeal return. A romance would attend your name wherever the Baltimore newspapers are taken. You would be as great a heroine as Betty Patterson."

"That disobedient girl?" Vesta exclaimed, still in astonishment.

"I saw her when the bride of Jerome Bonaparte. She was not half as lovely as you. If Jerome had seen you—you were not born then, and I was in society—he would never have looked at Betty. She forced a settlement out of the emperor, husbanded the income of it, and she is richer and freer today than if she had become a French Bonaparte."

"Weak as they may be in many things, I am a Custis," Vesta said with pale scorn. "I would not drag my name through the tobacco-stained lobbies of Annapolis to wear the crown of Josephine. The word I gave to the man who is now my husband, in pity of my parents, I would not take back to my dying day, unless he first denied his word. I believe there is such a thing as honor yet, Mother. You fret my father by such principles."

"They are the principles of your uncle, Allan McLane."

"A man I shrink from," Vesta said, "although he is your brother. His unfeeling respectability, his unchangeableness, his want of every impulse but hate, his appropriation of our family honor—as if he was our law giver and high sheriff, his secretiveness, formal religion, and mysterious prosperity I do not appreciate, much as I have tried to be charitable to him. I do not like Baltimore as I do the Eastern Shore. It is fierce, hard, and suspicious."

"You shall not run down Baltimore before me," Mrs. Custis cried hotly. "It is a paradise to this region, and comparing Meshach Milburn to your uncle is blasphemy."

"I have on my finger, Mother, his mother's ring."

"A pretty object it is," said Mrs. Custis, taking a peep at it and another at her check. "It requires a microscope to find it. Next you will be walking through Baltimore on your bridal tour, followed by a mob of small boys to see Meshach's old hat. Then I shall feel for you, Vesta."

The cruel blow struck home. Vesta's reception, so unexpected, so acrimonious, affected her with a sense of gross ingratitude and with a greater disappointment—she had failed to restore joy to her parents by her desperate sacrifice.

She began to feel that she might have done wrong. Looking back upon the broad sight of her act from this momentary revulsion seemed a frightful flood, like the mouth of one of the little Eastern Shore rivers, that expands to a gulf in the progress of a brook. Last night she saw the misunderstandings and ruin she could prevent by her ready decision. Now she saw the misunderstandings she never could correct, the prejudices stronger than parental sympathy, the wide separation her marriage had effected between two classes of her duty—to think with her husband's affection and her mother's interests at the same time.

It also occurred to her that her father, the darling of her thought, had seemed slow to appreciate her marriage sacrifice and was testy at her willingness to loosen her heart towards her husband.

The whole day had passed with such relief, such satisfaction, that she expected to end it in the tranquillity of Teackle Hall like some young eagle returned to her nest with abundant prey for the old birds there, worn out with storm and time. In place of love and healing nature, Vesta had found worldliness, resentment, intrigue, and aspersion, concluding with a reference to the one object she feared and shrank from—the hat of dark entail, the shadow upon her future life. Her eyes filled up. She lisped aloud, "I wish I had stayed with my husband."

"Has he become so necessary to you already?" asked Mrs. Custis.

"He does appreciate my sacrifice," Vesta said, and her low sobs filled the room. In a moment Virgie entered, alert to her playmate's pains, and threw her arms around her mistress and kissed her like a child.

"Oh, missy," she said to Mrs. Custis, "to make her cry after what she has done for all of us—to save your home, to save me from being sold."

No scruples of race made Vesta reject this sympathy, precious to her parched breast despite the quadroon taint, as the golden sand in the brooks of Africa give at once wealth and cooling. The slave girl's long white arms, scarcely less pale than ivory, drew Vesta into her lap and laid her head upon the fair maiden shoulder as if it was a babe's.

On such a shoulder, only a shadow darker, Vesta had often lain in infancy and sucked the milk that was sweet as Eve's—the common fount of white and black—at the breast of Virgie's mother. That faithful nurse was gone—the wild plum grew upon her grave—but Virgie inherited the motherly instinct and added her sisterly sympathy. Her rich hair, half unbound, streamed down on Vesta's temples among the dark ringlets there, while she looked into her own spirit for a word to check those tears and found it:

"The Lord knows you did right. Don't let anybody make you lose your faith till your master, your husband, does wrong to you. He wouldn't like to have you cry."

There was a nervous chord in the slave's throat that trembled on the key of the heroic, and her nostrils, slightly rounded, her head free of carriage as the wild colt's, and a light from her soft eyes that seemed to be reflected on their long silken lashes, bore out a spirit tamed by servitude, which still could kindle to everything that concerned woman in her birthright.

Vesta kissed Virgie and ceased to sob. She rose and kissed her mother also.

"It was very wrong in me to say what I did not wish to say about Uncle Allan, Mamma. I hope Papa was kind to you today."

"Dear me!" Mrs. Custis cried, "everything is turned upside down by that bog iron ore. A new element has come into the family to disturb it. Nobody believes anything respectable any more. Your father is an infidel or a radical or something perverse. You are defending those wild foresters. What will become of the Christian religion and society and good principles?"

"What did Papa say before he left home?"

"He acted in the strangest manner, Vesta. He came right in and kissed me like a great booby and sat down and wanted to talk about our courting days. I thought at first he was drunk again or that the Methodists had got hold of him and fed him on camp meeting straw. How do you account for it?"

Virgie had slipped out as soon as the talk became confidential.

"He wants to do better, dear Mamma. Do respond to his contrition and affection. If we could all humble our hearts, it would be so easy to start life better and turn this accident to joy and comfort. I have found new engagements and relieves already. There is a young girl, Mr. Milburn's niece, whom I shall bring home this evening and occupy myself teaching her. She is an orphan, without a mother's knowledge, barely able to read, but pretty and quaint."

"Bring a forester in here?" Mrs. Custis exclaimed, fairly shivering. "What will Allan McLane's daughters say? Your sister from Talbot has been here all this day, and you have scarcely given her an hour. Between this fatal marriage and your neglect, she left with her husband, positively pale with horror. I do not know what is to follow this marriage. I have posted a letter already to my brother Allan, telling him of your betrayal by your father and this bridegroom. All our connection will be up in arms."

Vesta's heart sank again, but she felt no fears of her husband's ability to meet mere family opposition, secured by law and form in his rights. She feared only that hostility might rouse severity and defiance in him, which would neutralize her present influence upon him and change his accommodating, almost gentle disposition as a husband.

Blacker than any object in her path, she saw a trivial thing like a wild boar closing her hitherto adventurous excursion into the forest where her husband grew—the hat that had covered his head!

Her mother's thoughtless mention of that object made it formidable to her fears as some iron mask locked round her husband's countenance, making day hideous and the world a dungeon to all who must walk with him.

She discerned that if it should become the subject of family rancor, his combative spirit would start to the defense of his hat because no man forgives an insult to his personal appearance. This article of wear had ringed his brain with gangrene, and war made upon it would be met by war, while Vesta had expected to induce forgetfulness of the old tile, charm away the remembrance of it, and have it laid forever aside.

"I am not the daughter of Uncle McLane," Vesta protested. "I am, besides, a woman free of my minority. Mr. Milburn is hardly the man to submit to any trespass. I warn you, Mamma, to put my uncle at no disadvantage. My husband has already beaten Papa, and he will smile at your brother when he knows that I do not support any of his pretensions."

"The first thing," answered Mrs. Custis stubbornly, "is to see that he pays this check. Oh, my dear money!" She pressed it to her heart. "How delightful it is to see you again. Science, love, glory, ideas—how vulgar they are without money. With this check paid, I think I shall never read a book again, and as for the bog ores, why, I shall scream if there is an iron article in the house. This house, I believe, is yours now, Vesta. I had forgotten. Well, no wonder you defend the man who took your father's roof from over his head and gave it to you!"

"That is unkind, Mamma. I value it only as a sure home for you and Papa. If I gave it to him, it might be in risk again."

"But suppose you continue to defend this monster of a Milburn; he and you may require the whole house. I am too well bred to be converted to any of his impious ideas. I am a Baltimorean and stand by my colors."

"Let us speak of that no more," Vesta said, almost in despair, "but talk of dear Papa. I know he loves you."

"It is too late," Mrs. Custis remarked solemnly with another fondling of her check. "He has neglected me too long. I expect his attention and respect and that he shall behave himself, but no lovey and no honey for me now. Life has passed the noon and the early afternoon for him and me, and I live to be respectable, to appreciate my security, to keep upstarts at arm's length, to enjoy my life in its appointed circle, taking care of my income, and never—no, never—give any human being the opportunity to make me a beggar again."

"Oh, Mamma," Vesta said, "think of Judge Custis. Have you not made home cold to him by this formalism? We must study men and please them according to their tastes, else we are false to the companionship God gave us to man for. Therein lies our joy. Yield to your husband's boyish-heartedness. Fly with him like the mate by the bird. He has repented. Welcome him to your love again and stay his feet from truant going, or he may dash down the precipice of everlasting dissipation and the death of his noble soul."

Vesta stood above her mother, deeply moved, deeply earnest. Her mother stole another look at the bank check.

"Well, Daughter, I will be humbugged by him if you desire," she said, "but if I had my life to go over again, I would marry a businessman and let the aristocracy go. There is the second knock at the front door. I believe I will dress myself and go downstairs too."

There were two ladies in the parlor when Vesta went there— Grandmother Tilghman and the Widow Dennis.

"Good evening, Vesta," said the old lady, who was stone blind but easily knew Vesta's footstep. "William thought you would not go to evening service on account of Mr. Milburn's illness, so I came to sit till church is over. But what is that I hear in this parlor, like somebody sniffling?"

"It's me, Aunt Vesty," said the voice of Rhoda Holland from the background.

"This is Mr. Milburn's niece, who has come here to stay with me," Vesta said.

"Ah, then it is no Custis. The last sniffle I heard was at the ball to Lafayette in the spring of 1781. The marquis had marched from Head of Elk to the Bald Friars' Ferry on the Susquehanna and inland among the hills to Baltimore, and we gave him a ball, which, at his request, was turned into a clothing party. He snuffed so much that he kept up a sniffle all the evening, like. . . ."

Here Rhoda's sniffle was heard again.

"Yes, that's a good imitation," said Grandmother Tilghman, "but I don't like it."

"Did the gineral dance at the ball?" asked Rhoda. "What did he do with his swurd? Did he dance with it outen his scibburd?"

"He danced like a gentleman," Mrs. Tilghman replied, as if she would rather not have, "and led me out in the first set. You danced with him, Vesta, at the ball in '24, forty-three years afterwards. Does he sniffle yet?"

"I don't recollect, Grandaunt. I was a little girl and so much flattered that I thought everything he did was perfect."

"Ah me," exclaimed Mrs. Tilghman, putting the feather of her turban up and looking as much like an old belle as possible at eighty years. "You danced before Lafayette with my grandson Bill. Bill hardly remembers Lafayette at all, thinking of you that night, so wonderful in your girl's charms. I told him Vesta would never marry him, as he was too plain and poor, but I never thought you would marry that. . . ."

Here Rhoda sniffled warningly.

"Yes," exclaimed the old lady, catching the sniffle, "I never thought you would marry *that!* But Bill is as dear a fool as ever. He says now that Meshach Milburn is a good man, too. I never thought he was above a. . . ."

Rhoda sniffled earnestly.

"Precisely that," exclaimed the old lady. "That was my estimate of the stock. Bill says he is a financial genius. I don't see what is to become of girls in this generation. Here is Ellenora, too good to marry

Phoebus the sailor man, too poor to marry anybody else. Now, if Milburn had married her and taken her son Levin into his business, it would have been reasonable, but to take you and pervert your happiness almost makes me. . . ."

Sniffle from Rhoda.

"Yes," said the old lady snappishly, "almost! But I never did do it yet."

"Did you ever see Gineral Washin'ton, mem?" Rhoda asked. "I thought maybe you was old enough. Misc Somers, she see him up yer to Kint River a-crossin' to 'Napolis. He was a-swarin' at the cappen of the piriauger an' a-dammin' of the Eas'n Shu. He said they wan't no good rudes in Marylan' nohow, that the Wes'n Shu was all red mud an' the Eas'n Shu yaller mud, an' the bay was jus' pizen. Misc Somers say she don't think it was Gineral Washin'ton caze he cuss so. She goin' to find out when she kin git a book an' somebody to read outen it to her, caze she dreffle smart."

"Grandaunt Tilghman," Vesta interposed to the blank silence of the room, "knew General Washington intimately."

"Do tell us!" cried Rhoda. "You kin be a right interestin' ole woman, I reckon, ef you air so quar."

In the midst of a smile, in which the blind old lady herself joined, and during which Mrs. Custis entered the room, Mrs. Tilghman offered the following story:

"Several years before the Revolution I went to visit Cousin Martha Washington at Mount Vernon. I had seen her while she was the widow of Cousin Custis, and we occasionally corresponded. In those days we visited by vessel, so a schooner of Robert Morris's father set me ashore at Mount Vernon. Colonel Washington was then forty years old and having his first portrait painted by Wilson Peale. Washington and Peale used to pitch the bar, play quoits, and fox hunt, while Cousin Martha, who was only three months younger than the colonel, knitted and cut out sewing for her colored girls, and listened to her daughter play the harpsichord. Poor Martha had the consumption. Washington often carried her along the piazza and into the beautiful woodlands near the house, but she died, leaving him all her money—nearly twenty thousand dollars. We Custises rather looked down on Colonel Washington in those days. He was not of the old gentry. His poor mother could barely read and write, and once, when we went to Fredericksburg to see her, she was riding as her own overseer out in the field among her few Negroes, wearing an old sunbonnet and sunburned like a forester."

"Dear me," exclaimed Mrs. Custis, "I should think she was a great impediment to Washington."

"I reckon that's the way her son got big," exclaimed Rhoda. "If his mar had laid in bed all day, he couldn't have killed King George so easy with his swurd."

"I often said to Cousin Martha, 'What did you see in this big horse of a man?'

"'He's the best overseer in Virginia,' she replied. 'He looks after my property as no other man could.'"

"Then," said Mrs. Custis emphatically, "he was one man out of a thousand."

"That's the kind of man you married, Vesta," said Mrs. Dennis.

"*Her* husband," said Mrs. Custis, "looked after her father's property, I am sure, for he got it all."

"And returned it all," exclaimed Vesta.

Mrs. Custis then remarked that Washington certainly was a blue-blooded man.

"Is thar people with blue blood come outen 'em?" Rhoda asked. "Lord sikes! I should think it would make 'em cold."

"I wonder if men are ever great," Vesta mused, "or whether it is not great occasion and trial that project them. A crisis comes in our lives, and finding what we can endure, we incur greater risks, and finally delight in such adventure."

"That is the way with my poor boy, Levin," said Mrs. Dennis quietly.

She was a pretty woman, somewhat past thirty, with rosy cheeks, blue eyes, neat but rather poor attire, and a simple, artless manner. She might have passed for the sister of her son.

"Is Levin coming for you tonight?" Vesta asked.

"No," the widow blushed, "James Phoebus will see me home. Levin has gone off in his boat, and I have been worried about him all day. Sometime, I am afraid, he will go and never return. Oh, Cousin Vesta, this waiting for a husband neither alive nor dead is very trying."

"Norah," Mrs. Custis remarked, "you ought to be ashamed to keep that faithful fellow waiting for you, when you could give yourself a good husband and reward him so easily."

"I think you had better look out for old age," Mrs. Tilghman added, "while you have youth and good looks to obtain the provision. Oden

Dennis is probably dead. If not dead, he does not mean to return, for I can think of no circumstances in this age which would forcibly detain a man from his wife for fifteen years. Even if he was in a prison, he would be allowed to write to you. He may not be dead, Norah, but he is not coming back. Get a father for your son. You cannot manage Levin."

"Maybe he has been stoled by the Injins," exclaimed Rhoda with great fervor. "Thar was a Injin captive in a shew at Nuark that had been kept nineteen years. He forgot his language an' whooped dreffle. But Misc Somers say he was an imploster an' worked on the brekwater up to Lewistown. She's always lookin' behin' the shew to find out somethin'," Rhoda added.

"Do get that girl a handkerchief and show her how to use it," exclaimed Mrs. Tilghman. "I have been a widow for thirty years and never gave up the expectation of marrying again till I lost my eyesight. And even after that, at sixty-five, I had an offer of marriage. But I said to my gallant old beau, 'I will not take a man I cannot compliment by seeing him and admiring him every day. I love you, but my blindness would give you too much pain.' In our quiet towns all the life worth living is domestic joy. Do not lose it, Ellenora. Do not put it off too long."

"I could love Mr. Phoebus," the widow said, "if I could persuade myself that Oden is dead, but that I cannot do. A person—spirit or man—is watching over me closely. The very shoes I wear tonight came from that mysterious agent. It is not my son nor James Phoebus, and no stranger would so secretly assist me. I am bound up in the fear and wonder that it is my husband."

"That does beat conjecture," said Mrs. Tilghman. "Have you no friend you might suspect?"

"None," the widow answered, "who have not worn out their means of giving long ago. Can I marry with this ghostly visitation coming so regularly? Should I not have faith in a husband's living if I receive a wife's care from an unseen hand?"

"Oden Dennis," Mrs. Tilghman remarked, "was hardly a man to do charity and not be seen. He was rather self-indulgent, demonstrative, and restless. I cannot think of his nocturnal visits in the body. Besides, he would not supply you in that way, Norah, if he meant to come back. And if he cannot himself come to you, neither could he send."

Not relishing Mrs. Tilghman's reproof, Rhoda spoke up, saying, "Lord sakes, all the women has to talk about when they is gone is the men. When the men comes, they talks as if they never missed of 'em.

Misc Somers, she never had no man, an' she talks mos' about the women that has got one. I think Aunt Vesty has got the best man in Princess Anne. He's the richest; he's the freest; he never courted no other gal; an' he ain't got no quar old women runnin' of him down."

"I begin to think my fortune is better than I deserve," Vesta replied, as wine and cake were brought in. "Now, dear friends, as I am Mr. Milburn's wife, let us all be Christians this Sunday night and drink his health and happy recovery, and that he may never repent his marriage."

They drank with some hesitation, except the bride, Rhoda, and Mrs. Dennis. Mrs. Tilghman needed the wine too much to wait long, and Mrs. Custis, finding she was observed, took a sip from her glass also, excusing herself from drinking heartily on the ground of a recent headache.

As the conversation proceeded, now by general participation, again by couples apart, Vesta found herself more and more a subject of sympathy with no little curiosity interwoven. She also imagined that an undertone of belief was abroad that she had made a mercenary marriage.

Mrs. Tilghman, a most caustic belle in her prime and worldly as three marriages, all shrewdly contracted, could make her, seemed determined to hold that Vesta had rejected her grandson for the money lender on the consideration of wealth. Vesta's own mother, who should have known her well, had twice hinted the same. Even the inoffensive Ellenora had accepted the idea, or one kin to it, and Rhoda Holland had remembered that her uncle was the richest of bridegrooms in Princess Anne.

Vesta felt the injustice but said to herself, "I must make the sacrifice complete and incur any harsh judgment it may bear. I see that I shall be driven for sympathy to the last place in the world I anticipated—to my husband's heart. Yes, there is something besides love in marriage. If I cannot love him, he can understand me."

Vesta had come to a place where all arrive who volunteer an act of great sacrifice—to have it put upon a low motive by many otherwise kind people. We give our money to an institution of charity, and some say that it was for notoriety or self-seeking or at the expense of our kin. We lead a forlorn hope in politics or some other arena to establish a cause or assist a principle, and we are said to be jealous or malignant. Perhaps we make a book to illustrate some old region off the highways of observation, drawn to it by kindred strings or early patterings, and the politician there regards it as an attack, the old family fossil as an intrusion, the youth as if it were a gratuitous thing from such an outer source. So we wince a little, but feel that it was necessary to be misunderstood to complete the sacrifice.

The feeling of despondency increased after the little company separated, and Vesta went to her room and laid herself upon her still maiden bed. She had said her prayer and asked the approval of God, but her nervous system, under the tension of almost two days' excitement, was alert and could not fall to slumber. Old passages of Testament haunted her soul: "Thy desire shall be to thy husband, and he shall rule over thee. A man shall leave his father and his mother and shall cleave unto his wife." She began to see that marriage was not merely the solution of a family trouble and the giving of her body as a hostage for a pecuniary debt, but that it was a rendition of all her liberty, even the liberty of sympathy and of sorrow, to the man to whom she must cleave.

In marrying him, she had left her father and mother at a greater distance than she ever dreamed, and they resented the desertion to the degree that they now confounded her with her new interest, let go their claim upon her, and could scarce conceive of her except in the dual relation of a woman subject to her husband and selfish as himself.

"I wonder if he will grow weary of me, too," she thought with anguish, "after his possession is established and I shall have no other source of confidence? What did I know of this world only yesterday? Every way seemed clear and open for me then, my friends abundant and love profuse. Today, I am in awful doubts, yet I must not lose my will and drift with every passing fear and confusion into the fickleness which makes woman contemptible after she has given her hand. I will never give up two persons—my father and my husband!"

As she turned down the lamp, it being nearly midnight, a short, fierce cry, quickly stifled, seized on her ears and chilled her blood, as if some wild animal had howled once in nightmare and fallen asleep again. Vesta started up in bed and listened. She seemed to hear footsteps, but they passed away, and she listened in vain for other sounds till sleep fell deep and dreamless upon her.

Long Separations

Chapter 21

Vesta was awakened by her mother and Roxy and Virgie, together exclaiming something unintelligible. It was late morning, the whole family having slept long after the experiences of the past two days, and the sun was shining through the great trees before Teackle Hall and burnishing the windows so that Vesta could hardly see.

"The kitchen servants have run away," Mrs. Custis shrieked, after Vesta's request that her mother alone should talk. "Old Hominy is gone, and she has taken all her herbs and witcheries with her, and Ned and Vince and little Phillis, too."

"I heard a strange cry last night as I dropped to sleep," Vesta exclaimed, rubbing her eyes.

"Dear missy," cried Virgie, falling upon the pillow, "it was your poor dog, Turk. His throat has been cut."

"Yes, missy," Roxy blubbered, "poor Turk lies in his blood upon the lawn. There is nobody to get breakfast but Virgie and me. Indeed, we did not know about it."

"That is not very likely," said the suspicious Mrs. Custis.

"I know you did not, girls," Vesta said. "You have too much intelligence and principle. Nor could Hominy have been so inhuman to my poor dog. The first thing to be done is to have breakfast. Roxy, go at once to Mr. Milburn's and bring his man Samson here, and awake Miss Holland to take Samson's place by her uncle. Tell Samson to make the fire, and you and he get the breakfast. No person is to speak of this incident of the servants leaving us on any pretense."

"Won't you give the alarm the first thing?" cried Mrs. Custis, not very well pleased to see Vesta keep her temper. "They may be overtaken before they get far away. Those four Negroes are worth twelve hundred dollars!"

"They are not worth one dollar, Mamma, if they have run away from us, because I should never either sell them or keep them again if they had behaved so treacherously."

"I say sell them and get the money," Mrs. Custis cried. "Are they not ours?"

"No, Mamma, they are mine. Mr. Milburn and Papa are to be consulted before any steps are taken. Papa deeded them to me only last Saturday. Why should they have deserted at the moment I had redeemed them? Virgie, can you guess?"

Virgie hesitated only a moment.

"Miss Vesty, I think I can see what made Hominy go. She was afraid of Meshach Milburn and his queer hat. She believed the devil give it to him. She thought he had bought her by marrying you and was going to christen her to the bad man or do something dreadful with her and the little children."

"That's it, Miss Vessy," Roxy added. "Hominy loved the little children dearly. She thought they was to become Meshach's and she must save them."

"Poor, superstitious creature," Vesta exclaimed.

"More misery brought about by that fool's hat!" cried Mrs. Custis. "If I ever lay hands on it, it shall end in the fire."

"No wonder," Vesta said, "that this poor, ignorant woman should do herself such an injury on account of an article of dress that even disturbs liberal and enlightened minds. Now I recollect that Hominy said something about having 'got Quaker.' What did it mean?"

The two slave girls looked at each other significantly, and Virgie answered, "Don't the Quakers help slaves to get off to a free state? Maybe she meant that."

"Do you suppose the abolitionists would tamper with a poor old woman like that, whose liberty would neither be a credit to them nor a comfort to her? I cannot think so meanly of them," Vesta reflected. "Besides, could she have killed my dog?"

"A gross, ignorant, fetish-worshipping Negro would kill a dog or a child or anything when she is possessed with a devil," Mrs. Custis insisted.

"I don't believe she killed Turk," Roxy remarked, as she left the room. "There was a white man in the kitchen last Saturday night. I think he slept there. Master gave him leave."

"Yes, missy," Virgie continued, after Roxy had gone to obey her orders. "He was a dreadful man and looked at me so coarse and familiar that I have dreamed of him since. It was the man Mr. Milburn knocked down for mashing his hat. He was afraid Mr. Milburn would throw him into jail, so he asked master to hide in the kitchen. But Hominy was almost crazy with fear of Mr. Milburn before that."

Vesta held up her arms with a look of despair. "What has not that poor old hat brought upon everybody?" she cried. "Oh, who dares to contest the sunshine with the tailor and hatter? They are the despots that never will abdicate or die."

"The idea of your father letting a tramp like that sleep in the kitchen among the slaves!" cried Mrs. Custis. "What obligation had he incurred there, too? Teackle Hall has become a cave of owls and foxes. It is time for me to leave it. Here is my husband, gone, riding fifty miles for his worst enemy, leaving us without a cook or a man's assistance. I know what I shall do. I will start this day for Cambridge to meet my brother and visit the Goldsboroughs there till some order is brought out of this attempt to plant wheat and tares together."

Vesta stopped a moment and kissed her mother. "That is just the thing, dear Mother," she said. "Let me straighten out the difficulties here. Go, and come back when all is done and you can be yourself again."

"I shall do it, Vesta. Brother Allan gets to Cambridge tomorrow afternoon. I will go as far as Salisbury this day and either meet him on the road tomorrow or find him at Cambridge. Oh, what a house is Teackle Hall—full of male and female foresters, abolitionists, runaways, and radicals, all made crazy by the bog ores and that fool's hat!"

Descending to the yard, Vesta found Turk lying in his blood, his jaws and shaggy sides clotted red, and the howl in which he died, as it seemed, still lingering in the air. The Virginia spirit rose in Vesta's eyes. "Whoever killed this dog only wanted the courage to kill men," she exclaimed. "James Phoebus, look here."

The pungy captain had already been abroad for hours, and the masts of his vessel were just visible across the marshy neck in the rear of Teackle Hall. He touched his hat and came in.

Long Separations 191

"Early mornin', Miss Vesty. Hallo! Turk dead? By smoke, yer's pangymonum!"

Coming from the kitchen, Samson Hat remarked, "He's stabbed, Jimmy. See whar de dagger struck him right over de heart. Dat made him howl an' fall dead. His froat weren't cut dat sudden. It's gashed as if wid somethin' blunt."

"Right you are, nigger. The throat cuttin' was make believe; the stab will tell the tale. But who's this yer, lurkin' aroun' the kitchen do'? If it ain't Jack Wonnell, I hope I may die. Sic!"

With this, Jimmy rushed on Jack Wonnell, chased him to the fence, and brought him back by the neck. Wonnell wore a bell-crown, and his hand was full of fall blossoms. As he observed the dead dog, Roxy came out of the kitchen and stood blushing, yet frightened to see him.

"What yo' doin' with them rosy-posies?" Jimmy demanded. "Who're they fur? What air you sneakin' aroun' Teackle Hall fur so bright of a mornin', lazy as I know you is, Jack Wonnell?"

"They are flowers he brings every morning for me," Roxy spoke up, coming forward with a pretty simper.

"For you?" exclaimed Vesta. "You are not receiving the attentions of white men, Roxy?"

"He offered to get flowers for me, so I might give you as pretty ones as Virgie, missy. I let him bring them. He's a poor, kind man."

"I jess got 'em, Jimmy," Jack Wonnell interjected with his peculiar wink and leer, "caze Roxy's the belle of Prencess Anne, an' I'm the bell-crown. She's my little queen, an' I ain't ashamed of her."

"Courtin' niggers, air you!" Jimmy exclaimed, collaring Jack again. "Now whar did you go all day Sunday with Levin Dennis an' the nigger buyer? What hokey-pokey wair you up to?"

"Mr. Wonnell," Roxy had the presence of mind to say, "take care you tell the truth for my sake. Aunt Hominy is gone with the kitchen children, and Mr. Phoebus suspects you."

"Great lightnin' bugs!" Jimmy Phoebus cried. "The niggers stole an' the dog dead, too?"

"I 'spect Jedge Custis sold 'em," Jack pleaded, twisting out of the bay captain's hands. "He's gwyn to be sold out by Meshach Milburn. Maybe he jess sold 'em an' skipped."

"Where is Judge Custis, Miss Vesty?" Phoebus asked.

"He has gone to Delaware, to be absent several days."

"Is it true what this bell-crowned fool says, Miss Vesty?"

"No. There was some fear among the kitchen servants of being sold, but there was no such necessity when they ran away, as it had been settled."

"It's unfortunate that your father's gone. He has been seen with a Negro trader, an' that trader an' he disappear the same evenin'. The trader lives about Delaware, too, Miss Vesty."

Vesta's countenance fell as she thought of the suspicion that might attach to her father.

"Who told you, Jack Wonnell," asked the bay sailor, "that Judge Custis was to be sold out?"

"I won't tell you, Jimmy."

"I told him," Roxy cried after an instant's hesitation, while Jimmy Phoebus was grinding the stiff bell-crown hat down on Wonnell's suffocating muzzle. "I did think we was all going to be sold and had nobody to pity me but that poor white man. I told him as a friend."

"An' I never told nobody in the world but Levin Dennis yesterday," Jack cried out, when he was able to get his breath.

"Whar did you go, Jack, wid the long man an' Levin all day yisterday?" Samson asked.

"Yes, whar was you?" Jimmy Phoebus shouted in one of his Greek fits of temper, his dark skin and black-cherry eyes flaming volcanic. "Whar did you leave Ellenora's boy an' that infernal soul buyer? Speak, or I'll throttle you like this dog!"

"You let him alone, sir!" little Roxy cried hotly. "He won't deceive anybody. He's going to tell all he knows."

"Let go, Jimmy," Samson said. "Don't you see Miss Vesty heah?"

"Don't scare the man, Mr. Phoebus," Vesta added. "But I command him to tell all that he knows, or Papa shall commit him to jail."

Wonnell took his place some steps from Phoebus, wiped his eyes on his sleeve, and whimpered for a few minutes to Roxy's great agitation. "I'm sorry, Jimmy, you accused me before this beautiful lady an' my purty leetle Roxy—bless her soul—of stealin' Jedge Custis's niggers. Thair's on'y one I ever looked sheep's eyes at, an' she's a-standin' here listenin' to every true word I says. I'm pore trash, an' I reckon the jail's as good as the porehouse, fur it's in town, an' Roxy kin come an' look at me every day through the bars."

Roxy was so much affected that she threw her apron up to her face, and Vesta and Phoebus had to smile. Samson, looking indulgently on, exclaimed, "Dar's love all froo de woods. Doves an' crows can't help it. It's deeper down dan fedders an' claws."

"That nigger trader," continued Jack Wonnell, bell-crown in hand, "hired me an' Levin to take him a-tarrapinin'. He had a bag of gold that big (measuring with his hand in the crown of the hat). He give Levin some of it, an' I took it to Levin's mother las' night an' told her Levin wouldn't be back fur a week, maybe. I thought Mr. Johnson was gwyn to give me some gold, too, so I could buy Roxy, but yer's all he give me. Everybody disappints me, Jimmy."

Jack Wonnell showed an old silver fi'penny bit, and his countenance was so lugubrious that the sailor exclaimed, "Jack, he paid you too well for all the sense you got. Now whar has Levin gone with the *Ellenora Dennis?*"

"I don't know, Jimmy. Johnson sailed her up to the landin' down yer below town, while Levin was sleepin'. Levin told me he was goin' off with the nigger trader to git some of his money fur mother.'"

"Poor miserable boy," Phoebus exclaimed, "he's led off easy as his pore daddy. The man he's gone with, Miss Vesty, is black as hell. Joe Johnson is known to every thief on the bay an' every Gypsy on the shore. He steals free niggers when he can't buy slave ones outen Delaware. He sometimes runs away Maryland slaves to oblige their hypocritical masters that can't sell 'em publicly, an' Johnson an' the bereaved owner divides the price. Go in the house, yaller gal," Jimmy Phoebus said to Roxy. "Jack Wonnell, you go too; I'm done with you! You needn't go, Samson; I know you're true as steel."

"I must git de breakfast, Jimmy," the Negro said, going in.

"Now, Miss Vesty, Joe Johnson has got old Hominy an' the little niggers, by smoke. That part of this hokey-pokey is purty sure. Did he steal 'em an' decoy 'em, or wair they sold to him by Judge Custis or Meshach Milburn?"

"By neither, I will risk my life," replied Vesta. "Mr. Milburn was taken to his bed Saturday evening, and on Sunday father went to Delaware on legal business for my husband."

"That is Meshach Milburn, I hear," the bay sailor remarked with a penetrating look. "Shall I go an' see him on this nigger business?"

"No," Vesta replied, "he is too sick, and it is a delicate subject to name to him. Virgie and Roxy think old Hominy ran away from a superstitious fear she had of Mr. Milburn."

"Yes, by smoke, every nigger in town, big an' little, is afraid of Milburn's hat."

"He has no ownership in those servants, nor has my father now. I will tell you, James—relying on your prudence—that Hominy belonged to me, as did those three children, having passed from my father to my husband and thence to me and back to my father, and from him to me again in the very hour of my marriage. I fear they have been persuaded away to be abused and sold out of Maryland."

Jimmy Phoebus looked up at the sighing trees and over the wide facade of Teackle Hall and exclaimed, "By smoke!" several times before making his conclusions. "Miss Vesty," he finally said, "send for your father to come home immediately. People will not understand how Joe Johnson, outlaw as he is, dared to rob a judge of his house servants unless they had some understanding. Your sudden marriage an' your pappy's embarrassments will be put together, by smoke, an' thar's some blunt enough to say that when Jedge Custis is hard up, he'll git money anyhow."

The charge, made with an honest man's want of skill, battered down all explanations.

"I confess it," said Vesta. "Papa's going away on Sunday and these people disappearing on Sunday night might excite idle comment. It might be said that he endeavored to sell some of his property before his creditor could seize it."

"I have seen you about yer since you was a baby, Vesty, an' Ellenora says you're better game an' heart than these 'ristocrats, fur who I never keered. That's why I take the liberty of callin' you Vesty. Now, let me tell you about your niggers. If they was a-gwyn to freedom in a white man's keer, I wouldn't stop 'em to be cap'n of a man-of-war. But Joe Johnson, supposin' that he's got of 'em, is a demon. Do you see the stab on that dog? Well, it's done with one of the bagnet pistols them kidnappers carries—hoss pistols with a spring dagger on the muzzle. When they come to close quarters, they stab with 'em. Joe Johnson killed your dog; I know his marks. He sails this whole bay, an' maybe he's run them niggers to Washin'ton or to Norfolk an' sold 'em south. If he has, with the wind an' start he's got an' your pappy's influence lost to us by his absence, it ain' no use to foller him to either of them places. But thar is one chance to overhaul the thief."

"What is that, James?" asked Vesta earnestly. "I do want to save those poor people from the abuse of a man who could kill my poor, fond dog."

"Joe Johnson keeps a hell trap—a reg'lar Pangymonum—up near

the head of Nanticoke River. It's the headquarters of his band, an' a black bunch they air. He has had good wind to get him out of Manokin last night an' into the sound, but he must beat up the Nanticoke all day. If that's his destination, we kin head him off by land an' make him show his cargo before he gits to Vienna. Then, with a messenger to follow Jedge Custis an' turn him back, we can swear these niggers on Johnson. We can't make no such oath till we git the evidence. An' then, by smoke, we'll bring ole Hominy an' the chillen back to Teackle Hall."

"Here is one you love to serve, James," said Vesta, as the Widow Dennis came in the gate.

"I came to meet you at the landing, James," said the blue-eyed, sweet-voiced widow with the timid step and ready blush. "Levin is gone for a week with a Negro trader. He sends me so much money I fear he is under an unusual temptation, and Wonnell says the trader is giving him liquor. What shall I do?"

"Make me his father, Ellenory. That'll give me an interest over him, an' you will command me. Levin kin make a fool of me if I chase him now, an' I can't measure money with a nigger trader, by smoke."

"Oh, James," the widow said, "you know my heart would be yours if I could control it. When my way is clear, you will have but to ask. Do go and find Levin."

"Norah, we suspect the same trader of having taken Hominy and the kitchen children in Levin's boat."

The widow listened to Vesta and burst into tears. "He will be accessory to the crime," she sobbed. "This is what I have ever feared. James Phoebus, you have always had the best influence over Levin. If you love me, arrest him before the law takes cognizance of this wild deed. Where has he gone?"

Virgie appeared on the lawn to say that Mrs. Custis wanted to know who should drive her as far as Salisbury, where she could get a slave of her son-in-law to continue on with her to Cambridge.

"I have been thinking all the morning where I can find a reliable man to bring back Papa," Vesta answered. "There are a few slaves at the furnace, but time is precious."

"Here is Samson," Virgie said, "and he has a mule he rides all over the county. Let him go."

"Go whar, my love?" asked Samson.

"To Dover, in Delaware," Vesta answered. "You can ride to Laurel by dark, Samson, and get to Dover tomorrow afternoon."

"An' I can ride with him as far as Salisbury," Jimmy Phoebus said, "an' get out to the Nanticoke some way, fur I see Ellenora will cry till I go."

"You can do better than that, James," Vesta said, thinking rapidly. "Samson can take you to Spring Hill Church or Barren Creek Springs by a little deviation, and at the springs you will be only three miles from the Nanticoke. Even Mamma might go on with the carriage to-night as far as the springs or to Vienna."

"If two are going," Virgie exclaimed, "one can drive Missy Custis and the other ride the mule."

Samson shook his head. "Dey say a free nigger gits cotched up in dat ar Delawaw state. Merrylin's good enough fur me. I likes de Merrylin light gals de best," looking at Virgie.

"Go now, Samson, to oblige Miss Vesty," Virgie said, "and I'll try to love you a little, black and bad as you are.'

"I'se 'fraid of Delawaw," Samson repeated. "Joe Johnson, dat I put dat head on, will git me whar he lives if I go dar, mebbe."

"No," Phoebus said, "I'll be lookin' after him on the banks of the Nanticoke, Samson, while you keep in the high road from Laurel to Georgetown an' on to Dover. Joe Johnson's been whipped at the post an' banished from Delaware for life. He dussn't go thar no more."

"If you are a free man," Virgie exclaimed, her slight figure expanding, "are you afraid to go into a freer state than Maryland? If I was free, I would want to go to the freest state of all. Behave like a free man, Samson Hat, or what is freedom worth to you?"

"It's wuth so much, pretty gal, dat I don't want to be a-losin' of it, 'cept to my wife when she'll hab me."

Samson watched the quadroon's delicate features, her skin almost paler than her young mistress's, her figure like the dove's after a hard winter—the more active though a little meager, her head small, and its tresses soft as the blackbird's plumage. The loyalty for her mistress, that lay in her large eyes like strong passion, turned to pride and nearly scorn when she listened to him.

"A slave, Miss Vesty says, is not one that's owned half as much as one that sells himself to hard drink or to selfishness or fear. You're not a free man, Samson, if you're afraid like these low slave Negroes who dare nothing if they can only get a little pleasure. All that can make a black man white in my eyes is a white man's enterprise."

As she often had before, Vesta felt the capable soul of her servant and did not resent her spirit as unbecoming a slave. Rather, she felt responsive chords in her own nature, as if Virgie was the more imperious of the two. Coming now into full womanhood, her character unrestrained by anyone in Teackle Hall, Virgie was her young mistress's shield bearer, like David to the princely Jonathan.

"Virgie," Samson answered with humility, "I never meant not to go, lady gal, after marster's wife asked me. I only wanted you to beg me hard, an' mebbe I'd git a kiss befo' I started."

"Wait till you come back and see if you do your errand well," replied Virgie. "I shall not kiss you now."

"I will," Roxy cried to the amusement of all, giving Samson a hearty smack from her little pouting mouth. "And now that you've got it, think it's Virgie's kiss and get your breakfast and start!"

As they went to their abodes to make ready, Jimmy Phoebus found Jack Wonnell playing marbles with the boys at the courthouse corner. "Jack," he said, "I'm a-going to find Levin an' that nigger trader. I may git in a peck of trouble up yonder on the Nanticoke. Tell all the pungy men whair I'm a-goin' an' what fur."

"Can't I give you one o' my bell-crowns, Jimmy? Thair's plenty of 'em left."

"Take my advice, Jack, an' tie a stone to all them hats an' sink 'em in the Manokin. Pore an' foolish as you air, maybe your ole bell-crowns will ruin you."

The road to Salisbury—laid out in 1667, when Cecil, Lord of Maryland and Avalon, erected a county "in honor of our dear sister, Lady Mary Somerset"—followed the beaver dams across the river heads, pierced the flat pine woods and open farms, and passed through two little hamlets before our travelers saw the broad millponds and poplar and mulberry lined streets of the most active town—albeit without a courthouse—in the lower peninsula.

The little party descended into the hollow of Salisbury at the dinner hour and stopped at the hotel. The snore of gristmills, the rasp of mill saws, the flow of pine-colored breast water into the gorge of the village, the cypress trees impudently intruding into the obliquely radiating streets, the humidity of ivy and creeper over many of the old, gable-chimneyed houses, the long lumber yards reflecting in the swampy harbor among the canoes, pungies, and sharpies moored there, the small houses sidewise to the sandy streets, the larger ones rising up the sandy hills, the old boxbush in the silvery gardens, the bridges close together, and the smell of tar and sawdust pleasantly inhaled upon the lungs made a combination like a caravan around some pool in the desert of the Nile.

"If there is any chance to catch my Negroes," Mrs. Custis said, "I will go right on after dinner. Samson, send my daughter's boy Dave to me immediately. He is working in this hotel."

Samson found Dave to be none other than the black class leader he had failed to overcome at the beginning of our narrative, but changes were visible in that individual which Samson had not expected. From having a clean, godly, modest countenance, Dave now wore a sour, evil look. His eyes were bloodshot, and his straight, manly shoulders and chest, which had once exacted Samson's admiration and envy, were stooped to conform with a continual cough from deep within his frame.

"Dave," said Samson, "your missis's modder wants you, boy, to drive her to Vienny. What ails you, Dave, sence I larned you to box?"

"Is you de man?" Dave exclaimed hoarsely. "May de Lord forgive you, den, fur I never kin. Dat lickin' I mos' give you made me a po', wicked, backslidin' fool."

"Why Dave, I jess saw you was a good man; I didn't mean you no harm, boy."

"You ruined me, free nigger," the huge slave said with a scowl, partly of revenge and partly remorse. "You set up my conceit dat I could box. I never struck a chile till dat day. After dat I went aroun' pickin' quarrels wid bigger niggers, an' low white men backed me to fight. I was turned out o' my church. I turned my back on de Lord. Whiskey tuk hold o' me. De debbil has entered into class leader Dave."

"Oh, brudder, wake up an' do better. Yer, I give you a dollar an' want to be your friend, Davy boy."

"I'll git drink wid it," Dave muttered, and as he passed out of the stable door, he looked back at Samson fiercely and exclaimed, "May Satan burn your body as he will burn my soul. I hate you, man, long as you live!"

Jimmy Phoebus remarked a few moments afterwards that Dave, dividing a pint of spirits with a lean little mulatto boy, put a piece of money in the boy's hands, who then rode rapidly out of the tavern yard upon a fleet Chincoteague pony.

At two o'clock they set forward again. Dave drove the carriage with Jimmy Phoebus beside him, while Samson easily kept alongside upon his old roan mule. As they ascended the plateau between the Wicomico and Nanticoke, the road became more sandy, and the carriage drew hard.

"If it's too late to keep on beyond Vienna tonight," said Mrs. Custis, "I will stop there with my friends, the Turpins, start again after coffee in the morning, and reach Cambridge for breakfast."

"I will turn off at Spring Hill," Samson said, "an' I kin feed my mule at sundown in Laurel an' go to sleep."

St. Paul's (Spring Hill) Episcopal Church

In an hour they came in sight of old Spring Hill Church at the source of a creek called Rewastico, a venerable relic of the colonial Established Church. Before they crossed the creek, Dave called, "Ho!" in such an unnecessarily loud voice that Mrs. Custis reproved him sharply. Dave jumped down from the seat and appeared to be examining some part of the breaching, though Samson assured him that it was all right. As Dave finished his examination, he raised both hands above his head twice and stretched to the height of his figure.

"Missy Custis," he apologized, "I's mighty tired dis a'ternoon. Dat stable keeps me up half de night."

"Liquor tires you more, David," Mrs. Custis spoke sharply, "and that tavern is no place to hire you to with your appetite for drink, as I shall tell your master."

At this moment, Jimmy Phoebus observed the little mulatto boy from the hotel come out of a swampy place in the road and exchange a look of intelligence with Dave, as he rode past on the pony.

"Boy," cried Samson, "is dat de road to Laurel?"

The boy made no answer, but, looking back once, timidly ground his heels into the pony's flank and darted into the brush towards Salisbury.

"Samson," said Dave, "you see dat ole woman in de cart yonder? I know her, an' she's gwyn right to Laurel. She lives dar. It's ten miles from dis yer turnoff, an' she knows all dese yer woods roads."

"Good-bye, den, an' may you find Aunt Hominy an de little chillen, Jimmy, an' bring dem all home to Prencess Anne," Samson cried, trotting his mule through the swamp and away.

Jimmy Phoebus saw him overtake the old woman in the cart and begin to speak with her, as the scrubby woods swallowed them in.

"What's dat he said 'bout Joe Johnson?" Dave asked, after they cleared the old church and entered the sandy pine woods.

Mrs. Custis spoke up more promptly than Jimmy Phoebus desired and told the Negro about the escape of Hominy and the children, and the hope of Mr. Phoebus to head the party off as they ascended the Nanticoke towards the Delaware state line.

"You don't want to git among Joe Johnson's men, boss," said the red-eyed Negro. "Dey bosses all dis country on boff sides o' de state line. All dat ain't in wid dem is afraid o' dem."

"How fur is it to Delaware, Dave?" asked Phoebus.

"We're right off de cornerstone o' Delawaw dis very minute. It's hardly a mile from whar we air."

Mason-Dixon Cornerstone

"Do you know Joe Johnson, Dave?"

"Yes, Marster Phoebus, you bet I does. He's at Salisbury; he's at Vienna; he's up yer to Crotcher's Ferry; he's all ober de country, but he don't go to Delawaw no more in de daylight. He was whipped dar an' banished from de state on pain o' de gallows. But he lives jess on dis side o' de state line, so dey can't git him in Delawaw. He calls his prace Johnson's Cross Roads. Ole Patty Cannon lives dar, too."

"What is the occupation of those people?" asked Mrs. Custis.

No answer was made for a minute. Then, glancing at both companions, Dave said in a low, frightened voice: "Kidnappin', I 'spect."

"It's everything that makes Pangymonum," Jimmy Phoebus explained. "That old woman Patty Cannon has spent the whole of a wicked life—ever sence she came to Delaware from Cannady as the bride of pore Alonzo Cannon—a-makin' robbers an' bloodhounds out of the young men she could git hold of. Some of 'em she sets to robbin' the mails, some to makin' an' passin' counterfeit money, but most of 'em she sets at stealin' free niggers outen the State of Delaware. An' when it's safe, they steal slaves too. She fust made a tool of Ebenezer Johnson, the pirate of Broad Creek, an' he died in his tracks a-fightin' fur her. Then she took hold of his sons, Joe Johnson an' young Ebenezer, an' made 'em both outlaws an' kidnappers. An' she married Joe to her daughter when Bruington, her first son-in-law, was hanged. When Samson Hat, who is the whitest nigger I ever found, knocked Joe Johnson down in Princess Anne the night before last, he struck the worst man in our peninsula."

Dave listened to this recital with such a deep interest that his breath, strong with apple whiskey, came short and hot, and his hands trembled as he guided the horses. At the last words he exclaimed, "Samson knocked Joe Johnson down? Den de debbil has got him an' means to pay him back."

"What's that?" cried Jimmy Phoebus.

The sweat stood on the big slave's forehead, as if his imagination was terribly possessed, but before he could explain, Mrs. Custis interrupted: "I think it was said that Patty Cannon corrupted Jake Purnell, who cut his throat at Snow Hill five years ago. He was a free Negro who engaged slaves to steal other slaves and bring them to him, and he delivered them up to the white kidnappers for money. Nobody could account for his prosperity till a Negro who had been beaten to death was found in the Pocomoke River, and three slaves who had been seen in his company were arrested for the murder. They confessed that they had stolen the dead Negro, and he had escaped from them. He was so beaten with clubs to make him tractable that when they gave him to Purnell, his life was all gone. He was thrown in the river, but his body came up, and the confession of the wretched tools explained to the slave owners where their missing Negroes had gone. They marched and surrounded Purnell's hut, and he was discovered burrowed beneath it. They brought dogs and fire to drive him out, and, as he came out, he cut his throat with desperate slashes from ear to ear."

During this narrative Dave had listened with rising nervous excitement and large beads of sweat all around his brow. He rolled his eyes as if in strong inward torment till the concluding words inspired such terror in him that he dropped the reins, threw back his head, and shouted, "Mercy! Mercy! Have mercy! Save me, oh, my Lord!"

"He's got a fit, I reckon," cried Jimmy Phoebus, grasping the reigns and pinning Dave to the carriage seat with his leg.

At that moment the road descended into the hollow of Barren Creek. Leaping down at the old Mineral Springs Hotel, a health resort of those days, Phoebus humanely procured water and freshened up the gasping Negro's face.

Mardela (Barren Creek) Mineral Springs

"I declare, I am almost afraid to trust myself to this man," Mrs. Custis observed with more distaste than trepidation.

"Every nigger in this region," exclaimed Jimmy Phoebus, "thinks Pangymonum's comin' down at the dreaded name of Patty Cannon, an' this nigger's gone most to ruin anyway."

"Oh, marster," exclaimed the slave, recovering his speech and glaring wildly around, "I hain't been always the pore sinner rum an' fightin' has made of me. I served the Lord in all my youth. I praised his name an' kept the road to heaven, an' thinkin' of the shipwreck I'se made of a good conscience, an' hearin' missis tell of the end of Jake Purnell, it made me yell to de good Lord for mercy, mercy, oh, my soul!"

Dave's frightful agitation increased, and Jimmy Phoebus soothed him good-naturedly, saying, "Mrs. Custis, I reckon you'd better let him come in the tavern an' take a little sperits. It'll strengthen his nerves an' make him drive better."

As they drank at the old summer resort bar, at that time in the height of its celebrity and the only spa on the peninsula south of Brandywine Springs, Phoebus said to the Negro, "Dave, somethin' not squar an' fair is a-workin' yer, by smoke. I've got my eye on you, nigger, an' sure as hokey-pokey, thair it'll stay. You know my arrand yer, to save a pore, ignorant, deluded black woman from Joe Johnson's band. Now, you've been a-cryin' 'Mercy!' I want you to show mercy by a-tellin' me whar I'm to overtake an' sarch Levin Dennis's catboat if it comes up the Nanticoke tonight with them people an' Joe Johnson aboard."

Having swallowed his liquor greedily, Dave lowered his head and avoided Jimmy's eyes. "You can't do nothin' as low down de river as Vienny," he replied, "caze de Nanticoke is too wide dar. An' if you cross it at Vienny Ferry, den you got de Norfwes' Fork 'tween you an' Johnson's Cross Roads, wid one ferry over dat at Crotcher's, an' Joe Johnson owns all dat place. But you kin keep up dis side o' de Nanticoke de same distance as from yer to Vienny, to de pint whar de Norfwes' Fork come in. Sometimes Joe Johnson sails up dat big fork to get to his crossroads. In gineral he keeps up de oder fork to Betty Twiford's wharf, right on de boundary line."

"How far is that?"

"It's five mile from yer to Vienny an' five mile from yer to a landin' opposite de Norfwes' Fork. Four mile furder on, you're at Sharptown, an' dar you can see Betty Twiford's house on de bank two mile acrost de Nanticoke."

"Nine miles, then, to Sharptown. He's had the tide agin him since he entered the Nanticoke, an' it's not turned yit. By smoke, I'll look for a conveyance."

"You can ride with me to the first landing," spoke up a noble-looking man, whip in hand.

Phoebus accepted the invitation, and cautioning Mrs. Custis to speak with less freedom in that part of the country, he bade her adieu and took the vacant seat in the stranger's buggy.

When Mrs. Custis came to Vienna Ferry, and the horses and carriage went on board the scow to be rowed to the little, shipping settlement of that name, the Negro Dave, standing at the horses' heads, exchanged a few sentences with the ferry keeper.

"Dave," Mrs. Custis called a little later on, "I see you have no love for old Samson."

"He made a boxer outen me an' a bad man, missis."

"Do you know the man he works for—Meshach Milburn?"

"No, missis, I never see him."

"He wears a peculiar hat—nothing like gentlemen's hats now-a-days. It is a hat out of a thousand."

"I never did see it, missis."

"You cannot mistake it for any other hat in the world. Samson is the only servant and watchman at Mr. Milburn's store, and he attends to that disgraceful hat. If you can ever get it from him, Dave, and destroy it, you will be doing a useful act, and I will reward you well."

The moody Negro looked up from his remorseful, brutalized orbs and said, "Steal it?"

"Oh, no, I do not advise a theft, David, though such a wretched hat can have no legal value. It is an affliction to my daughter and Judge Custis and all of us, and you might find some way to destroy it, that is all."

"I'll git it some day," the Negro muttered and drove into the old tobacco port of Vienna.

Vienna on the Nanticoke River

Nanticoke People

Chapter 22

A map would be out of place in a story, yet there are probably some who perceive that this is a story with a reality. If such will open an atlas at the "Middle States" of the American Republic, they will see that the little state of Delaware is fitted as nicely into a square niche of Maryland as if it were a lamp or piece of statuary standing on a mantelpiece. It stands there on a mantel shelf about forty miles wide and rises to more than three times that height, making a perfectly straight north and south line at right angles with its base. Thus mortised into Maryland, its ragged eastern line is formed of the Atlantic Ocean and the broad Delaware Bay.

The only considerable river within this narrow strip is the Nanticoke, which issues, like a crack in the wall, with breadth and tidal ebb and flow from the Chesapeake Bay through the Eastern Shore of Maryland into Delaware, and is there formed of two tidal sources, the one to the north continuing to be called the Nanticoke, and that to the south—nearly as imposing a stream—named Broad Creek.

Nature, therefore, as if anticipating some foolish political boundaries on the part of man, prepared one drain and channel of ingress at the southwestern corner of Delaware to the splendid bay of Virginia.

Around that corner of the little Delaware commonwealth, in a flat, poor, sandy, pine-grown soil, Jimmy Phoebus rode by the stranger in the October afternoon. The sun, an hour high in the west, shone upon his dark cheeks and neck, and he heard the fall birds whistle and cackle in the mellowing stubble and golden thickets.

The meadowlark, the boy's delight, was picking seed, gravel, and insect eggs in the fields. Large and partridge-like, its breast is washed yellow from the bill to the very knees, except at the throat, where hangs a brilliant reticule of dusky brown. Its head and back are of hawkish colors—umber, gray, brown—and something of the gamecock is in its carriage. It flies high, sometimes alone, sometimes in the flock, and is our winter visitor, loving the old fields improvidence has abandoned and uttering, as it feeds, loud sounds of challenge, as if to cry, "Abandoned by man; preempted by me!"

Jimmy Phoebus also heard the bold, bantering woodpecker with its red head, whose schoolmaster is the squirrel and whose tactics of keeping a tree between it and its enemy the Indian fighters adopted. It mimics the tree frog's cry and migrates after October, like other voluptuaries who must have warmth and fruit and eggs always in market. Dressed in its speckled, black, swallow-tailed coat, with a long pen in its mouth and its shirt bosom faultlessly white, the woodpecker works like some Balzac in his garret, making the treetop lively as it spars with its fellow Bohemians. Being sure itself of a tree and clinging to it with both tail and talons, it esteems everything else that lives upon it to be an insect at which it may run its bill or spit its tongue—that tongue which is rooted in the brain itself.

In the hollow, golden bowl of echoing evening, the sailor also noted the flicker with its golden penciled wings, back of speckled umber, mottled white breast with coal-black collar, and neck and head of cinnamon. Its golden tail drooping far below its perch, and running downward along the tree trunk, it flashes its pickax bill like a scepter over the wood lice it devours. "Go to the ant, thou sluggard," was an instigation to murder in the flicker, which loves young ants as much as wild cherries or Indian corn and is capable of taking any such satire seriously upon things to eat. Not so elfin and devilish as the small black woodpecker, it is full of bolder play.

The redbird, like the unclaimed blood of Abel, flew to the little trees that grew low, as if to cover Abel's altar. The jacksnipe chirped in swampy spots like a divinity student, probing the scriptures of the fields with its bill and critical eye. The quail, leading its mate to where the wild seeds were best, piped like an old bachelor with family cares at last, and voices of birds forsaken or on doctor's errands darted through the air, crying, "Phoebe? Phoebe?" or "Killed he! Killed he!"

"Are you a dealer?" the gentleman asked Jimmy Phoebus.

"Just a little that way," said Jimmy warily, "when I kin git somethin' cheap."

The stranger had a pair of keen, dancing eyes and a long, eloquent, silver-gray face that might have suited a great general, so fine was its command, yet too narrowly dancing in the eyes, like spiders in a well, disturbing the mirror there.

"Ha!" he chuckled, as if his eyes had chuckled, so poorly did that sound represent his lordly stature and look of high spirit. "Ha! That's what brings them all to my neighbor Johnson—a fair quotient."

"Quotient?" repeated Jimmy.

"Johnson's a great factor hereabout," the military-looking man continued, bending his handsome eyes on the bay captain as if there was a business secret between them. "He makes the quotient to suit, leaves the suttle large, and never stints the clot."

"He don't narry a feller down to the cloth he's got, sir?" assented Jimmy dubiously.

"Why should he? His equation is simple. I suppose you know what it is."

"Not ezackly," answered Phoebus, attentive to learn.

"Well, it is force and class sympathy against a dead quantity, laws which have no consignees, cattle which have no lawyer nor tongue, rights which have lapsed by their assertion being suspended till demand and supply, like a pair of bulldogs, tear what is left to pieces. Armed with his *ca. sa.*, my neighbor Johnson offsets everybody's *fi. fa.*, serves his writ the first, and makes to gentlemen like you a satisfactory quotient. But he cuts no capers with Isaac and Jacob Cannon."

"I expect now that you are Jacob Cannon," remarked the tawny sailor, not having understood a word of what preceded. "If that's the case, I'm glad to know your name an' thank you for givin' me this lift."

By a bare nod, just intelligible, Mr. Cannon signified that the guess would do, and in his grand way continued: "We let neighbor Johnson and his somewhat peculiar mother-in-law make such commerce as suits him, provided he studies to give us no inconvenience. That is his equation. With his quotient we have no concern other than our slight interest in his wastage, as when Madame Cannon rides down to change a bill and leaves an order for supplies—rum, chiefly, I believe. Gentlemen like you come into this country to deal, replevin, or what not, and we say to you, 'Don't tread on us—that is all.' We shall not look into your parcels nor lie awake of nights to hear alarms, but harm Isaac and Jacob Cannon one ha'pence and *levari facias, fi. fa.!*"

"And fee-fo-fum," responded Jimmy cheerfully. "I've hearn it before."

Looking again with some curiosity at his companion, Phoebus saw that he was not beyond fifty years of age, of a spare, lofty figure—at least six feet four—sitting straight and graceful as an Indian, his clothes well-tailored, his countenance both stern and refined. Every feature was perfected and keen without being hard or angular, and yet Jimmy did not like him. There seemed here to be a commodore or a general—someone designed for deeds of chivalry and great philanthropy—yet around and between the dancing eyes, spider lines were drawn, as if the fine, high brain of Jacob Cannon had put aside matters that matched it and meddled with nothing that ascended higher above the world than the long white bridge of his nose. His sentiments apparently fell no further towards his heart than that. His brain belonged to the bridge of his nose.

"Another Meshach Milburn, by smoke," Jimmy concluded.

After a little pause, Phoebus inquired into the character of the people in this region of the country.

"The lands on the Nanticoke are the quotient of much misplanting and lawyering," said the gray-nosed Apollo. "The piece of country directly before us in the rear of my neighbor Johnson's crossroads was old Indian reservation for seventy years, and so were three thousand acres to our right on Broad Creek. The Indian is a bad factor to civilize his white neighbors. He does not know the luxury of the law, that grand contrivance to make the equation between the business man and the herd."

Mr. Cannon chuckled as if he, at least, appreciated the law and turned the fine horsy bridge of his nose, all gray with dancing eyelight, enjoyingly upon Mr. Phoebus.

"The Indians were long imposed upon, and when they went away at the brink of the Revolutionary War, they left a demoralized white race. Others who moved in upon the deserted lands of the Nanticokes were, if possible, more Indian than the Indians. This peninsula never produced a great Indian, but when Ebenezer Johnson settled on Broad Creek, it possessed a greater savage than Tecumseh. He took what he wanted and, like the Indian, appealed to nature. He stole nothing; he merely took it. He served his *fi. fa.* and his *ca. sa.* upon wondering but submissive mankind with anything convenient from his fists to a blunderbuss. Need I say that this was before the perfect day of Isaac and Jacob Cannon?"

"They would have socked it to him, I reckon," Jimmy exclaimed consonantly.

Mr. Cannon gave a smile such as the gray horse emits at the prospect of oats and continued, "Such was the multiplicand to make the future race. Here, too, raged the boundary-line debate between Penns and Calverts with occasional raids, broken heads, and a noble suit in chancery for fifty years, till no man's title was known. Instead of improving their lands, our voluptuous predecessors improved chiefly their opportunities. You cut sundry cords of wood and hauled it to the landing, and Ebenezer Johnson coolly scowed it over to his paradise at the mouth of Broad Creek. You had a little parcel of Negroes, but the British warships lay in the river mouth and beckoned them off in two successive wars. Having no interest in any certain property, the foresters of the Nanticoke would rather trade with the enemy than fight for foolish ideas. So this region was more than half Tory and is still half passive—the other half predatory. To neither half of such a quotient belongs the house of Isaac and Jacob Cannon."

His nostrils swelled a trifle with military spirit, and he raised the bridge of his nose delicately, turning to observe his instinctive companion.

"If it's any harm, I won't ask," the easy-going mariner said, "but air you two Cannons ary kin to ole Patty Cannon?"

Mr. Cannon smiled. "In Adam all sinned. There we may have been connected," he said. "The question you ask may one day be actionable, sir. The Cannons are a numerous people in our region of fair substance, such as we have, but they showed nothing to vary the equation of subsistence here till there arose the mother of Isaac and Jacob Cannon. She was a remarkable woman. Unassisted, she procured the charter for Cannon's Ferry and made the port settlement of that name by the importance her ferry acquired. When she died, there were found in her house nine hundred dollars in silver—for she never would take paper money—the earnings of that sequestered ferry to start her sons on their career. She knew the peculiar character of her neighbors—how lightly *meum* and *tuum* sat upon their fears or consciences—but she kept no guard except her own good eyes and dauntless heart over that accumulating pile of little sixpences. There was but one spirit as bold as she in all this region of the world."

"And that, I reckon," observed Jimmy Phoebus, "was ole Patty Cannon herself."

Mr. Jacob Cannon slightly bowed his head and spoke aloud from an inner communion: "Forgive me, Mother, that I make the comparison. Thy frugal oil that burned with pure and lonely flame at Cannon's Ferry window, the traveler hailed with comfort in his heart and blessed the enterprise. But to compound the equation, another unknown quantity of female force arose beside my mother's lamp. A certain young Cannon, distantly of our stock, must needs go see the world. He returned with a fair demon of a bride and also settled at Cannon's Ferry. He lived to see the wondrous serpent he had warmed in his arms and died, they say, of the sting. But she lived on, and shrinking back into the woods to a little farm my mother's sons rented to her, she lighted there a Jack-o'-lantern which many a traveler has pursued who never returned to tell. With Ebenezer Johnson's progeny and her own siren sisters, who followed Madame Cannon to the Nanticoke, the nucleus of a settlement began and has existed for twenty years, that only the Almighty's *venire facias* can explore."

"That's my arrand, Jacob Cannon," remarked Jimmy Phoebus quietly. "I'm a pore man from Prencess Anne. If you took me for a nigger dealer, you did me as pore a compliment as when I asked if you was Patty Cannon's kin. I have got just one gal to love an' just one life to lose, an' if God takes me thar, I'm a-goin' to Johnson's Crossroads."

Mr. Jacob Cannon turned and examined his companion with some twinkling care but showed no personal concern.

"Every man must be his own security, my dark-skinned friend, till he can find a bailsman. That place I never take—neither the debtor's nor the security. The firm of Isaac and Jacob Cannon allows no trespass and further concern themselves not. But we are at the Nanticoke."

"I'm obliged to you for the lift, Mr. Jacob Cannon," Jimmy said, springing down, "an' hope you may never find it inconvenient to have let such a pack of wolves use your neighborhood to trespass on human natur."

Twiford's Island

Chapter 23

Some piles of wood and an old wharf were at the riverside. A little scow, half filled with water and with a broken piece of paddle in it, was the only boat the pungy captain could find. The merchant's buggy was soon out of sight, and the gray Nanticoke, several hundred yards wide at this point and made wider by a broad river that flowed into it immediately opposite, was receiving the strong shadows of approaching night, and the tide was running up it, violent and deep.

Long lines of melancholy woods shut both these rivers in. An osprey suddenly struck the surface of the water like a drowning man and rose as if it had escaped from some demon in the flood. The silence following his plunge was deeper than ever till a goatsucker, noiselessly making his zigzag chase, cried his solemn command to "*Whip* poor Will." Those notes repeated—as by some slave ordering his brother to be lashed, or one sympathetic soul in perdition made the time caller to another's misery—floated on the evening light as if the oars of Charon echoed on the Styx, and broken hearts were crossing over.

Alone, unintimidated, but not altogether comfortable, Jimmy Phoebus proceeded to bail out the old scow and wished he had accepted one of Jack Wonnell's hats to do the task. When he had finished it, the stars and clouds were maneuvering around each other in the sky, the clouds the more aggressive, and finally some drops of rain punctured the long, bare muscles of the inflowing tide, making a reticule of little pittings like a net of beads on drifting women's tresses.

As night advanced, a puffing something ascended the broad, black aisle of this forest river, and slowly the Norfolk steamboat rumbled past with passengers for the Philadelphia stage. Then silence drew a sheet of fog around herself and passed into a cold torpor of repose, affected only by the wanes that licked the shores with intermittent thirst.

Regretting that he had not taken his stand at Vienna, where assistance might have been procured, the waterman fought sleep away till midnight, straining his eyes and ears for some sign of sail, but nothing drew near. He had insensibly closed his lids and might have soon been in deep sleep, but suddenly, between his dreams and this world, he heard something like a little baby moaning in the night.

He sat up in the damp scow and listened with all his senses wide open, and once again the cry was wafted upon the river zephyrs. Before it died away, the sailor's paddle was in the water, and his frail, awkward vessel was darting across the tide.

He saw in the black night what none but a sailor's eyes would have seen, a thing not visible but divined, coming along on the bosom of the river. His ears saw it the clearer as that little cry continued—now stopped—now stifled—now rising—now nearly piercing. Then there was a growl, momentary and loud, and a rattle of feet over wood and a stroke or thud or heavy concussion. Then a white thing rose up against the universal ink and rushed on the little scow, sucking water as it came— the catboat under full sail.

Phoebus had paddled for the opposite shore to prevent the object of his quest from escaping up the Northwest Fork, yet to be in its path if it beat up the main fork. By a piece of instinctive calculation, he had run nearly under the catboat's bow.

"Ahoy there!" cried Jimmy, standing up in his tipsy little skiff. "Ahoy the *Ellenory Dennis!* I'm a-comin' aboard."

With this, the paddle still in his hand, the sailor threw himself upon the gunwale and let it glide through his palms till he could see the man at the helm. There was no light to be called so, but the helmsman was perceived by the sailor's experienced eyes. Phoebus grasped the gunwale firmly and prepared to swing himself on board, shouting hoarsely, "You, Levin Dennis, I see you, by smoke! You know Jimmy Phoebus is your friend. Come out of this Pangymonum an' stop a-breakin' of your mother's heart! I see you, my son!"

If he did see Levin Dennis, Levin did not see Jimmy Phoebus, nor apparently hear him, but stood motionless at the helm as a frozen man, looking straight on in the night. The rigging made a little flapping, the rudder creaked on its hooks, but every human sound was still as the grave, and the boy at the helm seemed petrified and deaf and blind.

The pungy captain's temper rose, his superstition not being equal to that of most people, and he cried again, "You're a disgrace to the woman that bore you! Hell's a-waitin' for your pore tender body an' soul! Heave ahoy an' let drop that gaff an' take me aboard, Levin!"

Still silent and passive as a stone, the youthful figure at the helm did not seem to breathe, and the catboat cut the water like a fish hawk.

A flash of bright fire lighted up the vessel's side. A loud pistol shot rang out, and the sailor's hands loosened from the gunwale and clutched at the air. He felt the black night fall on him as if he had pulled down its ebony columns upon his head.

He knew no more for hours till he awoke lying in cold water and saw the gray morning coming through tree boughs over his head. He had a thirsty feeling and pain somewhere. For a few minutes he lay there on his shoulder and did not move, holding to something and guessing what it might be and where he might be making his bed in this chilly autumn dawn.

His hand was clutching the stern plank of the old scow and was so stiff he could not open it for some time. The scow was aground upon a marshy shore on which some large trees grew, the fringes of a woods that deepened farther back.

"By smoke," muttered Jimmy, "if yer ain't hokey-pokey, but I reckon I ain't dead, nohow."

With this he lifted the hand that had been stretched beneath his head and was also numb with cramp and cold. It was full of blood.

"Well," said Jimmy, "that feller did hit me, but if he'll lend me his pistol, I'll fire a straighter slug than his'n."

Feeling around his head, the captain came to a raw spot, the touch of which gave him acute pain and made the blood flow freshly as he withdrew his hand. He could just speak the words, "Water, or I'll. . . ," when he swooned away.

The sun was up and shining cheerily in the treetops as Phoebus, who was its name bearer, recovered his senses again. He bathed his face, still lying down, and tore a piece of his clothing off for a bandage. By the mirror of a still, green pool of water, he examined his wound—a little groove or gutter where the ball had plowed a line in the fleshy part of his cheek. It had probably struck a bone but had not broken it, and this had stunned him.

"I was so ugly before that Ellenory wouldn't more than half look at me," mused Phoebus. "Now, I 'spect, she'll never kiss that air cheek agin."

He bandaged his cheek roughly, sat up, and took a survey of the scenery. The river was a full quarter of a mile wide. The opposite shore was bluffy and bold in places, but on the side where Phoebus had drifted, there extended a point of level woods and cripple, as if by the action of some backwater. This low ground appeared to have a considerable area and was nowhere tilled nor gave any signs of being visited.

But the opposite or northern shore was quite otherwise. There, the river had a wide bend to receive two considerable creeks and changed its course almost abruptly from west to southwest, giving a grand view of its wide bosom for the distance of more than two miles into Maryland. The prospect was closed in that direction by a whitish-looking something—lime or shell piles standing against the background of pale blue woods and bluffs.

Opposite the spot where Phoebus had been stranded, a cleared farm came out to the Nanticoke, affording a front of only a single field on the crest of a considerable sand bluff—elevations looking magnified here where nature is so level. At one end of this field, which was planted in corn that clung dry to the naked stalks, an old lane descended to a shell-paved wharf of a stumpy, square form. Almost at the other or western end of the clearing stood a respectable farmhouse of considerable age. It had a hipped roof, three queer dormer windows slipping down the steeper half below, and two chimneys which naturally rose from the old English brick gables. All between the gables was built of wood. A porch of one story occupied nearly half the center of that side of the house facing the river, and to the right, against the house and behind it, were kitchen, smokehouse, corncribs, and other low tenements in picturesque medley. To the left, an old, low building crouched on the water's edge, looking like a brandy still or small warehouse. The road from the wharf and lane passed along a beach and partly through the river water to enter a gate between this shed and the dwelling, and on the lawn arose two tall and elegant trees, a honey locust and a stalwart mulberry.

"I never been by this place before," Jimmy Phoebus muttered, "but, by smoke, yon house looks to me like Betty Twiford's wharf, an' I can't help thinkin' yon white spots down this side of the river air Sharptown. If that's the case, which state am I in?"

Site of Betty Twiford's Wharf

He rose to his feet, bailed the scow, which was nearly full of water, and began to paddle along the shore. Seeing something white, he landed, parted the bushes, and found it to be a stone of a bluish marble bearing on one side the letter M and on the other the letter P, and a royal crown was also carved upon it.

"Yer's one o' Lord Baltimore's boundary stones," Phoebus exclaimed. "Now see the rascality o' them kidnappers. I know yon house is Twiford's becaze it's a'most on the state line, but I'm ashamed to say it's a leetle in Maryland. An' that lane comin' down to the wharf is my way to Joe Johnson's Pangymonum at his crossroads."

The sound of someone singing came from the woods nearby. Listening, Phoebus concluded that it was further along the water, and he paddled softly forward till he came to a small cove which led into the swamp. Nowhere did its shores offer a dry landing, yet there were recent footprints deeply trodden in the bog and disclosed up the slope into the woods. The mysterious chanting seemed to come from their direction.

"My head's bloody an' I'm wet as a muskrat, so I reckon I ain't afraid o' gittin' a little muddy." With this the navigator stepped from the scow into the swamp and pulled himself up the slope by main strength.

The trees increased in size as he went on and entered a noble grove of pines, through whose roar, like an organ accompanied by a human voice, the singing was heard nearer and nearer. Following the tracks of previous feet, which had almost made a path, Phoebus came to a space where an axe had laid the smaller bushes low around a large loblolly pine. There, fastened by a chain which only allowed her to go around the tree and tread a nearly bare place in the pine droppings or shats, a black woman sat, singing in a long, weary, throatsore wail. Jimmy listened to a few lines:

> Deepen de woun' dy han's have made
>   In dis weak, helpless soul,
> Till mercy wid its mighty aid
>   Descen' to make me whole;
>   Yes, Lord!
>   Descen' to make me whole.

A Negro child, perhaps three years old, was lying asleep on the ground at the woman's feet in a tattered gray blanket that might have been discarded from a stable. Nearby was a wooden box in which were a coarse loaf of cornbread and some strips of bacon. A wooden trough, hollowed out of a log, contained water. The woman's face was scratched and bruised, and as she chanted through swollen lips, her teeth were revealed with several freshly missing in front.

As Phoebus came in sight, she glanced up, looked at him in blank curiosity, as if she did not know what kind of animal he was, then continued her song wearily, as if she had been singing it for days and her mind was out of her control. As she moved her feet from time to time, the chain rattled upon her ankles.

"Well," said Jimmy, "if this ain't Pangymonum. Git up gal, an' let me see what ails you."

The woman rose mechanically, still singing in the shrill, cracked, weary drone. As she rose, the baby awoke and began to cry. She stooped and took it up and, patting it with her hands, sang on as if she would fall asleep singing but could not.

The chain, strong and rusty, had been very recently welded to her feet by a blacksmith. The fresh rivet attested that, and there were also pieces of charcoal in the pine strewings, as if fire had been brought there for smith's uses. Jimmy Phoebus took hold of the chain and examined it link by link till it depended from a powerful staple driven to the heart of the pine tree. Though rusty, it was perfect in every part, and the condition of the staple showed that it was permanently retained in its position as if to secure various and successive persons. The staple itself had been driven above the reach of the hands, as by a man standing on some platform or on another's shoulders.

Phoebus took the chain in his short, powerful arms and, giving a run from the root of the tree, threw all the strength of his compact, heavy body into a jerk, letting his weight fall upon it. He did not produce the slightest impression.

"There's jess two people can unfasten this chain," exclaimed the sailor, blowing hard and kneading his palms after two such exertions. "One's a blacksmith, an' t'other's a woodchopper. Gal, how did you git yer?"

The woman, a young and once comely person of about twenty-eight years of age, sang on a moment, as if she did not understand the question.

Phoebus repeated it with a kinder tone. "Pore, abused creatur, I ain't none of these kidnappers. Git your pore, scattered wits together an' tell a friend of all women an' little childern how he kin help you, fur time's worth a dollar a second, an' bloody vultures are nigh by. Speak, Mary."

The universal name seemed timely to this woman. She stopped her chanting and burst into tears.

"My husband brought me here," she said between her sobs. "He sold me. I give him everything I had an' loved him, an' he sold me—me an' my baby."

"I reckon you don't belong down this way, Mary. You don't talk like it."

"No, sir, I belong to Philadelphia. I was a free woman an' a widow. My husband left me a little money an' a little house an' this child. Another man come an' courted me, a han'some mulatto man, almost as white as you. He told me he had a farm in Delaware an' wanted me to be his wife. He promised me so much an' was so anxious about it that I listened to him. Oh, he was a beautiful talker, an' I was lonesome an' wanted love. I let him sell my house an' give him the money an' started a week ago to come to my new home. Oh, he did deceive me so. He said he loved me dearly."

She began to cry again, and her mind seemed to wander, for the next sentence was disconnected. Jimmy took the baby in his arms and kissed it without any scruples, and while he handled the child tenderly, it's large, black eyes looked into his as if he might be its own father.

"The foxes has come an' barked at me two nights," said the woman. "They wanted the bacon, I 'spect. The water snakes has crawled around here in the daytime, an' the buzzards flew right down before me an' looked up as if they thought I ought to be dead, but I wasn't afraid. That man I give my love to was so much worse than them. I just sung an' let them look at me."

"You say he sold you, Mary?"

The woman rubbed her weary eyes and slowly recollected where she had left off.

"We moved our things on a vessel to Delaware an' come up a creek to a little town in the marshes, an' there we started for my husband's farm. He said we come to it in the night. I couldn't tell, but I saw a house in the woods an' was so tired I went to sleep with my baby there. In the night I found men in the room, an' one of them—a white man—was tyin' my feet."

A crow cawed with a sound of awe in the pine tops, and squirrels ran tamely round about as she hesitated.

"I thought then of the kidnappers of Delaware. I had heard about them, an' I jumped out of bed an' fought for my life. They knocked me down, an' the rope around my feet tripped me up, but I fought with my teeth after my hands was tied, an' I bit that white man's knees. He picked up a fire shovel an' knocked my teeth out. My last hope was almost gone when I saw my husband comin' in. I cried to him, 'Save me! Save me, darlin'!' He had a rope in his hand, an', before I could understand it, he slipped it over my neck an' choked me."

"Your own husband? I can't believe it to save my life."

"I didn't believe it neither till I heard him say, 'Eben,' he said, 'I've took down every mole an' spot on her body an' can swear to 'em. You won't have no trouble a-sellin' her, as she can't testify.'"

"The imp of Pangymonum!" Jimmy cried. "He married you to note down your marks an' by 'em swear you to be a slave."

"The white man tried to sell me to a farmer, an' I told what I had heard them say. He believed me an' told them the mayor of Philadelphia had a reward out for them for kidnappin' free people. Then they talked together—a little scared they was—an' tied me again an' brought me on a cart through the woods to the river. They fetched me here an' chained me an' told me if I ever said I was free to another man, they meant to sell my baby an' drown me in the river."

She finished with a tremor and a low wail like an infant, but the sailor passed her baby into her arms to engage her and said, "The Lord is still a-countin' of his sparrows, or I wouldn't have been on this arrand, by smoke. To drift yer, hangin' senseless to that ole scow, must have been to save you, Mary. This is a island where they chains up property, I reckon, that is bein' follered up too close. Time's very precious, Mary, but I've got a sailor's knife yer, an' I'll stay an' cut the staple out o' this ole pine, if they come an' kill me. You take an' wash my face off outen that water trough, while I bite a bit of bacon."

He took the child and amused it while the woman carefully cleaned his wound and rebandaged it so that he could see and eat, though the cotton folds wrapped in much of his face like a mask. He then examined the chain and a large iron ball weighing several pounds, which was also affixed to her ankle. Her ankle had been blistered by the redhot rivet, smithed so barbarously close to the flesh.

"Oh, don't leave me here to die," the woman pleaded, as he started into the woods.

"I'll stay by you, Mary, an' we'll die together if we must, but it's not my idee to die at all. I'm goin' to bring that scow ashore an' cut a hickory—if I can find one—to break this yer chain."

Plunging again into the mud nearly to his waist, Phoebus pulled the scow into the woods. He had barely concealed himself when he saw a catboat like the *Eleanora Dennis* come out of the creek below Twiford's house and stand towards the island in the cripple.

"The tide's agin 'em, an' they must make a tack to get yer," Jimmy muttered. "I'm afraid this knife will have to go to the heart of some son of Pangymonum in ten minutes, or Ellenory Dennis will never agin be pestered by her ugly lover."

Phoebus was seized with a frenzy of strength at the danger he was in. As he carried the heavy scow across the wooded island, he noted a small hickory tree. Throwing himself against it, he bent it down and plunged his knife into the straining fibers so that it crackled and splintered in his hand.

Returning to the woman, Phoebus scaled the tree to which she was chained, as he had often climbed a mast. Clutching the pine with his knees, he trimmed the sapling to a point with his knife and thrust it under the staple. Then, catching the hickory like a lever, he dropped down and brought his weight desperately against it. The staple bent but did not loosen.

At that instant the scraping of a boat on mud was heard, and the black woman fell to her knees.

"Pray, but do it soft," Jimmy whispered. "An' not a cry from the child, or there'll be a murder."

While he spoke, Phoebus rapidly trimmed the hickory of its branches so that it could penetrate the limbs of the tree from above. Climbing higher, he worked the point of the lever downwards into the now crooked staple, throwing himself out of the tree against the sapling, which bent nearly double but did not break. As the staple yielded, the chain and the deliverer fell together on the soft pine litter.

"Hark!" exclaimed a voice through the woods.

"What was it?" asked another voice.

"Come," Phoebus murmured, gathering together the woman, the child, the ball and chain, and, as a rabbit leaps with long and silent steps, he carried the whole burden on his shoulders through the pines.

He sat them in the scow, which sank to its edges. Covered by a protruding point of woods, he pushed off into the deep river, guiding the frail vessel into the sides of the stream, away from the influence of the outrunning tide. As the scow turned the first elbow in the river, it began to sink.

"If you make a sound, you are a slave fur life," the waterman whispered as he slipped overboard and began to swim with his hand upon the stern. As he did this, straining every muscle of his countenance to keep afloat, the wound in his cheek began to bleed again, and he felt his strength going. He began to sink, and, as the water reached his nostrils, the woman heard him sigh, "I'd do it an' die agin fur Ellenory. God bless her."

The scow, now full of water, turned upside down and threw mother and child into the stream, and the child was gone beneath the surface before the woman could catch herself upon the sunken branch of a tree. As she gasped there, the body of the pungy captain swept past her. She caught him by the hair, and he clutched her with the drowning instinct, and down they went together.

They went to the very bottom, but not to drown. The old tree, having fallen where it grew in other years, was sustained upon its limbs and made an invisible yet sure pathway to the shore. The long chain and iron ball fettered to the woman's foot, however, deprived her for the moment of all power to step along the slippery, submerged trunk. With her soul full of agony for her child, she was about to let go of her deliverer's body and throw herself also into the river to die with them, when the old scow reappeared at the surface and struck the woman a blow that altered the course of her thought.

"Pore, brave man," she gasped. "He's got a wife, maybe, an' he give his life for a poor creature like me. God has took my baby. I can't do nothing for it now, but maybe I can save this man's life before I die."

Indifferent to her personal fate, she pushed the scow down and under Phoebus with her remaining hand till it relieved her of a portion of the weight of his body. Gathering up the meshes of the iron chain from its termination at her feet, she threw a portion of it into the scow, so that it no longer became entangled in the cross branches and knots below. She could now lift the iron ball sufficiently to allow her to glide her feet along the tree.

With pain and difficulty she pushed the scow and the body to the foot of the tree. As she felt around its old roots for further support, the red-eyed terrapins, disturbed in their possessions, arose and swam around her. She feared no reptile any longer, since death, the mighty crocodile, had eaten the babe that she had nursed but that morning.

She had remembrance enough to think of all the precautions her deliverer had taken, and when she had dragged his body on the shore into the dense, scrubby woods, she also drew out the little scow an heaped some dead brush upon it. She had scarcely concealed herself when she heard a voice from the river and the report of a sail swung around upon its boom.

"If she's got off to Delaware," the voice said, "Joe Johnson won't have long to stay on his visit. All the beaks will gather fur him an' be started by John M. Clayton."

"I'm sorry fur Joe," answered another. "He hoped to make one more big scoop this trip an' quit the Corners fur good."

"Let's sail by ole Ebenezer Johnson's roost at Broad Creek mouth an' peep up both forks of the river," said the other voice, receding. "It's only a mile an' a half. If we find nothin', we'll run down the river and inquire at the landings as fur as Vienny."

The colored woman now worked with all her strength to revive the insensible sailor, rolling him, rubbing his body till her elbows seemed almost to be dropping off, and then rubbing his great, broad breast with her head and face. She breathed into his mouth the breath heaven vouchsafed to Hagar as bountifully as to Sarah, and wringing out portions of her garments and hanging them at sunny exposures to dry, she substituted them for the wet clothing of the man. As she worked with a hollow, desolate heart, she sobbed, "Gi' me this man's life, Oh Lord that took my chile. I will have this life back."

Crying and weeping, fainting and laboring, she watched the hours run by, and still he did not waken. And still, with all that noble strength that makes the fields of white men grow and blossom under the Negro's unthanked toil, the widow and childless one fought on for this cold lump of brother nature.

He warmed. He breathed. He groaned. He spoke!

His voice was like a happy sigh, as of one disturbed near the end of a morning nap in summer: "You thar, Mary?"

He stared around with difficulty, his wounded face clotted and stained with blood, and his eyes next looked an inquiry so kind and apprehensive that she answered it to save him breath.

"Baby's drowned. God does best."

He reached his hand to hers and put his little strength into the grasp. She was almost naked to the waist, having sacrificed all she had—the greatest of which was modesty—to bring back the life in him.

"Mary," he exhaled, "why didn't you ketch the baby an' leave me go?"

"Oh, dearly as I loved it," the woman answered, "I'm glad you come up under my hands instead. You can do good; you're a white man. Baby would have only been a poor slave or a free Negro nobody would care for."

"I mean to do good if the Lord lets me," sighed the sailor. "I mean to go an' die agin for human natur at Johnson's Crossroads."

Old Chimneys

Chapter 24

The day had far advanced when Jimmy Phoebus was strong enough to rise and walk and leave the refuge in the woods. He advised the colored woman to crawl through the pine trees along the margin while he paddled the scow in the shadow of the forest, which now lay strong upon the river's breast.

At the distance of about a mile, Broad Creek flowed into the Nanticoke from the east, fully a quarter of a mile wide. Half a mile up this stream an old, low, extended, weather-blackened house faced the river. It seemed to grin out of its broken ribs and hollow window sockets like a traitor's skull discolored upon a gibbet. It was falling to pieces, and along its roof ridge a line of crows balanced and croaked, as if they had fine stories to tell and weird opinions to pass upon the former inhabitants of the tenement.

"There, I have hearn tell," said Jimmy, drawing in to the bank and taking the woman into the scow, "lived the pirate of Broad Creek, ole Ebenezer Johnson, who was shot soon after the war of '12 at Twiford's house down yonder."

"For kidnappin' free people?" the woman asked without interest.

"In them days they didn't kidnap much; it was jest a-beginnin'. The war busted ever'thing on the bay, burned half a dozen towns, kept the white men layin' out an' watchin', an' made loafers of half of 'em. It brought bad volunteers an' militia yer to trifle with the poorer gals, an' some of 'em stuck yer after the war was done. I don't know whar ole Ebenezer come from. Some says this an' some that. All we know is that he an' the Hanley gals, one of 'em Patty Cannon, was the head devils in an' after the war."

"It's a bad-lookin' ole house, sir. Yonder's a coon runnin' out the door. Oh, I hear my child cryin' everywhere I look."

"The British begun to run black people off in the war," Phoebus continued. "The black people wanted to go to 'em. The British filled the islands in Tangier with nigger camps. They was a-goin' to take this whole peninsuly an' collect an' drill a nigger army to put down Amerikey. When the war was done, the British sailed away from Chesapeake Bay with thousands of colored folks, an' people yer begun to hate the free niggers."

"For lovin' liberty?" the woman sighed, looking at the ball which had galled her ankle bloody.

"They hated free niggers as if they was all Tories an' didn't love Amerikey. So seein' the free niggers hadn't no friends, these Johnsons an' Patty Cannon begun to steal 'em, by smoke. There was only a million niggers in the whole country, an' Louisiana was a-roarin' for 'em. Every nigger was wuth twenty horses or thirty yokes of oxen or two good farms 'round yer. These kidnappers made money like smoke, bought the lawyers, went into polytics, an' got sech a high hand that they tried a-murderin' of the nigger traders from Georgey an' down thar, comin' yer full of gold to buy free people. That give 'em a backset, an' they hung some of Patty's band—some at Georgetown an' some at Cambridge."

"If my baby's made white in heaven, I'm afraid I won't know him," the woman said, nodding and wandering in her mind.

"At last the Delawareans marched on Johnson's Crossroads an' cleaned his Pangymonum thar out. They guarded Johnson an' sixteen pore niggers he'd kidnapped to Georgetown jail. Young John Clayton was paid by the Phildelfy Quakers to git him convicted. Johnson was strong in the county—we're in it now—Sussex—an' if Clayton hadn't skeered the jury almost to death, it would have disagreed. He held 'em over bilin' hell an' dipped 'em thar till the courtroom was like a Methodis' revival meetin', with half that jury cryin', 'Save me, Lord!' while some of 'em had Joe Johnson's money in their pockets. Joe was licked at the post an' banished from the state. He was so skeered that he laid low awhile, goin' off somewhar to Missoury or Floridey or Allybamy. But Patty Cannon never flinched. She trained the young boys round yer to be her sleuth hounds an' go stealin' for her, an' till she dies, it's safer to be a chicken than a free nigger. They stole you, pore creatur', from

Phildelfy, an' they steal 'em in Jersey an' away into North Carliney; fur Joe Johnson's a smart feller fur enterprise, an' Patty Cannon's deep as death an' the grave."

Phoebus looked at the woman sitting in the scow and saw that she was fast asleep, his tale having no power to startle her senses, now worn out by every infliction.

"I must git that ball an' chain off,' the sailor said, "but iron is scarce as gold in these ole sandy parts."

He lifted her out of the scow, laid her in the shade, and began to explore the old house. To his joy he found the iron crane still hanging in the chimney and signs of recent fire.

"These yer ole cranes was valleyble once," Jimmy said, "an' in the wills they left 'em to their children like farms. Lawsuits was had over the bilin' pots an' the biggest kittles. It broke a woman's heart to git a little kittle left her, an' the big-kittled gal was jest pestered with beaux. But, by smoke, we're a-makin' iron now in Amerikey. Kittles is cheap; that's why this crane is left by robbers an' gypsies after they used it."

He twisted the crane out of the bricks on which it was hinged, and some of the mantel jamb fell down.

"Hallo!" cried Jimmy, "what's this rollin' yer? A shillin', by George. I say 'by George' caze ole George the Third's picter's on it. Maybe thar's more of 'em."

He pulled a few bricks out of the jamb and raked the hollow space inside with his hand, bringing forth a steel purse of English manufacture, filled with shillings at one end and fifteen golden guineas at the other. They rolled out through the decayed filigree, rusted, probably, by rain percolating through the chimney. The purse crumbled to iron mold in his hand.

"The Lord is my shepherd," the sailor said reverently; "I shall not want. He leadeth me by the still waters. How beautiful Ellenory says it. Look thar at the waters of the Nanticoke, beautiful as silver. Lord, make 'em pure waters an' free to every pore creatur.

"Now, British money ain't coined by Uncle Sam. What is the date? I can make figgers out easy—eighteen hundred an' fifteen. I was about to do Ebenezer Johnson the onjustice of sayin' that he'd sold his country out to ole Admiral Cockburn, but the war was done when this money was coined. Whose was it?"

He removed more of the bricks to put his hand in the hollow depository left there. Feeling around and higher up, he brought out the bronze hilt of a sword, on which was a name.

"By smoke, maybe they've murdered somebody yer. I reckon he was British. I can't read it, but Ellenory kin, if I live to see her agin."

As he left the rotting old house, a crash and a cloud of smoke rose up behind him, and the chimney fell into the middle of the floor.

With the crane's sharp point and long leverage, the pungy captain succeeded, after tedious efforts, in breaking the links of the chain and removing the cannonball from the woman's foot, but he could not remove the iron band around her ankle.

"God bless you," she exclaimed. "It's a sin to say so, but I feel as if I could fly since that dreadful weight is off. Oh, I want to fly, for I dreamed of my baby, an' he smiled at me from heaven as if he said, 'I'm happy, Mamma.'"

"You don't owe me nothin', Mary. I love a widder who begged me to come yer. When you git to Prencess Anne, whar I want you to go, find Ellenory Dennis an' tell her I've seen her boy, an' I'll bring him back if I kin."

"Princess Anne, where is it?"

"It's maybe forty mile from yer, Mary, halfway between sunrise and sunset."

"Right south, sir?"

"That's it. Now, I'll tell you how to git thar. You take this old woods road along Broad Creek an' walk to Laurel—five miles. It's a little town on the creek. Keep in under the woods, but don't lose the road. Every foot of it's dangerous to niggers. You kin git thar by dark. I don't know nobody thar, an' I can't write, but you go direct to the house of some preacher of the Gospel an' tell him a lie."

Mary opened her eyes.

"I wouldn't have you tell a lie to nobody but a good man," Phoebus continued, "fur it's close to the Lord then an' won't git fur an' pizen many, as lies does. You tell that preacher you're the runaway slave of Judge Custis of Prencess Anne, an' you're sorry you run away an' want to go home."

"Oh, sir, you are not like my wicked husband, trying to sell me too?"

"No, Mary, bad as you've been used, faith's your only sure friend. If you was to tell the preacher you had been kidnapped, he'd maybe be afraid to help you. They're a timid set down yer on any subject concernin' niggers. These preachers will help save black folks' souls but never rescue their pore broken bodies. When you tell him you are the slave of a rich man like Judge Custis, he'll jump at the chance to do the judge a favor an' tell you that you do right to go back to your master. That's whair he's a liar, Mary, so he'll scratch your lie off."

"They'll turn me back at Princess Anne and wont know me, maybe."

"Not if you do this: Make them take you to Judge Custis's daughter —the one that's just been married. Tell her you want to speak to her privately. Tell her the nigger-skinned man—I'm him—that she sent away with her mother found you whar you was chained in the woods. Take this link of the chain to show her. Tell her you want to be her cook till the one that run away is found."

"I'll do it, sir. I've got no home to go to now."

"Tell her all you remember. Tell her not to tell Ellenory any of my troubles. Tell her I'm a-startin' for Pangymonum, an' if I die, it's nothin' but a bachelor keepin' his own solitary company. Yer's a gold piece an' three silver pieces to pay your way."

"Won't you give me your knife?" asked the woman.

"What fur, Mary?"

"To kill myself if they kidnap me again."

"I have nothin' else to fight for my life with," said Phoebus. "You must not do that. Keep in the woods to Laurel."

She fell on the ground and kissed his knees and bathed them with her tears.

"I do have faith, master," she said, "faith enough to be your slave."

"I'd cry a little, too," said Jimmy, twitching his eyes as the woman disappeared in the forest, "if I knowed how to do it, but the wind on the bay's dried up my tear ponds. I'll bury these curiosities right yer an' put some old bricks around 'em outen the chimney they come from."

He dug a hole with his knife, carefully cutting out a piece of the sod and restoring it over the buried articles, and, after notching some trees to mark the place, he pushed the scow again into Broad Creek and descended the Nanticoke on the falling tide to Twiford's Wharf.

Dragging the scow up a creek bed to conceal it, Phoebus discovered another boundary stone. A beach led under the cover of a sandy bluff to the river gate of Twiford's comfortable house, and he boldly entered the lane and lawn, saying to himself, "I reckon a feller can ask to buy one squar meal a day in a free country, fur I'm hungry."

Even in that day the house was probably seventy years old. The roof, capacious as a land turtle's back, had been done by an artistic shingler in lines like old lacework, with the short roofs over the three dormers like laced bib aprons. Half of the roof was almost as straight as the walls, and the small, foreign bricks in the gables, glazed black and dark red alternately, had been laid by conscientious workmen and bade fair to stand another hundred years.

Standing beneath the locust tree at the lawn gate, the sailor beheld an extensive prospect of the river, bending in a beautiful curve like the rim of a silver salver. Towards the south the blue perspective of the surrounding woods faded into azure bluffs on the farther shore, where, as he now identified it, the hamlet of Sharptown assumed the mystery and similitude of a city by the enchantment of distance. A large brig was riding up the river under the afternoon breeze, carrying the English flag at her spanker. Wildfowl, flying in V-formed lines like Hyads astray, reflected from the surface of the river. Some distant fishermen appeared human, yet nearly stationary, as if to enliven a dream, and bees murmured nearby from a row of hives, increasing the restful sense in the heart and the ears.

Phoebus crossed the lane to a squatty structure of brick by the waterside and peeped in.

"A still, by smoke," he said. "If it ain't apple brandy, may I forgit my compass. No, it's peach brandy. Well, anyway, it's hot enough. This, I 'spect, is what started the Pangymonum."

He took a stout drink, and it revived his weakened system. He bathed his head in its strong alcohol and returned to the lawn. Walking around the house, he peeped into the two lower rooms but saw nobody. The porch in the rear extended the full width of the house, unlike the smaller shed in front, which only covered two doors, standing curiously side by side.

Completely sheltered by the long porch, Phoebus looked into a window and saw a table set with a clean cloth, bread, cold chicken, and a pitcher of creamy milk with a piece of ice floating in it. On either side of a large fireplace were doors, one open and leading by a small winding stair to the floor above.

With a sailor's quiet, sliding feet, Jimmy walked into the low hall, and a catbird in a cage there immediately started such a shrill series of cries that his steps were unheard by himself.

"Nobody bein' yer," thought Jimmy, "an' the flies gittin' at the victuals, I reckon I'll do as I would be done by."

He began to eat and soon heard a female voice sound down the stairs, as if reciting to another person.

"Aunt Patty says Aunt Betty's first husband, Captain Twiford, was a sea captain and a widower. She was one of the beautiful Hanley girls, brought up by old Ebenezer Johnson at his house across on Broad Creek. Captain Twiford courted her there and brought her here to live. He died early—all my aunties' husbands died early—and is buried in the vault out here behind the pound. You can go in and see him in his shroud, lying by Aunt Betty. Her next husband, John Gillis, left her, and then she lived with William Russell, a Negro trader. Aunt Patty governed all her sisters and the Johnson boys, too. Oh, how I fear her when she looks at me sometimes with her bold, black eyes. I can't help it."

Another voice, not a woman's, yet almost as gentle, seemed to ask a question, but the catbird made such a furious screaming at seeing a stranger drinking the milk that Phoebus could not hear it well.

The pleasant female voice spoke again. "Yes, he was killed in the room under this before I was born, Aunt Patty says. Sometimes she likes to tell such dark and bloody tales and laughs with joy to see me frightened at them. Aunt Betty got in debt, and this house and farm were sold under executions and bought by a Maryland man. While the men were away, he set his goods in the house and set Aunt Betty's goods outside upon the lawn. It's only a mile or a little more from here to Ebenezer Johnson's, and the news of the seizure was sent there."

Jimmy tore off a piece of chicken with his teeth, listening voraciously.

"Did you hear anything?" continued the voice. "I thought I did. Bad people often come here, and the dogs are chained up in the smokehouse."

"I'll go turn the dogs loose."

"Be dogged if you do," Jimmy reflected.

Something in the other voice sounded familiar to the uninvited guest, but the catbird broke in again.

Then the female continued: "While the men were removing Aunt Betty's goods, throwing many of them out of the windows, a sound was heard in the room below, where your meal is now ready. Like a panther skipping and lashing his tail, and before the men could breathe, old Ebenezer Johnson was up the stairs and laying about him. His eyes were full of murder. One man jumped right through that window and rolled off the porch, and another pitched down the stairs. The third was a boy, Joe King, barely grown. He lives not far from this house now. Ebenezer Johnson dashed him down the stairs and started after him.

All his life the boy had been taught to dread that terrible man, and now he was flying before him. As he reeled through the room below in the agony of the fear of death, the boy's eyes beheld a rifle leaning at the door that opens on the back porch."

"Mighty good thing if it was thar now," Jimmy inwardly remarked, finishing the chicken and still hungry.

"Oh, there *is* a noise somewhere in this house," the voice exclaimed. "I never tell this story but it makes me startled at every sound. The boy, as he whirled past, grasped the long rifle, drew it to his shoulder, and with a young volunteer's skill—he had been drilling to fight the British —put the two balls in that old man's brain. Both balls entered over the left eyebrow, and one passed through the head and was found in the wall. The other never was found. The lawless giant gave a trembling motion through his frame, his eyes glazed, and he sank dead upon the floor without a sound. The wicked had ceased from troubling. Aunt Betty, Aunt Patty, and Aunt Jane—three sisters shaped by him in soul— fell on his body and wept and almost prayed, but it was too late. They buried him in the field behind the pound."

Undertaking to rise from his chair, Jimmy Phoebus made a loud scraping on the floor, and the table knife fell with a ringing sound.

"Who's there?" cried the female voice and added, "I knew the dogs ought to be loose."

"Who's there?" the other voice also asked with something very familiar to Phoebus in its sound.

"Ebenezer Johnson!" Jimmy answered in his deepest bass tones, mentally considering that a ghost might carry more terror than a robber after that tale.

A little scream and a whispered consultation followed, and then a girl's bare feet, beautifully molded, slowly descended the steep stairway. Next, a slender, graceful body came into view, and finally a face— delicious as a ripe peach—looked once at the intruder below. All the pink and bright color faded from it to see, standing where Ebenezer Johnson had given up the ghost, a stalwart effigy, bandaged in white all around the head. And over the left eye and cheek, where the dead river pirate had received his double bullet, the blood was hideously matted and not wholly stanched even yet. The girl sank slowly down upon the steps and saw no more.

"Now if I don't git out, the dogs *will* be set loose," Jimmy muttered, as he disappeared up the lane, putting the barn between him and the house. Scarcely had he done so, when Levin Dennis, unconscious of the apparition, appeared coming down the stairs. Finding the beautiful girl insensible, he raised her in his arms and stole a kiss.

In a level field of deep sand between the cattle pound and the pines, an old burial lot lay under some low cedar trees. Jimmy Phoebus stopped a minute. There were several little stones over Twifords who had died early and a large heap of sand planted with flowers, which Phoebus believed was the resting place of the river buccaneer. There was also a vault of brick and plaster with its door ajar, where prurient visitors, themselves with Saul's own selfish curiosity to raise the dead, had poked about until the coffin lids had been drawn back and the dead pair exposed to the humid peninsular air.

The bay captain looked in and beheld his predecessor, Captain Twiford, lying in his shroud—not in full clothing as men are buried now, for clothing was too valuable in this scantily peopled country to feed it to the worms. Twiford lay shriveled up, shroud and flesh making but one skin. His face was a walnut color, the hair complete, the teeth sound, and with a severe dignity unrelaxed by the exposure he was condemned to for his evil alliance with Betty Hanley.

She also lay exposed, who had lived so shamelessly, respecting not the mold of beauty God had given her. Now men leered to look upon her nearly kiln-dried bosom, glued into its winding sheet. The glory of her hair that had been handled by bantering outlaws covered the grinning coquetry of her skull in a rippling wave of unbleached coal.

"Them that mocks God shall be mocked of him," Phoebus said, closing the door and putting some of the scattered vault bricks against it. "Now, I reckon, I kin git to the crossroads by a leetle after dark."

Patty Cannon's

Chapter 25

Phoebus walked along a large, shaded millpond and found the old boundary stone again. Taking the angle from its northern face as a compass point, he proceeded in that direction and soon fell in with a path which ran almost on the line between Maryland and Delaware, passing within sight of several of the markers. As he proceeded, no dwelling was visible, not even a clearing. There were no streams except one mere gutter in the sand, and he saw no man nor hardly an animal or bird. The monotonous sand pines, too low to moan, too thick to expand, too dry to give shade, grew like poor folks' sandy-headed children, keeping company with scrubby oaks. Pine cone and acorn seemed to have bred upon each other, and the wild hogs disdained the progeny.

"Maybe I'll git killed up yer in this Pangymonum," Jimmy reflected. "Though I 'spose it don't make no difference whair you plant your bones, I don't want to grow up into ole pines. Big, preachin' kind of pines, I could go into their sap and shats fust rate, but to die yer an' never be found in these wastes is pore salvage for a man that's lived among the white sails of the bay an' loved a woman elegant as Ellenory."

It was dark, and in half an hour he could hardly see his way. Sometimes a crow, as it heard strange sounds go past, would caw like an old watchman's rattle. The stars became bright, however, and the moon was new, and when Phoebus came to an open area in the pines, the lambent heavens broke forth and bathed the sandy fields with silver, showing a house in the clearing. It had outside chimneys, one thicker than the other, and a porch of two stories facing the east.

Site of Joe Johnson's Tavern

Though not a large dwelling, it was large for those days and for that unfrequented region. Its roof seemed to Phoebus remarkably steep and long, and yet, while enclosing so much space, had not a single dormer window in it. The southern gable was turned towards the intruder, and in it were two small windows at the top, crowded between the thick chimney and the roof slope. The two main stories were well lighted, and the porch was enclosed at the farther end, making a double outside room. No sheds, kitchens, or stables were attached to the premises, but an old pole well, like some catapult, reared its long shaft at half an angle between the crotch of another tree. Roads marked by tall worm fences crossed at the level vista where this tall house presided, and a quarter of a mile beyond the crossroads, to the northeast, was another house, smaller and hip-gabled like Twiford's, standing up a lane and surrounded by small stables, cribs, orchard, and garden.

"I never 'spected to come yer," Phoebus observed, "but I've hearn tell of this place considabul. The big, barn-roofed house is Joe Johnson's Tavern for the entertainment of Georgey nigger traders that comes to git his stolen goods. It's at the crossroads, three miles from Cannon's Ferry, whar the passengers from below crosses the Nanticoke fur Easton an' the north, an' the stages from Cambridge by the King's road meets 'em yonder at the tavern. The tavern stands in Dorchester County with a tongue of Caroline reaching down in front of it, an' Delaware State hardly twenty yards from the porch. Thar ain't a courthouse within twenty miles nor a town in ten, 'cept Crotcher's Ferry, whar the people goin' to church every Sunday mornin' kin pick up a basketful of ears, noses, fingers, an' hair bit off a-fightin' on Saturday afternoon. They call the country round Crotcher's 'Wire Neck' caze no neck is left thar that kin be twisted off, an' the country in lower Car'line they calls 'Puckem' caze the crops is so puckered up. They say Joe's a great man among his neighbors an' kin go to the legislater. T'other house out in the fields is Patty Cannon's own, whar she did all her dev'lishness fur twenty years till Joe got rich enough to build his palace."

With the rapid execution of a man who only plans with his feet and hands, the bay sailor observed that there was a grove of good, high timber—oaks and pines—only a few rods from the crossroads, under cover of which he could draw near the tavern. As he proceeded to gain its shade, he heard extraordinary sounds of turbulence from the front of the tavern: the yelling of men, the baying of hounds, oaths, and laughter. Listening, as he crossed the intervening space, he inadvertently fell into a ditch at the edge of the timber.

"Hallo," cried Jimmy, lying quite still for a minute in the perfectly dry channel to draw his breath, "this ditch seems to pint right for that tavern."

He crawled along its bed till it crossed under a road by a wooden culvert or little bridge of a few planks. The noise at the tavern was now like a fight, and as Phoebus continued to crawl forward, he heard voices crying:

"Gouge him, Owen Daw!"

"Hit him agin, Cyrus James!"

"Chaw him up!"

"Give 'em room, boys!"

Having crawled to what he judged to be the nearest point of concealed approach, Phoebus took a single glance only. Then, drawing his old slouched hat down to hide the bandaging, he muttered, "Now's jess my time," and crept up to the back of the crowd. They were all facing inwards in a circle, and he was not observed.

A fully grown man, as it seemed, was fighting with a boy hardly fifteen years old, but the boy was the more reckless and courageous of the two. The man, with three times the strength of the boy, lacked the stomach or confidence to avail himself of it. Having had the boy down, he was now being turned by the latter amid the shouts of the spectators:

"Three to two on Owen Daw!"

"Bite his nose off, Owen Daw!"

"Five to two that Cyrus James gits gouged by Owen Daw!"

The boy, with a Celtic face and supple body, was full of zeal to merit favor and inflict injury, and as the circle of vagrants and outlaws of all ages reeled and swayed to and fro, Phoebus put his head down among the rest and searched the faces for those of Levin Dennis or Joe Johnson.

Neither was there, and the only face which arrested his attention was a woman's. She was standing in the door of the enclosed space at the end of the porch. The whole building was without paint and weather stained, but this room on the porch was newer. Its two windows revealed the crude appendages of a liquor bar, as a fire within flashed up and lighted it.

By this fire the woman's face was also revealed. She was interested in the fight, slapping her hands together, laughing like a man, dropping her oaths at the right places, and crying, "I bet my money on Owen Daw! Cy James ain't no good, by God! Yer's whiskey a-plenty for Owen Daw if he gouges him. Give it to him, Owen Daw! Shame on ye, Cy James!"

There was occasional servility and deference to this woman from members of the crowd. She was what is called a "chunky" woman, short and thick, with rosy skin, low but pleasing forehead, coal-black hair, a rolling way of swaying and moving herself, a pair of large black eyes at once daring, furtive, and familiar, and a large neck and large breast, uniting the bulldog and the dam, cruelty and full womanhood.

Behind the woman, whom Phoebus thought to be Patty Cannon herself, the moonlight came through the door in the older and main building, shining through the house, and Phoebus saw that the rear door was also open and unguarded.

He took the first chance of dodging around the corner of the bar, intending to pass around the north gable of the house and dart up the stairs by the unwatched door. He had barely got out of sight when a loud hurrah burst from the crowd, and a feeble voice was heard crying,

"Enough, enough!" followed by jeers rapidly approaching.

The outside chimney, being the chimney of two rooms within, contained an arched cavity large enough to conceal a man. Phoebus dodged into this cavity in time to avoid the beaten party to the fight—the grown man—as he staggered blindly by towards a well, his face dripping blood. He was sobbing childishly, and the concealed sailor heard him say in a whining tone, "She set him on me; I'll make her pay for it."

Several of the partisans or tormentors of this craven followed after him, and Jimmy himself fell in at the rear. But instead of going with the rest towards the well, where the loser was bathing his face, Phoebus softly stepped over the low sill of the back door. As he had anticipated, a stairway ascended out of a large room containing tables, dishes, cards, bottles, whips, arms, and saddles, answering the purposes of parlor and hall, dining and gambling room.

Satisfying himself that there was no cellar under the tavern, the sailor slipped up the stairs, intent to discover where Judge Custis's property and Ellenora's wayward son had been concealed. The second story had a hall, which opened at the front of the house and upon the upper piazza, and four doors on this hall indicated four bedrooms. One of them was ajar. Peeping through, Phoebus saw the Negro trader Joe Johnson extended on a bed and oblivious to all the fighting and din outside, his form revealed by a lamp and an open fire.

An impulse, immediately repressed, came on the sailor to draw his knife and stab Johnson to the heart, as probably the villain who had shot him from the catboat. As the Negro trader wearily turned his long length in the bed, Phoebus slipped along the hall to the only other door that was not closed, which led into the room at the rear, southern corner of the house.

This door creaked as it opened, and a man lying on a pallet was revealed by the bright moonlight streaming in at two windows. Jimmy crouched where a large clothespress rose between the intruder and the occupant.

"Who's there?" exclaimed a voice with a slight lisp.

Discovering that a door opened into this remarkable closet, Jimmy slipped inside and drew his knife. The man moved about the narrow room and finally seemed to walk into the hall and down the stairs.

Feeling around the dark closet, Phoebus found a deep indentation in it—as of a smaller closet—and the sound of crooning voices came from above.

"By smoke," Jimmy mentally exclaimed, "this big closet is nothin' but a blind fur a stairway in the little closet, to climb up to the dungeon under the roof."

He stole out again and found the moonlight now streaming upon an empty pallet. The light also streamed upon a door in the closet, opposite the indentation he had felt. This door was secured by a padlock through a staple fastening an iron bar, and a key was in the lock. Jimmy turned the key, drew off the lock, and dropped the bar. The moment he opened the door an almost insupportable smell came down a hatchway within, up which leaned a rough stepladder of stout construction.

Phoebus went up the steep steps and entered a large garret, which was divided by a heavy partition with a door at the middle. From beyond this partition came the crooning sounds he had heard.

The bright night, shining through a small gable window, revealed this outer half of the garret empty, with no furniture or other appurtenance than the hole in the floor up which he had come. The door into the place of wailing was fastened by a long iron spike dropped into a staple that overshot a heavy wooden bar. As he slipped up the spike and took the bar off, Phoebus heard someone in the room below mutter and lock the great padlock upon the other door, effectually barring his escape by that egress.

"We must take things as they come," thought Jimmy grimly, "partickler in Pangymonum, whar I am now."

He also reflected that the arrangements of this kidnappers' pen, simple as they seemed, were quite sufficient. If authority should demand to search the house, the double clothespress below, with the ladder pulled up into the loft, became a harmless closet hung with wardrobe matters, and the inner closet a storeroom for articles of bulk. No one could go up or come down without passing two inhabited floors and three different doors, besides the door to the slave pen.

Phoebus now threw this last door open and walked into the pen itself, stooping his head to avoid the low entrance. As there was no window whatever, he was unable for some minutes to see the contents. He inhaled the strong, close air of many breaths exhausting the oxygen supply and heard various voices and chains and irons being moved against the boards of the floor. A man in some part of the den was praying in a highly nervous, excited way, slobbering out his agonizing sentences: "Lawd, descen'! Descen', oh my Lawd! I will not let dee go, oh, my Lawd! Come, save me! Yes, my Lawd, come walkin' on de waters! Come outen Lazarus's tomb! Come on de chario'f fire! Come in de power! Descen' now, oh my Lawd!"

Phoebus's entrance made no excitement, and he crouched to await the strengthening of his eyes. The place appeared to be nearly twenty-five feet square and was cross-boarded both the gable way and under the roof, the eaves of which were planked up a foot or two above the floor. A man standing in the middle could scarcely touch the ridge beam with his hands, while along the sloping sides he could barely sit upright.

The man continued to express his absolute subjection of spirit in a frenzy of words, while several little children cried and shouted responsively. After asking him kindly to do so several times, Phoebus ordered the man to cease, and when the command was disobeyed, he slapped the praying one with his open hand. The poor wretch rolled over in a kind of feeble fit.

A child continued to cry, and Phoebus took it in his arms and held one of the shillings from the cabin on Broad Creek between the child and the starlight. Seeing something shine, the child seized it and held fast. Phoebus next passed his hand over the face of a man who was snoring calmly and strenuously on the floor beside him. Making room for the faint light to shine upon the sleeper's face, he exclaimed, "If it ain't Samson Hat, I hope I may be swallered by a whale!"

Calling his name, "Samson! Samson!" Phoebus observed a most dejected mulatto person crawl forward from the shadows, rattling his manacles. When spoken to, this man replied with refinement and accuracy. His face, however, betokened a great inward misery. The sailor took as careful a survey of him as the moonlight coming in by the attic window permitted. The man had shaved recently, and his dark, curling side whiskers, clean lips, tuft of goatee in the hollow of his chin, and intelligent, high forehead seemed altogether out of place in this darksome eyre of the sad and friendless.

"Is he your friend, sir?" asked the man, turning towards Samson. "He must have a good conscience if he is, for he slept soon after he was brought here and has never uttered a single complaint."

"And you have, I reckon?" said the waterman.

"Oh, yes sir. I have been treated with such ingratitude that it would break any gentleman's heart to hear my tale. Who is your friend, sir?"

"Samson, wake up old bruiser!" cried Phoebus, shaking the sleeper soundly. "You didn't give in to one or two, by smoke."

"Is it you, Jimmy?" the old Negro finally said with a sheepish expression. "Why, neighbor, I'm glad to see you, but I'm sorry, too. A black man dey don't want to kill caze dey kin sell him, but a white man like you dey don't want to keep, and dey dassn't let him go."

"A *white* man here?" exclaimed the superior-looking person. "What can they mean?"

"I'm ironed so heavy, Jimmy," Samson continued, "dat I can't set up much. My han's is tied togedder wid cord, an' my feet's in an iron clevis, and a ball's chained to de clevis."

"Give me your hands," exclaimed Jimmy; "I'll settle them cords, by smoke."

In a minute he had severed the cords at the wrist, and the intelligent yellow man pleaded that a similar favor be done for him, to which the sailor acceded ungrudgingly.

"If it's ever known in Prencess Anne," said Samson, "as I 'spect it never will be—fur we're in bad hands, neighbor—dar'll be a laugh instid of a cry fur ole boxin' Samson, dat was kidnapped an' fetched to jail by a woman."

"You, licked by a woman, Samson?"

"Yes, Jimmy, a woman all by herseff frowed me down, tied my hands an' feet, an' brought me to dis garret. I hain't seen nobody but her an' dese yer people sence I was tuk."

"Ha!" exclaimed the dejected mulatto, "that's a favorite feat of Patty Cannon. She is the only woman ever seen at a threshing floor who can stand in a half-bushel measure and lift five bushels of grain at once upon her shoulders, weighing three hundred pounds."

"I ain't half dat," Samson smiled quietly, "an' she handled me shore 'nough. You remember, Jimmy, when I leff you by Spring Hill Church to git a woman on a little wagon to show me de way to Laurel?"

"Why, it was only yesterday, Samson."

"Dat was de woman, Jimmy. She was a chunky, heavy-sot woman, right purty to look at an' maybe fifty year ole. She was de nicest woman mos' ever I see. She made me git off my mule an' ride in de wagon by her an' take a drink of her own applejack. She said she 'stilled it on her farm. She said she knowed Judge Custis an' asked me questions about Prencess Anne, an' wanted me to work fur her some way. We was goin' froo pore, pine country, a heap wuss dan Hardship, whar Marster Milburn come outen, an' hadn't seen nobody on de road till we come to a run she said was name de Tussocky Branch, whar she got out of de wagon to water her hoss. At dat place she come up to me an' says, 'Samson, I'll wrastle you!'

"'Go long,' says I. 'I kin't wrastle no woman like you.'

"'You got to,' she says, swearin' like a man an' takin' holt of me jess like a man wrastles.

"I felt 'shamed an' didn't know what to do. Befo' I could wink, Jimmy, dat woman had give me de trip an' shoved me wid a blow like de kick of an ox, an' was atop of my back wid a knee like iron pinnin' of me down."

"The awful huzzy of Pangymonum!"

"De fust idee I had was dat she was a man dressed up like a woman. I started like lightnin' to jump up, an' my legs caught each oder. She had carried de cord to tie me under her gown an' clued it aroun' me in a minute. As I run at her an' fell hard, she drew de runnin' knot tight an' danced aroun' me like a witch, windin' me all up in de rope. De sweat started from my head. I yelled an' fought an' fell agin, an' as I laid with my tongue out like a calf in de butcher's cart, she whispered, 'Maybe you de las' nigger ole Patty Cannon'll ever tie.'

"At dat name I jess prayed to de Lord, but it was too late. She put me in de cart an' gagged me so I couldn't say a word, an' blood come outen my mouth. I heard her talkin' to people as we passed by a town an' over a bridge. Nobody looked in de cart whar I laid kivered over till we come to a ferry, an' dar we passed over. I heard her talkin' to a man on dis side of de ferry. He come to de side of de wagon an' peeped at me layin' helpless dar, my eyes jess a-prayin' to him. He had a elegant eye in his head, Jimmy, an' he says softly to hisself, 'Dis is no consignment, manifes'ly, to Isaac an' Jacob Cannon,' an' he kivered me up again. The woman fetched me yer, put on de irons, an' shoved me into dis hole in de garret."

"I reckon that was Isaac Cannon, t'other Levite that never sees anything that ain't in his quoshint."

"How's the purty gals, Jimmy? I 'spect I shall see 'em in my dreams if I'm sold Souf. I ain't got long to stay, nohow, fur I'm mos' sixty. If you ever git out, tell my marster to buy dat gal Virgie an' make her free. She ain't fit to be a slave."

"Gals has their place," said Phoebus, "but not whair men has to fight for liberty. How many fightin' men are we here?"

"I 'spect you's de only one, Jimmy. We's all chained up. Dese nigger dealers is all blacksmifs an' keeps balls, hobbles, gripes, an' clevises, an' loads us wid iron."

"Who is that woman back yonder so quare an' still?"

"Why, Jimmy, don't you know Aunt Hominy, Jedge Custis's ole cook? Dey brought her in dis mornin' wi' two little children outen Teackle Hall kitchen. Hominy ain't said a word sence she come."

Jimmy Phoebus went back to the corner of the den where the old woman cowered and called her name with kind assurances: "Hominy, ole woman, don't you know Jimmy? Jedge Custis is comin' for you, aunty; I'm yer to take you home."

She did not speak, and Phoebus lifted her without resistance nearer to the moonlight. Her lips mumbled unintelligibly. Her eyes were dull, and she did not seem to know him.

Samson crawled forward and also called her name kindly: "Aunt Hominy, Miss Vesty's sent fur you. Dis yer is Jimmy Phoebus."

Little Ned spoke up: "Aunt Hominy ain't spoke sence dat Quaker man killed little Phillis."

"Jimmy," Samson whispered solemnly, "Aunt Hominy's lost her mind."

"Yes," the dejected mulatto said, "she's become an idiot. They sometimes take it that way."

Phoebus bent his face close to the poor old creature, sitting there in her checkered turban and silver earrings, clean and tidy as servants of the olden time. He studied her vacant countenance, her tenantless eyes, her lips moving without connection or relevance, and felt that cruelty had inflicted its last miraculous injury—whipped out her mind from its venerable residence and left her body yet to suffer the pains of life without the understanding of them.

"Oh, shame," cried the sailor, tears finally falling from his eyes, "to deceive an' steal this pore, believin' intellec—to rob the cook of the little tin cup full o' brains she uses to git food fur bad an' fur good folks. Why, the devils in Pangymonum wouldn't treat the kind heart that briled fur 'em that a-way."

"De long man said he was Quaker man," exclaimed Vince, the larger boy, "He said Hominy was sold, an' he come to take us to de free country. De long man had a boat—Mars Dennis's boat—an' in de night little Phillis woke up an' cried. Nobody couldn't stop her. De long man picked little Phillis up by de leg an' mashed her skull in agin de flo'. Aunt Hominy ain't never spoke no mo'."

"Did you hear the long man speak after that, Vince?"

"Yes, mars'r, I heerd de long man tell Mars Dennis dat if he didn't steer de boat an' shet his mouf, he'd shoot him. I heerd de pistol go off, but Mars Dennis wasn't killed, fur I saw him steerin' afterwards."

"Thank God!" said the sailor, kissing the child. "Ellenory's boy was innocent, by smoke. That nigger trader shot me an' threatened Levin's life if he listened to me hailin' of him. The noise I heard was the murder of the baby, whose cries betrayed the coming of the vessel. Samson, thar's been treachery ever sence we left Salisbury, an' that nigger Dave's a part of it."

"He said he hated me caze I larned him to box. Maybe my fightin's been my punishment, Jimmy, but I never struck a man a foul blow."

"An' what was your hokey-pokey?" the pungy captain asked of the man who had been making so much religious din. "Did they sell you fur never knowin' whar to stop a good thing?"

The man hoarsely explained: "I was slave to a local preacher in Delaware an' de sexton of de church. It was ole Barratt's chapel, up yer 'tween Dover an' Murderkill—de church whar Bishop Coke an' Francis Asbury fust met on de pulpit stairs. My marster an' me was boff members of it, but he loved money bad, an' I was to be free when I got to be twenty-five years ole, accordin' to de will of his Quaker fader dat left me to him. Las' Sunday night dey had a long class meetin' dar, an' when nobody was leff in de church but my marster an' me, he says to me, 'Rodney, le's you an' me have one more prayer togedder befo' you put out dat las' lamp. You pray, Rodney.' I knelt an' prayed for marster after I must leave him to be free next year, an' while I was prayin' loud, people crept in de church an' tied me, and marster was gone."

"He sold you fur life to them kidnappers, boy, becaze you was goin' to be free. Don't your Bible tell you to watch *an'* pray?"

"Yes, marster."

"Well then, boys, it's all watch tonight and no more prayin'," cried Jimmy Phoebus cheerily. "Here are four men, lovin' liberty an' bound to have it or die. Thar's one of 'em with a knife, an' the first kidnapper that crosses that sill, man or woman—fur we'll trust no more women, Samson—gits the knife to the hilt! The blessed light that shone onto Calvary an' Bunker Hill is a-gleamin' on the blade. Work off your irons if you kin. I'll git you rafters outen this roof to jab with if you can't do no better. Are you all with me?"

"I am, Jimmy," answered Samson quietly.

"I'll die with ye, too," exclaimed the praying man with rekindled spirit.

"We will all be murdered, gentlemen," protested the dejected mulatto. "I know these desperate people."

"Then you crawl over in the corner," Phoebus commanded, "and see three men fight fur you. We don't want any fine buck nigger to spile his beauty for us."

The man crawled back into the blackness of the den, and Phoebus began to search the open half of the garret for implements of war. He found two long pieces of chain with which determined men might beat out an adversary's brains.

"Now boys," Jimmy said, "I hain't lost my head yesterday nor today neither, by smoke. I'm goin' to kill the first person that comes yer, git the keys of this den from him, an' lock all of you in fast—the dead kidnapper, too. Then they won't git at you to ship you off till I kin git to Seaford—it's not more than six mile—whar I know three captains of pungies, an' all of 'em's in port thar now—all friends of Jimmy Phoebus. They's all armed, an' their crews is enough to handle Pangymonum."

A noise was heard at the lock of the lower door, and Phoebus slipped into the enclosed den and took his station just within the door. "Remember," he whispered, "I open the fight."

The lock snapped at the door below the stepladder, the bolt fell, and the light of a lamp flashed up the hatchway upon the naked roof and through the cracks of the garret pen.

The sailor's knife was in his belt pouch, where he carried it over the hip. As he leaned down to look through a crack in the low door, he felt a hand from the gloom behind touch him. Instinctively, he felt for his knife, and it was gone.

"Captain," cried the voice of the dejected mulatto, as the door of the pen flew open and a bandit-looking stranger appeared with the lamp, "there's a white man here going to kill you. I've taken his knife from him and saved your life. It's a rebellion, Captain!"

"Help! Patty! Joe!" the man cried, as Jimmy Phoebus threw himself upon him, extinguishing the lamp.

The two men rolled on the floor in a grip of mortal combat. Phoebus was a man of great power, but his antagonist was also strong and slippery and a rough-and-tumble fighter. The pungy captain was on top. The bandit locked him fast in his arms and legs and tried to stab him in the side. Phoebus felt the handle of a clasp knife strike him repeatedly around the groin in strokes that would have killed had the blade not been slow to obey its spring.

While the two Negro assistants beat down the traitor with their chains and searched him vainly for the knife he had filched, Phoebus attempted to drag his antagonist to the hatchway and force him down it. At last he prevailed, and the man rolled down the ladder, seven feet or more, keeping his desperate hold on Phoebus and dragging him along. Both might have cracked their skulls but for a woman who was hurrying up the ladder, against whom their bodies pitched and were cushioned.

The shock, however, stunned both of them, and when Phoebus collected himself, he was tied hand and foot and lying on the garret floor again. Over him stood Joe Johnson, flourishing a cowhide. The bandage had been torn from Phoebus's face, and he was bleeding from the flesh wound in his cheek and breathless from his conflict.

The man called "Captain" and the woman—the same Phoebus had seen downstairs—subdued and tied the black insurgents, and both of them flourished whips over the backs and heads of the prisoners, big and little.

The woman turned her lamp on the sailor's swarthy, injured countenance and looked him over with dark, bold eyes.

"Joe, this is a nigger, by God!"

Johnson and the captain also examined him carefully, and, uttering an oath, the former kicked the prostrate man with his heavy boot.

"I popped this bloke last night," he said, "and thought the scold's cure had him. He's a sea crab, playin' the setter fur niggers. He sang beef to me in Princess Anne. I told him thar he'd pass for a nigger, an' we'll sell him fur one to Georgey."

"All's fish that comes to our net, Joe," the woman chuckled. "He'll sell big, too."

"That white man," spoke the voice of Samson from within the pen, "has hunderds of friends a-lookin' fur him. You'll ketch it if you don't let him off."

"What latitat chants there?" Joe Johnson demanded of Patty Cannon.

"That's my nigger, Joe," the woman answered.

"Fetch him to the light."

The captain propped Samson up, and Joe Johnson glared into his face, then struck him down with the handle of his heavy whip.

"Patty," he growled, "that nigger's scienced. He's the champion scrapper of Somerset. He knocked me down, an' I marked him fur it. Now, by God, I'm a-goin' to burn him alive on Twiford's island."

He swore an oath, half blasphemous, half blackguard, and the captain murmured with a lisp, "The white man is the only witness. Make sure of him!"

Irons were produced, and the captain speedily fastened Phoebus's hands in a clevis, hobbled his feet, and chained him to a ring in the joist below.

As the door was closed and bolted, a voice from the darkness of the pen cried out, "Aunt Patty, let me out. I saved the captain's life. I took the white man's knife. I'll serve you faithfully if you only let me go."

"He blowed the gab," said Joe Johnson, "but it won't serve him."

"Zeke," the woman cried, "it's no use. You go to Georgey with the next gang—you an' the white nigger thar."

The man threw himself upon the floor, moaning and praying as the lamplight disappeared. The hatchway slid over the stairs with an echo, and the lower bolts were drawn. As he lay there in horror and amid contempt, a voice arrested his ears, singing so low that it seemed a hymn from the roads and fields far down beneath:

> Deepen de woun' dy hands have made
> In dis weak, helpless soul.

The man listened in awe and silence, as if a spirit had hummed the tune. For a moment he forgot his doom of slavery in the deeper anguish of a treacherous heart, which that simple hymn bestirred.

It was only Jimmy Phoebus, thinking what he could say to punish this double traitor most, who had turned his back upon his race and upon gratitude. Jimmy had remembered the poor woman chained to the tree on Twiford's island and her oft reiterated hymn and had come to the conclusion that the mulatto wretch who decoyed her away and sold her was none other than his renegade fellow prisoner, in turn made merchandise of because he was too dangerous to set at large in the probable hue and cry for her.

"Poor Mary," Phoebus said in his deepest tones and with solemn cadence.

The wretched man listened and trembled.

"Mary's sperrit's callin', 'Zeke!'" Phoebus continued, awful in his inflection.

The miserable procurer's heart stopped at the words, and his eyeballs turned in torment.

"Come, Zeke, poor Mary's a-waitin' for ye!" cried the sailor in a voice of thunder, and as suddenly relapsed into the low singing of the quiet hymn again:

> Deepen de woun' dy hands have made
>   In dis weak, helpless soul,
> Till mercy, wid its mighty aid,
>   Descen' to make me whole;
>   Yes, Lord!
>   Descen' to make me whole.

At the thunder of the invocation the elegant Iscariot reached into a place between two of the cypress shingles in the roof, where he had hidden the sailor's knife, overlooked in the excitement of the preceding minutes and now remembered as superstitious passions rolled like dreadful meteors across the black and hopeless chasm of his despairing soul.

When the low drone of the hymn again crossed his maddened ears, he raised one shriek of "Mercy!" to which no answer fell. Then he drew the blade across his throat and fell dead in the kidnappers' den.

Van Dorn

Chapter 26

A thin fur of frost lay on the level farmlands, and the saffron and orange leaves were falling from the trees almost audibly when Levin awoke in the long, low house standing back in the fields from Johnson's Crossroads. He drank in the cool, stimulating morn, the sun already having made its first relay, and its postilion horn was blowing from the old tavern that reared its form so broadly in plain sight.

Levin had been brought up from Twiford's wharf the night before by the pretty maid whom Jimmy Phoebus had so much frightened. Having slept off the liquor fumes of Sunday, the exciting watches of Monday, and the mingled pleasure and pain, illness and interest, love and remorse of Tuesday, this was his first day of restful feeling.

He had already felt the earliest twinges of youthful fondness for the girl with whom he had spent the day at Twiford's, lying sick there from a disordered stomach and nervous system. More than the temptation of unhallowed money, her amiability and charms had changed his purpose to escape and give information of the injury inflicted upon Judge Custis's property.

It hardly seemed real that he had been an accessory to a felony and a witness to a murder, yet so it had happened. He felt the danger he was in but hesitated how to act. He had accepted the money of the trader and passed his mother's noblest friend on the river without recognition, while a dastardly ball had probably ended poor Phoebus's career. To these deeds he was the only white witness, the only one on whose testimony redress could be meted out.

He felt, therefore, that he was a prisoner and that his life depended on his cordial relations with the bloody Negro dealer and his band, and Johnson had reiterated his promise that if Levin joined them in equal fraternity, he should make money fast and become a plantation proprietor.

This coming night a raid on free Negroes in Delaware was to be made by the band in force. Levin had been told that he must be one of the kidnappers, and his frank cooperation would forever relieve him of any suspicions of defection and bad faith.

"Steal one nigger, Levin," Joe Johnson had said, "an' then if ever caught in the hock, you can never snickle." Levin interpreted this thieves' language to mean that he must do a crime to get the kidnappers' confidence.

He had divined a little of the power of this band at points along the river, especially around Vienna, when there had been mysterious intercourse between Joe Johnson and people on the shore, and the Negro ferryman at that old Dorchester village had spoken with Johnson only half an hour before the trader's encounter with Jimmy Phoebus in midstream. It was then the grim passenger had produced his pistol and said to Levin, "Now, my teller prig, honor's what I expect from you, an' to remind you of it, I'm a-goin' to pint this barking iron at your mummer. If you patter a cackle, a blue plum will go right down your throat."

Johnson had tried to evade an expected someone on the river. At the awakening and wailing of the child, he had hushed it forever in a fit of rage, and then he had shot Phoebus down.

Poor Hominy had sincerely believed that Johnson's peculiar slang was the language of the good Quakers, followers of Elias Hicks, who sheltered runaway slaves and spoke with a "thee" and "thou" and "verily." The keen dealer had made use of that misapprehension in the old woman's ignorant mind to decoy her into Levin's vessel and waft her into a distant country.

"We didn't steal her, Levin," Johnson said. "She wanted to mizzle from a good master, an' we jess sells the crooked moke an' makes it squar."

When Aunt Hominy came on board the *Ellenora Dennis* at Manokin Landing with the children, Levin had been asleep and knew nothing of the theft till it was too late to protest. Johnson himself had sailed the catboat into broad water and, bearing through Kedge's Strait, had cruised up the open bay out of sight of the Somerset shore. Towards night he had entered the Nanticoke by way of Harper's Strait and run up on the night flood, but the instinct of Jimmy Phoebus had cut him off at the forks and added another crime to Johnson's suspected record. He had never been indicted for murder, though it was thought to be none too formidable a crime for him.

There was a zest of adventure in this guilty errand, which, but for its crime, would have pleased Levin moderately well. Not being a reader, he knew little of the Delaware kidnappers, and in those days little was printed about Patty Cannon's band except in the distant journals like *Niles's Register* or *Lundy's Genius of Emancipation*. Levin had never sailed up the Nanticoke before, and its scenery was agreeable to his sight, while his heart was just fluttering in the first flight of sentiment towards the interesting creature he had so unexpectedly discovered there.

Arriving at Twiford's in the night, Johnson had sent Levin to bed there and pushed on himself to his crossroads. When he awakened the next day, Levin had found a beautiful wildflower of a young woman sitting by his pallet, looking into his large, soft eyes with her own long-lashed orbs of humid gray, and brushing his dark auburn ringlets with her hand. As he looked up wonderingly, she had said to him, "I have never seen a man with his hair parted in the middle before, but I have dreamed of one."

"Who air you?" Levin asked.

"Oh, I'm Hulda. I'm Patty Cannon's granddaughter."

"That wicked woman!" Levin exclaimed. "Oh, I can't believe that!"

"Nor can I, sometimes, till the sinful truth comes to me from her own bold lips. But, sir, I am not as wicked as she."

"How kin you be wicked at all," Levin asked, "when you look so good? I would trust your face in jail."

"Would you? How happy it makes me to be trusted by someone. Nobody seems to trust me here. My mother was never kind to me. Captain Van Dorn is kind, but he is too kind; I shrink from him."

"Where is your mother now?"

"She has gone south to live in Florida for all the rest of her life, and we are all going there after father gets one more drove of slaves. You are one of father's men, I suppose?"

"Who is your father?"

"Joe Johnson."

"That man!" murmured Levin. "Oh no, it is too horrible."

"Do not hate me. I have watched you for hours, almost hoping you might never wake up, so beautiful and pure you looked asleep."

"An' you—that's the way you look, Huldy. How kin you look so an' be his daughter?"

"I am not his child, thank God. He is my stepfather."

"What is your name, then, besides Huldy?"

The girl blushed deeply and hesitated. Her fine gray eyes were turned upon her bare feet, white as the river that flashed beneath the window.

"Hulda Bruinton," she said, swallowing a sigh.

"Bruinton—where did I hear that name?" Levin asked. "Some tale has been told me about him, I reckon?"

"Yes, everybody knows it," Hulda said in a voice of pain. "He was hanged for murder at Georgetown when I was a little child."

Levin could not speak for astonishment.

"I might as well tell you," she said, "for others will if I conceal it. I can hardly remember my father. My mother soon married Joe and neglected me, and Aunt Patty, my grandmother, brought me up. She was kind to me, but oh, how cruel she can be to others."

"You talk as if you kin read, Huldy," Levin said, wishing to change so harsh a topic. "Kin you?"

"Yes, I can read and write as well as if I had been to school. Colonel McLane taught me the letters around the tavern. I had a gift for it, I think, because I began to read very soon, and then Aunt Patty made me read books to her—such dreadful books!"

"What wair they, Huldy?"

"The lives of pirates and the trials of murderers—about Murrell's band and the poisonings of Lucretia Chapman, the execution of Thistlewood, and Captain Kidd's voyages. The last I read her was the story of Burke and Hare, who smothered people to death in the Canongate of Edinburgh last year to sell their bodies to the doctors."

"Must you read such things to her?"

"I think that is the only influence I have over her. Sometimes she looks so horribly at me and mutters such threats that I fear she is going to kill me, so I hasten to get her favorite books and read to her the dark crimes of desperate men and women, and she laughs and listens like one hearing pleasant tales. My soul grows sick, but I see she is fascinated, and I read on, trying to close my mind to the cruel narrative."

"Huldy, air you a purty devil drawin' me outen my heart to ruin me?"

"Oh, do not believe that! I suppose all men are cruel, and all I ever knew were Negro traders, but I should believe you too gentle to live by that brutal work. I looked at you lying in this bed, and pity and love came over me to see you, so young and fair, entering upon this life of treachery and sin."

Levin gazed at her intently, then raised up and looked around him, peering down through the old dormers into the green yard, and the floody river hastening by with such nobility.

"Air we watched?" he inquired.

"By none in this house. All the men are making ready for the hunt tomorrow night. The river is watched, and you would not be let escape very far, but in this house I am your jailer. Joe told me he would sell me if I let you get away."

"Hear me, Huldy, lady with such purty eyes: I never stole anything in my life nor trampled on a worm if I could git out of his path. How shall I save myself from these wicked men and the laws I never broke till Sunday? Tell me what to do, Huldy."

"Do anything but commit their crimes. Promise me you will never do that," she answered. "Let us be the friends I wished we might be before I ever heard you speak. What is your name?"

"Levin—Levin Dennis. My father's lost to me, and mother too."

"Then heaven has answered my many prayers, to give me something to cherish and protect. What is my dreadful doom—to become a woman among these wolves who meet around my stepfather's tavern to buy the blood and souls of people born free? Joe Johnson sells everything. He has often threatened to sell me to some trader whose bold and wicked eyes stared at me so coarsely. I have heard them talk of a price, as if I was the merchandise to be transferred—I, in whose veins every drop of blood is a white woman's."

"I want you to watch over me, Huldy. I'm a poor drunken boy. My boat is chartered to Joe Johnson fur a week an' paid fur. Tell me what to do, an' I'll do it."

"First," she said, "you must eat something and drink milk—nothing stronger. Their brandy, which they still themselves, sets people on fire. I will set the table for you."

It was after the table had been set that Jimmy Phoebus slipped in and devoured the milk and meat, overhearing the continuance of the conversation just given, and when his awkward motions had disturbed these new friends.

Levin now looked out of a small window upon a little garden, where a short, stout, powerfully-made woman was taking up some flowers from their beds and putting them into boxes full of earth.

"Yer, Huldy," exclaimed this woman, "sot 'em all under the glass kivers, honey, so grandmother will have some flowers for her hat next winter. They wouldn't know ole Patty down at Cannon's Ferry ef she didn't come with flowers in her hat."

A mischievous bluejay, apparently domesticated in a large cherry tree, occupied himself by alternately mimicking the cries of a little bird in terror and a hawk's scream of victory.

"Shet up, you thief!" said the woman, looking up. "The niggers is afeard of them bluejays, gal, an' kills 'em as Ole Nick's eavesdroppers an' tale carriers. That's why I keeps 'em round me. They's better than a watchdog to bark at strangers, an' caze they steals all their life, I love 'em. Bluejay, by God, is ole Pat Cannon's bird."

"Grandma," Hulda said, "I wish you had a large, elegant garden. You love flowers."

"Purty things I always would have," exclaimed the bulldog-bodied woman with an oath. "Bright things I loved when I was a gal an' traded what I had fur 'em. Direckly I got big an' traded ugly things fur 'em, like niggers. I'd give a shipload of niggers fur a apern full of roses."

"They say Florida is beautiful, Grandma, and flowers are everywhere there."

"Yes, they says so, but I don't never expect to go thar. Your mommy, Margaretty, likes it thar, but Delaware's my home, whar I've been cock of the walk sence I was a gal. Some of 'em hates me yer, an' the lawyers tries to indict me, but I'll live on the line till they shoves me over it."

Hulda was barefooted, but her feet, molded like flowers, seemed as natural as naked roots. She carried the boxes around to the glass beds encircling a chimney—dahlias, autumnal crocuses or saffrons, tricolor chrysanthemums, and orange marigolds. Resting on her hoe, the older woman smelled the turpentine of a row of tall sunflowers and twisted one off and put it in her wide-brimmed Leghorn hat.

"When I hornpipe on the tight rope," Levin heard her chuckle, "one of these yer big flowers must die with me."

She disappeared into the peach orchard, which tinted the garden with its pinkish boughs, and Levin improved the chance to look over the cottage and the landscape.

Site of Patty Cannon's House

The farm, level as a floor, was part of a larger clearing in the primeval woods, where only fire or age had preyed before man had come. Although there seemed more land than belonged to this property, Levin could see no other house over all the prospect except the bold and tarnished form of Johnson's castle with its long porch sliding forward. Its tall, blank, inexpressive roof seemed suspended like the drab curtain of a theater between the solemn chimney towers—the northern chimney, huge and broad and bottomed on an arch, the southern leaner, but erect as a perpetual sentry on the king's road.

The house where Levin had slept was a double frame cabin with three small rooms. There were beds in every room but the kitchen, and the hip roof provided considerable bed accommodation in the attic besides. Around the house extended a pretty garden with cherry and plum trees and wild peach along its boundaries. The fields contained many stumps, showing that the clearing had been made not many years before, while here and there some heaps of brush had been allowed to accumulate instead of being burned. As Levin looked at one of those brush heaps in a low place, a pair of buzzards slowly circled up from it, then flew low, round and round, as if they might be rearing their young there and hated to go far.

He drew his head back inside the dormer casement and was making ready to go down to the breakfast he smelled cooking, when he heard his name spoken in the garden and paused to listened.

"You lie!" exclaimed the old woman's voice. "I'll mash you to the ground!"

"He said so, Grandma, indeed he did."

Levin peeped from the garret depths and saw Mrs. Cannon standing with her hoe raised over Hulda's head, while a demoniac expression of rage distorted her not unpleasing features.

Levin walked at once to the window and whistled, as if to the bird in the tree. The older woman immediately dropped her hoe and cried out to Levin, "Heigh, son. Ain't you most a-starved fur yer breakfast? It's all ready fur ye, an' Huldy's waitin' fur ye to come down."

Levin went down the short, winding stairs to a table spread in the kitchen, while the old woman blew a tin horn towards Johnson's Crossroads, as if summoning other boarders. Then she said to Levin with a very pleasing countenance, "Son, these yer no-count people will be askin' you questions to bother you, an' I don't want no harm to come to you. You tell everybody you see yer that Levin Cannon is your name, an' they'll think you's juss one o' my people an' won't ask you no more."

Hulda raised her eyes slightly, which Levin took to mean assent.

"Cannon's good enough for a body pore as me," he said.

"You're a-goin' with Joe tonight, ain't ye?"

"Yes'm, I b'leeves so."

"That's right, Cousin. You'll git rich an' keep your chariot yit. Captain Van Dorn's gwyn to head the party. As Levin Cannon, ole Patty's pore cousin, he'll look out fur you. Now have some o' my slappers an' jowl with eggs, an' the best coffee from Cannon's Ferry. Help yer Cousin Levin, Huldy gal. He won't be yer sweetheart ef ye don't feed him good."

The breakfast was brought in by a white man with a scratched face, and one of his eyes was full of congested blood.

"Cy," Patty Cannon cried, "with that red eye Owen Daw give you, I 'spect you had hard work to turn them slappers."

"I'll brown both sides of him yit when I git the griddle ready for him," the man exclaimed, half snivelling.

"Before you raise gizzard enough for that, Cy, little Owen'll peck outen yer eyes like a crow. He's game enough to tackle the gallows. You may git even with him thar, Cy."

The man turned his cowardly, serving countenance on Levin inquisitively, then looked sullen and ashamed when Hulda observed, "Cyrus, you are not fit for the rude boys around father's tavern. They always impose on you. Please don't go there again."

"Where else kin he go?" Patty Cannon inquired. "Thar ain't no church left nigh yer sence Chapel Branch went to rot for want of parsons' pay. Let him go to the tavern an' learn to fight like a man, an' if the boys licks him, let him kill some of 'em. Then Joe an' the captain kin make somethin' of Cy James, an' people around yer'll respect him.

"Why, Captain, honey, ain't ye hungry?"

This was addressed to a man with several bruises on his forehead and an enormous flaxen mustache as soft in texture as a child's hair. He was wearing delicate boots with high, Flemish leggings that curled over and showed full women's red hose. Over these, covering his thighs only, were buckled trousers of buff corduroy, fastened above his hips by a belt of hide. His shirt was of blue figured stuff, and his loose, unbuttoned coat was a kind of sailor's jacket of tarnished black velvet. He hung a broad, slouched hat of a yellowish-drab color, soft, like all his clothing, upon a peg in the wall. He bowed to Hulda first with a smile of welcome, to Madame Cannon cavalierly, and to Levin with a graceful reserve that attracted the boy's attention from the notorious woman at the head of the table and held him interested during all the meal.

"Pretty Hulda, I salute you. Patty, *buenos dias*. I hope I see you well, friend," the last to Levin.

As he took up his knife and fork, Levin observed a pure white diamond ring flash upon the captain's hand. He was a blue-eyed man with a blush and a lisp at once, as of one who is shy. At times he would look straight and bold at someone in the group, and then he seemed to lose his delicacy and become coarse and cold. One such look he gave to Hulda, who bowed her eyes before it and looked at him but little again.

To Levin this man had the greatest fascination, partly from his extraordinary dress and partly from his countenance, in which was something very familiar to the boy, though he racked his memory in vain for the time and place. The stranger was hardly more than forty to forty-five years of age, but the mistress of the house treated him with all the blandishments of a husband.

"Dear Captain, pore honey," she said, "to have his beautiful yaller hair tored out by the nigger hawk. Honey, he fell onto me, and I thought a bull had butted me in the stummick."

"He broke no limbs, Patty," the captain lisped, feeding himself in a dainty way, while Levin observed that his fork was silver, and the knife he had taken from his pocket was a clasp knife with a silver handle. "*Chis! Chis!* If he had snapped my arm, the caravan must have gone without me tonight. I am sore, though, for senior was a valiant wrestler."

"He'll git his pay, honey, when they sot him to work in Georgey an' flog him right smart, an' we'll spend the price of him fur punch, lovey lad."

"I took this from him today when I searched him carefully," the captain said, handing Patty Cannon a piece of silver coin.

The woman drew out spectacles of silver from an old leather case, and putting them on, spelled out the coin: "George—three—eighteen—eighteen hunderd and fifteen!"

She threw up her head so quickly that the spectacles dropped from her nose. Hulda caught them, and Mrs. Cannon turned on her with a ferocious expression, snatching the spectacles from her hand.

"Whar did the devil git it?" Patty Cannon asked.

"Ah, who knows?" the captain lisped with pale nonchalance, giving one of those strong, piercing looks he sometimes afforded, right into the hostess's eyes. "It might be a coincidence. A shilling of a certain year is no rare thing. But, Madame Cannon, it becomes slightly curious when six such shillings, all numbered with that significant year, come out of the same pocket."

With this he passed five shillings of the same appearance to the hostess. She put on her spectacles again and looked at them all, then dropped them in her lap with a weary yet frightened expression and muttered, "Van Dorn, who kin he be?"

"That is of less consequence, my dear, than whether we can afford to sell him."

The captain was now looking at Hulda with the same strong intentness, but her eyes were on her plate, and though Madame Cannon looked at her, too, with both interest and dislike, Hulda quietly ate on, unconscious of their regard.

"Shoo!" the woman said. "People kin scare theirselves every day if they mind to. We've got him, an' if he knows anything, it's all in that nigger noddle. So eat an' be derned!"

"My guardian angel," the captain remarked with a blush and a stronger lisp, "you may not have observed that I never ceased to eat, while you immediately lost your appetite. What will you do with the shillings?"

Patty Cannon took them from her lap and rose, as if she meant to throw them out of the window.

"Stop, remarkable woman," the captain said, pulling his soft, flaxen mustache with the diamond-flashing hand. "Let your fecund resources stop and counsel. I am only looking to your happiness, that which has so abundantly blessed my life and banished every superstition from my heart till I believe in neither ghosts nor God nor devil, while you believe in all of them and give yourself many such unnecessary friends and intruders. *Chito! Chito!* as the Cubans say, and hear my suggestion before you throw those shillings away."

"Take care how you mock me!" cried Patty Cannon, her dark, bold eyes furtive, like one both angered and troubled, and her ruddy cheeks full of cloudy blood.

"Sit down. Give the shillings to pretty Hulda there."

"To her?"

"*Ya, ya,* to pleasing Hulda. What will trouble us then, her sinless bosom being their safe depository and her long-lashed eyes melting our ghosts to gray air?"

With a look of strong dislike, Patty gave Hulda the shillings, saying, "If you ever show one of 'em to me, gal, I'll make you swaller it."

Hulda took the silver pieces and looked at them a moment with girlish delight. "Oh, Grandma, how kind you are! Why do you speak so mad at me when you give me these pretty things? They seem almost warm in my bosom, like things with life. Let me kiss you for them."

She rose from the chair and approached the mistress of the house, who sat in a strange terror, not forbidding the embrace, yet almost shuddering as Hulda stooped and pressed her pure young lips to the blanched and dissipated face of Patty Cannon.

The captain looked at the kiss with his peculiar, strong, cold look, then smiled at Hulda graciously and said, "There, ladies, repose in each other's confidence. A few shillings for such a kiss is shameful pay. Do you remember as well as I do, Madame, that once you missed some money and thought your mother had stolen it, and hunted everywhere for it, and it never came to light?"

"Yes," cried Patty Cannon, "I do," and she swore a man's oath.

"Has senior been in that direction, do you think? I think he has, for Melson and Milman are up from Twiford's with the news that Zeke's last hide has burst her chain and fled. All the lower Nanticoke gives no trace of her, and Zeke has passed the heavenly gates." The captain drew the back of his silver clasp knife across his throat, smiling, and placed a sailor's sheath knife on the table. "Zeke only was untied. It was a too generous omission," he said.

"The senior says he set the Philadelphia woman free, and she has gone to start an alarm against us. The senior is a cool man. He told me that and laughed, and says he will live to see us all in a picture frame."

With her face growing longer and longer, the woman heard these scarcely intelligible sentences—wholly unintelligible to the younger people. To Levin it seemed that she grew suddenly old and yet older till her cheeks became dead and wrinkled.

"Van Dorn, I'm dying," she muttered. Her eyes glazed, and she settled down in her chair like a lump of dough.

"Hands off, fair Hulda," the captain cried joyfully, as Hulda moved to relieve the poor old woman. "No one shall assist at these ceremonies of expiation but Van Dorn himself, whose rights in Mistress Cannon are of priority. She's dropsical and hastening to perdition too soon, which I must arrest and let her comfort me still more. Young gentleman, you shall help me."

Levin took hold of Patty Cannon's feet and found that she seemed made of bone, so tough were her sinews. Van Dorn easily lifted her broad shoulders, and she was laid on a bed in the next room, where the elegant captain rubbed her limbs. Handling a bottle of leeches, he allowed one to crawl over the hand that wore the diamond, making it look like a ruby in living motion. As this voracious blood lover took his fill around the straight ankles of the hostess, the dainty captain held her in his arms like an ardent lover.

"Honey," the woman sighed, "my rent is due, an' Jake Cannon never waits. Take Huldy an' this yer new recruit, my cousin Levin Cannon, an' drive 'em to the ferry. An' watch that boy, Van Dorn; I want him broke in! Give him a pistol an' a knife an' have him cut somebody. Put the blood mark on him an' he's ours."

Prolific of his kisses, the captain lisped, "Great woman—Maria Theresa! Semiramis! Agrippina! Cleopatra—ever fecund in great ideas and growing youthful by nightshade. *Alto quedo*, but I love thee."

"Am I young a little yit, honey?" asked Patty Cannon. "Oh, don't deceive me, Van Dorn. Can my eyes look love an' hate like old times?"

"*Si, quiza!* More and more I see your deep eyes flame, dark angel, entering into black age like torches in a cave, but never do they please me as when they flash on some new, wicked idea, like this of marking the boy for life. Who is he?"

"He's a Cannon, one of the stock that my Delaware man belonged to. His mother looked down on me fur coming in their family. I have remembered her."

"You want your young cousin made a felon, then?"

"Yes, honey, I want him scorched so the devil will know him fur his own."

The captain reached down to the lady's feet and pulled off the leech and held it up against his hollow palm, gorged with the blood of the fair patient.

"The boy shall drink blood like this, Patty, till he can hold on no more and drops into our fate as in this vial."

As he spoke, he let the leech fall into the bottle, where its reflection in the glass seemed to splash blood.

"Ha, Van Dorn, I love you!" the woman cried and smothered him with caresses.

Cannon's Ferry

Chapter 27

Levin and Hulda were talking in the garden, dangerously near the subject of love, when it was announced that they were to be given a ride to Cannon's Ferry with Captain Van Dorn, and Aunt Patty also sent them a handful of half cents to spend. They were both delighted, though Hulda said, "Dear Levin, how happy we might be if it was only ourselves going for good. I could live with your beautiful mother and work for her, and knowing me to be always there, you would bring your money home instead of wasting it."

"Can't we do so some way?" asked Levin. "Oh, I wish I had some sense! I wish Jimmy Phoebus was yer to take me out thair in the garden an' whip me like my father, but if I hadn't come yer, how could I have seen you, Huldy?"

"And how could I have spent such a heavenly night of peace and hope if you had not come? The Good Being must have led you to me."

"Huldy," said Levin, after thinking to the range of his knowledge, "maybe thar's a post office at Cannon's Ferry, an' you kin write a letter to Jack Wonnell fur me."

"Why not to your mother, Levin?"

"Oh, I am ashamed to tell her. It would kill her."

"If we should be found out, Levin, Aunt Patty would kill me. There is no paper here, no ink that I can get. The postage on a letter is almost nineteen cents. These half cents are short of the sum by two."

"I have gold," cried Levin, thinking of the residue of Joe Johnson's bounty. He put his hand into his pocket, but the money was no longer there.

"Hush!" cried Hulda, "you have been robbed. Everybody is robbed who sleeps here. Grandma can smell gold like the rat that finds yellow cheese."

The individual who had served breakfast was seen coming towards them, a man with a low forehead, no chin to speak of, a long, crane neck, and a badly scratched and festered face.

"Mister," he said to Levin, "come help me hitch the horses; I'm beat so I can't see how."

Levin started at once, suggesting to Hulda to make a search for his missing money.

When they were in the little stable, the man observed to Levin in a whisper: "By smoke!"

Levin continued putting the bridles and breeching on the horses, when the man, with an insinuating grin, again said, "By smoke!"

"Heigh?" exclaimed Levin.

"By smoke!" the man remarked again with a very ardent emphasis.

"You must have been in Prencess Anne," Levin said, "to swar 'by smoke.'"

The ill-raised man with such an inferior head and cranish neck now slipped around to the front of Levin and looked down on him and whispered, "Hokey-pokey."

The idea crossed Levin's mind that the scullion of Patty Cannon must have gone crazy.

"Whair did you pick up them words, Cy?" Levin asked.

"Hokey-pokey," answered Cy James with a more mysterious and impressive sufflation; "hokey-pokey, by smoke, an' Pangymonum, too."

"Why Cy, what do you mean? Jimmy Phoebus never swars but in them air words. Do you know Jimmy Phoebus?"

"Pangymonum, too!" hissed Cy James with every animation. "Hokey-pokey, three, an' by smoke, one."

He put his long arms on his knees, bent down like a great goose, and stared into Levin's eyes.

"I never had sense enough," Levin said, "to guess a riddle. Them words I have hearn a good man use so often that they scare me. My mind's been a-thinkin' on him night an' day. Oh, is he dead?"

"By smoke, hokey-pokey, an' Pangymonum, too," the long, lean, excited fellow whispered with the greatest solemnity.

"They're Jimmy Phoebus's daily words, dear Cyrus. He was killed on the river night before last; I saw him fall. It is my sin an' misery."

"He ain't dead," Cy James whispered very low and carefully. "I won't tell you whar he is till you make Huldy like me."

"How kin I do that, Cy?"

"She thinks I'm a coward an' gits whipped by Owen Daw. Tell her I ain't no coward. Tell her I'm goin' to fry all these people on my griddle—all but Huldy. Tell her I'm only playin' coward till I gets 'em all in batter an' the griddle greased, an' then I'll be the bully of the crossroads."

"Do you hate me, Cy Jeems? I ain't done nothin' to you. I'm a prisoner here till I kin git my boat back from Joe an' go to Prencess Anne."

"I won't hate you if you kin make Huldy love me," Cy James replied. "Tell her I ain't no coward, that I'm goin' to be free an' rich too." He dropped his palms to his knees again and whispered, "Fur I know whar ole Patty buries her gole an' silver."

"Come with those horses, you idle lads," the lisping voice of the captain was heard to call. "*Ya, ya! luego!* The morning passes on."

"All ready," Cy James replied, and as they left the stable door, he whispered once more, looking significantly towards Johnson's Crossroads, "By smoke, hokey-pokey, an' Pangymonum, too."

The captain, looking like a gentleman of the knightly ages misplaced in this forest lair, held the reins, and with a grace, a blush, and a lisping laugh that Levin thought were very fascinating, handed Hulda into the seat beside his own.

"Now, Master Cannon, take your place in the tail of the vehicle," Van Dorn said, bowing to Levin and darting a cold, coarse look at him.

The vehicle was an old wagon without springs, and Levin's seat was a piece of board. Hulda's had a back to it and was padded with a bearskin robe. The captain looked with the most delicate attention at Hulda and blushed when she looked at him. Scarcely noticing the horses, yet having them under complete control, he drove out of Patty Cannon's lane and turned into the woods.

Levin cast one long, prying look at Johnson's tavern, wishing he might have the gift to see through its weather-stained planking and tall blank roof. Then he turned his attention to the road of hard sand and piney litter, as it unraveled like a ribbon behind the wheels and among the thick pines.

He observed the skill with which the captain threw his long, cowhide whip, a mere strip of rawhide fastened to a stick. While it might be awkward in other hands, Van Dorn could brush a fly from either of the short, shaggy horses with it, while hardly looking where he struck or disturbing the horse. He could also deliver a blow with it by mere sleight that made the animal stagger and tremble with abrupt pain.

At a little, sandy rill, the only one they crossed, a long water snake endeavored to escape before the wagon could strike it, but the captain rose to his feet, quick and cat-like, and projected the long lash into the roadside. The snake writhed and bounded in the air, almost cut in two. Then sitting again and bending so close to Hulda that his long, downy mustache of gold touched her cheek, Van Dorn said softly, "*Que hermoso*, young wildflower, let me take a snake out of your path also?"

"Which one, Captain?"

"It does not matter. Name any one."

"Alas," said Hulda, "I am of them. How can I wish harm to my stepfather and my grandam? They are not what I wish, but I am commanded to honor them."

"By whom, fair Hulda?"

"By God. I read it in The Book after I heard it from a slave."

"*Donde esta!* What slave that we know was so God-read?"

"Poor drunken Dave. He was a good man before he knew us. He told me the commandments for a drink of brandy. I wrote them down, and afterwards I found them in a book."

"*Chis! chito!* How graceful is your mind, Hulda. It comes out of the absolute blank of your condition and discovers things, as the young osprey, untaught before, knows where to dive for fish. Who that ever comes to Johnson's Crossroads brings a Bible?"

"Colonel McLane."

"He? The self-righteous crocodile! He gave you The Book?"

"Yes. He told me that Joe and Grandma were good people—conservative good people, I think he called it—but he said you believed in nothing, and there was no basis for conservative good in you."

"Oh, *hala hala*, but this is good," the captain softly remarked, stroking his golden mustache with the hand that carried the lustrous ring. "Patty Cannon may be saved, but I must be damned, and Allan McLane will sit in judgment. I believe nothing because such as they believe!"

"That is why nobody likes you," Hulda observed frankly, "agreeable as you are."

"And can you believe in anything after the surroundings of your childhood, touching crime like the pond lily that grows among the water snakes?"

"The lily cannot help it and is just as white as if it grew under glass, because...."

"Because the lily has none of the blood of the snake," the captain lisped. "Do you enter that claim?"

"No," said Hulda. "I know I am born from wicked parents, a daughter of crime—my father hanged, my mother of dreadful origin—but never have I felt that God held me accountable for their works if I kept my heart humble and my hands from sin. And never have I been tempted yet from within my own nature to enjoy a single moment of such hideous selfishness. I thank my kind Maker that something to love and believe in has come down the sad pathway I looked along so many years and found me waiting for him."

The captain kept his thoughts for several minutes, then finally sighed, "I know one thing in which I might believe, pretty child."

"Then embrace it," Hulda said, "and give your faith a single straw to cling to."

Van Dorn's hand slipped around her waist, and his florid cheeks and blue eyes bent beneath her Leghorn hat. "I find it here, perhaps. Shall I embrace your youth with my strong passion? I fear I love you."

"Yes," she answered, looking up with her long-lashed eyes of such entrancing gray. "Kiss me if it will give you hope."

The blush and high color went out of his face as he stared into those passive, large gray orbs, wide open beneath his pouting, rich, effeminate lips. As he hesitated, Hulda repeated, "If it will make you hope, kiss me."

"No," he answered. "Of all places, I am most hopeless *there*."

"I knew you would not kiss me," Hulda said, "if I gave you the right for any pure object. The kiss you would give me does not see its mate in my soul."

"You hate me, then?" said Van Dorn.

"No, I pity you. I pray for you, too."

"For me? What interest have you in me?"

"I do not know," said Hulda. "I have often wondered what made me think of you so often, yet never with admiration. You are the only person here who appears to have lost something by being here. Some portion of you seems to have disappeared. I have felt that you might have been a gentleman, though you can never be again. I shrink from you, and still I pity you. With all your handsome ways, I would never love you, while I loved the boy who is riding with us as soon as he came."

"*Chis! chito!* You can shrink from me and not from a Cannon? Why, girl, you have put him in my power."

"I have been in your power for a long time, Captain Van Dorn. You have looked at me with bold and evil eyes many a time but never came nearer. When I gaze at you as I did just now, you fly from me. That boy I love is as safe in your hands as I am."

"Why, dear presumer? Tell me."

"Because I love him, and you require my pity. As long as you protect that poor orphan boy, I shall carry your name to God for pardon. If you ever do him harm, my prayers for you will be dumb forever."

"Oh, *ayme! ayme!*" Van Dorn laughed softly, his blush not coming now. "You forget, Hulda, that I believe in nothing."

They had hardly gone four miles, when a low-pitched town of small square houses, strewn about like toy blocks between pairs of red, outside chimneys, appeared in the soft, humid, October morning, lying along the rim of a marshy creek which skirted the hamlet and flowed into the Nanticoke River a few miles above Twiford's Wharf. Two streets formed by two roads ended in a third street along the sandy, flattish river shore, where stood several larger dwellings. Like their humbler neighbors, they, too, were built of wood, but with greater, bolder chimneys rising as if in rivalry of four ships lying at anchor or beside two wharves. The ships threw their masts and spars into the sailing clouds, making the low forest that closed in river and village stoop to its humility. And the beautiful river, bordered by sandy bluffs and woods, flowed two hundred yards wide in stately tide, bearing up fish boats and pungies, Yankee schooners and wood scows to Cannon's Ferry.

The signs of life, floating in blue smoke from many hearths and sounding in oars, rigging, and lading, seemed human joy and power to Hulda. She cried to Levin, "Oh, look! Did you ever see as big a place as this? Yonder is the road to Seaford, just as far as we have come. The big ships are taking corn for the West Indies and bringing sugar and molasses. That is the ferry scow, and on the other side it is only five miles to Laurel."

"Do you like to travel that road?" asked the captain, his pleasing lisp and blush returned again.

"It makes me sad," replied Hulda, "but I do not mutter when I go past the spot like Grandma does."

"What spot?" asked Levin.

"Where father killed the traveler," Hulda said. "He died shamefully for it. You could almost see the place but for yonder woods, where the road to Laurel climbs the sandy hill."

"What's this?" said Van Dorn, seeing a little crowd around one of the single-storied cabins and turning his team into the parallel street.

A very tall, grand-looking man, who towered above the others and seemed unable to stand upright in the low cottage, took his place on the grassy sand without and gave his directions to someone within: "Levy on the spinning wheel! Simplify the equation! Stand by your *fi. fa.*! Don't be chicken-hearted, constable. She's had the equivalent; now she sees the quotient, too."

Van Dorn looked on and saw a spinning wheel come out of the door and a little wool in a bag after it.

Jacob Cannon put his foot on the wheel and poked his head in the door. "I see an axe and a coffee mill there, constable. Levy onto 'em with your *distringas. Experientia docet stultos!* Pass out that pair of shoes!"

The voice of a woman crying was heard, and Van Dorn and Levin both leaped out to look. Hulda also stepped down and disappeared.

A woman, white as illness and anguish could make her and barely able to stand, staggered to the door to beg that her shoes be given back, pointing to her naked feet.

"Now she's off the bed, levy on that!" cried the military figure with the long, eloquent face and twinkling eyes. "Shove it out the window. Mind your *fi. fa.*, and I'll take care of the quotient."

"Have mercy!" cried the woman. "My child was born only last week."

"Fling out that good chair, constable. Levy on the green chest. Don't you see a whole quilt or blanket anywhere? Allow neither tret nor suttle when you serve a writ for Isaac and Jacob Cannon!"

"Where shall I lie with my babe?" cried the poor woman, looking around the naked cabin, where neither bed, nor blanket, nor chair, nor chest, nor spinning wheel remained.

"*Li-vari facias!* and *fi-eri facias!* If there's a mistake, a replevin lies, but no mistakes are made by Isaac and Jacob Cannon. Constable, I think I see an iron pot on that crane!"

"It's got meat in it, sir—meat a-bilin'," answered the constable.

"Turn out the meat! Levy on the pot! Make the quotient accurate! Eliminate the pot from the equation!"

Out came the pot, the material inside extinguishing the fire, and it was thrown in the miscellaneous heap at Jacob Cannon's feet.

"Now take the cradle, hard-hearted man," the woman cried, "and turn the baby into the fire, too, since I can cook nothing to make its milk in my breasts."

"Is the cradle worth anything, constable?" asked the magnificent-looking man with the gray, silvery lights around his horsy nose. "If it's worth taking, I want it. People who can't pay their debts must live single like Jacob Cannon and not be distrained."

A boy, whose face was scratched and dissipation settled in it, bounded suddenly into the aghast group of spectators and made a vicious dive to recover the effects around Jacob Cannon's feet, but that mighty worthy took him by the collar, held him up, and dropped him over a fence like a bug. "Owen Daw," he said, "here be witnesses to an assault *insultus*, actionable as a trespass *vi*, the quotient, whereof, is damages or the equivalent in Georgetown Jail. Take heed, good citizens, and especially I note you, Captain Van Dorn."

"I'll kill him," shouted the young bully of Johnson's Crossroads, seizing an ugly stick.

"Justifiable as *son assault demesne*," remarked the creditor, as he wrenched the bobbin from the spinning wheel and knocked the boy down with it.

Deeply pained by the scene, Levin Dennis fervently and impulsively cried to Van Dorn, "Oh, Captain, can't you pay her debts! I'll give all Joe's going to give me to pay you back. See how she lays on the bare floor and hear her child crying for her. Oh, I think I hear my mother's voice a-callin' of me home as I listen to it."

Van Dorn, feeling Levin's hands grasp his own with simple confidence, heard but did not turn his head, while blushes, like roses, bloomed successively upon his fresh, effeminate cheeks. He did not repel the boy's hands but looked at the scene with worldly and unpitying curiosity.

"To pay the distraints of Isaac and Jacob Cannon," he murmured softly, "would keep a poor slaver poor. You must grow accustomed to such cries; I had to do so. Learn to love money like that merchant and me, and you will think them music."

"When we cry to God for mercy, Captain, maybe our cries will sound like that. I can't bear to hear it."

"You told Mother when she rented this ole house," Owen Daw exclaimed, "that she needn't pay the rent till the day of judgment."

"I've got the judgment," Jacob Cannon answered, his whitish eyes seeming to chuckle to the bridge of his nose, "and this is the day it's due. All legal days are judgment days to Isaac and Jacob Cannon."

"My son, my son," the woman's voice wailed to Owen Daw, "I see the end of your going to Patty Cannon's—my baby to the grave, myself to the almshouse, and you to the gallows."

"Captain," Levin cried, "pay the debt for me! Mother's never been poor as this. Pay it, and I will work fur you anywhair."

"How much is the debt?" asked Van Dorn lispingly.

"Ten dollars," said the constable, also moved to shame.

"Cannon, will you take me for it?"

"I'll take your judgment bond or cash, Captain—nothing less."

"Put back her stuff," the captain said, slightly pressing Levin's hand. "Put it back, and I'll settle with Isaac Cannon."

"God bless you!" cried the woman, taking her babe from the cradle and hushing its hunger at her breast. "They call you a wicked man, but blessings on you for all the good you do."

"*Chito! chito!*" smiled Van Dorn. "I did it for this foolish boy. I pity none."

Hulda had resorted to the strand or river street of Cannon's Ferry, where there were two storehouses. She had borrowed quill and ink and written a letter addressed to Mrs. Ellenora Dennis, Princess Anne, Somerset County, Maryland, saying:

> *Madam: Levin, your son, is near this place against his will, among dangerous men and in great temptation, but he has found a friend. In one week this friend will try to write again, and if not heard from, seek Levin Dennis at Johnson's Crossroads.*

This letter, written with all her unproficient speed, had just been folded, wafered, and endorsed, and she had put down one of the shillings of 1815 to pay the postage, when a shadow fell upon the store counter, and the letter was withdrawn from her hand. Van Dorn stood by her side.

"*Chis! chito! Es Posible?* A spy, perhaps. Now you will love Van Dorn, or Grandma Cannon shall hear your letter read."

"Give it to me," Hulda pleaded. "She will kill me if she reads it."

"If it were sent, we all might die. No, you are too dangerous."

"He looked at the shilling she was putting back in her bosom, and his eye was cold and fierce. Hulda's heart sank down.

"Brother Isaac," cried Jacob Cannon to a man at the desk—a man shorter than Jacob and not so much of a king in appearance, but with the same whitish eyes dancing around the bridge of his nose and a covert and thoughtful brow—"Captain Van Dorn is chicken-hearted and wants to settle the debt of the widow O'Day."

"By cash or judgment note, Captain?"

"Cash," answered Van Dorn modestly. "Take it out of this double eagle with Madam Cannon's rent for your farm."

"There's a tree—a bee tree, I think you said, Brother Jacob—cut down from Mrs. Cannon's field?"

"Yes, actionable under statute made and provided: to willfully spoil or destroy any timber or other trees, roots, shrubs, or plants. Value of said bee tree is three dollars; *levari facias!* The quotient is unsatisfactory to Isaac and Jacob Cannon."

"Oh, Brother Jacob," he chuckled, "what an executive help you air. Captain, isn't he a perfect Marius?"

"Madam Cannon," observed the captain, "throws up the farm with this payment, gentlemen. She has already moved her effects across the line to son-in-law Johnson's. I know nothing about the bee tree."

"Brother Jacob," said Isaac Cannon, "Moore takes the farm. Let him be notified that his rent commences without delay."

"Execution made, Brother Isaac," answered the Marius of the family. "This morning, perceiving Patty Cannon about to move her effects, my bailiff seized on her plough as security for the aforesaid bee tree, and Moore is ploughing with it already to put in his wheat. Time is money to Isaac and Jacob Cannon."

"Ha! What an executive comfort! Brother Jacob never adds an item to profit and loss."

"Gentlemen," said Van Dorn, "I recommend you not be charging bee trees to tenants in the vicinity of Johnson's Crossroads. It is an unusual item, and we are raising young men there who may not understand it."

"Captain," said the elder Cannon, chuckling as if still in admiration of Marius's subtlety, "I recollect that our ferryman brought over a man from Laurel this morning with some news. A woman with a broken shackle reported there last night and said she was the slave of Daniel Custis of Princess Anne. She came from Broad Creek."

"Where did she go?"

"A Methodist preacher put her in his buggy and started to her master's with her."

"Then she'll beat the wind," said Van Dorn. "These preachers are all horse jockeys and can outswap the devil. *Hola! ya, ya!* I must see to this."

He strode out and glanced at Hulda with a cold eye.

"Come, young people," said the grand head of Jacob Cannon to Levin and Hulda, "I will show you my museum."

He led the way to a warehouse overhanging the river, unlocked a door, and told them to walk carefully till they could see in the dark of the interior.

Levin kept Hulda's hand in his, as there slowly emerged from the shadows a great variety of dissimilar things heaped together. The house could hardly hold the vast aggregate of pots and kettles, spinning wheels and cradles, bedsteads and beds, harrows and plows, chairs and gridirons, rakes and hoes, silhouettes and picture frames, handmade quilts of calico and pillows of home-plucked geese feathers, fishermen's nets and oars—whatever made the substance of living in an old country without minerals and manufactures in the early part of the nineteenth century.

"Whare did you git 'em, sir?" Levin asked.

"Executed of 'em," said the warrior head and stature of Jacob Cannon; "pounced on 'em; satisfied judgments upon 'em. *Fi. fa.!* We call this Peale's Museum Number Two or the Variegated Quotient."

"All these things taken from the poor?" asked Hulda. "How many miseries they tell."

"Mr. Cannon," said Levin, "what kin you do with 'em? People won't buy 'em. They're just a-rottin' to pieces."

"We keep 'em," Marius answered, "to show all who trespass on Isaac and Jacob Cannon that there is a judgment day!"

With a look of more than childish contempt in her long-lashed gray eyes, Hulda said, "I should think you would fear that day, Mr. Cannon, when you say the prayer, 'Forgive us our trespasses as we forgive those who trespass against us.'"

The wind from the river appeared to bend the old warehouse, and the noise it made through the chinks and around the corners stirred the loosely disposed pile of cottage and hut comforts and seemed to arouse low wails among them, as when they were torn from the chimney side and the family.

"Where is my baby," the cradle seemed to say, "that I received warm from the womb of pain? Oh, I am hungry for his little smile."

"Why do I rest my busy wheel?" the spinner seemed to creak, "when I know my children are without stockings? Who keeps me idle while Mother asks for me?"

"Where is the old gray head," sighed the feathers, sifting in the breeze from a broken pillowcase, "that every night and in the afternoons dozed on our bag of down and picked us over once a year and said her prayers in us? Is she sleeping on the cold, bare floor, and we so useless."

The pot seethed to the kettle, "It is dinner time, and the little boys are crying for food, and still there is no one to lift me on the crane and start the fire beneath me. What will they think of me, they who gathered around so many years and watched me boil and poked their little fingers in to taste the stewing meat? I want to go! I want to go!"

The kettle answered to the pot, "I never sung since the constable forced me from Grandmother's hand and robbed her of the cup of tea."

The old quilt of many squares fluttered in the draught. "Take me to the young wife who sewed me together and showed me so proudly, for I fear she is cold since her young husband died."

The thrilled young lovers, standing so poor on the brink of what they knew not, seemed to hear these sounds in awe and drew closer to each other, like young Eve and Adam in the great wreck of Paradise and at the voice of God.

Hand in hand they stepped forth into the bright light of day and walked along the sandy street beneath the tall locust, maple, and ailanthus trees that grew in line along the front yards of the Cannons. Four large houses stood sidewise, end to end. First, Cannon's business house; next, Isaac Cannon's comfortable home, where he dwelt, a married man; third, the elegant frame mansion of Jacob Cannon, the bachelor, whose house, built for a bride, had never yet been warmed by a fire; and, finally, the old, low, bow-roofed dwelling of the mother of the Cannons, opposite which was the ferry wharf and Van Dorn talking to the Negro ferryman.

"Levin," Hulda said gravely, "this noble house is like that noble-looking Mr. Cannon, hollow and cold. Because he loved money too much to find a wife, he lives with his brother Isaac and keeps his own dwelling empty and locked."

"Let us love each other," Levin said. "It's all we've got."

"It is all there is to get," Hulda answered. "I do love you, Levin, and I will try to save you, though suffering may come to me."

The Woodland (Cannon's) Ferry and Cannon Hall

As Captain Van Dorn came from the wharf, blushing like a schoolboy and tapping his white teeth together under the long flax of his mustache, his attention was arrested by a proclamation pasted on a post:

Five Hundred Dollars Reward for
JOSEPH MOORE JOHNSON, KIDNAPPER
The above reward will be paid by me to any person or persons —and they will be exempted from detention—who will deliver to me the body of the above-named miscreant, that he may be brought to trial in Pennsylvania.
JOSEPH WATSON, *Mayor of Philadelphia.*

"Chis! he!" Van Dorn sighed. "The end must soon be near. Now, young people, come!"

As they passed Cannon's place going out of town, the familiar voice of Jacob was heard to cry, "Owen Daw's escaped, Brother Isaac, but we'll clap it to him on a *de bonis non*. I'll never take my eye off him till I die."

"Brother Jacob, what an executive help you air!"

As Van Dorn drove the horses up the slight ascent in the rear of the ferry, past an ancient double puncheon house with an arch in the center, Hulda pointed back and said to him, "Captain, it was there my father killed the traveler, where we see the road beyond the ferry enter the pines."

"Yes," said Van Dorn, giving her a cold look. "We might see the place but for the woods. It is at a hill, a short mile from the Nanticoke."

"Tell Levin about it, Captain."

"*Quedo, quedo!* It would not be pleasant."

"If it is true," said Hulda, "I can hear it. I want Levin to hear it, too, so that no deceit shall be between us."

Her smooth, moist hair, gray, humid eyes, complexion born between the rose and dew, straight, lithe figure, and air of dignity and truth impressed Van Dorn curiously.

"How bold you grow, wildflower. Cannot you stoop to recreate me? I, too, would live without deceit, but I will not tell you that story."

"You are afraid," spoke Hulda, feeling that nothing but this man and three miles of level road separated her from the vengeance of Patty Cannon, and that she must assert herself strongly over him.

"*Ya, ya!* are you not harsh? Remember, you may be whipped by your grandma."

"No, you will whip me or kill me if it is to be done. You dare not give me to her to punish."

"Dare not, again? Why?"

"Because you are my guardian. Between us is an instinct different from love, but strong. I feel it. I lean towards you but not on you. What is it?"

"*O Dios!*" lisped Van Dorn, his blush suspended and his warm blue eyes fascinated by her. "Is this a child or echo?"

"Tell us of my father's crime. I want Levin to know the wretched thing he has affection for."

"*Ayme! ah!* Well, listen, young lovers, and see what grisly things walk in these pines. There was a man named Brereton—they call him Bruington here, where their noses are twisted and their chins weak. He came from old Lewes, off to the east by Cape Henlopen, of a stout family in which was a grain of evil ever smoking through the blood. Do you sometimes feel it, Hulda?"

"No, not evil like that."

"He was apprenticed to a blacksmith and held the iron while the master struck. One day a man came in the shop to have a shoeing, and when he paid for it, he took a handful of money from his pocket. One piece—a dollar—fell in the soft soot of the shop, unperceived but by the boy. *Chis!* He covered it with his foot. When the man departed, the boy raised his foot and uncovered the dollar. His master said, 'Smart boy,' and they divided the stolen dollar."

"Jimmy Phoebus says the fust step is half of a journey," Levin noted.

"The boy looked avariciously on travelers ever after, who might possess a dollar. He took the empty shop of Patty Cannon's first husband, years after that saint died, and worked on hobbles, clevises, and chains to hold the kidnapped articles of commerce. Naturally, he kidnapped too, and while she was yet a child, Patty's daughter became Brereton's wife, bestowed by the fond, appreciative mother. Master Levin, if you fall into his path, Brereton's daughter may be bestowed on you. *Hola!* Behold her in Hulda."

"I can't see any of that sin in Hulda, Captain. She ain't even ashamed."

"No," affirmed Hulda, looking sincerely at Van Dorn, "it is too true to make me ashamed. I feel as if God's hand covered me like the silver dollar under my father's foot because he let me survive such parents." As she spoke, she took one of the silver shillings of 1815 and covered it with her hand in Van Dorn's sight.

Van Dorn continued: "There were two brothers named Griffin from about Cambridge, in Maryland—spoiled boys who had taken to the flesh trade. They stole men and gambled the proceeds away, and Brereton was their leader. One day a traveler came by from Carolina, hunting contraband slaves. He was your boastful sort, dropping the hint that he had fifteen thousand dollars to be invested. No later had he spoken than he felt his folly from the burning eyes and watering mouths telling him to stay, and slaves would be fetched. He started in a fright for Laurel, by way of Cannon's Ferry, intending to deposit his money and make them deal with him there. The word was passed to Brereton, and by Brereton to the Griffins, to mount and intercept the gold. Some say," lisped Van Dorn, "that Mistress Cannon dressed in man's clothes and commanded the band."

A deep, chuckling interest, like the sound of a hidden brook, attended Van Dorn's recital, and he blushed like a girl.

"At Slabtown, a nondescript spot a mile above Cannon's, the band crossed in a rowboat. They piled brush and bent down saplings in the traveler's road, and when the fleshmonger halted at the obstacle, *chis, hola!* they let him have it on both sides, sending icicles to his heart. He drew a pistol, but in a dying hand. His horse, in fright at bursting firearms in the evening shades, leaped the brushy barriers, galloped to Laurel, and delivered there an ashy-visaged effigy. As he sat stiff in death in the buggy, the red dye of his life dripped down his beard audibly. His name was only guessed."

"And what was the fate of the murderers?" Hulda asked with less horror than Levin showed.

"Three of them were arrested. One of the Griffins exposed his brother and Captain Brereton. Those two died on the gallows at Georgetown, young Brereton exerting himself under the noose to prevent his injudicious comrade from saying too much about Patty Cannon and her fair sisters, thinking on their interests more than on this living child, Hulda Brereton."

"The other Griffin also suffered death?" suggested Hulda with a pale, unevasive countenance.

"Yes. Your fond grandma, then in her blazing charms, drew him to her band again with the lure of Widow Brereton's hand. He killed a constable to recommend himself the better and died on the gallows at his native Cambridge. *Hala hala*, wildflower Hulda, next she gave your mother to Joe Johnson."

"It is an awful story," Levin said, "but Hulda never saw it."

"I can remember my father," said Hulda. "He was a large, strong man with a slow, heavy face, but he never smiled on me."

"Well, here is the crossroads," said Van Dorn. "What shall I do with this letter, bad wildflower?"

"Read it, if you will, or take this shilling and post it."

Van Dorn shrank back, rejecting the money. "Will you not buy it back, Hulda," he whispered, "with love?"

"Never."

"You may pay for this letter with your life or modesty."

"You dare not kill me," Hulda said.

"You will see," said Van Dorn.

Pacification

Chapter 28

For several days Princess Anne had missed some conspicuous citizens, such as Daniel Custis and wife, Captain Phoebus, Levin Dennis, and the free Negro Samson—large components of a small town, but, with the exception of Vesta Milburn, it had gained what everybody admitted to be the most beautiful woman in the place —the tall, brown-eyed, roguish niece of Meshach Milburn. In externals Vesta had made her a lady, correcting some of her faults, such as the sniffle, and was daily teaching her the mysteries of grammar and address. In these activities she was aided by the rector of the parish, whose heart was roused to partial animation again by the young visitor.

Loyally, William Tilghman pressed his friendship on Vesta's semi-social husband, determined to like him. He found little resistance and, happily, no suspicion there. Vesta was so grateful that she indulged the hope that her cousin and late lover would find compensation for her loss in Rhoda Holland.

Love came easily as a topic of talk to Rhoda, who said one evening as they sat in the library at Teackle Hall, "Mr. William, do preachers love jus' like other folks? Misc Somers say they is drea'fle sly boots. She say thar was a preacher down yer to Girdle Tree Hill that preached the meal-an-the-yum was a-goin' to happen right off."

"Millennium?" suggested Tilghman.

"Maybe so, but Misc Somers called it the meal-an-the-yum. Anyway, they was all goin' to rise right off, an' he with 'em. Lord sakes, they had frills put on thar nightgowns to rise in, an' the night before they was a-goin' up, that ar scamp run off with a widder an' her darter —jilted the widder an' married the darter. They couldn't rise at Girdle Tree Hill caze the preacher wa'n't thar, an' they didn't know when."

"And I suppose Mrs. Somers tells it on him," William Tilghman added.

"That she do. Now, was you ever in love, Mr. William?"

"I have been thinking, Rhoda, that when you are a good scholar and grandmother and you grow to like each other, as I believe you will, I might fall in love with you."

"Lord sakes—me loved by a preacher? Couldn't I never stay home from the preachin'? But then, to hear your own ole man a-barkin' away at the other gals, I think it would be right good."

The subject had now gone to that length that in a few days, to Grandmother Tilghman's slight indignation, Rhoda called the rector "William," and he answered her, "Dear Rhoda."

The triple widow, however, had one lane to her consideration, up which the artful Rhoda strayed as soon as she saw the gate ajar.

"Misc Tilghman," she said one day, "I been a-lookin' at you, an' I 'spect you was a real beauty. If you wasn't a little quar, nobody would see you was a ole woman now."

"I was a belle," the blind old lady said emphatically. "General John Eager Howard said he would rather talk with me than hear an oration from Fisher Ames. Charles Carroll of Carrollton proposed to me when I was old enough to be your grandmother, and after Susan Decatur, the commodore's widow, had tried in vain to get an offer from him. Said I, 'Carroll, is this another Declaration of Independence?' I said, 'No, Carroll, I won't reduce the last signer, it may be, to obedience on a wife going blind. That would be worse slavery than George the Third's.' He said I was a Spartan widow."

"Every widow I ever see was a sparkin' widow," Rhoda naively concluded, at which Mrs. Tilghman had to join in the laughter, and there was no evil feeling.

Jack Wonnell now held the temporary post of cook and woodchopper at Teackle Hall. Roxy saw him every day, sewed his tattered clothing, put the germs of self-respect in him, and caused Vesta to say to her husband one afternoon, "Such rapid changes have taken place, Mr. Milburn, that they have disturbed my judgment. As I see that white man the happy domestic servant of my pure slave girl, I hardly know whether my oldest prejudice is assured. She seems to have no greater affection than pity and interest for him, while he is made more of a man by his undisguised devotion to her. No man could work better than he does now."

"Love is so great, so occult," the husband replied, his brown eyes searching his wife's face over, "that its combinations have centuries left to run before they shall beat every prejudice down and prove, in spite of sin and dispersion, that of one blood all the nations are made."

Beginning of the Raid

Chapter 29

Organization of the raid into Delaware was completed when Levin and Hulda returned to Johnson's tavern, and the arrival of Van Dorn called forth cheers, as that blushing worthy threw his trim figure out of the wagon and bowed to Joe Johnson on the tavern porch.

"*O hala hala!* Do you go, son-in-law?"

"I'll ride with ye, Captain, a split of the Maryland way, but sprat for that Delaware! I'll go in it no more. I'll stand whack with you, however, fur the madges I give you and fur my stalling ken."

"*Quedito*," lisped Van Dorn. "We never leave your interests out, son-in-law. How is Aunt Patty?"

"She's made a punch fur the population an' calls fur young Levin thar to lush with her."

"I'll take mine along," Levin cried, "an' drink it in the chill o' the night."

"No," commanded the voice of Patty Cannon, "it's a-waitin' fur you, son—a good stiff bowl of apple and sugar. Him as misses his drinks yer, we sets no account on."

As Van Dorn and Levin pushed through the motley crowd on the little porch into the bar, Mrs. Cannon set before them two fiery bowls and cried, "Come in yer, Colonel McLane, an' jine my nug an' my young cousin Levin."

"No, Patty," answered a voice from the next room, "I've drunk my share. There's nothing like a conservative course."

As Patty put her head into this inner room, Levin saw an open window at his elbow and threw the whole of his liquor into the yard, smacking his lips heartily and saying, "Good!"

"Ha!" exclaimed Van Dorn, noticing Levin's deceit. "Smart people are around us, Patty—beware!"

He took from his pocket the fateful letter and glanced at its endorsement. As he did so, Levin heard an exclamation in the yard from a man who had received the whole of the apple brandy in his face. He was furious, but as soon as he recognized the thrower, he muttered apologetically, "Hokey-pokey, by smoke, an' Pangymonum, too!"

When Levin looked at Van Dorn again, the blush was on his face, but the letter had disappeared.

"Beware of the conservative course, Colonel," lisped Van Dorn, "except when generous Patty makes the punch, for she holds such measure of it that she does not see our infirmities."

"Honey," cried Patty Cannon to Levin, giving him an affectionate hug, "have ye swallered yer liquor so smart as that? I love to see a nice boy drink."

"But no more for him now, *cajela*," the captain protested. "Two such will make him fall off his horse. *Bebamos*, Patty. *Esta excelente!*" as he drank.

"How purty the captain says them things," the madam said to the gentleman within. "Maybe he's a-mockin' his ole sweetheart. Oh, Van Dorn, if I thought you could forget me, I would kill you!"

Levin noticed the rapid temper and demoniac face of this engaging lady as she spoke, her whole nature turning its course like a wheeling bat. From plausibility to an instant's jealousy and then to a dark tide of awful rage took but a thought.

"*Que disparate! hala o he!*" Van Dorn lisped sweetly, chucking the hostess under the chin. "But I do love to see thee so, thou charmer of my life. Never will I desert thee, Patty, whilst thou can suffer."

Her dark clouds slowly passed away, but her small head and abundant raven hair showed the blood troubled to the roots. Her eyes, once rich with midnight depths, now glazed like old window panes by age, searched the bandit's face with a strange fear.

"Van Dorn, time and pleasure cannot kill you; how well you look today. I think you are a boy to be ruined again every time you love me. You blush so modestly. Where is that pot of color you paint your cheeks with even before me, whose blushes none can recollect? Why do you love me?"

"*O dios!*" said Van Dorn. "I love thee for these spells of splendor, dark night and noonday passion, the alternations of earth and hell that eclipse heaven altogether. I love to see thee fear, though fearing nothing here. You hate this boy?"

"I hate him worse than wrinkles. Let him not come to me a child tomorrow. Let him see ghosts as long as he lives."

"How are the prisoners, Patty?"

"Why, the white nigger, dovey, is sick today. Blood loss and blisters have give him fever. My nigger that I tied—ha! a good job for Patty Cannon at her age—says t'other's a pore coaster named Jimmy Phoebus."

"Joe must be ready for a quick departure when we come back from Dover," the captain exclaimed. "It is a bold undertaking, and the whole of the state will be aroused like a blacksnake uncoiling in one's pocket."

The woman pointed from her shoulder towards the inner room and spoke even lower than before: "Van Dorn, I have a customer."

"For Negroes?"

"No, for Huldy. He shall have her."

∞

As Levin Dennis stood without, he saw a strange man plowing on the farm so recently deserted by his hostess for the gayer crossroads. The afternoon light fell on the sandy fields and struck a polish from the plowshare, and as the plowman passed the brambly spot, the buzzards circled up as if to protest that he came too near their young.

The long, lean servant who had waited on the breakfast table came out to Levin and watched his eyes.

"Plowin', plowin'," he said. "Levin, I kin show you how to plow. I can't do it, but you're the man."

"Huldy don't hate you, Cyrus. She says you're the nighest to a friend she's got."

"Oh, I love her like sugar cane," the lean, cymlin-headed servant said. "Tell her I'm goin' to be a great man. I'm goin' to spile the game. They lick me, but Cy Jeems has courage, Levin."

"Cyrus, tell Huldy all that's goin' on agin her. You kin go an' come an' nobody watches you. Huldy will be grateful fur it."

Putting his long arms on his knees and bending down, the scullion stared close to Levin's eyes, and looking towards the field, he whispered,

"Plowin', plowin'." Then turning partly and gazing over the old tavern with a look of wisdom, Cy James whispered, "Hokey-pokey, by smoke, an' Pangymonum, too."

"I reckon he's crazy," Levin thought, as the queer fellow turned and fled.

It was about three o'clock when the cavalcade was reviewed by Captain Van Dorn from the porch of the hotel. It consisted of about twenty persons, white and black, some riding mules, some horses, and there was one wagon in the line—the same that had been driven to Cannon's Ferry, intended to carry Van Dorn, Joe Johnson, and Levin. Van Dorn stood blushing, pulling his long mustache of flax and resting on his cowhide whip.

"Dave," he called to a powerful Negro, "get down from that mule; you're too drunk to go. Jump up in his place, Owen Daw."

The widow's son gladly vaulted on the animal.

"Sorden," continued Van Dorn, "you know all the roads; lead the way. Whitecar, go with him. We rendezvous at Punch Hall at eight o'clock. The order of march is in pairs, a quarter to half a mile apart. If any man acts in anything without orders, or halloos upon the road, he may get this lash or he may get my knife."

"Captain, where do we feed?" asked a small, wiry mulatto.

"Water at Federalsburg," answered Van Dorn; "feed at the Punch Hall."

They rode off in pairs at intervals of ten minutes, Van Dorn's vehicle to bring up the rear. A moment before he departed, Cy James touched the captain's sleeve and whispered, "Huldy." Turning to see if he was observed, Van Dorn followed to the deep-arched chimney at the northern gable and dismissed his guide with a look.

"Captain Van Dorn," Hulda said, her large gray eyes strained in tenderness and nervous courage, "do that boy Levin no harm; I love him. God forgive all your sins, many as they are, if you disobey Grandmother's wicked commands about my darling."

"Ha, wildflower, you have been listening?"

"No, I have only looked. I know Aunt Patty's petting ways when she means to ruin. She is no cousin of Levin; he is Joe's gentle prisoner. His very name she made him hide when she saw you coming this morning."

"*Creo que si*, Hulda, let me kiss you."

"Yes, if you dare."

She gave him that pure, soul-driven, child's strong look again, exerting all the influence she had ever felt she exercised over him.

Nevertheless, he kissed her for the first time.

"Today, *bonito*, I dare to kiss thee. Believe me, my kiss is a tender one."

"Yes, sir, there is something like a father in it. Oh, my father, art thou in heaven?"

"If there be such a place, wildflower, I think he is."

"Thank you, Captain Van Dorn; there may you also be and find the faith I feel in my one day's love on earth. I pray for you every day."

"*Ayme*, poor weakling, pray now for thyself. If thou canst save thyself sinless a brief day or two, it may be well for thee and Levin. Thy grandmother is dreadful in her joys this night."

"I can die," said Hulda, "if Levin be saved."

He kissed her again, and something wet dropped down his blushes.

"Eternal love," he sighed. "I've lost it."

Africa

Chapter 30

The captain took his place at the reins, his picturesque appearance deserving all of Patty Cannon's encomiums as he made a polite adieu. Then he threw his whip like a thunderbolt, and a cheer rose from the discarded volunteers loitering about the tavern as he drove Joe Johnson and Levin away.

The road was nearly dead level for five miles. As it was the commonly traveled highway from Laurel and the south to Easton and pointed towards Baltimore, numerous farms and clearings were seen, and tobacco fields alternated with the dry corn and newly plowed wheat patches. Here and there, like a measure of gold poured upon the ground, the yellow ears lay in the gaunt corn rows, to become the ground meal of the slave and the cattle's winter substance.

Johnson's popularity was apparent everywhere, and many a shout was given:

"Good luck to ye, Joe!"

"Tote us a nigger back from Delaway, Joe!"

"Don't be too hard on them ar black, Blue Hen's chickens, Joe!"

Van Dorn was too far above the comprehension of his neighbors to be familiarly addressed. "Patty Cannon's man" was the term of injured inferiority directed towards him after he had passed.

At Federalsburg they crossed the branch of the Nanticoke which pierced to the center of Delaware state and saw one large brick house of colonial appearance dominating the little wooden hamlet. Here, as generally within the Maryland line, hunting Negroes was either a "lark" or the serious occupation of many an idle or enterprising fellow. These men trained their Negro scouts like setters and crossed the line on appointed nights as ardently and warily as the white trader in Africa takes to the trails of the interior for human prey.

View from the River Crossing in Federalsburg

"Joe," said Van Dorn, "what is to be your disposition of the prisoners we have?"

"All goes to Norfolk but one—the nigger boxer. I burn him alive on Twiford's Island. If the white chap is too pickle to sell, I'll throw him overboard. He ain't safe."

"*Ea! sus!* It is boyish to burn the old lad. I have had many a blow from a black, and stab, too. A dog will bite you if you lasso him."

"No nigger can knock me down an' git off with sellin'."

"Then you are a bad trader. The Negro's price is all the Negro is. Why make him your equal by hating him?"

"I'm a Delaware boy," Joe Johnson said. "It's the pride with me to give no nigger a chance. In Maryland you pets 'em, like ole Colonel

Ned Lloyd over yer on the Wye. He's give his nigger coachman a gole watch an' chain because he's his son. What a nimenog! Some day he'll raise a nigger that'll be makin' politikle speeches, an' then I don't want to live no more."

"*Chito!* Since the Delaware lawyer sent you to the post, son-in-law, you're morose. I have had to eat with Negro princes, dance with their queens, and be ceremonious as if they had been angels."

"It would be the reign of Queen Dick for me! I couldn't do it, nohow."

"And by the way, Joseph, I may see your friend, the lawyer Clayton, at Dover tonight. He may send me to the post, too, and I fear no Delaware governor will take off the cropping of my ears, as was done for you in state patriotism."

"Beware of that imp of Tolobon!" Johnson muttered. "How I wish you could kill him. He's got to be a senator. Some day he'll be chief justice of Delaware. What'll niggers be wuth thar then?"

"I fancy, Joseph, you might be a legislator in Delaware if your inclinations ran that way."

"Easy enough, but I makes legislators. My wife Margaretta—her first husband's sister is the wife of the chancellor."

"*Hola! oh!* How came that great alliance?"

"She was housekeeper, an' he was a close old bachelor an' must break a leg. 'Well,' she says, 'you're a daddy. Justice is your trade, an' I must have it.' So, from bein' his peculiar, she becomes the madam, but she invented the kid."

"I have never been in Dover. How shall I tell where Lawyer Clayton dwells?"

"It's on the green a-middle of the town an' a-standin' by the Statehouse—a long, rough-cast house in the corner, three stories high, with two doors. The door next to the Statehouse is his office. Go past the Statehouse, which has a cupola onto it, an' you see the jug an' whippin' post. He's got 'em handy fur you."

Levin listened with all his ears. The liquor was now well out of his system, and he thanked God he had refused Patty Cannon's burning dram, else he might this night be the reckless mate for Owen Daw, whose own mother had predicted the gallows for him.

"An' now, Van Dorn, I turn back," Joe Johnson said. "I have a job to do down the Peninsuly. McLane has become the owner of a gal thar an' wants her sneaked. I takes black Dave with me, an' when I'm back, my boat will be ready an' my cargo packed. Then hey fur Floridey!"

He unhaltered his horse at the tail of the wagon, mounted him, and rode back across the stream. Van Dorn touched his horses and entered the dense woods on a byway to the north.

"Get up here, Master Levin, and ride by me," the captain soon said. He lifted Levin's old hat from his head and looked at his bright hair parted in the middle, his fine, large eyes, needing the light of knowledge, and his soft complexion and marks of good extraction.

"Where is thy father, Levin, to let thee go so ragged?"

"Shipwrecked," said Levin. "Gone down, I 'spect, on the privateer."

"A sailor was he? Well, he should be home to clothe thee and see that thou dost not cheat. I marked how Madam Cannon's punch was tossed out of the window."

"I thought you would not want me drunk beside you all night, sir, an' then I might enjoy your company. I don't want to drink no more liquor."

"You like my company?"

"Yes, sir."

The captain blushed and asked, "Why do you like me?"

"Not fur nothin' you do, sir. I like you fur somethin' in your ways. I reckon you're a smart man."

"*Si, senor*, that I am. I have gained the whole world and lost two."

"Two worlds, sir?"

"Yes, two immortal worlds—that is to say, two unaccountable worlds. I am no Christian."

"Maybe you're Chinee or Mahometan, then, sir. I 'spect everybody's got a religion."

"I was a Mahometan for business ends," Van Dorn said. "Having become a slaver, it was nothing to be a renegade. Stealing a man's soul every day, I put no value on mine. Yes, Mahomet is the prophet of God. So are you."

"You have been in Afrikey, I 'spect," suggested Levin.

"A few years only, long enough to be rich and to be ruined. I know the Negro coast from the Gambia to Cape Palmas and inland to Timbo. I have had an African queen and the African fever. I went to conquer Africa and became a slave."

"In Africa, I 'spect, Captain," Levin remarked without inference, "a nigger trader is respectable."

Van Dorn shook his head: "I doubt if the trade is respectable anywhere on this globe, unless it be here. No, I will say for these people, too, that while they do it low, lip homage, they look down on it. I was once the greatest guest in Timbo, housed with its absolute prince, attended by my suite, looking like an ambassador. He called me his son and drew me to his breast. Proclamations were made that I should be respected as such, yet every human object fled before me. As I rode out alone to see the gardens and cassava fields, the roaming goats and oxen, the rich mountain prospects, the sloe-eyed girls bathing in the brooks, the cry went round, 'Flesh buyer is coming.' Huts were deserted, and fields forsaken. The gray patriarchs and the little children ran, and I was left alone with the dumb animals, despised, abhorred."

"Don't they have slavery thair, sir?"

"Yes, slavery immemorial, yet the slave buyer is no more respectable than the procurer. The coin of Africa—its only medium—was the slave. He paid the debt of war, of luxury, and of business. Yet in the familiar study of such universal slavery, the soul of man grovels with it and points no more to bright destiny with the head erect. I died in Africa."

"Ain't you in the business now, sir?"

"Now I am a mere forest thief and bushman, Levin. He who begins a base trade rises early to its fullness, and in subsequent life must be a poor wolf rejected from the pack, stealing where he can sneak in. Such is the kidnapper, eking out the decayed days of the slaver. Such is the ruined voluptuary, living at last on the earnings of some shameless woman. Such am I—behold me!"

Van Dorn's eyes turned on Levin in their cold, heartless light, and yet he blushed as usual.

"You ought to be a gentleman, Captain. What made you break the laws so an' be a bad man?"

"*Ayme! ayme!*" mused Van Dorn, "shall I tell you? It was Africa. I was a high-minded youth, cool and bold and with a thread of pleasure in me. I went to sea in a manly trade, and fortune being slow, they whispered to me in the West Indies that my clipper was just the thing for the slave trade. I made the first venture out of virtue, which is all the voyage. In Africa I fell prey to the voluptuous life a white man leads there, to which the very missionaries are not always exceptions. Young, pale, graceful, brave—my blushes were as instant as my passions. The ceaseless intrigue of that climate circled around me like a harem dance around the young intruder. I forgot my native land and every obligation in it. I was enslaved by Africa to its swooning joys. I went there like the serpent and was stung by the woman."

"Ain't they all right black an' ugly in Africa, Captain?"

"The world has not the equal of Senegambia for beauty," Van Dorn said. "The Fullah beauties are often almost white, and the black admixture is no more than varnish on the maple tree. Even here, my lad, where civilization builds a wall of social fire around the slave, you often mark the idolatry of the white head to captive Africa."

"Did you make money?"

"For some years I did, plenty of it, but degradation in the midst of pleasure weighed down my spirits. The thing called honor had flown from over me like the heavenly dove, and in its place a hundred painted birds flocked joyfully—the dazzling creatures of that thoughtless world. Oh, that I could have been born there or never have seen it! At last I started home, but the world had adopted a new commandment: 'Thou shalt not trade in man.' They took my ship and all its black cargo, and I came home naked. Then my heart was broke, and I turned kidnapper."

"Home is the best place," said Levin, "even if folks is pore. When Jimmy Phoebus give me a boat, I thought I was rich as a Jew."

"What is that name?" asked Van Dorn.

"James Phoebus. He's mother's sweetheart."

"*Ce ce ce*," the captain mused. "Your mother lives, then?"

"Yes, sir. She's pore, but Jimmy loves her, an' the ghost of father feeds her."

"*Quedo*, a ghost? What kind of thing is that? Aunt Patty sees them; I never do."

"It comes an' puts sugar an' coffee in the window, an' sometimes a pair of shoes an' a dress. Mother says it's father. I guess it is."

"*O Dios*," lisped Van Dorn. "This Phoebus, is he a good man?"

"Brave as a lion, sir, an' pore as any pungy captain. He's the best friend I ever had. I hoped mother would marry him—he's been a-waitin' fur so long. She's afraid father ain't dead."

"*O hala, hala*, women are such waiters, but this man can wait too. Is he strong?"

"He come mighty nigh givin' Joe Johnson a lickin' in Princess Anne last Sunday, sir. He hates a nigger trader. Him an' Samson Hat, a black feller, thinks as much of each other as two brothers."

"And he gave you a boat?"

"Yes, sir. Joe Johnson hired it of me, but I didn't know he was goin' to run away niggers. He's got my boat an' ruined my credit in Princess

Anne, I 'spect. An' what will Mother do when I go to jail?"

"Why this other man, Phoebus, is there to marry her or look after her."

"Oh, Captain," sobbed Levin, putting his hands on Van Dorn's knees and laying his head there too, "pore Jimmy's dead; Joe Johnson shot him."

The captain did not move or speak.

"I've been a drunkard, Captain," Levin sobbed again in the confidence of a child. "That's whair all our misery comes from. I've got nothin' but my boat, an' people hires it to go gunnin' an' fishin' an' spreein'. They takes liquors with 'em, an' I drinks. God help me, I never will agin, but die first."

"Are you not afraid to lean on me?" lisped Van Dorn.

"No, sir."

"I have killed people, too."

"The Lord forgive you, sir. I know you won't kill me."

A sigh broke from the bandit's lips in place of his usual soft lisp, followed by a warm drop of water that splashed on Levin's neck as from the forest leaves now bathed in night.

"Oh, God," a soft voice said, "may I not die?"

Then Levin felt the same warm drops fall many times upon him, and his nature opened like the plants to rain.

"I have found a friend, Captain," the boy said after several minutes; "I feel you cry."

"*Chito, chito,*" lisped Van Dorn. "Here is Punch Hall."

Levin raised his head and saw an old house standing in the trees with a faint light streaming from the door and heard the hilarity of drinking men. The whole band poured out to receive Van Dorn's commands.

"One hour here to feed and rest!" Van Dorn exclaimed. "Let those sleep who can. Let any straggle or riot who dare!"

Peach Blush

Chapter 31

Judge Custis, whom we left riding out of Princess Anne on Sunday afternoon, kept straight north, crossed the bottom of Delaware in the early evening, and went to bed at Laurel on Broad Creek, a few miles south of Cannon's Ferry.

At daylight he was a-horse again, scarcely stiff from his exertion and feeling the rising joys of a stomach and brain becoming clear of alcohol. His mind had been bathed in sleep and temperance, the two great physicians, and exercise, natural to a Virginian, awakened his flowing spirits. He fancied the air grew purer as he advanced into the north, though there was hardly any perceptible change of elevation. Receding from the Chesapeake and approaching the tributaries of the Atlantic, the country grew drier as he turned the head springs of Cypress Swamp, the counterbalance of the Dismal Swamp of Virginia. At nine o'clock he entered the courthouse cluster of Georgetown, a little place of a few hundred people, pitched nearly at the center of the county a generation before, or about ten years after the independence of the country.

It was a level place of shingle-boarded houses assembled around a sandy square in which were both elm and Italian poplar trees. A double-storied, wooden courthouse rose on the farther side, surrounded by little cabins pitched here and there for the county offices. In the rear was a jail of two stories, containing family apartments below and the dungeon, debtors' room, and a family bedroom above. Near the jail and courthouse stood the whipping post with a pillory floor some feet above the ground.

Young maple, mulberry, and tulip trees grew bravely to make shade along the two streets which pierced the square and four parallel streets —pretty lanes to which loamy gardens ran. As the judge stopped at the tavern near the court, he was told that it was "returning day," and the place would soon be filled with constituents assembling to hear how she'd gone. "She," the judge knew well, meant Sussex County, and "gone" intimated the decision expressed at the polls.

"She's gone for Adams an' Clayton, ain't she, Jonathan Torbert?" asked the innkeeper.

"Yes," said a plain, religious-looking man, the teller of the bank, "Clayton's kept Sussex and Kent in line for Adams. Jeems Bayard and the McLanes have captured Newcastle. Clayton goes to the senate, Louis McLane to the cabinet, and the country to the alligators."

"Hurrah for Jackson!" answered the host. "He suits me ever since he whipped the British."

At breakfast Judge Custis recognized a gentleman wearing small-clothes, with his hair in a queue, who said with a passively kind expression, "Judge."

"Ah, Chancellor."

The chancellor was nearly seventy years old and wore a humble, meditative, yet gracious look, as one whose relations to this world are those of stewardship, and whose nearly obsolete dress represents the badge of perished joys and contemporaries, not of worldly pride. His unaffected countenance seemed to say, "I wear it because it is useless to put off what no one else will wear, when presently I shall need nothing but a shroud."

Judge Custis looked at the meek old gentleman closely, sitting at his plate like a lay brother in some monastery or infirmary, indifferent to talk or news or affairs. He had been keen, accumulative, with youthful passions long retained.

The remembrance impressed the Virginian to say to himself, "What, then, is man? At last old age asserts itself and bends the brazen temple of his countenance in almost pious remorse. There sits twenty-five years of equity administration, and behind it, thirty years of jocund and various life. No newspaper shall ever record it because none are printed here. He is indifferent to that forgetfulness and to all others because the springs of life are dry in his body, and he no more enjoys."

"Are you traveling north, Judge Custis?" the old man asked for politeness' sake.

"Yes, to Dover."

"There is a seat in my carriage. You are welcome to it."

"I will take it a part of the way, at least, to feel the privilege of your society, Chancellor."

The old man gave a slow, sidewise shake of his head.

"Too late, too late," he said, "to flatter me. I was fond of it once. I have been a flatterer, too."

The chancellor's black boy was put on the judge's horse, and the two men, in a plain, light, square vehicle, turned the courthouse corner for the north. As they passed the door, they heard the sheriff knock off two slaves to a purchaser, crying, "Your property, sir, till they are twenty-five years of age."

"Ha, ha!" a nearly chinless villager laughed in a great horse laugh, "say till ole Patty Cannon can git 'em!"

The purchaser gave a cunning, self-convicted smile to the passing chancellor, whose look of resignation only deepened and grew more humble.

The judge changed the subject: "We see each other but seldom, Chancellor, though we divide the same little heritage of land. I suppose your people are all proud of Delaware."

"Yes," the old man said, "being a mere foundling in the band of states, our people have the pride of their independence. The laws are administered, more farms are opened in the forest every year, blossoms come, old men die and are buried on their farms and their bones respected a few years. Our history is so pastoral that we must show some temper when it is assailed or we might let out our ignorance of it."

They rode in silence some hours through an older, settled, and more open country with large millponds and a better class of farm improvements. The sense of large water near at hand was mystically felt.

At one place the judge followed the old man's eyes, raised in an expression of tranquil satisfaction. From the slight elevation they had reached, a beautiful landscape of soft green marsh lay under their gaze, showing cattle and sheep roving in it, tall groves where cows and horses found midday shade, and winding creeks carrying sails of hidden boats, as if in a magical cruise upon the velvet verdure. Haystacks and farm settlements stood out in the long levels, and sailing birds speckled the air. In the far distance lay something like more marsh, yet like the clouds.

"It is the Delaware Bay," the chancellor said.

They entered a well-built little town on a navigable creek with a large millpond, sawmills, several vessels building on the stocks, and an air of vitality superior to anything Judge Custis had seen in Delaware. Here the chancellor pointed out the late home of Senator Clayton's father.

After the horses had been fed, the pair continued northward, passing another small town on a creek near the marshes, and came to a venerable brick church sitting a little off the road in a grove of oaks and forest trees.

Barratt's Chapel

"Here is Barratt's Chapel," said the chancellor, "celebrated for the plotting of the campaign between Wesley's native and English preachers for the conquest of America as soon as the crown had lost it."

They looked up over the broad-gabled, Quakerly edifice with its wide, low door, high roof, double stories of windows, a higher window in the gable, trim rows of arch bricks over door and windows, and belt masonry. The tall trees hushed it to sleep like a baby left to them. Nearly fifty feet square and probably fifty years old, it looked to be good for another hundred years.

"Through a mistaken conservatism my family in Accomack was harsh with the Methodists," Judge Custis said. "They are a good people and seem to suit this peninsula like the peach tree."

A small funeral procession was turning into the chapel, and the chancellor interrogated one of the more indifferent followers as to the dead person.

Having mentioned the name, the citizen said, "His death was mysterious. He was a Methodist and a good man, but it seems that avarice was gnawing his principles away. A slave boy, soon to become free by law, disappeared from his possession. He gave it out that the boy had run away, but suddenly our neighbor began to drink and to display money, and they say he had the boy kidnapped. He died like one with an attack of despair."

As they turned northward again in the genial afternoon, Judge Custis said, "What a stigma on both sides is this kidnapping."

The old man meekly looked down and did not reply. Judge Custis, feeling there was some sensitiveness on this and kindred subjects—yet why he could not understand—continued: "The night before I left Princess Anne, Joe Johnson, one of your worst kidnappers, boldly came to my house for lodging. Why I let him stay there is a subject of wonder and contempt even to myself, but there he was, perhaps, when I came away."

"Not a prudent thing to permit," the old man groaned.

"His wife was the widow of a gallows' bird, one Brereton. He was hanged for highway robbery and murder."

A muffled sound escaped the old gentleman of Delaware.

"*You* should remember the murder, Chancellor. It happened in this state. Brereton killed a slave buyer for the money he brought upon his person to buy kidnapped free people and slaves. Brereton was the son-in-law of Patty Cannon, that infamous pander between Delaware and the South."

The old chancellor looked up. "I wish to anticipate you," he said, "in what you might further say with truth, but perhaps do not fully know. The murderer Brereton was the son-in-law of Patty Cannon, it is true, but he was also the brother-in-law of myself."

"Impossible!" Judge Custis said.

"Yes, sir. I married his sister."

The old chancellor again turned his eyes to the ground.

"Great heavens!" exclaimed the judge. "How many curious things can there be in such a little state?"

Delaware State Capitol

It was in the middle of the afternoon that Judge Daniel Custis rode into a small town on an undulating plain, around two sides of which, at hardly half a mile distance, a creek ran through a pretty wooded valley, and a third side was bounded by a branch of the same creek, all winding through copse, splutterdock, lotus flower, and marsh to the Delaware Bay.

On a swell of alluvial soil at the center of the town, an oblong public square, divided by a north and south street, contained the principal buildings of the place, one of which was the Delaware State Capitol, a red, brick building a little older than the American Constitution, with a bell-crowned cupola above its center from which could be seen the Delaware Bay.

Near the Statehouse stood the whipping post, as humble as a hitching post, and the brick jail, like an unpresentable servant ever cringing near his master's company, hid out of the way there also. Various buildings surrounded this prim, Quakerly square, some brick and with low portals, others remodeled to suit the times. Some were mere wooden offices or huts with long dormers falling from the roof ridge nearly to the eaves, like a dingy feather from a hat crown.

State Offices on Dover Square

At diagonal corners of this square, as far apart as its space would permit, two venerable doctors' homes still stood, which had given more repute to Delaware's little capital than its jurists or statesmen—the former residences of Sykes the surgeon and Miller the pathologist and writer. It was at the former of these houses, a many-windowed, tall, side-fronting house of plastered brick, with side office and center door, that Judge Custis stopped and hitched his horse to a rack. The sound of twittering birds fell from the large elms, willows, and maples on the square, and Custis could see the robins running in the grass.

From the door of the two-storied side office, the sound of a violin came tenderly, and the judge waited until the tune was done. Loud exclamations of pleasure—the clapping of hands and the stamping of feet—showed that the fiddler was not alone. Presenting himself at the door, Judge Custis was immediately confronted by a large, tall man, fully six feet high, with a strong countenance and sandy hair, who carried the fiddle and bow in one hand and with the other seized Judge Custis almost affectionately and drew him in.

"Why, how is my old friend? Goy! How does he do? Who could have expected you on this simple occasion? Sit down there and take my own chair! Not that little one—the big easy chair for my old friend! Goy!"

As Judge Custis cast his eyes around to note the company, the demonstrative host whispered with a flash of his gray-blue eyes, "Who is he? Who is he?"

"A Custis," whispered a person hardly the better off for his drams. "I reckon he is by the lips and skin."

"Goy!" said the fiddler. "Friend Custis, I know my heart does not deceive me! Let me introduce you to the very essence of grand, old, little Delaware. Here is Bob Frame, the ardent spirit of our bar. This is James Bayard, our misguided Democratic favorite. Here is Charley Marim and Secretary Harrington and my esteemed friend, Senator Ridgely, and my cousin, Chief Justice Clayton. We are all honored by such a rare guest. Goy!"

As the judge went through the hand-shaking process, the tall, well fed host stooped to the convivial person again, and with his hand to the side of his mouth and an air of solemn cunning, whispered, "Where from?"

"Accomack or Somerset, I reckon," muttered the other.

"Now," exclaimed the host, taking both of Judge Custis's hands, "how do our dear friends all get along in Somerset and Accomack? Where *do* you call home, now, Friend Custis? How are our old friends Spence and Upshur and Polk and Franklin and Harry Wise? Goy! How I love our neighbors below."

There was a strength of articulation and physical emphasis in the speaker that the judge noted at once, and it was attended with a beaming of the eyes and a fine fortitude of the large jaws that made him nearly magnetic.

"And this is John M. Clayton?" said the judge. "We are not so far off that we have not fully heard of you. And now, since I belong to a numerous family, let me identify myself as Daniel Custis, late judge on the Eastern Shore."

"Judge Custis! Daniel Custis! Friends, what an honor! Think of it! The eminent American manufacturer! The creator of our industries! The friend of Mr. Clay and the home policy! Bayard, you need not shake your head! Ridgely, pardon my patriotic enthusiasm! Look at a *man*, my friends, at last! Goy!"

As the judge listened to various affirmations of welcome, Mr. Clayton, with one eye winked and the other resting on Lawyer Frame, the ardent spirit of the bar, made the motion with his lips: "Cambridge?"

"No, Princess Anne."

"And dear old Princess Anne, how does she fare?" He had again turned to the judge. "How is the little river Wicomico—no, I mean Manokin—how does it flow? Does it flow benevolently? Does it abound in the best oysters I ever tasted? In tarrapin, too? How is she now? Goy!"

"Are you on your way north, Brother Custis, or going home?" the keen, black-eyed chief justice asked.

"No, my journey is ended. I came to Dover to be acquainted with Mr. Clayton."

"Aunt Braner! Hyo! Come yer, Aunt Braner!" the host cried loudly, and an old colored woman entered, closely followed by some of her grandchildren. "Take this gentleman and give him the best room in my house. The best ain't good enough for him! Take him right up and give him water and make your son bresh him, and we'll send him the best julep in Kent County. Goy!"

"De bes' room was Miss Sally's, Mr. Clayton," the old woman answered.

A sudden change came over the highly prompt and sanguine face of the host. He hesitated, wandered in the eyes, and caught himself on the words, "No, give him the Speaker Chew room. That'll suit him best."

As the judge followed the servant out, the young senator emptied his mouth of a large piece of tobacco into a monster spittoon that a blind man could hardly miss, and with a face still long and silent and much at variance with his previous spontaneity, he absently inquired, "What can he want? What can he want?"

One of the Negro children had meantime toddled in at the door, and with large, liquid eyes in its solemn, desirous face, laid hands on the fiddle and looked up at Mr. Clayton.

"Bless the little child," he suddenly said; "he wants a tune? Well!"

Placing himself in a large chair, the young senator tilted it back till his hard, squarish head rested against the mantel, and he felt along the strings almost purposelessly till the plaintive air came forth:

> Ye banks and braes o' bonnie Doon!
> > How can ye bloom so fair?
> How can ye chant, ye little birds,
> > And I so full of care?
>
> Thou'lt break my heart, thou bonnie bird,
> > That sings beside thy mate;
> For so I sat, and so I sang,
> > And wist not of my fate.

He closed his eyes on the strains, and as he continued the air, a thickening at his throat and movement of his broad, athletic chest showed that he was inwardly laboring with some strong emotion.

His cousin, the chief justice, made a signal with his hat, and one by one the sitters stole noiselessly out into the square and went their ways, leaving the young man playing on with the Negro child at his knee, leaning there as if to spy out the living voice in his violin.

Other children came to the door—white children from the square and black children from the garden. Some ventured a little way in to hear the tender wooing of the sympathetic strings. He moved his bow mechanically, but the music sprang forth as if it knew its sister, grief, was waiting on the chords. At last a bolder child than the rest came and pushed his elbow and said, "Papa!"

"My dear boy," the fiddler cried. Tears streamed down his cheeks, and he lifted the lad to his heart and kissed him.

Judge Custis, though no word passed upon the subject, saw the solitary canker at the Senator's heart—his wife's dead form in the old Presbyterian kirk yard.

From this and other silent things it was soon apparent to Judge Custis that a light-hearted, affectionate, strong, yet womanly engine of energy constituted the young Delaware lawyer-politician. Keen, cunning, impulsive, hopeful, his feet provincial, his head among the birds, he combined facility and earnestness in almost mercurial relations to each other, and the judge saw that these must constitute a remarkable jury lawyer.

His face was shaven smooth. His throat and chin showed an early tendency to flesh. The poise of his head, the thoughtful darting of his eyes, and the slight aqualinity of his nose indicated one who loved mental action and competition, yet drew that love from a great, healthy body that had to be watched, lest it relapse into indolence. The loss of his wife so soon after marriage had been followed by nearly complete indifference to women. He had made politics his consolation and mistress, harnessing her like a young mare with his old roadster of the law and driving them together in the slender confines of his principality, then locking the law up among his office students to drive politics into the national arena at Washington.

"You require to be very neighborly, Clayton, in a small bailiwick like this?" the judge inquired, as they strolled along the square in the soft evening.

"We have the best people in the world in Delaware, friend Custis— few traders, little law, scarcely any violence. They are easy to please, but it is a high offense in this state not to be what is called 'a clever man.' You must stop, whatever be your errand, and smile and inquire of every man at his gate for every individual member of his household. The time lost in such kind, trifling intercourse is, in the aggregate, immense, but I do love these people. Goy!"

"It seems to me that you encourage that exaction."

"Well, I do—Why, Jim Whitecar, Lord bless your dear soul!" This was addressed to a thickset, uncertain-looking man who was retreating into the Capitol Tavern. "What brings you to town, Jim?"

"It's a free country, I reckon," exclaimed the suspicious looking man.

"Goy! That's so, Jimmy. We're all glad to see you in Dover behaving of yourself. Now don't give me any trouble this year, friend Jimmy. Be an honor to your good parents that I think so much of. Oblige me now."

As they turned to cross the middle of the square, Clayton said, "I'll have him at that whipping post—hugging of it—one of these days."

"What is he?"

"A kidnapper down here in Sockum, and a bad one—dangerous fellow, too. I hear he says if I ever push him to the extremity of his co-laborer, Joe Johnson—whom I sent to the post and then saved from cropping—that he'll kill me. Goy!" Clayton looked around a trifle apprehensively. "I'm ready for him."

"Delaware kidnapping is a great institution," Custis said.

"It has an antiquity you would hardly believe, friend Custis. Long before our independence, in the year 1760, the statutes of Delaware had to provide against it. Our laws have never permitted the domestic slave trade with other states."

The little place seemed to have a good society, and the beauty of the young girls sitting at the doors or walking in the evening showed something of florid North European skins, Batavian eyes, and rotund Dutch or Quaker figures.

The Tavern on Dover Square

As they returned to the public square, a room in the tavern, brilliantly lighted for that day of candles, displayed its windows to the gaze of Clayton, who exclaimed, "Goy! That is surely John Randel, Junior."

"The distinguished engineer?" observed his visitor, who had been waiting all the evening to broach the subject of his errand. "I have the greatest admiration of him. Shall we call on him?"

"Why, yes, yes," answered Clayton dubiously, "I'm not afraid of him. I—goy! I owe him nothing. He is such a litigious fellow, though, and so persistent with it. He's the wildest man of genius alive, but come on."

Knocking at a door on the second floor resulted in a sharp, prompt reply: "Come!"

A middle-sized man with a large head, broad shoulders, and cloth leggings buttoned to above his knee sat in a nearly naked, carpetless room, writing. His table was surrounded by burning wax candles, and his countenance was proud and intense. Mr. Clayton rushed upon him and seized his hand. "How is my friend Randel, the indefatigable litigant, the brilliant engineer to whom ideas are like persimmons on the tree, abundant but seldom ripe, and only good when frosted? How is he now and what is he at?"

"Stand there," said the engineer, "and look at me while I read the sentence I was finishing upon John Middleton Clayton of Delaware."

"Go it, Randel. Now, Custis, he'll put a wick in me and set me afire. Goy!"

"'It is the curse of lawyers,'" the unrelaxing stranger began, "'to let their judgment for hire to easy clients or to suppress it in the cringing necessities of popular politics; hence that residue and fruit of all talents, the honest conviction of a man's bravest sagacity, perishes in lawyers' souls ere half their powers are fledged. They become the registers of other men; they think no more than wax.'"

Here Mr. Randel blew out one of the candles. The illustration was cogent. Clayton lighted it again with another candle and said with a wink, "There's method in his madness, Custis," and turning to the host, "Let me introduce my great friend to you, Randel."

"Stop there," the engineer repeated sternly, "till I have read my sentence. 'Seldom it is that a lawyer of useful parts in a community as detached and pastoral as the State of Delaware has a cause appealing to his manliness, his genius, and his avarice like this of John Randel, Junior, civil engineer. No equal public work will probably be built in the State of Delaware during the lifetime of the said Clayton. No fee he can earn in his native state will ever have been the reward of a lawyer there, like his who shall be successful with the suit of John Randel, Junior, against the Canal Company. No principle is better worth a great lawyer's vindication than that these corporations, in their infancy, shall not trample upon the private rights of a gentleman and treat his scholarship and services like the labor of a slave.'"

"Well said and highly thought," interposed Judge Custis.

"'The said Clayton,'" continued John Randel, still reading, "'refuses the aid of his abilities to a stranger and a gentleman inhospitably treated in the State of Delaware.'"

"No, no," cried Clayton. "That is a charge against me I will not permit."

"'The said Clayton,'" Randel read inflexibly, "'with the possibilities of light, riches, and honor for himself, and justice for a fellow man, chooses cowardice, mediocrity, and darkness. He extinguishes my hopes and his.'"

With this, by a singular fanning of his hands and waft of his breath, Mr. Randel put out all the candles at once and left the whole room in darkness.

Judge Custis was the first to speak after this extraordinary illustration.

"Clayton, I believe he has a good case."

"That is not the point now," Mr. Clayton said with rising spirit and emphasis. "The point now is, am I guilty of inhospitality? Goy! That touches me as a Delawarean and is a high offense in this little state. It is true that this suitor is a stranger. He comes to me with an introduction from my brilliant young friend, Mr. Seward of New York, who vouches for him, but the corporation he menaces is also entitled to hospitality. In the main it is Philadelphia capital. Girard himself, that frugal yet useful citizen, is one of its promoters. My own state and Maryland, too, have interests in this work. Is it the part of hospitality to take advantage of our small interposing geography and lay by the heels a young, struggling, indeed national undertaking through our local courts?"

"Let the courts of the state, which are pure, decide between us," said John Randel, Junior, relighting the candles with his tinder box.

"No lawyer ought to refuse the trial of such a public cause because of any state scruples," Judge Custis interjected in his grandest way. "That is not national, and it is not Whig, Brother Clayton." The judge here gave his entire family power to his facial energy and expressed the Virginian and patrician in his treatment of the Delaware bourgeois and plebeian. "Granted that this corporation is young and untried. Let it be disciplined in time that it may avoid more expensive mistakes in the future. No cause is like a human cause to a true lawyer. The time may come when the talent of the American bar will be the parasite of corporations and monopolists, but it is too early for that degradation for you and me, Senator Clayton. The rights of a man involve all progress. Progress, indeed, is for man, not man for progress. As a son of Maryland, if he came helpless and penniless to me, I would not let this gentleman be sacrificed."

"If I were a rich man, Clayton would take my case," the engineer said. "My poverty is my disqualification in his eyes."

He again essayed in a dramatic way to fan out the candles, but his breath failed him. His hands became limp and hastily covered his eyes, and he sank to the table with a groan, putting his head upon it convulsively.

"Oh gentlemen," he uttered in a voice touching by its distress, "professional life—my art—is, indeed, a tragedy."

The easy sensibilities of Judge Custis were at once moved. Senator Clayton, looking from one to the other in nervous indecision, seeing Custis's dewy eyes and Randel's proud breaking down, was himself carried away and shouted, "Goy! This is a conspiracy, but I'll take your case, Randel. I can't see a man cry. Goy!"

As they all arose sympathetically and shook hands, a knock came on the door. There was a call for Mr. Clayton.

He returned in a few minutes with a grim countenance and said, "Randel, I have just declined a big, round, retaining fee to defend the very suit your tears and Brother Custis's have persuaded me to prosecute, but, goy, a tear always robbed me of a dollar."

"This sympathy today will make you an independent man for life," exclaimed the engineer.

"I have done Milburn's first errand right," thought Judge Custis. "Five minutes' delay would have been fatal."

Garter Snakes

Chapter 32

At Princess Anne, Vesta had moved her husband to Teackle Hall. He occupied her father's room and seemed to be growing better, though the doctor said that he had best be sent to the hills somewhere.

The free woman Mary, whom Jimmy Phoebus sent to Vesta, had arrived very opportunely. She took Aunt Hominy's place in the kitchen, where all the children's echoes were gone. The poor woman's own bereavement thrilled the ears of Virgie, Roxy, and Vesta herself, but her tale could not be used as legal testimony because she was a little black.

Jack Wonnell had found unexpected favor in Meshach Milburn's eyes and was appointed to sleep in the store and watch it. Roxy came down in the twilights and listened, with pity more than affection, to him weave the illusion of his love for her, willing to be amused by it because he was so sincere. Jack was all lover, meek and artful, bold and domestic, soft and outlawed as the houseless Thomas cat that makes highways of the fences and woos the demurest kitten forth by the magic of his purring.

"Roxy," said Jack, "I'm a-goin' to git you free, gal, fur I 'spect Meshach Milburn will give me a pile o' money fur a-watchin' of the sto'. Then we'll go to Canaday, whar I hearn tell color ain't no pizen. We'll love like the white doves an' the brown that makes the same coo, so happy they is."

"Jack," said the soft-eyed, pitying maid, "you're a pore foolish fellow, but I like to hear you talk. I reckon there is no harm in you. Virgie is in love with a white man, too, but you mustn't breathe it."

"Never," said Jack, making solemn motions with his eyes and cuddling closer in dead earnest. "Hope I may die; can't tell to save my life. Whooop! Tell me, Roxy."

Pore sister Virgie, she was made to love, and though it's hopeless, I think she loves Mr. Tilghman, our minister. He loved Miss Vesty once, and Virgie worships Miss Vesty like her sister."

∞

Vesta told the story of the free woman Mary to her husband, who listened closely.

"I know of but one thing," he said, "that will make such ignorance and cruelty fade from the forests of this peninsula—an iron road. A new thing called the railroad engine has just been made by an Englishman, one George Stephenson, and a specimen has been sent to New York, where I have had it examined. The errand your father went to do for me, he has done well. I shall send him to Annapolis next to get a charter for a railroad up this peninsula that will pass inside the line of Maryland and penetrate every kidnapping settlement hidden there. Intercourse, light, and law shall exterminate such barracoons as Johnson."

Vesta was glad to hear her husband praise her father, and hopes rekindled of a happier family reunion, when she should feel the heartache die within her. A letter came on the fourth day, which dashed these hopes to the ground:

Dorchester County, MD, October, 1829

Darling Niece, idol of my heart, let me begin by entreating you to take a conservative course when I break the sad intelligence to you of the death of my dear sister, Lucy, at Cambridge, yesterday, of the heart disease. She was the star of the house of McLane. She is gone. 'Vengeance is mine,' saith the Lord, and I shall take a conservative though consistent course on the parties who have inflicted this injury upon you, my dear niece, and upon your calm and collected, if stricken, uncle.

The Lord moves in a mysterious way, his wonders to perform, and his humble instruments require only to be inflexible and conservative to do all things well. Be assured that righteousness shall be done upon the adversaries of our family, and that right speedily. My own grief is composed in the satisfaction I shall take, and the assurance that your sainted mother is where the wicked cease from troubling.

The financial arrangements of my dear sister were of the most conservative and high-toned character, as was to have been expected of her.

You may be desirous, my outraged but still, I hope, spirited idol, to hear the particulars of Lucy's death. She did not reach Cambridge till near midnight, having made the journey from Princess Anne without fitting companions and in the excited state of her feelings. After she left Vienna in the evening, a depression of the spirits accompanied by a fluttering of the heart came on and rapidly increased. By the time she arrived at our relatives', she was nearly dead with nervous apprehension and weakness. On seeing me, she revived sufficiently to make her will in the most sisterly and conservative manner.

A physician was procured, but he pronounced her system so debilitated that he could not expect her to outride the shock, the nervous centers being depressed and atrophy setting in.

She talked incessantly about the Entailed Hat and said it was a permanent shadow and weight upon your heart, and made me promise to mash it if it could conservatively be done.

I read to my dear sister from the Book of Books and tried to compose her feelings, but she broke out ever and anon, "Oh, Brother Allan! To think I have raised children to be bought and sold and married to foresters and trash." She was deeply sensitive as to what would be said about it in Baltimore.

Just before she died, she said, "Do not bury me at Princess Anne where that fiend can come near me with his frightful hat! Take me to Baltimore, where there are no bog ores nor old family chattels to disturb the respectability of death. Apologize for my daughter and do her justice."

And so this grand woman died in the confidence of a blessed immortality, leaving us to vindicate her motives and contin-

ue her conservative course, and to meet at her funeral next Friday at our church in Baltimore, where Rev. John Breckenridge will preach the funeral sermon over this murdered saint.
With conservative, yet proud grief,
Affectionately, your uncle,

Allan McLane.

"Oh, sir," Vesta exclaimed, turning blindly towards her husband, "Mother is dead. Where can I turn?"

"Where but to me, poor soul," Milburn replied, knowing nothing of Mrs. Custis's late feelings against him. Your father shall be notified, and I am able to attend the funeral with you."

"It is in Baltimore," Vesta sobbed.

"Well, honey, I am ordered to go there by the doctor and get above the line of malaria. I can make the effort now."

Her grief and loneliness deprived her of the will to refuse. Roxy was selected to be her mistress's maid upon the journey, and William Tilghman and Rhoda Holland were to take them in the family carriage to Whitehaven landing to catch the evening steamer.

In officious zeal to be useful, Jack Wonnell gathered flowers and hung around Teackle Hall to run errands, and in order not to exasperate Vesta's husband, appeared bareheaded as the party set off.

"There is a dollar for you, Mr. Wonnell," Milburn said. "I rely upon you to watch my old store and conduct yourself like a man."

"I'll do it," answered Jack, grinning and blushing. "Hope I may die! Good-bye, Miss Vesty. Don't you forget me, Purty Roxy, way off thair in Balt'mer. I'll teach Tom to sing your name befo' you ever see me agin."

He waved his arms with real tears dimming his vision, and Roxy affected to shed some tears also as she waved good-bye to Virgie, whose eyes were turned with wistful pain upon the beautiful face of her mistress. Vesta threw her a kiss and reclined her head upon her husband's shoulder.

That evening, an hour before the carriage was to return, Virgie and the free woman Mary walked together down to Milburn's store to see if Jack Wonnell was on the watch. As they trode in the soft grass and sand under the old storehouse, they saw the bell-crowned hat—a new one brought from the ancient stock that very day—shining glossily on Wonnell's high, eccentric head. He sat in the hollow window of the old storehouse and talked to the mockingbird, which he was feeding with a clam shell full of boiled potato, egg, and some blue haws.

"Say Roxy, Tommy, an' I'll give ye some. Now, boy. Roxy, Roxy, purty Roxy. *Purty* Roxy. Poor ole Jack. Poor ole Jack."

Tom flew around Wonnell's head, biting at the hat, which stood in such elegant irrelevance to the remainder of his dress, and cried, "Meshach, he! Vesty, she! Vesty, Meshach! Vesty, Meshach!" but said nothing the village vagrant would teach it.

He showed the patience which idleness can well afford, feeding it or withholding the food, while continuing to plead, "Roxy, Roxy. Purty Roxy. Poor Jack. Pore Jack. Now, Tom, say Roxy, Roxy, pore Jack."

The bird flew and struck and sang a little, very niggardly. As the lights in the west sank and faded, the shiftless lover continued in vain to give the bird one note more than his master had taught.

The stars modestly appeared in the soft heavens, and Princess Anne gathered its roofs together like a camp of camels in the desert. With an occasional bleat or bark or human sound, the town seemed to doze in the soft fall night, perhaps absorbed in the spreading news of Mrs. Custis's death and Vesta's wedding journey that had to be taken at last.

"Miss Virgie," said Mary—ten years her senior but comely still—"have you ever loved like me? I had a kind husband, and helpless as I was, I tried to love once more. Maybe it was a sin."

"I love my mistress as if she was myself," Virgie said. "I feel as if in heaven, before we came here, I was with her. I love her father, too, as if he was not my master but my friend. Oh, how I love them all, but what can I do to show my love—poor naked slave that I am? They say they will soon set me free. How do people feel when they are free?"

"They don't appreciate it," Mary sighed. "They just go and put themselves in captivity again. Like selfish things, they falls in love."

"But to love and be free," Virgie said, her bosom glowing in the thought till her rich eyes seemed to shed warmth and starlight on her companion's face, "to give your own free love to someone and feel him grateful for it—what a gift and what a joy is that. He might be thankful for it, and seeing how pure it was, he might respect me."

"Who is it, Virgie?" Mary asked.

"Whoever would love me like a white girl," the ardent slave softy exclaimed. "It must be someone who does not despise me. I hear Miss Vesta's beau, Master William, read the beautiful service, and I think to myself: 'How freely he might have my heart to comfort his if he would take it like a gentleman.' I would be his slave to make him happy if he could love me purely like my mother. Oh, my mother, whose name I do not know, where is the tie that fastens me to heaven? Did my father love me?"

"Pore Jack, pore Jack," Wonnell coaxed to the sleepy bird. "Sing Roxy, Roxy, Roxy, Tom."

"Whoever your father was, Virgie, your mother's love for you was pure. God makes the wickedest love their children because he is the Father to all the fatherless."

"Could my own father have brought me into the world and hated me?" Virgie said. "They say I am almost beautiful. Will he who gave me life never call me his and say, 'My daughter, come to my respect; rest on my heart and take my name?'"

"Poor Virgie," Mary sighed. "Remember that we are black. We hardly ever have fathers; they is for white people."

"Dog my hide," Wonnell mumbled above, "ef a bird ain't a perwerse critter. Purty Roxy won't think I'm smart a bit ef I can't make Tom say Roxy, Roxy, Roxy. Pore Jack."

"I am almost white," Virgie continued. "I want to be all white. Why can't I be so? The Lord knows my heart is white and full of holy, unselfish love."

"Pore chile," Mary said. "We shall all be washed and made white in the Lamb's blood, Virgie. That's where your soul pints you to. I know it ain't pride and rebellion in you. It's like I'm looking at my baby, white as snow to me and God now."

"Hush!" said Virgie, suddenly trembling. "What voice is that?"

There was an old willow tree in a recessed spot at the end of the store, and by it were two sheds, now disused. Mary drew Virgie into one of them, and they listened.

A low voice said, "Dave, air your pops well slugged?"

"Yes, Mars Joe."

"Allan McLane pays well fur the job?"

"Yes, Mars Joe."

"You can't mistake him, Dave. No shap is worn like that nowadays. Look only fur his headpiece an' aim well."

"Yes, Mars Joe."

"Fur me," continued the other voice, "I'll go right to the tavern an' prove an alibi. My lay is to take the house gal that old gripefist's young wife thinks so much of. I'll snake her out tonight. She's the property of Allan McLane, left him in his sister's will. They found the paper on her body givin' the gal to the dead woman only two days before. She's Allan's tomorrow, but tonight she's mine!"

A sensual, sucking, chuckling sound like a kiss made upon the back of his own hand followed this significant threat. Mary placed her hand over the sinking slave girl's mouth and held her motionless.

"Tommy! Sing Roxy, Roxy, Roxy. Pore Jack. Pore Jack. Sing, Tommy, sing!"

"There," the white man whispered softly and was gone.

Mary breathed the words to Virgie, "Kidnappers—come," and they glided from the old tenement unobserved and entered the copse along the stream.

The mourner at the window above chattered sleepily to the nodding bird, "Pore Jack. Pore Jack. His leetle Roxy's gone away. Pore Jack. Roxy, Roxy, Roxy."

The Negro, half covered by the willow's shade at the corner of the old warehouse, peered up with bloodshotten eyes to distinguish the covering on the bird tamer's head. He saw Jack Wonnell sitting backward on the window frame, swaying in and out as he lazily tempted the mockingbird to sing, and the bell-crown, so singular to view, came in full relief against the gray sky.

"It's ole Meshach," said the Negro silently. "I hoped it wasn't, but dar is de hat, sho." He cocked his huge horse pistol and took aim directly from below.

"Pore Jack. I reckon Roxy won't have pore Jack caze Tommy won't sing. Sing, Tommy. Pore Jack. Pore. . . ."

The great horse pistol boomed on the night, and in its smoke the Negro rushed into the bush and sought the fields.

Down from his seat on the windowsill the witless villager fell backward, all bestrewn, measuring his body in the sand. There he lay silent as the other shadows, his arms extended in the frenzy of death and his mouth wide open and flowing blood. Jack Wonnell had paid the penalty of being out of fashion.

Aroused by the loud report, the mockingbird leaped onto the empty windowsill to seek his tutor. "Poor Jack! Poor Jack! Roxy! Roxy! Roxy!" came screaming on the night; then all was still.

∞

Returning from Whitehaven, William Tilghman was absorbed in the melancholy thoughts inspired by the departure of his cousin, when the carriage was arrested at the ancient Presbyterian church by a woman almost throwing herself under the wheels.

"Why, Lord sakes, it's our Virgie!" cried Rhoda Holland.

The girl sprang into the carriage by William Tilghman's side and threw her arms around him, crying, "Save me!"

"What ails you, Virgie?" the young man asked assuringly. "You are in no danger, child."

"I am sold," the girl gasped with terror in her voice and her wild eyes. "Miss Vesty's sold me to her Uncle Allan. He's sent the kidnappers after me. They're yonder in Princess Anne. Drive me to the North, to the swamps, anywhere but there!"

"I know your mistress made you over to her mother, Virgie, for a precaution, fearing you might not be safe in her own hands. She told me so and asked if the death of her mother could possibly affect you."

"Oh, it has! Mary knows the kidnapper that's come for me. He is the same that stole Hominy and the children. He kept her chained on an island. He says he'll have me tonight to do as he pleases. Master McLane lets him have me!"

The carriage had already descended the hill and crossed the Manokin when, in her terror, Virgie seized the reins from Tilghman's hands and drew them with such frenzy that the horses were pulled into the open area before Milburn's store. There, something frightened them, and they dashed at a gallop into Front Street, the wheels passing over an object that nearly upset the carriage.

The street they took for their run crossed a small arm of the Manokin and led up to a gentleman's gate, but before this brook was reached, Tilghman, an experienced horseman and driver, had reined the flying animals into a nearly unoccupied street called Back Alley, parallel with the main street of Princess Anne. In little more than a moment of time the whole town had been cleared, and hardly a person in it was aware of the vehicle going past.

Tilghman, in a cool, gentle voice, told the girls to sit perfectly still. As he could not force the animals to stop without danger to their harness, and seeing that they had a clear, level road ahead, he waited for their power to wear out and their fears to subside.

Rhoda Holland was too ashamed to scream, and her pride was aroused in the presence of the muscular young minister, sitting there like an artillery teamster driving into battle, his nostrils and jaws delineated in the gray air. He expressed almost the same joy he had long experienced by following the hounds in the autumn fox hunts, where Judge Custis had said he was the perfect pattern of a rider.

Since they were leaving behind the bloody hunters of men and women, Virgie felt no fear of the horses, but the young man, mindful of her mistress and feeling that this poor quadroon was dear as a sister to Vesta's heart, bent down and kissed the slave girl pityingly. With a great torrent of tears, a sense of rest and respect fell upon Virgie, and she paid no heed to time or danger till the carriage came to a stop in the deep forest sands several miles east of Princess Anne.

"William," said Rhoda Holland, "what air we to do to save Virgie? Uncle Meshach's gone. Jedge Custis is nobody knows whar. This yer Allan McLane, Aunt Vesty says, is dreffle snifflin' an' severe. I think it's a conspliracy to steal Virgie when they's all away. Misc Somers would take keer of her, but I'm afraid she'd tell somebody."

"Are you sure that you saw and heard truly?" the minister said to Virgie.

"Oh, yes! I saw the same man at Mr. Milburn's the day he was taken sick. He looked at me a low, familiar look and muttered something evil. Mary knew him too. Oh, do not take me back to Princess Anne; I will never go there again."

"It may be true," Tilghman reflected. "It probably is true. Vesta has no faith in Allan McLane. She says that in spite of all his religious formality, he makes money in the Negro trade. He is the trustee already of Mrs. Custis's estate and no doubt the administrator by will. He may have sent Joe Johnson to kidnap Virgie under color of his right, and Johnson would abuse anybody. Vesta will never forgive us if we let Virgie go to him."

"But I am a slave," Virgie sobbed. "Oh, my Lord, to think I am not Miss Vesta's, but a strange man's slave. How could she give me away!"

"It was an error of judgment," Tilghman replied. "She could not anticipate her mother's immediate death. There, where she thought you safest, you were most in peril."

They had now crossed Dividing Creek into Worcester County. Here they halted to cool the horses at the same old spring under the gum tree where Meshach Milburn stopped on the evening he went to the furnace village.

"William," Rhoda Holland said, "if Virgie is McLane's slave, you can't keep him from a-takin' her. She can't go back to Prencess Anne at all."

"I don't mean that she shall, Rhoda. I know you are a brave woman. We will drive her to Snow Hill tonight and leave her with a nurse, a free woman once belonging to my family. This nurse has a husband who is said to be a conductor on what is called the Underground Road to the free states."

"Lord sakes, a abolitionist?"

"I hope so," Tilghman said. "I know Vesta wants to set this girl free. There is no way to do it and respect her womanhood except to give her a wild beast's chance to run."

"My, my, and you a minister of the Gospil, William!"

"Yes," he answered, "of the Gospel that tells me how to be a neighbor to my neighbor." The young man's eyes flashed. "I never felt so humiliated for my cloth and for my country as now. To think how many men preach the Gospel of God all their lives long and have never set a living soul free. By the help of Christ I will do one such Christian felony."

As he spoke, the sound of a cornstalk fiddle and of foresters' naked feet dancing on the floor of the old Milburn cabin came crooning out in the night.

In another hour they were at the furnace village; its blast gone out; its lines of huts deserted; no human soul to be seen. The millpond, lying like a parchment under the funereal cypress trees, seemed stained with the blood of the bog ores that oozed upward from the depths like the corpse of murdered enterprise, suffocated in Meshach Milburn's foreclosure.

The horses toiled through the sand till an open country of farms provided better roads, and at ten o'clock they crossed the Pocomoke at Snow Hill and stopped at a gate before a neat, one-story, whitewashed house.

Virgie kissed Rhoda and descended with Mr. Tilghman, who knocked at the vine-environed door. A window opened, and after a parley the door admitted them.

"May God let you know some night the pure bed and sleep you have brought me to," Virgie whispered. "God bless you for the kiss you gave me, my dear white playmate, that you are not ashamed of. My heart is bursting. What can I say?"

"The people here will hide you or slip you forward tomorrow night," the young minister said. "Here is money to pay your way. You can write. Write to your young mistress wherever you go."

"Tell her," said the runaway girl, "that I loved her dearly. Oh, dear old Teackle Hall—shall I ever see you again? William, I shall get my freedom or die on the road to it."

"That is the spirit," the minister said. "We will buy it for you if we can, but get it for yourself if you can do it."

He kissed her again with the instinct of a father to a child and hastened to his horses.

With dawn breaking, Tilghman and Rhoda started back to Princess Anne. The young girl suddenly turned and kissed her minister. "Thar," she said. "I think you just looked magnificens last night, sittin' behin' them critters like death on the pale horse, an' lovin' Aunt Vesty enough to fight for her pore, brightskinned gal, though she's gone away an' quit you. I wish somebody would love me like that."

"So you could quit him, too, Rhoda?"

"I likes beaus that's couragelis, William. You're splendid a-preachin', but I like you better drivin' and showin' your excitemins."

"You are a beautiful girl," the clergyman said. "Suppose you try to like me better."

Being thus opened, the great question was not disposed of when they reached Princess Anne and quietly stabled the horses.

Honeymoon

Chapter 33

The steamer, meanwhile, was taking Vesta and her husband across the Chesapeake Bay in the night—that greatest, gentlest indentation in the coast of the United States, at once river and sound, fjord and sea. Smooth as a millpond and full of life as the nutritious milk of the mother, it suckles on its breast a brood of rivers without rivalry. To the wild swan its arborage looks like a vast pine tree, climbing from its roots in the land of corn and cotton for two hundred miles into the golden cloud of northern grain and hay.

Upon one broken horn of this fruitful bay hung Baltimore, like an eagle's nest upon the pine, seizing the point of indentation that brought it nearest to the fertile upland and valley outlets of the North and West, where toil-loving Germans burnished their farms with woman's hands and sent their long-bowed teams to market on as many turnpikes as the Chesapeake has rivers.

In the morning Vesta looked upon a fleet of little sails lying among larger ships in the basin of the city. Federal Hill's red clay rose a hundred feet above the piers, and the spotless monument to Washington rested its base as high above the tide on a nearly naked bluff. The rich sunrise fell on the streaked flag of the republic at the mast on Fort McHenry, and the garrison band was playing the very anthem that lawyer Key had written in the elation of victory, while a prisoner in the enemy's hands.

At Barnum's Hotel Vesta heard with both satisfaction and regret that her husband was too ill to attend the funeral and must keep to his room and fire. In her sorrow she needed his comfort and devotion, but the injunction against that fateful hat he had brought with him seemed to stand upon her dead mother's bier. She pitied him that he must stay alone, unknown, unrelated, chattering with the chill or burning without complaint.

"God send you sympathy from the angels like you, my darling," Milburn said. "I know what it is to lose a mother."

At the news that her uncle Allan McLane had not arrived and would not, probably, be present, she felt another blending of relief and apprehension. Her husband might not be exasperated by him, yet his relations to her mother's property would still remain unknown, and Vesta feared for Virgie.

In the same impulse which had made her retain Teackle Hall, securing it against her father's careless business methods, she had made Virgie over to her mother to place her farther from danger, never supposing that in those prudent hands the enemy might insinuate. But death, the deathless enemy, was filching everywhere, and though she could not see why Virgie could be persecuted, Vesta now wished she had set her free.

The girl belonged to her mother's estate. Suppose Allan McLane was the administrator of it? Suppose, indeed, he was the heir? Vesta's heart fell as she considered that a woman had best let business alone.

The young bride-mourner was an object of mingled admiration and sympathy as she leaned on the arm of a kinsman and entered the Presbyterian kirk. She was considered one of the great beauties of Maryland, and the young Robert Breckenridge, fresh from Kentucky to visit his brother, the pastor, thought he had never seen Vesta's equal, even in Kentucky. As he gazed through her mourning veil, the pastor's Delaware wife heard him whisper, "Divinity itself!"

The clear olive skin, eyes of gray twilight, eyebrows like midnight's own arches, and luxuriant hair were touched by grief as if a goddess suffered, and in her mourning robes Vesta seemed a monarch's daughter about to pass through some convent to her sainthood. She had the height to give dignity to this beauty and the grace to lift pathos above weakness.

The minister's musical tones were wrought to consonance with this noble human model. He spoke of that ideal motherhood which, to every child at the bier, seems real as the dripping bucket at the fairy's well—of mother's love, trials, weakness, and immortality; of the absence of her sympathy making the first great bereavement in life's progress; of her nature abiding in us and her spirit hovering over while we live.

Painted in the soft hues of personal experience, prescribed to her needs with a physician's art, doing all that funeral talk can do to raise the final tears from among the heartstrings and pour them in oblation upon the corpse, the pastor's consolation had the effect of some mesmeric hand that weakens our systems while it sublimates our feelings, and Vesta's female nature was almost broken down.

Where could she lean for the close sympathy befitting such grief? Her father was not here, and she had none but her husband—the husband of less than a week, but still the nearest to her need.

She allowed herself to rest on him that solemn evening after her mother's body had sought the ground. For the moment he was well again.

For the first time she was alone with him, and as the shadows narrowed their chamber and they sat with no other light than a little wood smoldering in the grate, he came to her and began to talk of childhood and his own mother. He spoke of the little sorrows his mother had shared with him, of domestic disagreements and happy love making anew, how men feel when the partner of life is taken away, of children who know not the meaning of death that has done so awful a thing upon the inoffensive one. "But above all," Meshach said, "is shining the star of motherhood, faintly lighting our way, mellowing our souls, and basking on the waters."

As he continued, she could not see him but only hear the plaintiveness of his voice, and it became comfortable to listen to him speak, and she grew more passive. A sense of resignation fell upon her heart and of gratitude to him that could divine her loss so touchingly. Like a child she rested upon his side, upon his knee, and in his arms at last; not yet fond nor infatuated, but subsiding and consenting, accepting her destiny like a myriad of women that are neither oppressed nor tender, but yield with reluctance. She passed out of grief to wifedom, like one tired and in a dream.

Visits of consolation were made by a few old friends for a day or two succeeding. The Rev. Henry Lyon Davis, late president of the college at Annapolis, brought his handsome boy of twelve, Master Harry Winter Davis. The attorney general of Maryland, Mr. Roger Taney, came with Mr. George Brown, the banker. Commodore Decatur's widow sent a mourning token, and the Honorable William Wirt brought Mr. Robert Smith, once the secretary of state at Washington.

Looking at Meshach Milburn a little oddly, these and others found him, on acquaintance, to be a man of sense, but McLanes who called were either supercilious or studiously avoided the groom.

Vesta received an invitation to Arlington House, and as they proceeded out the Washington road in a private carriage, they observed Mr. Ross Winans' friction-wheel car with nearly forty people in it making its trial trip behind a horse at a gallop.

At the relay house, where the horses on the railroad were changed, Milburn gazed up the Patapsco valley and remarked, "My wife, we are here at the birth of this little iron highway. If our vision was great enough, we might see the mighty things that may happen upon it—servile insurrection, sectional war, armies riding to great battles, thousands of emigrants drawn to the West. We shall die, but this road will grow and continue for generations after us—a vein of iron whose length and uses no man can measure."

The road to Washington was good in places and often turned in among the pines. At Riverdale they saw the deer of Mr. George Calvert, a descendant of one of the Lords Baltimore, browsing in his park, and his great four-in-hand carriage was going in the lodge gates from a state visit to the Custises. Passing directly to Georgetown from Bladensburg, they encountered General Jackson taking his evening ride on horseback, and saw the chasm of the new canal being dug along the Potomac. Then, crossing Mason's ferry, they were set down at Arlington House an hour after dark.

The hospitable proprietor welcomed them into the huge edifice among his elaborate daubs of pictures and furniture and relics of Custis and Washingtonian times. He was nearly fifty years of age, having Indian features but a rather weak face, like one whose only substantiality was in his ancestors. Placing him beside her husband, Vesta reflected that similar inbreeding had produced a similarity in the two men, both of a sallow and bilious attenuation. Milburn, however, beside her kinsman Custis, was like a bold wolf beside a vacant-visaged sheep.

Yet these men liked each other immediately. They strolled through those beautiful woods—one day to become a grove of sepulture for an army of dead—while Vesta talked with her cousins and with the graceful Lieutenant Lee, who was courting Mary Custis.

It was suggested they go to the capitol, and Mr. Milburn, daily growing better in the hill region, went also. He wore his steeple hat to the great edification of Mr. Custis, who reveled in such antiquities. When they returned, Vesta heard the ladies whispering that a parcel of boys and Negroes had followed the hat, jeering and laughing, and had finally driven the party to their carriage. This and her husband's impatience to return to his business hastened their departure from Arlington.

They took the steamer down the Potomac, and as they came off the mouth of St. Mary's River, Milburn donned his Raleigh hat and stood on deck, looking at the lights. Here, on a naked plain within sight of a sandy point that faced the Eastern Shore, lay the capital of Lord Baltimore with a few starveling mementos.

"My hat," Milburn said to himself, "is as old as yonder town and better preserved. The Calverts and Milburns have married into Mrs. Washington's kin. Does my wife love me?"

The Ordeal

Chapter 34

When Levin Dennis awoke in the bottom of the old wagon, it was being rapidly driven, and Van Dorn's voice, without its usual lisp and Spanish interjection, was heard to say from the driver's seat, "Whitecar, is your brother at Dover sure of his game?"

"Cocksure, Cap'n. Got 'em treed! Best domestic stock in the town thar, an' the purtiest yaller gals. I know that suits you, Cap'n."

"Have they arms?"

"Not a trigger. We trap 'em at one of their festibals. No sir, niggers won't scrimmage."

"We assemble at Devil Jim Clark's," Van Dorn said and passed by with a crack of his whip.

Levin, whom some friendly hand had wrapped in a bearskin coat—he had seen one like it upon Van Dorn—next heard the slaver speak to another party he had overtaken:

"Melson?"

"Ay yi!"

"Milman?"

"Ah, boy."

"You get your orders at Devil Jim Clark's."

The stars were out, yet the night was rich in large, fleecy clouds, as if heaven were hurrying onward too. Levin lay on his back, jostled by the rough wagon. Perfectly sober now, he was more reasoning and courageous, and his new-found love impelled him to self-preservation. He might have rolled out of the vehicle and into the woods and at least saved himself from committing further crime, but how would he see Hulda again—Hulda, in danger, perhaps. Thus love brings understanding even to ignorance, and Levin began to ask himself the cause of his own misery. He knew it was liquor, yet what made him drink if not a disposition too easily led? Even now he was under almost voluntary subjection to the bandit in the wagon, whose voice he again heard issue commands to a pair they had overtaken:

"Tindel?"

"Tackle 'em, Cap'n Van. Tackle 'em!"

"You are not to be in peril tonight, so keep your spirits. I expect you to look out for the cords, gags, and fastenings generally."

"Tackle 'em, Cap'n. Oh, tackle 'em!"

"You and Buck Ransom there!"

"Politely, Captain. Politely, sir," exclaimed an insinuating voice from a Negro rider.

"Meet us all at Devil Jim's."

"Tackle 'em, Cap'n!"

"Politely, Captain!"

As Van Dorn urged his way to the head of the line, Levin silently looked out upon the flat country of forest and a few poor farms, drained imperfectly by some ditches of the Choptank. He supposed it might be almost midnight from the position of those brilliant constellations, which shone down equally upon his mother and himself—she in her innocence and he in his anxiety—and also, perhaps, upon his poor father's grave in isle or ocean.

Within an hour, no doubt, blood would be shed and rapine done, and he knew not the road by which to escape nor the hole to hide in. Yet in that hour he had to make his choice: to fight for liberty or go to jail, the whipping post, or, perhaps, the gallows.

Levin ruefully considered his vagrant past and how little could be said in extenuation of him in a court of justice, except by his mother's faith, which was no more evidence than a Negro's oath.

Once it arose in his mind to surprise Van Dorn, overcome him, cast him in a ditch, and drive to one of the little farmhouses where he could rest till day should give him his whereabouts and remedy.

Levin was not a coward, but his heart relented to the fierce, soft man who so unsuspectingly sat with his back to him. This very day Van Dorn had paid a debt for him to the widow whose son was next overtaken and who forwardly cried without being addressed, "What are you goin' to give me, Van Dorn, if I git a nigger?"

"This!" said Van Dorn, reaching the boy a measured blow with his whip that made him literally fall from the mule and grovel with pain. "Discipline is what your mother failed to give you, *reprobo*. Manners, I shall teach you. Fall in the rear!"

Owen Daw crawled desperately on his mule and obeyed without parley, but his audacity soon recovered enough to force his animal up to the wagon tail and open whispered communications with Levin there.

Nothing had passed them for hours that Levin had seen, when suddenly a horseman at a rapid lope stopped the wagon, and a hoarse, Negro voice muttered, "How de do, now? See me! See me!"

"Derrick Molleston?" questioned Van Dorn.

"See me! see me!"

"Get down and ride with me. Levin, are you awake?"

"Yes, Captain."

"Take this man's horse and ride him a while. It will stretch your chilled limbs. John Sorden is ahead."

"May I go with him?" asked Owen Daw in his Celtic accent, quite cringing now.

"Not unless he wants you."

"Come then," Levin obligingly said.

While the two youths were still lingering by the wagon, they heard Van Dorn say, "Have you arranged everything with Whitecar and Devil Jim?"

"See me! See me!"

"Is Greenley ready to make a diversion if an attack be made upon us?"

"See me! See me! His gallows is up and he'd burn de world."

"This Lawyer Clayton?"

"See me! See me! He gives a big party, Aunt Braner tole me. A judge is dar from Prencess Anne an' liquor a-plenty. See me! See me!"

"The white people absolutely gone from Cowgill House?"

"See me! It's nigh half a mile outen de town. Dar's forty tousand dollars if dar's a cent at dat festibal—gals more'n half white, men dat can read an' preach—de cream of Kent County. See me! See me!"

"And not a suspicion of our coming?"

"See me! Oh, see me!" the Negro said hoarsely. "Innercent as de unborn. Tonight's deir las' night!"

Levin trembled as these merciless words reached his ears, but Owen Daw seemed to forget his affront at the tidings and chuckled to Levin as they trotted away, "Bet I git a better nigger nor you!"

"Oh, shame, Owen Daw. Your mother was saved today from bein' turned out of doors by my pity. Think of robbin' these niggers of their freedom. What have they done?"

"Been niggers!" exclaimed Owen Daw. "That's enough!"

"What will you do, Owen, to help your poor mother?"

"Wait till I git big enough, bedad, an' kill ole Jake Cannon for this day's work."

As they rode on, they came to the man called Sorden, riding as guide to the invading column, a person of more genteel address than any other beneath Van Dorn, and young, pliable, and frolicking.

"My skin!" he said. "Now, boys, Van Dorn oughtn't had to brung you. You're too sniptious for this rough work. I love the captain better than I ever loved a male, but he oughtn't to spile boys."

"Van Dorn told me to come," Owen cried. "I'm big enough to buck a nigger."

"I love him better than I ever loved a male," said Sorden apologetically. "Who is t'other young offender?"

"I'm a stranger to your parts," Levin replied. "Mrs. Cannon made me come. I didn't want to."

"Are you afear'd?"

"Yes," Levin said.

"Well, I love the captain better than I ever loved a male, but boys is boys, and I hate to see 'em spiled. If you was nigger boys, I wouldn't keer a cent, but white's my color, and I don't want to trade in it."

They halted at a small, sharp-gabled brick house of one story with a kitchen and garret. The corner of a piece of oak and hickory woods came up to it shelteringly, while in the rear several small barns and cribs enclosed the triangle of a field. A door in the middle, towards Maryland, seemed very high-silled, and low grated windows were at the cellar on each side of the steps.

The place had a suspicious appearance, and a pack of hounds in full cry rushed from the kitchen. While in the act of leaping the stile and palings, they were arrested almost in mid air by a chuffy voice from within: "Hya! Down! Spitch!"

The whole pack meekly sneaked back to the house, whining low, and a few blows of a switch and short howls completed the excitement.

"What place is this?" asked Owen Daw.

"Devil Jim Clark's," said Sorden.

The dwelling stood about forty yards back from the road, drawing nearly into the cover of the woods. Its little yard was made cavernous by thick-planted mulberry and maple trees, while a line of cherry trees and an old pole well rose along the road and hedge. As they proceeded to the rear of the house, they could see a little dormer window, low along the roof, and a light was shining from it.

"Devil Jim's business office," nodded Sorden.

"What's his business?" asked Levin freshly.

"Niggers. He keeps 'em up thar 'tween the garret and the roof. Sometimes in the cellar."

"Does he want a business office for that?"

"He's a contractor on the canawl, too, Jim is. He raises race horses, farms, gambles a little, but nigger runnin' is his best game. My skin, yer comes Captain Van Dorn. I love him as I never loved a male."

"Van Dorn," a voice called from the house, "remember my family is particular. Your men must go to the barn. Come in."

A quiet remark from somewhere—"Spiced brandy at the barn"—was sufficient to lead the herd away.

Giving the order to "water and fodder," Van Dorn passed into the kitchen, thence through a bedroom to the chief room of the house and up a small winding stair to a scrap of hallway hardly two feet wide.

The man who led pointed to a trap above one end of this hall and exclaimed, "Niggers there; family yonder." The last reference was to a door closing the little passage.

He then opened a wicket at the side of the hall, admitting Van Dorn to a small closet or garret room, barely large enough for the men to sit, and lighted by a lamp in the little dormer window.

"Drink," said the man, uncorking a bottle of champagne. "I had it ready for you."

He poured the foaming wine and set the bottle on a sort of secretary or desk, then looked anxiety and avarice together out of his liquid black eyes and broad, heavy face.

"*Buena suerte, senor,*" Van Dorn lisped as they drank together.

"Hya! Spitch!" Clark muttered nervously, cutting his own boots with a dog whip. "I wish I was out of the business; the risk is too great. My wife is religious—praying now, mebbe. My daughters is at the seminaries, spendin' money like the canawl company on the lawyers. Nothin' pays like nigger stealin', but it's beneath you and me, Van Dorn."

"*A la verdad!* This is my last incursion, Don Clark. Pleasure has kept me poor for life. Today I did a little sacrifice, and it grows upon me."

"If they should ketch me and set me in the pillory for what you do tonight, it would break Mrs. Clark's heart."

"I want this money tonight," said Van Dorn, "to make two young people happy. They shall take my portion and take me with them out of the plains of Puckem."

"Oh, it is nervous business." Clark's eyes of rich jelly made the pallor on his large face look like a winding sheet. "Hya! Spitch! The Quakers are a-watchin' me—Ole Zekiel Jinkins over yer, ole Warner Mifflin down to the mill, an' these durn Hunns look me through every time they ketch me on the road. But the canawl contract don't pay like niggers. My folks must hold their heads up in the world. Sam Ogg won't let me keep out of temptation."

"Do you fear me, Devil Jim?"

"No. If all in the trade was like you, I could sleep in trust. If you go out of it, so will I."

"Then tonight, *penitente*, we make our few thousand and quit. Give up your cards and I my *doncellitas*, and we can at least live."

They shook hands and drank another glass, and then Van Dorn said, "Send up to me, *hermano*, the lad who will reply to the name of Levin. I would speak with him while you give directions."

After his host had descended the stairs, Van Dorn said, "Poor coward, he can never be less than a thief with that irksomeness under such fair competence."

At that moment a beautiful maid in a white night robe appeared in the little doorway, with eyes so like the richness of his just gone that it must have been his daughter. She fled as she recognized a stranger, and Van Dorn pursued till a door was closed in his face.

"Poor fool," he said, sinking into his chair again. "I will never be more honest than any woman can make me."

As Levin entered the little hallway, Van Dorn smiled and offered, "Here is a glass of real wine to inspire you, *junco*."

"No, Captain. I would rather die than drink it."

"Do you repent coming with me?"

"Bitterly, Captain. I don't want to steal poor, helpless people, if they *is* black."

"Listen, lad!" Van Dorn's face ceased to blush, and a coarse look came into his blue eyes. "This night's excursion is for your profit. I like your gentle inclination for me and the good acts you have solicited from me, as well as the confidence you have shown me as to your love for pretty Hulda. Join me in this work willingly, and I will give all my share for your marriage settlement."

"Never," Levin exclaimed.

Van Dorn drew his knife and rose to his feet.

"Levin," he lisped, "I promised Patty Cannon that I would bring you back spotted with crime or dead. Now choose which it shall be."

"To die, then," cried Levin, with one hand brushing the long, silken hair from his eyes and with the other drawing his own knife. "But I will fight for my life!"

Van Dorn seized Levin's wrist in a vise-like grip, but as he did so, threw his own knife upon the floor.

"Oh, *huerfano*, waif," Van Dorn murmured, while his blush returned, "take heed thou ever sayest '*No*' with courage like that, when cowardice or weak acquiescence would extort thy '*Yes*.' This moment, if thou hadst consented, thy heart would now be on my knife!"

He drew the knife from Levin's hand and put it in his ragged coat again, setting the boy on his knee as if he were a little child.

"Oh, God be thanked I did not kill you, sir," sobbed Levin, his tears quickly following his courage. "Twice I have thought of doin' it today."

"I never would have put you to that test, my poor lad, but that I saw your conscience at work all this day under the stimulation of virtuous love. Think nothing of me. Build your own character upon some good example and—sweet as life is—fight for it on the very frontiers of your character. Die young, but surrender only when you are old."

"Captain," Levin said, "how kin I git character? My father is dead. Everybody twists me around his fingers."

"Then think of some plain, strong, faithful man you may know and refer every act of your character to him. Ask yourself what he would do in our predicament, then, go and do the same."

"I do know such a man," Levin said. "It is Jimmy Phoebus, my poor, beautiful mother's beau."

"*El rayo ha caido*," Van Dorn said, low and calm. "Yes, Levin, any man worthy of your mother will do."

"Captain, turn back with me. Is it too late?"

"Too late these many years, young *senor*. I shall lead the war on Africa again tonight at Cowgill House."

He rose and finished the wine.

"Clark shall give you a horse, Levin. I present it to you. Ride on with Sorden at the lead, and a mile from here, at Camden Town, take your own way. Good night."

Levin looked at the miserable band of whites and blacks revealed by lantern light in the barn. In the excitement of drink and avarice or the familiarity of fear and vice, some were inspecting gags of corncob and bucks of hickory. Others trimmed clubs or blackjacks with the roots attached or loaded horse pistols and greased the dagger slides thereon. They whetted their hog-killing knives upon harness and cut rope and cord into lengths to bind men's feet. Clark set Levin on the loping horse he had been riding, and soon he met Sorden on the road.

"Where is Van Dorn?" Sorden asked. "I love him as I never loved a male."

"He sends me to Camden of an errand," Levin answered. "Is it far?"

"About a mile. Three miles, then, to Dover. My skin, how fresh your critter is. Ain't it Dirck Molleston's? I thought so. He'll be wantin' to turn in at Cooper's Corners."

"Does Derrick live there?"

"Yes. That's whar he holds the forks of both roads from below and watches the law in Dover. I hope Van Dorn will git away with the loot and not git ketched, fur I love him as I never loved a male."

At his easy gait, Levin's horse soon left Sorden far behind, and the strange events of the night and his wonder what to do next kept Levin's brain whirling till he saw the form of a few houses rise among the trees. A line of arborage indicated a main road from north to south, and the scent of cold, wide waters and marshes filled the night.

"Here's Camden," Levin thought; "where shall I go? If I turn south, I shall get no bed nor food all night, and I'll be picked up in the mornin' fur a kidnapper. I can't go back. The big river or the ocean, I reckon, is before me. What would Jimmy Phoebus do?"

He held the animal in as he asked the question and paused at the crossing of the great state road. The idea slowly spread upon his whole existence that James Phoebus would, in Levin's place, ride instantly to Dover and give the alarm.

While Levin tried to construct Phoebus in a mood to give other advice, the resolute pungy captain's form rose more and more stalwart and appeared to lead towards Dover. There, so many poor souls in the joys of freedom were, like little birds, unaware of the hawks above, and no man in the world but Levin Dennis could save them from death or bondage. Would James Phoebus ever hesitate in the duty of a citizen and a Christian under such circumstances or forgive another man for withholding information that might be life and liberty and mercy?

Yet there was also Van Dorn to be betrayed. What would Van Dorn do in Levin's place?

The words of Van Dorn, not a quarter of an hour old, spoke aloud in Levin's echoing consciousness: "Think nothing of me. Refer every act to some faithful man and go and do the same."

Levin looked up, and the very clouds, now swollen dark in spite of starshine, seemed hurrying on Dover. The night birds were crying, "Mercy! Mercy!" The lizards and tree frogs seemed to cross each other's voices, piping, "Time! Time! Time!"

"Huldy," Levin whispered and let the reins fall loose. His animal darted through Camden Town to the north.

He had gone by the small frame houses, the Quaker meeting, the stores, the outskirt residences, when suddenly his horse turned out to pass a large, dark object in the road ahead, and a horseman rode right across Levin's course, forcing his animal back on its haunches.

"High doings, friend," a man's voice spoke raspingly; "I'm concerned for thee."

"Git out of my way or I'll stab you!" Levin cried between his new ardor to do his duty and the idea that he had already been intercepted by Patty Cannon's band.

"Ha, friend, I'm less concerned for myself than thee. Thou wilt not stab a citizen of Camden Town at his own door?"

"For heaven's sake let me go then!" Levin pleaded. "Kidnappers is comin' to Dover in a few minutes. I want to tell Lawyer Clayton!"

The other person, a tall, lean man, wheeled immediately and dashed after the dark object ahead. Levin, following, found it to be a large covered wagon.

"Bill," the Quaker called to the driver, "spare not thy whip till Dover be well past. Here is one who says kidnappers are raiding even the capital of Delaware. I'm concerned for thee!"

The driver began to whip his horses into a gallop, and the cries of several persons were heard within the close-curtained vehicle.

"What's in there?" Levin asked the Quaker, who had rejoined him. "Niggers?"

"No, friend," the Quaker crisply answered. "Only Christians."

Without speaking, they crossed a millstream and soon afterwards a smaller run and came to a little log and frame cabin in a fork of the road, where Levin's horse tried to run in.

"Ha, friend, is it not Derrick Molleston's loper thee has—the same that he gets from Devil Jim Clark? What art thou, then? I feel concerned for thee."

"A Christian, too, I hope," answered Levin, forcing his nag up the road.

"Then thee is better than the youth in this dwelling we next pass," the Quaker said, pointing to a brick house on the left. "There lived a judge whose son bucked a poor Negro fiddler in his father's cellar and delivered him to Derrick Molleston to be sold in slavery. I hear the poor man tells of it in his distant house of bondage."

"What's this?" Levin inquired, seeing a structure of beams on a swell to the right, in sight of the dark forms of a town on the next crest beyond.

"A gallows," said the Quaker, "on which a horse thief will be hanged tomorrow. To steal a horse is death. To steal a fellow man is nothing."

As he spoke, the mysterious carriage turned down a cross street of Dover and stole into the obscurity of the town.

"Ha!" exclaimed the Quaker. "If Joe Johnson had not stopped to feed at Devil Jim's, he might have overtaken my brother's wagon full of escaping slaves. I tell thee, friend, because I'm scarce concerned for thee now."

Cowgill House

Chapter 35

It was long after midnight. Dover was in bed except at one large house on the capitol green, where light shone through the chinks and cracks of curtains and shutters, and some watchdog ran along curiously to see why.

The stars and clouds in the somewhat troubled sky looked down through leafless trees upon the pretty town and upon St. Jones's Creek circling past it. Hardly noticeable was a long band of creeping men and animals, stealing up from Meeting House Branch, past the tannery and the academy, and plunging into back streets to avoid the public square.

One file turned down to the creek and crossed it, returning further above to cut off escape by the northern road. A second file slipped silently through and around the compact little hamlet and waited for the other to arrive. Then both encompassed an old brick dwelling, which stood back from the road in a venerable, green yard, nearly half a mile from the settled parts of Dover.

The house was brilliantly lighted, and the rose bushes and shade trees were clearly defined as they stood above the swells of green verdure and the ornamental paths and flower beds.

One majestic tulip tree extended its long branches nearly to the portal of the quaint dwelling, and a luxuriant growth of ivy, starting between the cellar windows, clambered to the corniced carpentry of the eaves, making almost solid panels of vine between four, large, keystoned windows, which stood to the right of a broad door.

This door, at the top of a flight of steps, was placed so near the gable angle of the house that it gave the impression of but one wing of a mansion originally designed to be twice its length and size.

"Cowgill House," now Woodburn, the Delaware Governor's Mansion

Between this gable—which faced the road and contained four lines of windows besides a basement row—and the back or town door was one squarish window, out of relation to all the rest and perhaps twelve feet above the ground. This, as might be guessed, was on the landing of the stairs within, the great door and front of the residence being at the opposite side. The whole of the space at the townward gable, to the width of seventeen feet, was a noble hall about forty feet long, lofty, with pilasters in architectural style, and lighted by two great windows in the gable in addition to the square window on the stairway.

The stairway itself was a beautiful piece of work, rising from the floor in ten railed steps to the landing at the square window. Here, a space several feet square commanded the great front door, the windows in the gable, and also the yard behind. Thence, the flight of steps rose at a right angle along the back wall to a second landing and by a third leap returned to the floor above, making the well of the stairway exceedingly spacious.

Cowgill House

This great hall, no doubt, had been designed to be the center of a large mansion, but with its abundant daylight had lost nothing in agreeableness by becoming, instead, the largest room in the house. It was large enough for either a feast or public worship, and such was its frequent use.

Built by a tyrannical, eccentric man at the beginning of the century, it had passed through several families until a Quaker named Cowgill, superintendent of a tannery and mill nearby, made it his property.

He held no slaves and was kind to black people, allowing his domestics, during his frequent absences, to assemble their friends and the general race in the great hallway for such enjoyments as they might choose. In truth, he desired that the house gain a more cheerful reputation, for the Negroes in particular considered it haunted.

The first owner, it was said, had amused himself in the great hall by making his children stand on their toes, switching their feet with a whip when they dropped upon their soles from pain or fatigue. His own son finally shot at him through the great northern door with a rifle or pistol, leaving a mark to this day.

The third owner, a lawyer, often entertained traveling clergymen, and on one occasion the eccentric Reverend Lorenzo Dow met some one on the stairs and bowed to him, afterwards frightening the host's family by telling it, since they were not aware of any stranger in the house. The room over the great door had always been considered the haunt of peculiar people, who molested nobody living and vanished when pressed upon.

This main door itself had a church-like character and was battened or built in half, so that the upper part could be thrown open like a window, and yet the lock on this upper part was a foot and a half long, and the key weighed a pound.

This ponderous, elaborately constructed door opened upon a flight of steps and a flower yard surrounded by elms, firs, and Paulownia trees, the latter of a beany odor and nature. A lower, two-storied servants' dwelling stretched to the fields and had a verandah-covered rear.

Van Dorn called to a Negro: "Buck Ransom."

"Politely, Captain," the Negro's insinuating voice answered.

"Go to the front door and knock. As you enter, see that it is clear to fly open. Then, as you pass along the hall, throw the windows up."

"Politely, Captain." The Negro bowed and departed.

"Owen Daw."

"Yer honor."

"Climb softly into the big tulip tree and take this musket I shall reach you. Train it on the staircase window and fire only if you see resistance there."

The boy went up the tree with all his vicious instincts full of fight.

"Melson."

"Ay, yi."

"Milman."

"Ah, boy."

"Get yourselves beneath the two large windows on the hall and serve as mounting blocks to Sorden's party. I shall storm the main door. As we enter there, Sorden, order your men right over Melson and Milman into the windows Ransom has lifted."

"I love him," Sorden muttered admiringly, "as I never loved a male," and collected his party.

"Whitecar, you and your brother hold the back door with your staves. If it is forced, Miles Tindel. . ."

"Tackle 'em, Cap'n Van."

". . . will throw his red-pepper dust into the eyes of any that come out."

"Oh, tackle 'em, Cap'n Van."

"Derrick Molleston."

"See me, oh see me," the powerful Negro muttered.

"Take Herron, Vincent, and two more. Guard the kitchen and the front of the main dwelling. Knock any creature stiff, except—*ayme! ay!*—the young damsels, whose fears will soon trip them to the ground."

"See me, see me," the Negro said hoarsely.

"As we enter, I shall cry, 'Patty Cannon has come!' Spring in the windows then and beat any opposition down. *Relampaguea!* Ransom is slow."

The knocker on the great door sounded. Springing open, it quickly slammed again, and a stifled sound followed, as of a scuffle.

Agile as a panther, Van Dorn sprang on Milman's back and looked into a window in the gable, drawing his face away so as to be unseen in the night.

The bright interior was full of people sitting back against the wainscoting as if listening to a sermon. A table, lighted by whale-oil lamps and candles and filled with the remnants of a feast, stretched down the middle of the stately hall. Van Dorn could not see the stairway in the corner, and it was there the dusky audience faced, as if towards a preacher. The attention the inmates were paying seemed unusual, but Van Dorn's eyes were absorbed in the sight of several drooping and almost startled, dove-eyed quadroon maids. He could not see Ransom.

"Sorden," Van Dorn said, slipping down, "can Ransom have betrayed us? *Chis!* They all look as if a death warrant was being read."

"My skin, no, Captain. Air they all there?"

"All," answered Van Dorn. "I see thirty thousand dollars of flesh in sight."

"And niggers won't scrimmage nohow," said Whitecar. "Let's beat 'em mos' to death."

"Come on then," said Van Dorn softly. "If the windows are not lifted, break them in."

By main strength he twisted a panel out of the palings near the house and led the way to the great front door. A dozen desperate hands seized the heavy panel and ran with it. The door flew open, but at that moment every light in Cowgill House went out.

"Dar's ghosts in dar," the hoarse voice of Derrick Molleston was heard to say, and the Negro element stopped and shrank.

"Tindel, your torch!" Van Dorn exclaimed as the house and shady yard were illuminated by lightning, and sounds of thunder rolled in the sky. A blazing pine knot was procured, and Van Dorn, holding it in his left hand and a rude whip in his right, bounded in the door shouting, "Patty Cannon has come!"

At that dreaded name there were a few suppressed shrieks, and the great windows at the gable side fell inwards with a crash as the kidnappers came pouring over.

Van Dorn's quick eye took in the situation as he waved his torch. It lighted ceiling and pilaster, the close-fastened doors on the left, and the great stairway well beyond, filled with black forms in the attitude of defense.

"Patty Cannon has come!" he shouted again. "Follow me!"

An instant only brought him to the base of the staircase. Lightning flashing in the gaping windows revealed him to his followers, his yellow hair waving, and his long, silken mustache like golden flame.

A mighty yell rose from the emboldened gang as they formed behind him with bludgeons, iron knuckles, billies, slings, and whatever would disable but fail to kill.

Van Dorn made three murderous slashes of his whip across the human objects above, and with a toss of that formidable weapon, clubbed it and darted on.

At that instant, loud explosions, smoke, and cries filled the echoing house as a volley of firearms burst from the landing, sweeping the line of the windows and raking the hall. The band on the floor below stopped, and some were down, groaning and cursing.

"They're armed; it's treachery!" a voice cried in panic, and the cowardly assailants ran to places of refuge, some crawling out at the portal, some dropping from the windows, and others getting behind the stairway, out of fire, and seeking desperately to draw the bolts of the smaller door there.

"Patty Cannon has come!" Van Dorn repeated, throwing himself into the body of the defenders, who, terrified at his bravery, began to retreat upward around the angles of the stairs.

One man, however, did not retreat. Neither did he strike, but wrapped Van Dorn around the body in a pair of long and powerful arms, lifting him from the landing by main strength and saying, "High doings, friend, I'm concerned for thee."

Van Dorn felt at the grip that he was overcome. He tried to reach for his knife, but his arms were enclosed in the unknown stranger's, who now sought to push him through the square window on the landing into the grass yard below, where rain was falling and lightning making brilliant play among the herbs and ferns.

As the kidnapper prepared himself to fall, with all his joints and muscles relaxed, Owen Daw, lying bloodthirstily along the limb of the old tulip tree, aimed his musket at the contending forms and greedily pulled the trigger.

As the Quaker's arms enclosed Van Dorn, the cuff of his coat presented a large metal button, and the ball from the tree, striking this, glanced and entered Van Dorn's throat.

"*Ayme! Guay!*" Van Dorn muttered as he was thrown out of the window to the earth. And there he lay, limp and huddled together, till John Sorden bore him off, muttering, "I loved him as I never loved a male."

The desperate party beneath the stairs at last broke open the back door and rushed forth, only to receive handfuls of red pepper dust thrown by Miles Tindel, who cried, "Tackle 'em, Cap'n Van!" They screamed with anguish and rolled in the wet grass and, with fears stronger than pain, sought the road in blindness and some way to leave the town.

Young Owen Daw crept down the tree and mounted his mule. Seeing Van Dorn in Sorden's arms at the wagon, he contemptuously said as he vanished, "I reckon he'll never discipline me no mo'."

The rear of "Cowgill House" and the square window which opens on the first landing of the stairway. The young tulip poplar in the foreground replaces an ancient member of its species which succumbed to old age and the chainsaw in 1997.

Derrick Molleston bore to the wagon an object he had found striving to escape from the verandah. The man was gagged and skewered between his elbows and his back.

"See me! See me!" the Negro kidnapper said hoarsely. "He's mine an' Devil Jim Clark's. I tuk him!"

"Why, it's Buck Ransom," Sorden said.

"An' I'm gwyn to sell him, too," the Negro muttered, seizing the reins. "You see me now! Maybe he cheated us; anyway, he's tuk."

The old wagon started at a run through the driving rain, the black victim lying helpless on his back and Van Dorn bleeding in Sorden's arms, who continued to moan, "I loved him as I never loved a male!"

Van Dorn made several efforts to talk and coughed painfully. Finally, as they reached a lane gate, he was able to articulate: "The Chancellor's?"

The Chancellor's House

"Yes, dis is it," Derrick Molleston said. "See me, Cap'n Van; I's all heah."

As they advanced up a shady lane, fire from somewhere began to illuminate their surroundings.

"It's Bill Greenley; he's set de jail afire," the Negro exclaimed. "See me, oh, see me!"

The conflagration lent a dull, vapory red light to the secluded dwelling they now approached, and Sorden saw a woman of a severe aspect looking out of a window at the fire.

"What is the meaning of this trespass so late at night?" she called. "Are you robbers? My aged husband is asleep."

"No, Madam," answered Sorden, "here is the husband of Mrs. Patty Cannon. She was your brother's mother-in-law. I love this man as I never loved a male. He is wounded, and we want him taken in till he can have a doctor."

"Take him to the jail, then, if that is not it burning yonder," the woman exclaimed scornfully. "Shall I make the home of the Chancellor of Delaware a hospital for Patty Cannon's men as a reward for her sending my brother to the gallows?"

She closed the window and left them alone in the storm.

"Drive quickly, then, to your den at Cooper's Corners, Derrick," Sorden said.

As they left the lane, a flash of lightning, so near, so white that they seemed to be within the volume and crater of it, enveloped the wagon. One horse sank down on his haunches, and the other reared and tore from his harness, while the wagon was overturned.

The Negro picked up his helpless fellow African and lifted him on his back, starting off in mingled avarice and terror, saying, "Derrick's gwyn home, sho'. See me, see me!"

Van Dorn put his finger at his throat, where blood was all the while trickling, and with a gentle cough extorted, "Leave me under a bush to die."

"No," cried Sorden, raising Van Dorn also upon his back. "I love you as I never loved a male."

The fire of the burning jail lighted their return to the outskirts of Dover and to the gallows' hill, where the scaffold had been split by lightning from its cross beam to the death trap. As they halted to rest, a horse and rider came stumbling past, and Molleston, dropping his burden, shouted, "Bill Greenley, dat's our hoss. We want it."

"The hoss is his that's on him," cried the escaped thief, looking scornfully at his own gallows as he lashed the blinded animal along in the rain.

"Cheer up, Captain Van," John Sorden said, soaked through with the rain. "Tain't fur now to Cooper's Corners."

Two Whigs

Chapter 36

"Goy! Look at the trees, friend Custis," Clayton said as the rising sun innocently struck the treetops in the public square of Dover.

Judge Custis observed that many noble elms and locusts had been riven by lightning or torn by wind and wind-driven floods of rain. "What a night!" he exclaimed. "The jail burned, the lightning was appalling, and I thought I heard firearms."

As they entered the dining room, Clayton turned to his maid and said, "So, Aunt Braner, Derrick Molleston asked about my dinner, did he? And it's Bill Greenley that burned the jail? Goy! And the black people licked the kidnappers at Cowgill House?"

"Dat dey did; praise de Lord!" said Aunt Braner fervently.

Clayton then turned to a young man sitting at the table and said, "Now, friend Dennis, tell your tale."

The boy, whom the judge was startled to recognize, began at once:

"Jedge Custis, the man you left in the kitchen has stole Aunt Hominy an' your little niggers. They was at Johnson's Crossroads last night, but maybe they's gone before this. My boat was hired to take 'em off, an' I had to come along, but I run away from the band an' give warnin' last night to Mr. Clayton yer."

Before the judge could reply, Clayton exclaimed, "Brother Custis, now let my noble constituent and fellow Whig Jonathan Hunn resume."

"My friend," said a lean, healthy-skinned man, "this young man surprised me last night with intelligence that thy Maryland friends were marching on the very capital of Delaware to steal men. I was out in the road at that hour for another Christian purpose, and the Lord rewarded me with this good one. I brought friend Dennis to John Clayton's back door, and he lent us all his firearms. Just beyond the Cowgill House, at the little grocery of William Parke—where I am told he sells liquors to Negroes contrary to law, and so takes the name of 'Kind Parke' among them—I found several of our free Delaware Negroes, I fear on no good errand. So I remarked, 'If William Parke, contrary to law, has been selling thee brandy out of an eggshell, I shall pay him to repeat the vile enticement quickly, for ye who are of the world must fight this night.'"

"Goy!" said Clayton, warming up. "Quakers will set other people on, won't they? Goy!"

"Other arms were there procured, and we barricaded Cowgill House so as to make it at once a decoy and a hornet's nest. I despise war and men-of-war so much that I have studied their campaigns. I suggested, friend Clayton, that the stairway was a good tactical defensive position—is that the vain term?—to send a volley out the main door and a flank fire on every window along the sides of Cowgill's hall. The staircase also commanded the back yard by a window, and the door beneath it was barricaded. There was a festival and feast given last night by these folks of color with absent friend Cowgill's permission. I told the men-at-arms to leave their huzzies below in the feasting hall till the attack began and then to let them escape up the stairway and to defend that stair like sinful men. When a Negro spy knocked on the door, a loop was thrown over his neck, and two of the black boys gagged him. Then the attack was made, and at my order all the lights were put out."

"Jedge," Levin Dennis broke in, "it was short an' dreadful! Captain Van Dorn had got to the bottom of the stairs, when the niggers fired over his head an' shot mos' everything down. The Quaker man yer then pinioned the captain an' dropped him, wounded, out of the high window. I pity Van Dorn, but *he* says that he's in a bad business. I hope he ain't dead."

"Who is this Van Dorn?" asked Judge Custis. "I've heard of such a daredevil, but he has never pestered Princess Anne."

"I reckon, gentlemen," Levin continued, "the kidnappers will never come to Dover no more."

"Two things surprise me," Clayton said: "that Joe Johnson would venture to raid Dover itself after the licking I got him, and that free darkeys could make such a fight."

"Ah," said Jonathan Hunn, "there was a white witness there to affirm that they only defended their lives."

"It was Captain Van Dorn that raided Dover," Levin said. "Joe Johnson is a coward."

"Judge Custis," Clayton said, "you and I can save this peninsula at least from the sectional excitements that are coming. You must surrender old Patty Cannon and her household to Delaware. She now lives on your side of the line. Come to the Governor's office with me, and I will get a requisition for her on the business of last night. Young Dennis here knows the band, and friend Hunn saw the attack."

The judge's face grew suddenly troubled. "I would rather not appear in this matter. Indeed, you must excuse me," he said.

"What!" said Clayton. "You hesitate to do a little thing like this after the free opinions you have expressed?"

There was a long, awkward pause. The Quaker arose, looked well at Judge Custis, and said, "None but Almighty God knows the secrets of a slave holder's mind. No son of Adam is fit to be absolute over any human creature."

"Amen," Judge Custis said meekly.

∞

The news from Princess Anne confirmed the loss of Vesta Custis's slaves. Judge Custis was told to come home and take steps for their recovery, but he was strangely apathetic.

As law books were then scarce, the suit against the canal company required a great deal of research. Precedents for breaches of contract against corporations were few in that day. Clayton and Custis walked and ate together, comparing knowledge and suggestions, while the litigious mind of John Randel rather irritated both of them. Supplied with money by Meshach Milburn's draft, they resolved to visit the canal, which was about thirty miles distant.

After breakfast on a soft yet frosty morning, the three men started together in a carriage. They passed several tidal creeks, the Duck and the Little Duck, the Blackbird and the Apoquinimink. As they advanced, the barns became larger, the hedges more tasteful and trimmed like those in the French Netherlands, and the leafless peach orchards stretched out like the tea plantations in China. Several little towns studded the roadside. The woods gave way to small farms, and at a steep bottom called Fiddler's Bridge they turned across the fields to an old, four-chimneyed, galleried mansion at the end of a long lane. Here, John Randel, Junior, as he fully named himself on every occasion, had a fine dinner spread.

After dinner they launched upon the stream in a small boat, much to Mr. Clayton's trepidation, and bore to the Chesapeake and Delaware Canal through acres of splutterdocks, muskrats, wildfowl, and terrapins unnumbered.

Chesapeake and Delaware Canal Approaching the Delaware River

The Negro rower tied their boat behind a passing vessel, which towed them out to the locks at the Delaware River. At a point opposite a willowy island, where an embryo city had been started in the marshes, they waited for the packet from Philadelphia.

Mr. Randel took his Negro man, a person of sorrowful yet inexpressive countenance, to be a kind of piano or model on which to play his fierce gestures.

"Clayton," he said, sitting on a stone lock in the glow of evening, "I ought to have been a lawyer. Not that I am not the greatest theoretical engineer in the country, but my legal genius interposes, and I sue the villains who employ me."

Here he gave the melancholy Negro a violent shaking, who took it as stolidly as a bottle of medicine shaken by the doctor.

"Yes, you sued Judge Ben Wright, and he nonsuited you."

"I tell you a new axiom, Clayton," the engineer cried, putting the Negro down on his hams and sitting on him: "Whoever employs genius has to be a scoundrel. In the nature of their relations it is so. He deflects genius from its full expression, absorbs the virtue from it, and is a fraud."

Here he kicked the Negro underneath him, who hardly protested.

"Well then," said Judge Custis, "as Clayton is a man of genius, and you employ him. . . ."

"I'm a scoundrel, of course," Randel exclaimed. "His sense of law and right must yield to my ideas. Now look at this canal. Had I not been obliged to defer to the soulless corporation which employed me, I would have dug it to the depth that the tides of the two bays would have filled it, instead of damming up the creeks for feeders and pumping water into it by steam pumps. Then the war vessels of the country could go through it, and the channel would be purged by every tide."

He stood up and put his foot on the Negro, to the amusement of the boys gathering around.

The barge on which they embarked had numerous passengers. Soon it came to a small lock and turn bridge, and a few miles beyond cut through the ridge of the peninsula, which seemed almost mountainous to Judge Custis.

He was of that patriotic opulence just short of imagination which rejoiced in public works, and this little canal, only fourteen miles long, was, with two or three exceptions, the only achieved work in the Union, turnpikes and bridges omitted. Built by the national government, the three states it connected, and private subscription, it had involved two and a quarter million dollars of expense—no light burden when the population was less than eight million whites in all the land.

Judge Custis's family troubles faded from his mind as he looked up at the steep cut, nearly seventy feet in height, with banks of yellow and green sands, stains of iron, and strata of marl, some of which had fallen back into the excavation and threatened navigation. When he saw a bridge, which leaped the chasm ninety feet overhead by a span that then seemed sublimity itself, he touched Clayton and said, "Never mind my failures; I Thank God I'm a Whig."

Chesapeake and Delaware Canal Approaching Chesapeake City

"Goy! There's nothing like it," Clayton replied.

Not far from this point the canal passed an old church and graveyard, where Clayton said his namesake, the Revolutionary Governor of Delaware, was buried. Here Randel's plain conveyance took them in, and in the moonlight they drove a few miles to his estate near the banks of a river and under a long mountain of barren clay and iron stain on the farther shore.

"Here," Randel said, "is my future estate of Randalia. Here I shall see all the commerce of the canal pass by and garnishee every vessel that pays my tolls to the canal company."

"Randel," Clayton asked, "what were those stakes I saw some distance back, running north and south across the fields?"

"A railroad survey."

"Who is making it?"

"They say Meshach Milburn of Princess Anne."

"Goy!" exclaimed Clayton. "I'll beat him."

∞

For two or three days the three men, still studying the canal suit, drove over a picturesque country. They visited the old manor of the Labadists and their Bohemian patron, Augustine Herman, the homestead of the late treaty minister Bayard, and the ancient Welsh Baptist churches among the hills of the Elk and Christiana, where some of Cromwell's warriors lay. It was the favorite land of Whitefield.

In the neighborhood was an iron furnace, which Judge Custis examined with melancholy interest—one of the investments of General Washington's father more than a hundred years before, when the Indians made the iron.

They went also to Turkey Point, where the British army had been disembarked to capture Philadelphia, and Knyphausen's division obliterated the history of Delaware by carrying her records away from Newcastle.

Returning from one of these pleasant journeys, two messages from different points seared Judge Custis's eyes:

"Your wife died at Cambridge."

"Your daughter is very ill at Wilmington."

"To Wilmington!" cried Judge Custis, staggering up. "Oh, my daughter, I have killed her."

Spirits of the Past

Chapter 37

"What do they say, William, about Jack Wonnell being shot dead?"

"It is generally said that he was killed by the Negroes for gallantries to their color. Some talk of arresting little Roxy."

"What do you say, William?"

"The night I drove Virgie to Snow Hill I drove over poor Wonnell's body. A strange Negro was seen here—the enemy of your servant Samson. The new cook at Teackle Hall thinks he fired the shot."

The young rector could feel the searching look of those resinous, forester's eyes staring him through.

"That shot was meant for me, William Tilghman."

"Perhaps so."

"It was the shot of a hired murderer, who mistook Wonnell's unusual hat for mine, which was not well described to him, or the description of which his drunken and excited memory did not retain."

"Please save Vesta this suspicion, Mr. Milburn."

"Oh, that pure soul could not know it," Milburn continued with a moment's gentleness, "but some of her proud kin, to whom I am less than a dog, did send the assassin. I think I guess the man."

"Do not rush to a conclusion. Remember that Vesta has suffered so much for others' errors."

"Wonnell was killed in this room, where he never came before. The wound shows the shot to have come from a point below the window, where nothing of his features could be seen. The mistake of bell-crown for steeple-top shows that it was the job of a stranger. The poor fool died for me. Now, where did the bungler come from?"

"I will be frank with you; Joe Johnson was also here. Mary says so. To save Virgie from him, I helped her away."

"Now," said Milburn, "what enemy of mine delegated the kidnapper to procure a murderer?"

He waited for a moment, then answered his own question: "The man is now at Johnson's Crossroads. Letters from Cambridge tell me so. It was the deceased Mrs. Custis's brother, Allan McLane."

"I ask you again to think of Vesta and her many sacrifices."

"I do. I have promised her that she shall never receive a cruel word from me, but I shall not spare my assassins. To them I shall be as one they have killed and whose blood smokes for vengeance. I possess the only warrant that can drive them from Maryland."

He laid a roll of bank notes on the table suggestively. "No wealth is accumulated in vain," said Meshach Milburn, his delicate nostrils distended and his fine hand pointing to the bills. "Now, *war* on Johnson's Crossroads!"

He crossed the old room, opened the green chest, brought out the Entailed Hat, and took it in his hands with a grim smile. "I thought to lay this aside on my wife's account," he said, "but her people *compel* me to wear it! I thought all malice to this poor hat would be done with my social triumph here, but I am not a man to be frightened. Let them kill me, but it shall be under my ancestral brim."

"Oh, listen to your mockingbird sing: 'Vesta, Meshach, love!' Where is the bird?"

Meshach Milburn shook his head and put the Entailed Hat upon it. "Tom left me," he said, "when they began to fire bullets at my hat."

∞

Vesta's instinct had already found the explanation of Wonnell's death. From the first moment of knowing her husband, his hat had been a shadow across her life's path. His person had never been offensive to her, and something attractive or modifying in him had led her, when a child, to offer a flower to his hat, to give it consonance with himself, that seemed to deserve less evil. A fancied insult to his hat had made him quarrel with her father, a quarrel which involved her conquest, not by wooing, but by the treaty of war. The same hat had inspired the superstition which led her kitchen servants to leave their comfortable home and had been the insuperable obstacle to her mother's consent to her marriage. It had caused the only bitter words that ever passed between her and her father. At last it had spilled blood, and her uncle, she well knew from his implacable nature, had set the ruffians on. She knew as well that her husband had found him out. His intelligence, which would otherwise have been a matter of pride to her, now became a subject of fear.

The loss of Virgie was hardly less severe to Vesta than that of her mother's. It was true that Roxy, pretty and loving, now poured all her devotion at her mistress's feet, but there had been something in Virgie that Roxy could never rise to.

Vesta shed bitter tears at the news of that dear comforter's flight, and praying on her knees for the delicate, young wanderer, she felt God's conviction of the sins of slavery. Alas, thousands who felt the same would not admit the conviction nor agree to a lesser sacrifice, but were willing to give war.

A note from Snow Hill told Vesta that her maid had already departed and would only write again from free soil.

So the hat was worn more often than before, and Vesta suffered humiliation for it. Her husband moved actively to organize his railroad and visited the Maryland towns of the peninsula, taking her along and wearing his King James tile, now swathed in mourning crepe.

At Cambridge, which basked upon the water like an English Venice, he applied the sinews of war to a listless public sentiment, and the county press began to call for Joe Johnson's expulsion and Patty Cannon's rendition to the State of Delaware.

At Easton, which lay like a pearl oyster on her treasures of marl between the waters, people turned out to see the little man in the peaked hat with the beautiful lady at his side. Vesta was more pained for her husband than herself, to feel that his dress was prejudicing his railroad.

At the old aristocratic homes on the Wye River, more scowls than smiles were bestowed on the eccentric *parvenu*, and at Chestertown, where the Peales originated who drew his hat into their museum, boys burned tar barrels on the market and marched in hats of brown wrappers before the dwelling of Vesta's host.

The greater the opposition, the more indomitable Milburn grew to live it down. He wrote to Judge Custis to go to Annapolis and work for a railroad charter and state aid, and began grading for his line in the vicinity of his old store at Princess Anne. With the immemorial hat upon his sconce, he threw the first shovelful of earth himself. This time there were no shouts, and he almost regretted it, feeling that jeers carry no deep malice, while silence is hate.

Loyal to the least of her vows and wishing to love and obey him in spirit fully, Vesta felt that his own good nature was being darkened again by his obstinacy upon this single point of an obsolete hat. In their evening circle at Teackle Hall, dressed in a modern suit of clothes and slippers, he looked like a younger and knightlier person. His delicate hand well became the ring his wife put upon it, and when he talked high enthusiasm and sense and stood ready to back it with courage and money, Vesta thought her husband lacked but one thing to make him the equal of his supposititious kinsman, and that was another headdress. She almost feared to broach the subject, knowing that an old sore is ever the most sensitive, and she was too direct and frank to practice any arts upon him.

She was embroidering an evening cap of velvet for him one day, when Mrs. Tilghman sent a hatbox, and in it was a fine new hat of the current style. He answered her letter politely, put the new hat upon the rack of Teackle Hall, and never touched it again.

Next, Rhoda procured a beaver skin from some country beau, and beavers were growing scarce and dear in the peninsula. She had an elegant cap made of it for the cold weather coming, but Meshach only kissed her and put it on the rack, and there it tempted the moth.

His chills and fever continued at times, but more regularly, as he undertook to become the promoter of his region, he suffered the dislike and opposition of the old class of society. They regarded it as an audacity worse than crime. He had outstripped them in wealth and was now undermining their importance. Many avowed that they would never ride on a railroad built by such a man. Others hoped it would break him. Some took open ground against his work and wrote letters to Annapolis in an attempt to prejudice him with the legislature, where the Baltimore interest was already crying loudly that an Eastern Shore railroad meant to take Maryland trade and money to Philadelphia. Meshach fiercely responded that, unless the railway took the line of the Maryland counties, Delaware would build it and carry it to Newcastle instead of to Elkton, where Meshach meant to unite with a projected Baltimore system. While prudent of his fortune, he kept up a display of surveyors and graders in several counties, and his local patriotism at least had the appreciation of Vesta's little circle.

The continued absence of Samson surprised Milburn, and Judge Custis's letters were irregular and long coming.

Two letters received by the Widow Dennis were as mystical as they were assuring. One in a female hand told her that Levin was being tenderly watched, and another in man's writing enclosed money and said her son would soon be home. Mrs. Dennis was far from happy in this indefinite state of mind, and the absence of James Phoebus was a different strain. She loved that absentee already too well to forgive his silence.

One day before November Vesta said to her husband, "The air and sky are warm and sparkling yet, and the roses are out. You work too hard between the canal case and your railroad. Let us fill the two carriages and drive to old Rehoboth and eat our dinner there."

Milburn consented, and they took with them Grandmother Tilghman and William, Rhoda Holland, Roxy, Mrs. Dennis, and also the woman Mary.

The road passed in sight of the birthplace of Samuel Chase, the lion of independence in Maryland, who forced that hesitating state by threatenings and even riots to declare for permanent separation from England.

Near Chase's birthplace stood the old Washington Academy, raised in that early republican day when a generous fever for education followed the act of tolerance, making some noble schools that were ultimately discouraged by the growth of towns. With four great chimneys rising above a conical roof, pediments, cupola, and two wide stories, all laid in staid, dark brick, the academy had a mournful and neglected look, as if ruminating upon more brutalized times and lessening enlightenment, which false systems ever require.

"Ah," said Vesta's husband, "how many a poor boy thou hast sent from yonder, honey, mutilated for life like the lovers of the queen bee."

"How is that?" Vesta inquired.

"You never heard of the queen bee? Women, when they die, may turn to bees and reverse their hard conditions in this life. The queen bee has no rival in the hive. All other females there are immature, and all the males are dying for the queen. She has five hundred lovers, so lovesick for her that they never work, and forty times as many maids, like Penelope's, all embroidering comb and wax."

"How was that proved?"

"By putting the bees in a glass house and watching them. To God, all mankind may be in a glass hive, too, and every buzzer's secret biography be kept."

"And the queen bee's honeymoon?"

"From her that word is taken. She flies high into the air and meets a lover by chance. She has so many that one is sure to be met. She kisses him in that crystal eddy of sunshine, and in the transport he is wounded to the heart. How many young drones from the academy have seen thee once and swooned for life."

"But the queen bee also has a fate, sir?"

"Yes. She leaves the hive and settles upon some unsightly forest tree, and all that love her follow. The long-neglected herb becomes busy with music and sweetness and flashing of silver wings, till the farmer gathers the swarm into a gum tree cone, and it is their home."

Vesta looked up at the poetical illustration and saw her husband's conical hat, into which she had been hived, and her eyes fell to her mourning weeds.

"Oh, my father," she thought, "has he kept his good resolutions. It is all I have left to hope for."

Kingston Hall

They traveled down the aisles of the level forest, where the pine trees and holly enriched the brown concavity of oaks. At the scattered settlement of Kingston the Jackson candidate for governor, Mr. Carroll, bowed from his door. Crossing Morumsco Creek, they bore to the east and soon approached the still animate, ecclesiastical hamlet of Rehoboth, extending its two ancient churches across their vision.

The road ran to the Pocomoke River bank, where a ferry was maintained to the opposite shore and the Virginia land of Accomack, and the cold tide went winding to an oystery estuary of the bay, where the mud was so soft that vessels aground in it could continue sailing.

Close by were oyster shells piled high as a natural bluff by Indian gourmands before John Smith's voyage of navigation.

Vesta was set out at the great, ruined Episcopal church that made the gateway of Rehoboth, and while William and Rhoda strolled into the open door of the Presbyterian church farther on, Milburn put up the horses at the tavern.

"Was this the first Presbyterian church yer?" Rhoda asked William Tilghman.

Rehoboth Presbyterian Church

"The first in America, Rhoda. This was Rev. Francis Makemie's church. He lived in Virginia, not far from here, where no worship was permitted but ours, so he came over the Pocomoke and reared a church of logs at this point. This is the third or fourth church building upon the spot. Rehoboth came to be such a point for worship that the Established Church built yonder noble edifice in 1735, as if to overawe this Calvinistic one."

"It's a quare old house," said Rhoda. "The little doors that opens from the vlestiblule into the side galleries sent a draught right down the preacher's back when he give out the hymn, 'Blow ye the trumpet, blow.' He always blowed his nose twice. So they boarded up the galleries and let the ceiling down flat. If we go up thar, we can see the other old, round ceiling."

So they went up the narrow stairs from the door and came into the tubes of galleries, all closed from the congregation. Sitting in the obscurity, the preacher passed his arm around Rhoda's waist.

"Take keer," she said. "Maybe you was predestined to be lost yer. I'm skeered to be up yer half in the dark, even with a good man."

Nevertheless, she came a little closer to him and looked into his eyes, and the young rector suddenly kissed her.

"You've brought it on yourself by looking so pretty in this stern place of creeds and catechisms. Could you love me if I asked you?"

"You couldn't love me true, William. Your heart is in t'other old church among the bats and foxes, where Aunt Vesty sits this minute."

"No, my sorrow is there, Rhoda. I am trying to build a nest for my heart. We all must love."

"William, I don't think a young man in love can remember so much history when he's sittin' in the dark by his gal."

"Love among the ruins is always melancholy, Rhoda."

"Yes, William, and your love comes out of 'em—the ruins of your old, first love. I couldn't make you happy."

"Try," said William. "My fancy wavers towards you. You are a beautiful girl."

"Yes," said Rhoda, "it's time I was gittin' married. I think I'll take you on trial and watch Aunt Vesty to see if she is jealous of me."

Standing with this tall, willowy girl in his arms, all differences of education passed away, and the rector of Princess Anne felt that there was no medicine for love but love.

They walked together around the square old edifice, among the graves of Tilghmans, Drydens, Revells, and Beauchamps, and looked at the round-capped windows and double doors in arched brick. Then, passing back along the road, they entered the enclosure of the grand old Episcopal Church. Nearly eighty feet long, it presented its broadside of blackish brick and double tier of spacious windows to the absolute desertion of this forest place.

The churchyard was a copse of berry bushes, gum, and poplar suckers. Apple trees, cedars, and wild cherries rose above, and higher still the damp sycamores and maples, growing out of knee deep myrtle, which spread upon the waves of old graves.

Though the wall between them had fallen in, thirteen windows on the massive side held more than four hundred panes of dim glass in their hand-worked sashes, and two great windows in the gable, with fifty panes each, stood firm. In the opposite gable another door had been forced open, and as they crossed the sill, a crack, like thin ice stepped upon, went splitting the long and lofty vacancy with warning rumbles.

Ruins of Rehoboth Episcopal Church

At least seventy-five by fifty feet, the whole interior now stood exposed in fine perspective, a majestic hall unbroken by side galleries, with double stories of windows shedding a hazy light, and at the distant end was a low pulpit and spacious altar. The walls of this neglected temple were two feet thick, and its high ceiling was kept from falling by ten rude props of recent, rough carpentry. The pews were high-fenced and stately, and each four-sided to contain ten persons. The rotting damask cushions in many of them told of a former aristocracy, while now all the congregation could be assembled in a single pew, and worship was unknown but once a year when the bishop came to read his liturgy to dust and desolation.

So, on the opposite, western cape of the Chesapeake, the Roman priests of Calvert's foundation shivered in the waste of old St. Mary's. The folds had left the shepherds, and only fifty people came to worship in the kirk of the earliest Presbyterians.

Two tall, once elegant stoves stood nearly midway up the cracking church floor, and Mary had made a fire in one of them. The pine wood was roaring, and the long height of pipe was smoking. Startled by the fire, a venerable opossum came out of one of the pews and waggled down the aisle like a gray devotee who had said his prayers and feared no man.

Near the stove, Vesta read her prayer book aloud to the widow and Grandmother Tilghman. In a few moments the young rector, wearing his surplice, emerged from an old gallery for black people and read the service simply and plaintively, the small group responding in the room a thousand might have worshipped in.

"Cousin Vesta," the minister said after the service, "Miss Holland is going to try to love me. Mr. Milburn, may I address her?"

"She is a willful piece," Meshach said. "You must school her first. Let my wife give my consent."

Vesta went to both and kissed them. "I feel so encouraged, dear Rhoda and William, to see love beginning all about me. Now, Norah, if you could be just to James Phoebus, who is proving his love to you, perhaps with his life."

"Yes, that is a match I approve of," said Grandmother Tilghman, "but I don't want Bill to marry. Disappointed men make rash selections."

"Oh," said Rhoda, "don't conglatulate him too soon. I haven't tuk him yet. He's goin' teach me outen the books, and I'll teach him outen the forest."

They walked together to the river bank, and Mrs. Dennis had the poor woman Mary tell the adventures of Jimmy Phoebus to save her from slavery. All were deeply moved.

"Now, Norah," Grandmother Tilghman said, "the moment that man returns, you go to him and kiss him and say, 'James, you have been the only father to my son. Do you want me to be your wife?' This world is made for marrying, Norah. Women have no other career. Nature does not value the brain of Shakespeare, but keeps the seed of every vagrant plant warm, and marries everything."

"Well," said Vesta, "Norah loves James Phoebus; don't you, Norah?"

The widow blushed.

"Take him, my pretty neighbor," said Milburn.

As they all looked at her, she suddenly cried. "I want to. Indeed, I would have done so before, but I am superstitious. Who is it that feeds me so mysteriously?"

"Has he been coming of late?" asked Mrs. Tilghman.

"No, not since you were married, Vesta."

"Then I think he will come no more," Milburn said. "You have waited longer than I did." His eyes sought his wife's and he added, "Will I ever be more than your husband?"

"Yes," said Grandmother Tilghman with special effort, "when you wear a hat a young wife is not ashamed of."

All felt a cold thrill at these words from the blind woman, and Milburn said gravely, "How can you know about hats when you cannot see them?"

"Oh," said Grandmother, herself a little frightened, "that hat I think I can smell."

∞

That same night in Princess Anne, Mrs. Dennis undressed herself by a fragment of hearth fire that now and then flashed upon the picture of her husband as he had left her sixteen years before, when Levin was a baby—a rich, blonde, youthful man dressed in naval uniform, like Decatur, whose birthplace was so near his own.

His golden hair curled upon his forehead; his blue eyes were full of handsome daring; his red, pouting mouth was like a woman's. Upon his arm a corded chapeau was held; epaulettes tasseled his shoulders; his rich blue coat was slashed with gold along the wide lapels and stood stiffly around his neck. He seemed to be a mere boy, but of the mettle which made American officers and privateersmen of his day the only reward on the seas against the otherwise universal dominion of England.

This portrait, the last of her family possessions, was the young sailor's parting gift to her when he sailed in the *Ida*, leaving her a mere girl with his son upon her breast. The picture hung above the lowly door, the bolt whereof was never fastened in that serene society.

Mrs. Dennis knelt upon the bare floor and raised her arms, white as her spirit, to the lover of her youth: "Oh, thou I have adored since God gave me to feel the beauty and strength of man in my childhood, if I have ever looked on man but thee with love or wavering, rebuke me now for the offense I am to do, if such it be, in choosing another father for thy boy."

A low wail rose upon the midnight from somewhere near, and a sick man's cough broke the perfect silence. The widow's hand instinctively covered her bosom as she listened.

Then, deep in the spirit of her prayer, she continued: "Oh, Bowie, if thou livest, let me know. If thou art detained by enemies, by savage people, by foreign love—no matter what thy errors—I will still be true. Give me some token by the God that has thee in his keeping, whether thou liest on the ocean's floor or lookest from the stars. If thou art dead, love of my youth, assure me, I pray thee."

The wail and cough were repeated, and a footstep seemed to come. The door flew open, and a man stood in the moonlight, pale as a ghost, and with Spanish-looking garments and head and neck tied with cerements like wounded people in the cockpits of ships of war. He bent upon her the eyes of the portrait above the door.

Fascinated and frozen still, the widow let her arms fall and gazed in horror and astonishment.

The effigy, so like her husband, yet so altered, reached his hand towards her. A diamond caught the moon and seemed to drink it. A wail like the others she had heard broke from his lips and said, "To lose those charms—that heart. Oh, God!"

As he stood ghastly and supplicating, as if he would fall and die upon her threshold, another hand came forward and drew the door between them. A voice she had not heard before tenderly exclaimed, "I love him as I never loved a male."

"It is my husband's spirit," the widow breathed; "I cannot marry," and she swooned upon her floor before the dying fire.

Virgie's Flight

Chapter 38

*A*s Virgie looked upon it, Snow Hill seemed amost built on snow. The streets, gardens, and fields were composed of a white sand, though the humid air brought vegetation even from this. Vines clambered, willows drooped, flowers blossomed, and noble oaks and great speckled sycamores, like freckled giants, rose to heights suggesting rich nutrition at their roots.

Wind from a receded sea had piled up the sand long ago into mounds, and heat and moisture and salt had made the land habitable. Perhaps with memories of old Snow Hill in London, the manor owner called it a hill and put his own name thereto.

Upon this bank or hill stood two venerable churches, both of English brick. The Episcopalian was covered with ivy, and the Presbyterian, which had given its name to the first synod of the Kirk in the new world, now stood surrounded with gravestones. Here visitors might read Scottish names left to orphans at Worcester, which, as the court and jail indicated, was the name of the county.

As the sun rose into the old trees, waking the liquid-throated birds and putting a gleam on old brick and older white-washed houses, a golden luster, hidden in the sand like Benjamin's cup in the bag of flinty corn, seemed to betray Snow Hill. Virgie heard the sound of hoofs upon a bridge and saw the Custis carriage winding up a golden road across the lily-bordered river. "Alone," she said. "Love has gone. Now I must live for freedom."

Makemie Memorial Presbyterian Church

All Hallows Episcopal Church

"Breakfast, Miss," said a neat, kind-faced woman of Virgie's own size and color. "My husband is going to drive you out of town before any of the white people are up to see you." A mulatto man sat at the table, whom the woman introduced as her husband.

"Mrs. Hudson," Virgie said, "you are doing so much for me. May the good Lord pay you back."

"Oh, no," replied the woman, "I am always up at this hour. I work hard because I am trying to buy my mother, who is still a slave."

"How came you free?" Virgie asked wistfully.

"I saved a sick gentleman's life. He bought me for it and gave me my freedom. I have a pass that tells the color of my eyes and skin, my weight, and everything. With this I can go into Delaware and the free states. I wish you had one, Miss Virgie."

"Oh, Mrs. Hudson, I dearly wish I had. Let me read it. Why, from this description I could almost pass for you."

"Indeed," the housewife said. "We are not the same age, but white people don't read a pass very careful."

"How I would love anybody that could get me such a pass."

"I have given my word of honor that I will never lend it. Much as I like to help my color to freedom, I cannot break my word. Tomorrow I have to go into Delaware to nurse a lady."

"You attend the sick, Mrs. Hudson?"

"Yes, I have a kind of call that way, Miss Virgie. I pulled herbs and tried them on myself ever since I was a girl, and I studied 'tendin'' people, watchin' their minds—that is so much of sickness—and how to wrap and rub them. My husband oysters down in the inlets. Here is his wagon now."

"The Lord remember you in need, dear Mrs. Hudson."

The old wagon, an open thing to peddle oysters and fish, was driven across town to the south and was soon in the open country going towards Virginia. A smell of salt hay was in the air.

As they turned into a lane near a little roadside place of worship, a young white man rode by on horseback. Seeing Virgie, he reigned in and shouted, "Purty! Purty! Purty as peaches and cream! Ole Virginny blood is in them eyes, by the Ensign!"

The colored man muttered, "Go 'long, Mr. Wise."

"By the Ensign now," continued the man, who was young but of a cadaverous countenance, "if 'tis a Maryland huzzy, she is marvelous. What's the name, angel gal?"

"She's a Miss Spence, an' I'm a takin' her home yer," the mulatto man interposed, hastily going in the gate. With a shout like one intoxicated, the horseman galloped towards the north.

"I'm sorry he seen you, sho'," the conductor said. "That's Henry A. Wise, the big lawyer from Accomack. Maybe he'll inquire at Snow Hill, where he's goin' to court."

"What place is this?" Virgie asked, seeing a thick-set house at the end of the short lane with small farm buildings around it.

"It's ole Spring Hill, built by the first of the Milburns—the one that made the will leavin' his hat and nothin' else to he son. I'm goin' to leave you here with my sister till I see about gittin' a boat. If you is tracked to Snow Hill, it'll be found you come out this way. The inlets run up along the coast yer past the Delaware line. I'm a-goin' to double on 'em an' sail you past Snow Hill agin. I'll git you away, Miss Virgie, if it costs all I have got together."

Virgie was put in a loft over the kitchen of the house and left to her contemplations. The place was nearly dark, and she was jaded for want of sleep, the past night's excitement having shaken her. She began to doze fitfully and dream almost awake.

She saw Meshach Milburn, who seemed to have become a little, old-faced child, and he was reaching up to someone older, very like himself in features, and taking a steeple hat from his hand. This older child reached back and took a similar hat from one still older. The first two vanished, and two old men stood, giving and receiving the hat.

Then nothing was left but the hat, which was huge, and fire belched from it. A circle of wizards danced around and around the flame in dizzy glee, all wearing hats of similar form, but higher. The hats reached the sky and stars, and each was spouting flame. Among these riotous wizards Virgie recognized the features of the tall kidnapper and Judge Custis. Vesta was there, too, and old Aunt Hominy. All looked upon Vesta with shame or sorrow till she, fearful, yet fascinated, leaped into the circle and danced around and around with the rest. Her feet made a fiery path, and her head was burning hot. Finally, she lost her balance and fell into the great hat. It's high walls surrounded her like mountains, and she could see nothing in the bottom of the old tile but a little grave, and peeping from it was the face of the murdered child the kidnapper had taken away.

"Come," said a voice. Virgie awoke to see the head of her conductor looking into the loft. Her temples and hands were hot with fever.

She only knew that she was again in the old wagon, and a boy was in it. After a certain time—she could not tell how long—she was helped to the ground at an old landing and placed on board a boat.

The man Hudson watched the sail while the boy steered, and Virgie, covered with the man's greatcoat, lay in the middle of the skiff, sick and cold. It seemed to her to be afternoon and the ocean somewhere near, as she heard low thunder like breaking waves. Once, when she rose to look in a stupefied way, there were familiar objects on both shores, and she thought it was Old Town Beach near Snow Hill Inlet.

A little later the man brought her oysters and cold pork rib with cornbread to eat. Darting through a narrow strait, the skiff scraped bottom, and the shores grew closer and finally seemed almost to meet.

Then the stars were shining, and the waters grew wide again, and lying in a trance of flying lights and images, she thought she felt her lips kissed and a voice say, "Darling."

Finally, she felt lifted up and carried. When she could realize the situation, she found herself lying on a pile of shingles at an old wharf, and the man beside her was weeping as he watched the boat recede down a moonlit aisle of wave.

"My boy, my poor ole woman," she heard her conductor mutter, "I never can come back to you no mo'."

"Why?" asked Virgie, hardly realizing what she said.

"Because—*you* did it!" the man exclaimed, his eyes streaming tears.

"Oh, tell me where I am," Virgie said. "Is it far to freedom now?"

She looked at the sky, all agitated with clouds and stars moving across each other, and it seemed the nearest world of all. "Is my dear white father there?" she thought. "Can he see me here, sick and lonely, and hate me?"

"We're at de shingle landing. Yonder is St. Martin's," said the Negro cautiously. "There's two roads goin' to the North nigh whar we air. One is the stage road and t'other is the shingle trail through the Cypress Swamp."

"Take the road that's the safest to freedom," Virgie sighed.

In a few moments they came to a place where the cart trail crossed a sandy road and went beyond it along the edge of a small stream. The man walked a few steps up the better road undecidedly, then suddenly drew Virgie back into the bushes, but not quickly enough to be unobserved by two men coming on in an old, rattling wagon.

"My skin," cried the driver, "thar's a sniptious gal. Come out yer and show yourself!"

Virgie felt the man's eyes resting on her, but not with the coarse ardor of his companion, who wore a wide slouched hat and red shirt and bandages around the head and throat. Yet on his ghastly pale face, smeared with blood, lay a coarse leer. He kissed his mouth at her and uttered, "*O fexuosa! esquisita!* It is dainty, Sorden!"

"Now ef we was a-goin' t'other way, Van Dorn," the driver said, "we could give 'em a lift. Boy, what are you out fur? Where's your passes?"

"Yer they is. It's my wife an' me gwyn to nurse a lady in Delaware."

"Let me see!" He puffed his cigar upon the paper and exclaimed, "Prissy Hudson? Why, that's my wife's nurse, and that ain't the same woman! Where did you get this pass?"

"Go on, Sorden," coughed the other man. "I'm bleeding. Let me lie down."

His eyes had lost their wanton fire and were hollow and glazed. The driver caught him in his arms and said kindly, "I love him as I never loved a male."

"Give me back the passes," exclaimed the mulatto man, as the wagon started south.

"No!" shouted the driver. "I shall keep them as evidence against Prissy Hudson for assisting a runaway!"

"Lost, lost," muttered the mulatto. "Now the swamp's our only road."

He seized Virgie and pulled her up the cart track along the swampy branch.

"What have you done?" she cried.

"Come," answered the man. "Here is no place to talk."

With fever making her strong, and her fear absorbed by frenzy, the girl followed the man into the deep sand of the track, scarcely noticing the melancholy cypress trees rising around them out of pools that sucked poison from the starlight, basking there beside the reptile.

Flowers with such rich tints that night scarcely darkened them sent up their musky perfume, and vines, in silent festoons, drooped from the tips of giant trees like Babel's aspiring builders turned back and stricken dumb. They fell limp, and hanging there in death, their beards still seemed to grow in the ghastly vitality of an immortal dream.

The sounds of restless animation were more intense in the night, as if the moon were mistress here and had wakened every insect brain and tongue to industry. The volume grew prodigious in the sick girl's ears and seemed to deaden every word her male companion had to say. Like enormous pendulums of sound, the roaming crickets and amphibia swung their contradictions to and fro, like viragos doomed to wait for eternity, and each insisting upon the last word to say:

"You did!"

"You didn't!"

"You did!"

"You didn't, you didn't, you didn't!"

"You did, you did!"

Thus had the eternal quarrel, begun before Hector and the Greeks were born, raged in the Cypress Swamp, increasing in loudness every night till it pealed in the fleeing slave girl's ears like God and Satan disputing for her soul.

As this idea increased upon her fancy, she heard the very words these warring powers hurled to and fro, as now the myriad of angels cheered together, "Hallelujah! Hallelujah!" and, like an army of spiders assembled in the swamp, the deep refrain of "Hell, hell, hell!" groaned back.

"Hallelujah!"

"Hell!"

"Hallelujah!"

As she stumbled on, she found herself crying, "Hallelujah! Hallelujah!"

The swamp increased in depth and solemnity as they drew near the rushing sluices of the Pocomoke, the trail now being a mere ditch and chain of floating logs, where no vehicle could pass. The man seemed frightened as he led the way, sometimes balancing on a revolving log or again plunging nearly to his waist in vegetable muck.

But the light-footed girl had the step of a bird and hopped as if from twig to twig, seeming to slide where he would sink. Often, when he had fallen headlong from some treacherous perch, the man turned in terror to see her slender feet in crescent sandals play in the moonlit jungle like hands upon a harp.

He stared at her in wonder, but too wistfully. Cat briers hung across openings, and grapevines, like the cables of sunken ships, fell through the crystal waves of night, but the North Star seemed to find a way to peep through everything, and Virgie heard the words from Hudson, "Jess over this branch a bit we is in Delaware."

Then the crickets and tree frogs, the bullfrogs and whippoorwills, the owls and everything seemed to drown his voice and halloo, "We is in Delaware! We is, we is! We is in Del-a-a-ware!"

A warming, kindly light began to blaze their trail, as if some gentle predecessor with a golden adz had chipped the funereal trees and made them smile a welcome. Small fires were burning in the vegetable mold or surface brush, and the opacity of the forest yielded to the pretty flame, which danced and almost sang in a household crackle, like a young girl in love, humming tunes as she kindles a fire.

The mighty swamp now grew distinct, yet more inaccessible. Its inner edges seemed transparent in the line of fires, like curtains of lace against the midnight windowpanes. The Virginia creeper, light as the flounces of a lady, went whirling upward as if in a dance. The fallen giant trees were rich in hanging moss. Laurel and jasmine appeared beyond the bubbling surface of the long, green morass, where life of some kind seemed to turn over comfortably in the rising warmth, like sleepers in bed.

Suddenly, the man took Virgie up and carried her through a stream of running water, brown with tannin. "We is in Delaware," he said, as they reached a camp of shingle sawyers. The deserted outpost was lighted by the fire, with golden chips strewn around, and sawdust, like Indian meal, suggested to Virgie the warm pone at Teackle Hall.

She put her feet at a burning log to warm them and hardly saw a moccasin snake glide around the fire, stop, as if to dart at her, then glide away. Virgie's mind attributed this kindly fire to the presence of freedom.

"Oh, I should like to lie here and go to sleep," she said languidly. "I am so tired."

Wringing wet with the journey's difficulties, Hudson threw his arms around Virgie and drew her to his damp yet fiery breast. "We will sleep here, then," he breathed into her lips; "I love you!"

Virgie's incoherent state yielded to these sudden words, and she was startled to the reality she had not understood before: her guide was drunk with passion. She struggled with all her might but was as a switch in a maniac's hands.

"I stole my ole woman's pass fur you," the infatuated ruffian sighed. "You said you would love the man who got you one. Virgie, you is mine!"

A suffocating sense and a heat more than animal nature seemed to enclose them. The girl struggled free, her lithe figure exerting with all her strength to preserve her modesty.

"Hudson," she cried, "I will tell your wife! God forgive you for insulting a poor, sick, helpless girl in this wild swamp!"

"My wife is dead to me. You is the only wife I has now. Here we shall sleep and forget my children and my little home that was enough fur me, gal, till your beauty come and tuk me from it."

"Stop!" the girl called, her face blanched even in her fever. "If you do not keep away, I will throw myself in that pool and drown. I would rather die than cheat your good wife, as you have done."

"Nothing is yer," the Negro said, "but you an' me an' love. I would not let you drown; you are too beautiful. We will get to the free states together and live for each other. Kiss me!"

He darted upon her again and bent her fair head back by the fallen braids of her silky hair. The tall woods filled with majestic light. Something roared as if the winds had gone astray and were rushing towards them.

"Hark!" cried Virgie. "God is coming to punish you!"

As she spoke, the ground beside them burst into flames and black smoke. The man's arms relaxed. He looked around and exclaimed, "It's the underground fire; run fur your life!"

He led the way, running to the north as they had been going. Suddenly, fire, like a golden wall, rose across their path. They turned back, and the fire there was now like a lake of lava, and over it the enormous trees seemed to warm their hands. Up the dry vines like monkeys of flame, the forked spirits of the burning earth dodged and chased each other.

"Gal, I can't leave you to perish," the desperate man shouted; "you must love me, or we'll die together."

He threw his wet greatcoat around her head so that she could not breathe the smoke nor spoil her beauty and dashed into the fire ahead of them.

∞

Virgie awoke, lying upon the ground. Stars still stood in the sky, but streaks of light in the east betokened dawn. Her hands were full of soot. Her skirts were burned. Some smarting pains were in her legs and feet, but she was able to walk. "Where is that poor, deluded man?" she thought.

A groan came from the ground, and there lay something nearly naked, burrowing his face in a pool of swamp water.

"Thank the Lord you are not dead," the girl said, "but have lived to repent and be a better man."

He rose up and looked at her with a face all blackened and raw and hideous to see.

"Merciful Lord!" exclaimed Virgie, "what ails you?"

"The Lord has punished me for my wickedness," he groaned. "Virgie, you must lead me now; I am gone blind."

Virgie's Flight, Continued
Chapter 39

"Can you walk, Hudson?" Virgie asked, when her horror permitted her to speak.

"I can walk, I reckon, but both my eyes is burned out. Oh, my pore old wife, she could nurse me so well, an' I have lost her."

The girl comforted the sightless man and led him on, indifferent to danger. He waded the deep places, where the water soothed his wounds and filled his blistered sockets with cool mud.

"Blessed is the pure in heart," he murmured, as they reached some sandy ground and sank down. "You can see God, Virgie; I never can."

They had now reached the northern border of the great Cypress Swamp of Delaware. Probably once a shallow bay in the encroaching sandbar of the peninsula, it had been filled with oysters and fish, which in time were imprisoned to become the manure of a forest. For ages these trees had grown, dropping their leaves and branches and raising the level of the swamp higher and higher. With ages more than had dried the mummies of the Pharaohs, this deep, combustible mass had formed, often opening tunnels to burrowing fire, which at some point would belch forth and race for weeks. It was such a fire they had come through.

In the early daylight Virgie came upon a small, swarthy boy, driving a little cart and ox. "Are you a colored boy?" she asked.

"No," the boy answered proudly, "I'm Indian-River Indian. Reckon I'm a *little* nigger."

"Take this poor man in, and I will pay you. Where are you going?"

"To Dagsborough landing for salt."

"Leave me at the old Clayton house," said the blind man. "It's empty. I can die thar or git a doctor."

Before the people were up, they entered a small hamlet with a shingle-boarded church in the woods nearby. One large deserted house stood at the edge of town. "This is John M. Clayton's birthplace," the man said. "My wife used to work yer."

"Virgie!" exclaimed a familiar voice.

The girl turned, her ears still ringing with the echoes of the swamp, and saw a face she knew. She ran to the breast beneath it, crying, "Samson Hat! Oh, friend, love me like my mother. I am very ill."

"Pore darlin' chile," Samson said, "no love will I ever bodder you wid agin but a fadder's. Why air you so fur from home?"

"I'm sold, Samson, and I'm trying to get free. The kidnappers are after me. Oh, save me!"

"I've jist got away from 'em. De ole woman Patty Cannon set me free. I promised her I would kidnap somebody younger dan ole Samson. Bless de Lord I come dis way."

He led her into the oak trees of the old church grove, where English worship had been celebrated just a hundred years, and she gave him money to buy medicine and pay a doctor to tend the blind man. Then Virgie sank into a fevered sleep under the old trees.

When she awoke, she was in a boat with Samson, gliding down a broad stretch of water, and her head was in his lap.

"You air pure as an angel yit, my little creatur," Samson said. "Now I'm a-takin' you down the Indian River into Rehoboth Bay, and arter dark I'll git you up the beach to Cape Hinlopen. Maybe I kin buy you a passage on some of dem stone boats dat's buildin' de new breakwater dar, and dat goes back to de Norf."

"Oh, Samson, if I could love any man, it would be you," Virgie said, "but I cannot love any now except my dear white father. Who is he?"

"De Lord, I reckon, has got yo' pedigree, Virgie."

"Am I dying, Samson?" the girl asked wistfully, her brilliant eyes full of fever. "Oh, friend, let me die so good that Miss Vesty and my father can come and kiss me."

"Tell me about Princess Anne an' my dear old Marster Meshach Milburn dat I'se leff so long, Virgie," the old pugilist said, wiping his eyes of tears.

She tried to remember, but faces and events ran into each other, and she could not bring them back. The boat, sailing in sight of the ocean and stately ships there, grounded after noon, almost within sound of the surf.

After being sheltered in a piece of woods until dark, Virgie was carried in Samson's arms up a beach of yielding sand. Only at the very edge of the surf, which rolled ominously and with a roar, was the footing firm. Lightning played across the black sea, lifting it, it seemed, and showing vessels making either out or in. As thunder burst upon the gathering confusion, Samson said, "Dar's a gun in dat thunder."

The next lightning flash showed a vessel close to the shore, coming rapidly in on the southeaster. Her gun was fired again, and feeble hailing could be heard. The storm seemed to break all at once, and a wave threw Samson to the sand and nearly carried Virgie back with it to the boiling sea. The faithful old man fought for her, and she ran at his side, uttering no complaint. Once, when they stopped to get breath and the heavenly fire illuminated every foot of the vast ocean, cannonading it with majestic artillery, Virgie sighed, "Freedom is beautiful!"

"Oh, Virgie," Samson answered, covering her with his own coat, "if I could buy you free, pore chile, I'd a-mos' go into slavery to save you from dis night."

"I can die there," Virgie said, pointing to the waves; "they must not catch me."

A wail came out of the storm that hushed them both, and the lightning lifted a stranding vessel upon their sight, so close, it seemed, that they could touch it. She was full of people hallooing, but not in any intelligible tongue.

As black night fell again upon this magic-lantern sketch, they heard a crash of wave and wood and falling spars and awful shrieks. When the next vivid flash of lightning came, nothing was visible but floating debris. Spluttering cries came out of the bosom of the sea, and a black man, flung upon a wave as if out of a cannon, struck the ground at their feet. He looked into Samson's eyes as the convulsion of death seized his chest and feet.

Before they could speak to each other, the beach was full of similar corpses, and every one was naked and black.

"It's a slave ship foundered yer," cried Samson. He caught at a yawl boat driving past, and Virgie saw the word "*Ida*" painted upon its bow.

"Samson," she said, forgetting her own misery, "it's Mrs. Dennis's husband come home and shipwrecked."

∞

The Old Stone Breakwater from Cape Henlopen

When Virgie next remembered, she was on a vast hill of sand. A nearby lighthouse flashed sleepily upon a sullen break of day, and the mutual lights showed the tops of trees rising out of the sand, where a forest had been buried alive, like twigs in amber.

Almost naked from fighting the storm, Samson Hat slept at her side, peaceful in hale age and virtue.

"Happy are the black," the sick girl said to herself, "that take no thought on things this white blood in me makes so large—on freedom and my father. Father, do love me before I die?"

She knelt on the great hillock by Cape Henlopen and prayed till she lost her knowledge of self, then slept again at Samson's side. She dreamed of angels flying around her, and yet their voices were so harsh they awoke her at last, and still these seraphs were flying in the day. She saw their wings and moved the old man at her side to say, "Samson, why cannot these angels sing?"

The old man looked up and faintly smiled. "Poor Virgie, dey is wildfowls—geese an' swans—all bewildered by dat storm. Dey can't sing like angels."

"Something sings," the girl said. "What is it?"

"Maybe Jesus," the Negro answered, looking at her with his eyes full of tears.

∞

The great breakwater, which required forty years and nearly a million tons of stone to build, was just commencing. Here, within the shallow bight of Henlopen, they saw the wrecks of many vessels, some sunken, some shattered in collision, some stranded in the marsh—proof of the need for such a work and of the fury of the storm that had so innocently vanished like a sleeping tiger after his bloody meal.

In the gentle sunshine the American flag floated upon several vessels—the flag that first kissed the breeze upon that spot in 1776, when Esek Hopkins raised the dyes of the peach and cream over the *Alfred* in the center of his little squadron.

And there, along the low bluff of the kill, lay the shingle-boarded town of Lewes in the torpor of nearly two hundred years, ever since the Dutch De Vries had settled it in 1631. Lord Delaware, Argall and the Swede, Penn, Blackbeard, Paul Jones, Lord Rodney—a thousand heroes had known it well. The pilots, like sea gulls, had nests there. Marylanders had invaded it; Tories had seized it; pirates had been suckled there; and now the courts and lawyers had forsaken it to go inland to Georgetown.

"Virgie," said Samson, "I'll try to buy some of de stone boat captains to carry you to Phildelfy."

He waded the Kill, carrying Virgie, and left her in the old Presbyterian church at the skirt of Lewes. After procuring medicine for her, he labored in vain nearly all day to get her passage to a free state. The reply was invariable: "Can't risk the whippin' post an' pillory. Can't lose a long job like bringin' stone to the breakwater to save one nigger."

A colored man at the hotel—a fine-looking man of a gingerbread color—beckoned Samson aside, and they went into the old, disused courthouse in the middle of a street.

"Brother," the stranger said, "I see by your action that you're trying to git a passage North. Is it fur yourself?"

"No," Samson said, taking inventory of the other's fine chest and strength and mentally wishing to have a chance at him, "I'm a free man an' kin go anywhere, but I have a friend."

"Why, old man," the other said frankly. "I'm the agent of our society at this pint."

"What is it?" asked Samson warily.

"The Protection Society. They educated me right yer. I went to school with white boys. Now, where is your friend?"

"What kin you do fur her?" asked Samson.

"A gal, is it? Why, I can just put her in my buggy, made and provided for the purpose, and drive her to the Quaker settlement."

"Whar's that?"

"Camden—only thirty miles off. I've got free passes all made out. Give yourself no more concern, brother."

Samson looked at the handsome person long and well, and the man stood his gaze modestly.

"Oh, if only I had some knowledge," Samson said. "I might as well be a slave if I know nothin'. I wish I could read your heart."

"I wish you could," said the man; "then you would trust me."

"What is your name?"

"Samuel Ogg."

"I want you to hold up your hand and swear, Sam Ogg, that you will never harm the pore chile I bring you. Say, Lord, let my body rot alive an' no man pity me, if I don't act right by her."

"It's a severe oath," said the stranger, "but I see your kind interest in the lady. Indeed, I'm only doing my duty."

He repeated the words, and Samson added, "God deal with you, Sam Ogg, as you keep dat oath. Now, come with me."

Virgie lay upon the altar cushions of the church like young Isaac upon his father's altar, and the cruelty of the law flashed over her like Abraham's superstitious knife. As song and seed in the spring bird, this young creature was priceless, yet a hard, steely prejudice had shut her away from every institution and equality, let every crime be perpetrated upon her, and made the scent of freedom in her nostrils worse than the incentive of the thief.

She was delirious, and her large eyes, in which blue and brown tints met in a kind of lake color, were wide open and almost lost in their long lashes. Flood and fire, sun and frost had beaten upon the slender encasement of her gentle life, yet it continued to kept time, like some Parian clock saved from a conflagration, in whose crystal pane the golden pendulum still moves, though the hands point astray in the mutilated face.

Her teeth, like the alabaster sails of the wave-tossed nautilus, or an ear of Indian corn exposed in the gale that blows across the tasseled field, showed through the loving lips she parted in her stormy dreams. Her raiment, partly torn from her, exposed her supple figure and neck, and her white arm, like an ivory serpent beneath her mass of silky hair, sustained her head. Such as she had called Antony from his wife and Caesar from his classical selfishness, and on many an Eastern throne such beauty as hers had stirred armies to glory and conquest.

In the old churchyard that surrounded them, revolutionary officers slept, who had helped to gain the nation's freedom. They might be willing to rise with her but not to be buried in the same enclosure. How small is religion; how false democracy; how far off are the judgments of heaven! There stood over the pulpit an inscription, itself presumptuous with aristocracy, saying: "The dead in Christ shall rise first," as if those truly dead in the humility of Christ would not prefer to rise last.

Samson watched his new friend narrowly, whose countenance was profoundly piteous. Satisfied with the man, Samson knelt by Virgie and kissed her once. "Pore rose of slavery," he said, "forgive me dat I courted you like a gal instead of like an angel. I am old and ashamed of myself. We may never meet agin, dear, draggled flower. May de Lord—if dis be his holy temple—save you pure and find you a home. Good-bye, Virgie."

"Come," said the man, as Samson sat bowed and weeping, "the buggy is ready. I'll wrap you warm, Miss."

"Freedom," whispered the girl, awakening; "oh, I must find it."

∞

The next Virgie knew, she was in a cabin loft, and a voice was speaking in the room below.

"See me," it said. "We sell you, dat's sho'. See me now. You make de best of it. Sam Ogg yer, we sold twenty-two times. Sam will be sold wid you an' teach yo' de Murrell game."

"Politely, gentlemen," responded a feminine voice. "I don't know that I have the nerve for it. My occupation has been marrying them. It's true that the hue-and-cry has made that branch dull, but I had great talent for it."

"Kidnappin'," said a third voice, "is runnin' low. It surrounds the whole slave belt from Illinois to Delaware. The laws of Illinois were made in our interests till Governor Harrison, whose free man was kidnapped, raised an excitement out there six years ago. Newt Wright, Joe O'Neal, and Abe Thomas were the smartest kidnappers along the Kentucky line, but Joe Johnson, who is gettin' ready to go south, will be the last man of enterprise in the business. John A. Murrell's idea is to divide fair with black men—sell and steal 'em back—and I think it is sagacious. It's safer, anyway, than Patty Cannon's other plan."

"What is that, Mr. Ogg?" asked the feminine-voiced Negro.

"Making away with the Negro traders, they say."

"See me, see me," exclaimed the first voice. "Dey'll hang her some day fur dat."

"Now," resumed Mr. Ogg, "a man of intelligence like you and me, Mr. Ransom—pardon, sir, does your shackle incommode you? I'll stuff it with some wool."

"Politely, Mr. Ogg. I'm ironed rather too tight."

"I say, Mr. Ransom, you and I can always play the average slave holder for a fool. Why, I hardly get into a family before I make love to some member of it, and if I don't vamoose with a black wench, it's with her mistress."

"Ah, Mr. Ogg, they are perfectly fiendish in resenting *that!*"

"Of course, but there's a grand tit-for-tat going through all nature. Why, sir, to a man of art and enterprise like you, the pleasures of the deep South far exceed this poor, plain region. Take the roof off slavery and the blacks have rather the best of it. The whites would think so if they could see what is going on."

"Politely, Mr. Ogg, will not the entire institution some day blow itself out like one of their western steamboats?"

"No doubt of it, Mr. Ransom. When we have disposed of you, and you can see the country for yourself, observe how sensitive slave holding is. A thousand anxieties lie in it. They believe in insurrections, rapes, and incendiaries. A perfect sleep they hardly know, but go prowling around night and day, driven by their suspicions. It makes them warlike and unhappy, and the slaves eat the ground poor. Besides, they have terrible enemies in the Negro traders, whom they look down on socially and really drive into sympathy with the Negroes. Mr. Murrell, for instance, has a grand plan for a slave insurrection. He says white society is all against him, and he'll get even with it."

"See me, see me," another voice chimed in hoarsely. "Slavery is bad scared, sho'. Joe Leonard Smith, Catholic over on de western sho', has jess set twelve niggers free. Governor Charley Ridgely has set two hundred and fifty free. John Randolph, dey say, is gwyn to set more dan three hundred free. Dar's fifty abolition societies in Nawf Carolina, eleven in Maryland, eight in ole Virginny, an' two in Delaware. Ho! Dey set 'em free, and we'll steal 'em back! Ole Derrick Molleston will never be out of pork an' money."

"Politely, gentlemen," said the individual with the shackle. "Have you heard of the incendiary proclamation issued in Boston by David Walker, telling all slaves that it is their religious duty to rise?"

"Yes, and rise they will, but to what end? It will be a big scare but no war. Next they will stop reading among all slaves, prevent emancipation by law, and watch the colored meeting houses. The fire will be buried under the amount of the fuel, yet all be there."

"Mr. Ogg, your experience is remarkable, and you have been sold and run away in nearly every slave state? Politely, sir, are they not kidnapping white men, too? Who is this Morgan that was stolen last year in the State of New York?"

"Oh, that's a renegade Free Mason, Mr. Ransom. As much fuss is made over him as if we did not steal a hundred free people every day. It only shows that kidnapping of all sorts is getting to be unpopular. If a new political party can be made on stealing one white Morgan, don't you think another party will some day rise on stealing several millions of black Morgans?"

"See me! see me!" exclaimed the hoarse voice suddenly.

"Escaping, are you?" cried the second voice.

"Politely, gentlemen," was heard from the third voice, some distance off in the dark. Chasing footsteps followed, and Virgie arose and peeped below.

A fire was burning in a clay chimney beside a table on which were meat and liquor. The girl swung herself out of the loft to the ground floor, seized the meat and some bread, and rushed noiselessly into the night.

She hardly knew what she was doing until she had crossed a bridge and come to the edge of a small town, around which she took a road to the right. This she followed a mile or more till she saw a small brick house in the edge of woods by a stile and pole well.

The light from a dormer window in the garret beamed so brightly that it charmed Virgie with the fascination of warmth and home. Without thinking, she crossed the stile, bathed her hot temples at the well, and walked into the kitchen before the fire.

"Freedom," said Virgie, "have I come to it?" She fell upon the rag carpet before the fire, saying, "Father, dear father," and did not move.

"Well," said a man sitting there, "it's not often people in search of freedom walk into Devil Jim Clark's."

"She is white," exclaimed a woman, looking compassionately upon the stranger, "and she is dying."

"No," retorted the man, "she is too pretty to be white. This is the wench Sam Ogg was seen with. She belongs to Allan McLane, and there's a reward of five hundred dollars for her, but she'll bring two thousand in New Orleans for a mistress."

"Hush!" said the woman. "You may bring a judgment upon your daughters."

"Joe Johnson is about to sail," remarked Devil Jim Clark. "He shall take her with him."

The girl heard *that* name through the thick chambers of oblivion. She rose and shrieked and rushed into the woman's arms. "Save me, Mother, save me from that man!"

The woman's heart was pierced by the cry. She folded Virgie to her breast and kissed her, saying, "She shall sleep in our daughter's bed and rest this night—our daughter, James, that we buried."

The man's mouth puckered a little. He looked uneasy and drew his handkerchief to his eyes. "You're all agin me!" he bellowed and rushed from the room.

∞

The wife of Devil Jim Clark was a pious Methodist and spent the next day, with her daughter's help, at Virgie's bedside, hearing her cherished remembrances and broken mutterings for fatherly love.

"Your father is out for mischief," Mrs. Clark said to her daughter. "Jump on your saddle horse and ride to the Widow Brinkley's. Tell her to send for this girl."

"Mamma, they say she's an abolitionist."

"That's what I send you for. It's a race between you and your father. Be with me or with him!"

The girl tied on her hood, took her riding whip, and departed.

In an hour she returned with a tidy black woman, whom Mrs. Clark took into Virgie's chamber.

"My heart bleeds for this girl," the hostess said. "They say your son spirits Negroes north. I do not ask you if it is true, but as one mother to another, I give you this girl. She is too white to be sold. She looks like a dead child of mine."

"Bill is not due home till sunset. If she is alive then, he has just time to drive her to Mr. Zeke Hunn's vessel at the mouth of the creek, which lies there every trip for one hour."

"To let runaways come aboard?"

"I have never been accused of helping them, Mrs. Clark."

The trader's wife slipped a bank bill into the colored woman's hand. "Lend to the Lord," she said. "I depend upon you to save us the sin of selling this girl."

∞

Two horses came to the little black house and stopped at the stile. "Wait here," said Devil Jim Clark. "Will you take her if she is still delirious?"

"Bingavast! Why not? I'm delirious myself; it's my wedding night. I'll rest her at Punch Hall."

The tall ruffian proceeded to prepare some saddle ropes to tie his victim before him on his horse. He was interrupted by a woman's voice: "Come and see your work, Joe Johnson!"

Following up the short cupboard stairs, the kidnapper was pointed to an object with peaked face and sharpened feet, lying white as lime on the bed, with eyelashes folded and arms drawn to its sides.

"Take her to Patty Cannon now," said Mrs. Clark, "who is only fit for dead company."

"The dell dead and undocked?" Johnson exclaimed, slightly shrinking from the body. "Maybe she's counterfeited the cranke. I'll search her cly."

Just then a wagon and hoofs were heard.

"Joe," whispered the woman's husband, "you're only four mile from Dover. Maybe it's warrants for both of us."

"Hike, then!" the pallid murderer hissed. "The world's agin me." And he slipped away with his companion.

∞

"Now, Bill Brinkley," the wife of Devil Jim whispered, as a tall, ingenuous-looking colored boy came in the room, "you are just in time. She has had laudanum to keep her still. My daughter powdered her. Let me kiss her once before she goes."

As the woman departed, the black boy, looking around him, muttered, "Whar is dat loft I've hearn about?"

Some movements overhead in the low dwelling directed his attention to a small trap door. Standing on a stool, he unbolted it and pushed it upwards, whispering, "Any passengers for Philadelfy? De gangplank's bein' pulled in!"

First a woolly head, then another, and next two pairs of legs appeared above.

"Take hold yer and carry de sick woman to de Dearborn," the boy said, as two frightened blacks dropped from the loft with handcuffs on them.

∞

In the clear evening a wagon sped through the saffron marshes towards the east, tramping down the stickweed and ironweed and goldenrod, and while the people in it cowered close, the Negro driver sang as carelessly as if he was the lord of the country:

> De people of Tuckyhoe
>   Dey is so lazy an' loose,
> Dey sows no buttons upon deir clothes,
>   And goes widout deir use;
> So nature she gib dem buttons,
>   To grow right outen deir hides,
> Dat dey may take life easy,

> An' buy no buttons besides.
>
> But de people of Tuckyhoe
>   Refuse to button deir warts,
> Unless dey's paid a salary
>   For practisin' of sech arts;
> Like de militia sogers,
>   Dat runs to buttons an' pay,
> De folks is truly shifless;
>   On Tuckyhoe side of de bay.

A sail was seen in the starlight, rising out of the marshes at an old landing in the last elbow of Jones's Creek. Hardly had the fugitives been put on board when the anchor was weighed and the packet stood out for the broad Delaware, her captain a Negro, her owner a Quaker.

The girl was awakened by the cold air of the bay striking her face. "Freedom!" she murmured. "It must be this. Oh, I am faint for father's arms to take me."

∞

Was this Teackle Hall that Virgie looked upon—a square, bright room, and her bed beside a window. Below her, streets of cobblestone and brick, and roofs of houses stretched to green marshes filled with cows, and a river that seemed blue as heaven.

"How beautiful! It must be freedom," Virgie thought, but why was she so cold? Glancing around the room, her eyes fell upon a lady in a cap, reading a tract to a large, shaven, square-jawed man. This woman was of a silver kind of beauty, as if her mind had overflowed into her heart, and not affecting it, had made her face of argent and lily, milk and sheen.

"What sayeth Brother Elias, Lucretia?"

"He sayeth, Thomas, 'This noble testimony of refusing to partake of the spoils of oppression lies with the dearly beloved young people of this day. We can look for but little from the aged, who have been accustomed to these things like second nature. Without justice there can be no virtue. Oh, justice, justice, how art thou abused everywhere! Men make justice like a nose of wax to satisfy their desires. If the soul is possessed of love, there is quietness.'"

"Yes," the girl said from her bed, thinking aloud, "love is quietness. Will father come?"

She looked again upon the hill descending to the river, the stately sails, the farther shore—so like her native region—and asked with her eyes what land they might be in.

"Wilmington," the woman said. "This is the house of Thomas Garrett, a friend of slaves. When you can be moved, it shall be to the green hills of the Brandywine, where all are free."

"Hills? What are they?" mused Virgie, looking at her wasted hand. "Must I climb more? Must I wade the swamps again? I know I have a father somewhere."

She dreamed and wept unconsciously and told of things at Teackle Hall, of being a child again, playing with her little mistress Vesta. The stars stood in the sky over her pillow, and she talked to them. Some she seemed to know as little Vince or Roxy or Master Willy Tilghman, playmates of her childhood.

But they vanished, and the young Quaker woman was reading again from the sermons of Elias Hicks: "'Love is quietness. Light only can qualify the soul. If I go not away, the Comforter will not come unto you.'"

"What Comforter?" sighed Virgie. There seemed to be a great blank, then with all her might she was trying to get somewhere, trying again and again. Then a calmness like gentle awe spread over her, and she only listened.

"My daughter, my own child," a voice said, "call me father and say I am forgiven."

"Father, forgiven," she murmured, and felt a warm face shedding tears and kissing her. She threw her arms tightly around the figure as if she could never let go, and everything was music and wonderful.

She feared she must fall if she did not hold to him. Who was it that called her "daughter?" Why came those cold stars so close, as if to spy upon him? She wrestled with something like a rock of ice to move her eyes and see the eyes that gushed for her. They were her master's.

"Master," she said, "whose am I?"

"Mine before God. Pure to my heart as your white sister, Vesta. White as young love in fondness and trust forever."

"And mother?" gurgled the girl's low notes, "where is she?"

"Yonder," said Judge Custis. "She is in heaven—that will judge me—whither she winged in bearing thee to me."

A happy light came over Virgie's face. She kissed her father twice, as if the second kiss was meant for her happier sister, and raising her arms towards the sky, she whispered, "Freedom," and died upon his breast.

Hulda Beleaguered

Chapter 40

Owen Daw brought the news of the repulse from Cowgill House and the wounding of Captain Van Dorn.

"Where's the little tacker Levin?" Patty Cannon asked furiously.

"Arrested, I 'spect," replied O'Day. "Van Dorn's hit in the throat."

"He'll not talk much then," she muttered. "His time had to come. Now, where will I find another lover at my age? Why, honey," she chuckled to herself in a looking glass, "that son of his'n may come back. He's took a shine to Huldy, why not to me?"

At that idea another thought came to her mind: to settle Hulda's fate in the absence of her young lover and monopolize the power over Levin Dennis, if he ever lived to see Johnson's Crossroads again.

As individual fugitives returned, confirming the decisive repulse of the band, Patty Cannon's face grew dark and her oaths low and deep. Cyrus James heard her say, "If I could only hang someone for this. Joe Johnson's the white-livered sneak that wouldn't go. I've hanged a better son-in-law."

"Aunt Patty, I love your grandchild Huldy," Cy James ventured to say. "The captain's wounded, an' Joe's goin' away to Floridy. Maybe I kin git you up another band."

Without an instant's consideration of this ambitious proposition, Mrs. Cannon threw Cy James through the window of her bar. He bawled like a baby, yet came out of his grief muttering, "Plowin', plowin'. I'll make her into batter an' fry her yet," and hid himself for the remainder of the afternoon in some secluded part of the hotel.

Mrs. Cannon resumed her monologue on business: "They all think to give the old woman the go-by. A sick man's no good, and there's that wife of Van Dorn's hopin' to git him yit. By God, she shan't have him in his shroud. I'll recruit from young material an' ruin 'em when they's boys. While you kin pet 'em, they'll do your work. I have a nigger in the garret Joe wants to burn. He's my nigger, and I'll let him loose to bring me more niggers. Money is what I need to put on a bold front, an' Huldy must fetch it!"

With this resolution, Patty Cannon mounted the stairs to a room on the second floor and pushed her way in without knocking. There she confronted a man of voluptuous form and face, like one overfed, yet on the best. He bore stiff, military shoulders, displayed a color warm in tint yet cold in expression, had blue eyes and rich, wine-lined cheeks and lips, though they seemed hard and self-indulged.

"Always knock, Patty," he said at once, "it's more conservative. My way in life is to reach my point while respecting all the forms. What do you want?"

"When do you leave for Baltimore, Cunnil McLane?"

"As soon as Joe returns with my dear sister's property. Tomorrow, I hope."

"You can take Huldy Bruington if you pay my price for her—two thousand dollars down. If you won't give it, she shall be married to some young kidnapper, who will fetch twice that pile for her in niggers. They'll all fight their weight in black wildcats to git her."

"Very abrupt proposition, Patty. It's not conservative at all. What's the matter with you today, dame? Van Dorn not lucky?"

He gave her a vitreous smile and watched her over his round paunch, on which a crystal watch seal hung, more like a human eye than his own.

Patty's color began to rise. "I'm mad," she said; "don't worry me! Yes, Van Dorn has been whipped—by niggers, too. Will you pay my price or not?"

"Tut, tut, good woman. What can I want with a white girl. It wouldn't look conservative at all in Baltimore."

Patty Cannon stamped her foot. "Don't rouse me with any of your hypocritical cant, Cunnil! What have you been teachin' that child to read an' write fur—out of your Bible, too? What do you bring her presents fur an' hang around us, when we know you despise us, except fur the black folks we can sell you cheap? Haven't I been sold to men like you time an' again before I was a woman, an' don't I know the sneakin' pains old men take to look benevolent when youth an' beauty is fur sale, an' how they pet it to keep it pure fur their own selfish enjoyment?"

"Patty, you shock me," the rubicund gentleman observed. "I have always found you conservative before. Go, and send sweet Hulda here, and for heaven's sake, Patty, don't reveal this bargain to her."

"Is it a bargain, Cunnil?"

"It is, if she can be made willing to it."

"That she shall, or make her bed in the forest, where good looks are not safe round yer."

Hulda was found at a window, looking out upon her former home and at a plowman who had nearly completed the furrows in a large field, sparing only some low places piled with brush. Hard as that home had been to Hulda, she regretted leaving it for this tavern across the Maryland line, where the caution that her grandmother had to exercise in Delaware was quite unnecessary.

Hulda had felt a sense of privacy at the little hip-roofed cottage, and her ability to read often charmed Patty Cannon to a stillness, even making her acquiescent and cordial. Unmodified by the example of modest women, Patty had a bold tendency to outdo men and lead them to audacities they would have feared to follow but for her courage and policy.

Her grandmother's feats of strength and cunning, statecraft and desperation, reminded Hulda of a book she had read about the Norman knights in England who kidnapped and robbed the poor Saxons. One description of William the Conqueror suggested to Hulda that perhaps he was a Patty Cannon in his times, as his body and legs were short and powerful, like hers, and he could bend a bow riding on horseback that no other knight could bend on foot with legs firmly planted. He could neither read nor write and was superstitious and cruel as the grave.

Hulda was dressed in her best clothes, and her hair was tied in wide braids. Her fine features and large, tender, seeking gray eyes had never before been turned on Patty Cannon so directly.

Her grandmother abandoned any attempt to be complaisant and sternly ordered her to attend to Colonel McLane's chamber.

"I can support you no longer, huzzy," the dark-eyed woman said, her cheeks full of blood. "Make haste to find some easy life or Joe shall get you a husband. We are ruined. You must make money, do you hear!"

"Here is money, Grandma," Hulda said, producing some of the shillings of 1815.

At the first sight of these, Patty Cannon turned pale, but in an instant the blood rushed to her face again, and she swore a dreadful oath, chasing Hulda into McLane's chamber.

"Ah, Hulda, inflaming your poor grandmother again," the carefully clad gentleman said. "It's not conservative, lovely girl. Honor thy father and mother, and grandmother, of course. Didn't I teach you that?"

"What is it to be conservative?" Hulda asked, sitting before the fire, while the colonel's eyes roamed over her tall, willowy figure.

"Conservative? Why, it's never to rush on anything—to oppose rushing. To be a bulwark against innovations. To prefer something you have tried and know."

"Like you?" asked Hulda.

"Yes, your benefactor. Of course, you never loved in this place?"

"It is the only place I know. To be conservative, as you call it, I must take my life and opportunity as I find them, like something I have tried and know."

"Ah, Hulda, I see you have a radical, perverse something in you, to twist my meaning so close. You do not belong to this vile spot except by consanguinity. It would be perfectly conservative for you to look to a better settlement."

"You have hinted that before," Hulda said, serene in his presence as a young woman used to proposals. "I do want to change this life, but I cannot do it and be conservative. I must fasten upon a free impulse, a natural chance of some kind. God has kept my heart pure in this dreadful place where I was born. Why are you here, if you are conservative? It is not a gentleman's resort."

He grew a little angry at this thrust, but she continued to look at him quietly, unaware that she was impertinent.

"I often have business, Hulda, with Joe and Patty. Negroes are very high, and we must buy them where they are to be had. But a deepening religious interest in you often attracts me here."

"Why religious as well as conservative, sir?"

"I have been afraid, after the good instructions I have given you, that the sights you see here might make you an infidel."

"What is an infidel?"

"One who, being unable to explain certain evils in life, refuses to believe anything. That is the case with Van Dorn—a very bad man.

Stepfather Joe is always conservative on that subject. As much as he may deviate, he never disbelieves. Aunt Patty, too, erratic as she is, holds a conservative position on a Great First Cause."

Here McLane drew out his gold spectacles, turned the leaves of his Bible over, and pointed Hulda a place to read, beginning, "The fool hath said in his heart, 'There is no God.'"

At his command she read it with faith, yet observation, her mind being fully alert to the warning Van Dorn had left her, that in his absence she would face a great trial.

McLane was wearing a gray English suit, sleek over his entire body. His hair was a little gray. Gold glasses dangled in his hand. Patent, varnished slippers, silk stockings, a silk scarf with a cameo pin on it, and a cameo of his deceased sister upon his finger ring marked his attire. His bulging eyes were set much too far forward. They were blue as old china, but an animal rather than spiritual blue—the tint of washing blue, not of distance. A hare-lip was evident in his talk, though the fullness of his very red lips hardly allowed place for it. His nose and brows were stern and military, as if he had been a pudding stamped with the die of a Roman emperor or General Jackson.

He watched Hulda reading with censorship, yet desire—patronage and oiliness together.

Glancing up when she had read far enough, Hulda thought he was looking at her as if she was some rare kind of Negress.

"Beautifully read, Hulda. I never go to such places as theaters, but you might be, I should say, an actress. Don't think of it, however; it's a very unconservative profession. I take great pride in you, my lovely girl. Suppose I take you home with me!"

McLane walked to her and laid his warm hand on her neck.

Hulda bent her head back, looked fearlessly up at him, and spoke as clearly as a bell: "Something has happened to me, Colonel McLane, to make even Johnson's Crossroads good and happy. Can you guess what it is?"

"Not religious ecstasy?" he said. "Not camp-meeting or revival conversion, I hope. That's vile."

"No, Colonel. It is knowing a pure young man whose love for me is natural and unselfish."

"Great God!" said McLane, removing his hand, "not some kidnapper?"

"No," Hulda said, "no slave dealer of any kind. They cannot make him so. He is perfectly conservative, Colonel, as to that vileness. I believe he is a gentleman, too."

"You must have great experience in that article," he sneered, looking angrily at her.

"I have seen you and my lover. You have the best clothes and profess more. He has a nature that your opportunities would bring real refinement from. He respects me, wretched as I am. I can read it in his eyes. You are looking for a way to degrade me in my own feelings, yet to deceive me. Can you be a gentleman?"

She was as serene as if she had said nothing and rose up and stood at one side of the fireplace, opposite him. Between them was a print of General Jackson riding over the British.

In that moment Allan McLane felt that the girl was cheap at her grandmother's figure. He had always conceived of her as a flexible, peculiar child. In a few minutes she had grown years and become a rare and nearly stately woman, not now to be molded but to be tempted with large, worldly propositions.

"May I ask who this lover is that I am so much beneath—I, who have taught you the accomplishments you chastise me with? I found you sand and made you crystal." He drew out a large pongee handkerchief and actually dropped some tears into it.

Hulda continued, cool and unmoved: "My love is Levin Dennis from Princess Anne. I am not afraid to tell it."

"Why?"

"Because I want his danger and mine to be fully known to him and make him a man."

The colonel folded his pongee and came again to Hulda's side. "That dissipated boy. Oh, Hulda, where is your real pride? He has abandoned his mother. He is a poor gypsy. I must save you from such a mistake; it is my duty to do it."

"I thank you for teaching me, whatever made you do it. If I could awaken in you some unselfishness towards me and my new love, sir, it would be the greatest gratitude I could show you. You conceal so many hard, bad things under your word 'conservative' that the gentle feelings, like forgiveness, have forsaken you."

"No," the colonel said stiffly, his shoulders becoming more military, "insults to my honor I never forgive. People who do not resent have no conservative principle."

"As I hope to be forgiven, I forgive Joe, Aunt Patty, Van Dorn, and you. I hope pity and mercy and sweet, unselfish love, such as I think mine is, may grow in all of you."

She turned to him earnestly. "Oh, Colonel, the buying and selling of these human beings makes everybody unfeeling. It is stealing their souls and bodies, whether they be bought at the courthouse or kidnapped on the roads. My dream of joy is to have a husband who will work with his own free hands, till his little farm, and sail his vessel without a slave. Above that I expect and ask nothing from the dear God who has so long been my protector in this den of crime."

"Warm or cold, hectoring or tender, you are splendid, Hulda," McLane said. "Now let me show you a conservative picture of your real desserts. I am a bachelor. I keep an elegant house in Baltimore. My table is supplied with the best in the market. My servants are my slaves and never disobey me. My paintings are celebrated. I never run to books —they are radical things—but I can buy them. My carriage is the best Rahway turnout, and my horses are Diomeds. In Frederick County I have an estate in sight of the mountains. As a Christian act I will take you away from this spot, to which you seem but half kindred, and make you my wife."

"You ask me to marry you?"

"Conservatively! Continue to be my pupil and obey me. I will bring your mind out of its ignorance, your body out of rags, your associations out of crime. I will provide for you as you are obedient while I live and after I am dead. You shall travel with me and see bright cities—New Orleans, Charleston, Havana. If you remain here, you will be another Patty Cannon or go to jail. There! Look at it conservatively. Warmth, riches, pleasure, attention, change, dress to become you, a watch and jewels against villainy and lowness of every kind."

"How are you to be repaid for this?"

"By your love."

"But it is not mine to give. Levin has it."

"Pooh! that's beneath you."

"But it is gone, and I cannot get it back. It will not come."

"Give me yourself," McLane said, drawing her towards him; "the refinements I do not care about. Be mine!"

The girl allowed herself to be brought nearly to his side, but as he bent to kiss her with his large, complacent lips, she glided from his hands.

"I could never stoop," Hulda said, "to be the wife of a Negro dealer."

He colored to the eyes, yet with admiration of her almost aristocratic composure. "You could not stoop to me?" he said. "Not from your father's gallows?"

"No. He was a robber, but a bold one. You only receive the goods."

She was gone, and McLane stood with evil lights in his face but no shame. He drank some brandy from a flask and murmured, "Now I have an insult to revenge as well as a fancy to be gratified. Her father must have been a cool rogue. Well, everything has to be done by force here. Patty Cannon shall see my gold."

Aunt Patty's Last Trick

Chapter 41

Though she had not revealed them, Hulda's emotions were profoundly excited, and the stab to her modesty now brought bitter tears to her eyes. Opposite McLane's room was the vestibule to the slave pen in the garret, where Van Dorn usually slept. Hulda fled into this room to deliberate upon her dire circumstances.

There were now only three other persons in the house, each an interested party in her ruin—the man she had just left, Cy James, full of cowardly passion for her, and Patty Cannon, who would gloat to see Hulda's virtue sacrificed.

"Perhaps I can fly to our old house across the state line and take refuge with the new tenant there," Hulda thought. "I wish Van Dorn was here. He is so brave, and when he left me, his kiss was like my father's."

Chains clanked, and the drone of low hymns came down the hatchway from the slave pen.

"There is a white man up there," Hulda reflected. "Dare I go up to see?"

She unlocked the padlock, stepped up the ladder, and peeped at the pen door, but she could see nothing in the blackness. She pulled the peg out of the staple and walked into the sickly odor of the jail.

"How many are here?" Hulda asked. "I hear you, but I cannot see."

"Three men, one old woman, an' some little things makes the present contents of Pangymonum," replied a rough, cheery voice."

"Is it the white man that talks?"

"He says he's white, but they think it's goin' to be easy hokey-pokey to pass him off for a nigger."

Her eyes soon picked out the speaker as he said, "By smoke, miss, you're not much like a Johnson. I reckon you're Huldy."

"Yes, and you, sir?"

"I was Jimmy Phoebus before I was a nigger."

Hulda went to him and threw her arms around him. "Thank God you are not dead. My dear friend Levin Dennis wept to think you were at the river bottom. Quick, sir, I may be caught here. Are you all true to each other?"

"Yes, the traitor's cut his wizzen. You kin speak out."

"I heard Patty Cannon mutter that she was going to set her black man free to kidnap for her. Oh, listen! I must fly."

Hulda descended the ladder in time to surprise Cy James coming up. He bent his goose neck down as he leaned his hands upon his knees, and looking up into her face, he said, "Hokey pokey, by smoke, and Pangymonum, too."

∞

"Samson," said Jimmy Phoebus, as soon as Hulda disappeared, "git ready to be a first class liar. I want you to take up Patty Cannon's offer."

"An' leave you yer alone, Jimmy? I can't do it."

"Don't be a fool, Samson. Ironed here, we can't help nobody. Make your way to Seaford an' Georgetown an' go round the Cypress Swamp to Prencess Anne. Alarm the pungy captains. Johnson'll try to run us by sail, I reckon, down the bay to Norfolk. I've got a file that cymlin-headed feller give me, an' I reckon I'll git out of my irons about the time you git to Judge Custis's."

"Go, Samson," said the Delaware man. "I'm younger than you, and I'll fight as heartily under Mr. Phoebus's orders."

Aunt Hominy's voice came in blank monologue out of the background, "He tuk dat debbil's hat, chillen, an' measured us in wid little Vessy."

∞

That evening there was a long conference between Samson and Patty Cannon in her kitchen. Hulda heard laughing and invitations to drink and all the sounds of perfect equality, the Negro's piquant sayings and *bonhommie* seeming to disarm and please the designing woman. Her familiarity was at once her influence and her weakness, and she lavished her sociable nature on blacks and whites alike. Samson was so fearless and observing that he betrayed no interest in escaping and came slowly into the range of her temperament. As Hulda peeped into the kitchen towards midnight, she saw Samson kindly patting juba, while Patty executed a drunken dance. As the latter dropped on a pallet bed and fell into a doze, the colored man quietly raised the latch and walked off the tavern porch.

∞

At dawn Hulda heard horses and voices and recognized Joe Johnson's steps in the house. He shook Patty Cannon but could not awaken her. Then he looked into Van Dorn's room and found Hulda, apparently sound asleep, and heard Allan McLane call from across the hall, "Not so loud, Joe; be conservative. Is all done and fetched?"

"The bloke with the steeple felt will never snickle," spoke the ruffian.

"Good, good, Joe. Vengeance is mine, and it's a conservative saying. My dear sister is at peace."

"The yaller pullets have slipped you," Joe continued. "The abigail mizzled to the funeral with your niece, an' t'other dell must have smelt us an' hopped the twig."

"Not tasteful language, Joe; I don't understand you. Where are the two bright wenches, Virgie and Roxy?"

"Roxy's in Baltimore, an' Virgie's run away."

"Run? Where? Don't trifle with me, Joe! Conservative as I am, I don't like it, sir. Where could she have run?"

"There's no way for her to slip us but by water or through the Cypress Swamp, Colonel. She ain't safe this side of Cantwell's Bridge. Word has gone out, an' every road is watched."

"Van Dorn is beaten back and hasn't made a single capture. The niggers drove him out of Dover with firearms, and he is wounded somewhere."

The tall kidnapper turned pale, then consigned Van Dorn's shade to eternal torment.

"Don't swear before me, sir!" an irritated McLane exclaimed. "It's not conservative, and I won't permit it. How do I know Meshach Milburn is dead? Who did it?"

"Black Dave fired the barker an' saw him settled."

"Send him here."

The Negro came in, red eyed and hoarse with diseased lungs, the wreck of a once gigantic and regular man. "Gi' me a drink," he muttered. "I'm mos' dead wi' misery an' cold."

"Tell this man what you did," Joe Johnson said. "You waited till you saw the hat at the window an' fired, an' fetched hat an' man to the ground?"

Swallowing a thimbleful of McLane's brandy, the Negro grunted, "Blood!" and looked tremblingly at his hands.

"What shape of hat was it?" McLane asked, shaking the Negro savagely. Then, shaping his own soft, slouched hat to a point, he inquired again, "Was it like this?"

Black Dave looked and shook his head.

"Not like that? Damnation!"

"No swearing, Colonel, before us conservatives," ventured Joe Johnson. "What was the hat like, Dave?"

"Like dis, I reckon." He modeled the crown into a bell form with his finger.

Joe Johnson and McLane looked at each other a minute with mutual accusation and confusion, and the former unceremoniously knocked the Negro down with his great fist.

"No gold of mine for this job, Joe Johnson," said Allan McLane. "In your conservatism to save your own skin, you have let your tool kill an innocent man."

He waved his hand towards the door and shut it in the kidnapper's face. Then, with disappointed pride and revenge, McLane sat down, glanced around him as if to determine the next move, and instinctively reached for his Bible. He opened it to a marked page and softly read: "To everything there is a season, and a time to every purpose under the heaven: A time to be born and a time to die; a time to plant and a time to pluck up that which is planted; a time to kill and a time to heal; a time to break down and a time to build up. God requireth that which is past. Man hath no preeminence above a beast, for all is vanity. A man should rejoice in his own works, for that is his portion. For who shall bring him to see what shall be after him?"

Tears of pious vindictiveness and counterfeit humility closed the reading, and Colonel McLane spread his pongee handkerchief on the bare floor and knelt in silent and comfortably assured prayer.

∞

Black Dave had crawled into the room where Hulda had been waiting and entered the large closet under the concealed shaft to the prison pen. Here, his groans and mental agony touched Hulda's sympathy, and she opened the trap and crawled there too.

"Hush Dave," she whispered. "What makes you so miserable?"

"I'se killed a man, Missy. Dey made me do it. I'll burn in torment. Lord save me!"

"Dave," said Hulda, "my poor father died for his offenses. You can do no more, but you can repent."

"Oh, missy, I's black. Rum an' fightin' has ruined me. Dar's no way to do better. De law won't let me bear witness agin de people dat set me on. How kin I repent unless I confess my sin? De law won't let me confess."

"Confess your poor, wracked soul to me, Dave. Though you dare not turn your face to him, the Lord will hear you."

"Once I was in de Lord's walk, Missy. My han's was clean, my face clar, my stummick unburnt by liquor. I stood in no man's way. At de church dey put me fo'ward. My soul was happy. One day I licked a man bigger dan me. It made me proud an' sassy. I backslid an' wan't no good to hire out to steady people. So de taverns got me, an' den de kidnappers used me, an' now de blood of Cain an' Abel is on my forehead forever."

Hulda knelt by the murderer and prayed with all her heart, not the self-conscious pleading of the prayers across the hall, but the humble prayer of the penitent on Calvary: "Lord, we of this felon den ask to be with thee in Paradise."

∞

Patty and her son-in-law spent the whole of the next day in preparation for flight. A boat of sufficient size and a crew to man it had to be procured, and this necessitated two journeys, one by Patty to Cannon's Ferry, another by Joe to Vienna and Twiford's wharf.

During their absence Cy James was equally intent on something. Hulda saw him in the plowed field near the old Delaware cottage, directing the farmer where to guide his plow, and in a little while it seemed that one of the horses had fallen into a pit there.

Later on, Hulda observed Cy with a spade, digging at various places near Patty Cannon's former cottage. "All are at work for themselves," Hulda thought, "except Levin and me. How often have I seen Aunt Patty slip to secret places in the night or early dawn, looking every window over to see if she was watched. Her beehives were her greatest care."

A sudden thought drained the color from Hulda's cheeks: "If they go away, I shall be taken, too—or kept here for worse evil. My mother is in Florida and hates me; she has told me so. I know the marriage Allan McLane intends for me—to be his white slave. Levin and his mother are poor. They say Grandmother has buried gold. Perhaps God will point me to it."

She slipped down the road and walked up the lane in the fields she knew so well. There was no one in the cottage, so Hulda went among the outbuildings, inspecting the beehives and the big wooden flowerpots Patty Cannon had left behind.

∞

"I shall have one piece of fun in Maryland before I go," Hulda heard her stepfather say the next morning as he went past her bed to ascend the hatchway, "and that is to burn the nigger who mugged me. This is his day."

He returned almost immediately, cursing, followed by a jeering laugh and cry from above, "We'll all see you hanged yit, by smoke, an' mash another egg on your face, nigger buyer!"

In a moment a tremendous quarrel began below stairs between the kidnapper and his wife's mother. It sounded to Hulda as though they were murdering each other. Peeping to see, she observed Johnson holding Patty to the floor and stuffing her elegant hair, which had been torn out in the scuffle, into her mouth.

"I'll be the death of you, old fence, before I go," he shouted. "The verdict would be that I did the county a service."

"Come away!" cried Allan McLane, pushing past Hulda and between the combatants. "Shame on you, Joe! To whip your mother-in-law is hardly conservative. Here is an errand that will pay you well. My wench Virgie has been caught."

The kidnapper released the woman and turned to his guest. "Good news!" he said. "I'll fetch her fur you ef it puts my neck in the string."

His countenance had begun to assume a sensual expression, when Patty Cannon rushed upon him like a tornado, lifted him from his feet, and threw him through the back door into the yard, bolting him out.

McLane retreated by the other door.

"Thank heaven," Hulda reflected, "no one is murdered yet, and I have another day of grace to wait for Levin."

∞

"Cunnil McLane," Patty Cannon said that night, "what interest have you in the quadroon gal an' Huldy? You don't want 'em both, Cunnil?"

"No, Patty, all my views are conservative—quite so. I want Hulda to reform and model to my needs. She'll ornament me. By taking the girl from my niece Vesta, I desire to punish the latter for consenting to the degradation of our family by marrying the forester Milburn. She loves the quadroon; therefore I will deprive her of the girl."

His face expressed the indifference he felt to Virgie's safety, and the coarse suggestion gave Patty Cannon her opportunity: "Cunnil, there's but three in the house tonight; I am one."

"And I am two, Patty."

"And three is purty Huldy, Cunnil."

They looked at each other a few minutes in silence.

"There is two to one," said Patty Cannon with a giggle. "We have no neighbors that air not used to noises yer."

"I made a very conservative and liberal proposition to her, and she insulted me. She did so beautifully, but I owe her a grudge for it."

"Insulted you, Cunnil? Why, the ongrateful huzzy! Can't you insult her back? She never dared to disobey me. Once her pride is broke down, she'll be like other gals, I reckon."

"That's true, no doubt. But Patty, haven't you a little remorse about it, considering she's your grandchild?"

"My mother had none fur me," the old woman chuckled familiarly.

"What is that story, Patty, about your origin?"

"I don't know more about it than any pore, ignorant gal would. I've hearn my grandfather was a lord. A gypsy woman enticed his son, an' he married her. His father drove him from his door, an' his wife fetched him on her money to Canady, where they went into the smugglin' business at St. John's, halfway between Montreal an' the United States."

"And he was hanged for assassinating a friend who detected him?"

"They says so, honey. Anyhow, he was hanged. Says mother, 'It's a hard world, but don't let it beat you, gals. Marry ef you kin. Anyway, you must live, an' you can't live off of women.' I married a Delaware man, an' so I quit bein' Martha Hanley an' became Patty Cannon."

"And what a career you have led, Aunt Patty. Had you lived anywhere but in this old pocket between the bays, you would have had the reputation of Captain Kidd. Tell me now, conservatively, was not your own childhood the cause of your mistakes, and does it never make you feel for other sparrow birds like Hulda?"

The black-haired woman clapped her bold, black eyes on McLane's and replied, chuckling, "I don't know as it do, Cunnil. Before my mother pinted the way, I loved the men. I loved 'em to be bad. As fur Huldy, her mother throws her onto me. She's not like the Cannons an' Johnsons; she's full of pride. Let it be tuk out of her. Will you pay my price?"

"It's not the price, Patty," he hesitated; "it's the way. Isn't it cowardly?"

"Yes," said Patty saucily, "it's kidnappin'. That's the trade yer. Pay down the money, Cunnil, an' this bare room will brighten to be your wedding chamber. Pah! Are you a man?"

Her words aroused visions which self-love can reluctantly repulse, and which, entertained but an instant, grow irresistible. The limber, maturing form of Hulda stepped onto the footstool of his mind and exhaled the aroma of her youth like a subtle musk. He leaned back languidly, as if smoking a pipe with her bust painted on its bowl, and all her modesties dissolved into the intoxication. Brutality itself grew natural to this vision as a fiercer joy and substitute for the deceit he could no longer practice. The child had flown from her like a pale butterfly, but there remained a silken and nubile essence, fairy and humanity in one, clad in pure thoughts and sweet respect, the profanation of which would be as rare a game as Satan's struggle with the soul of Eve.

Her innocence and spirit, self-respect and womanly consciousness, weakness and sensibility, mettle and beauty presented themselves by turns. The cold, woodeny room, the neglected tavern, the autumn night wind coming down the chimney and starting the fire—all, like him, seemed instinctive with mischief, as if Patty Cannon's soul flew astraddle a broom and led a hundred witches.

McLane was fifty. His family was a stiff, commercial one that had generally kept demure, yet grasping, and practiced the conservatism he boasted of, but had departed from. He was the outlaw of the house, yet elevating its tenets into an aggressive shibboleth, the more so that he prospered by anti-progress.

He was a backer of domestic slave dealers and put his money into forms of gain where most men hesitated: loan sharking, behind pawnbrokers and sporting men, in lottery companies and liquor houses, and, it was said, in the open slave trade. His clippers occasionally stole out of the Chesapeake on affected trading errands to the East Indies and came home with nothing but West India fruits.

He strove to maintain his credit by ostentatiously declaring an abhorrence of everything unorthodox and liberal, and had the sublime hardihood to carry his Bible into every sink of shame, as if it was the natural baggage of a gentleman. He would rebuke blasphemy while bidding at the slave auction or sitting in a barroom full of kidnappers, among many of whom he passed for a religious standard.

No portion of that Bible gave him any delight or occupation, however, except the Old Testament with its thorough-going codes of servitude, concubinage, and eye-for-an-eye. He knew the Jewish laws better than the Scribes and Pharisees in the time of Herod and John and had persuaded himself that the mental endorsement and, wherever possible, the practice of these constituted a firm believer. Revenge, intolerance, formality, and self-sleekness had become so much his theory that he did not know himself whether he was capable of doing evil, provided he wanted anything.

Not particularly courageous, he was so destitute of sensibility that he felt no fear anywhere. Among his low, white inferiors he was in the habit of being looked up to and rather preferred their society. He had an opinion on everything and permitted no stranger in Baltimore to entertain any. The riot spirit, so early and so frequent in that town, reposed upon such vulturous and self-conscious social pests as he, ever claiming to be the public tone of Maryland.

"Patty," McLane said in his bland yet hard voice, like mush eaten with a bowie knife, "I may pay you this money, and you may fail to deliver the property. Will she be tractable?"

"I'll scare her most to death, Cunnil. She'll hide from me yer by your fire, and my voice outside the door will keep her in till day."

McLane went to his portmanteau, unlocked it, and took out a roll of notes and a buckskin bag of gold. The yellow luster flashed in Patty Cannon's rich, black eyes like the moon overhead upon a well.

"How beautiful it do shine, Cunnil," she said. "Nothing is like it fur a friend. Youth an' beauty has to go together to be strong, but gold kin go it alone."

With his spectacles upon his hawk nose, McLane counted out two piles, one of notes and one of gold, and said, "Patty, I've bought many a grandchild *with* the old woman, but this is the first child I have bought *from* the grandmother. Now fulfill your contract and earn your money."

He put his spectacles in his pocket, stretched his gaitered slippers before the fire, looked at his watch, and let the crystal seal drop on his sleek abdomen. His vitreous, blue-green eyes filled with color, like twin vases in a druggist's window. He was ready and anxious to substitute the ruffian for the tempter.

Patty Cannon glanced at the money on the table, took up a lamp, and started at once through the house calling, "Huldy! Huldy!"

Nothing responded to the name.

She searched from room to room, peering everywhere, making the circuit twice, then went into the windy night and around the bounds of the old tavern.

"I reckon she's heard us," the old woman muttered. "She's run away an' ruined me. Joe's cruel to me. Van Dorn is gone. McLane is pitiless. Without gold I go to the poorhouse."

With only an instant's hesitation, she turned into the tavern again and buttoned the outer door. She reached her hand beneath her feather bed and drew out a large object, then took a horn from the mantel and sprinkled it with something contained there. In a bold, masculine walk, stamping hard, she went up the stairs again, talking as if to some truant she was coaxing or forcing. At McLane's chamber she knocked hard, crying, "Open, Cunnil! Here's the bashful creatur! She daren't disobey no mo'. Step out and kiss her, Cunnil!"

"Ha!" said McLane, throwing open his door, "conservative is she? Well, let her enter."

As he made one step to penetrate the darkness with his dazzled eyes, Patty Cannon thrust a huge horse pistol against his heart and pulled the trigger. A flash of fire from the powder in the pan lit up the hall an instant, and the guest's heavy body fell backward before his chair. She leaned over him with the pistol clubbed, ready to strike if he should stir. He did not move, but only bled at his large lips, ghastly and unprotesting, and his cold blue eyes looked as natural as life.

Patty Cannon took the chair and counted the money.

Beaks

Chapter 42

The wind was blowing in spells, like crowds moved during an argument, now mute with awe, again murmurous, and sometimes mutinous and fierce. Hulda, having heard only a few words of her grandmother's overture, glided from the old tavern into the night, terrified but not unthinking. The large pines above her seemed to moan, "Where, oh, where in the cold, cold wilderness of the world. . .?"

"Anywhere!" Hulda answered, unafraid of cold or nature, so intense had become her fear of men and women. "Still, where?" she thought. "I might go to Cannon's Ferry and tell my tale to those hard-hearted merchants or to Seaford and beg shelter there, but first I will try our old cottage home again."

Hulda went so quietly up the lane that dogs could not have heard her. As she approached the little house, she heard voices and saw moving figures within, and she stopped in the dark a little distance from one of the low windows.

An old, moldered chest with earth clinging to it sat on a table in the middle of the main room, and beside the chest on its riven lid were bones and shreds of clothing.

"You swear that the evidence you give shall be the truth, the whole truth, and nothing but the truth, so help you God!" exclaimed a small, chunky, Irish-looking person, presenting a book to be kissed by a scrawny, chinless, goose-necked lad, whom Hulda immediately recognized as Cyrus James.

"Shall I take him, Doctor Gibbons?" a fine-lookin, easy-mannered man asked of the magistrate.

"Yes, Mr. Clayton."

"Do you know the nature of an oath?"

"I'll be fried like a slapper on the devil's griddle ef I don't tell right," whined Cy James zealously.

"No you won't. At least not *first*. If you don't tell me the truth, I'll have your two ears cut off on the pillory, and no slapper shall enter that hungry stomach of yours for a month. Goy!"

He looked at Cy James as if he had a mind to bite his nose off as a mere beginning.

"Now, Holliday Hicks—you and Billy Hooper and the other constables—as soon as the witness has sworn to it, take away this box; it smells too loud here. When did you last see this box, James?"

"About ten year ago, sir, when I had been bound to Patty Cannon four year, I reckon. I see Patty an' Joe Johnson an' Ebenezer, his brother, all totin' this chist to the field an' a-buryin' of it."

"What did you see them put in this chest?"

"A dead man—a nigger trader. I can't tell whether his name was Bell or Miller. She killed two men nigh that time, an' I was so little that I've got 'em mixed."

"Did you see her kill this man?"

"No, sir, I wasn't home. I got home in time to see 'em packin' him in the box. I hearn Patty tell the boys how she killed him. Oh, she was proud of it, sir, becaze she didn't have no help in it."

Half a dozen constables, some of whom Hulda knew, leaned forward together to hear the witness, while others removed the unsavory remains.

Mr. Clayton continued: "How did she say she killed him?"

"She said he come to Joe's tavern with a borreyed hoss from East New Market, where he told the people he was buyin' niggers and would take fifteen thousand dollars wuth if he could git 'em. He was follered out, an' Ebenezer Johnson got in ahead of him. They told him the tavern was full, an' he would be better tuk care of at a good woman's little farm close by. They made him think, she said, that a gentleman with much money wasn't allus safe at the tavern. Aunt Patty got him supper. He sit at the table after it a-pickin' of his teeth. She got her pistol an' went out in her garden a-hoein' of her flowers. Once she come up on him at the window to shoot, but he turned quick, an' she says to him, 'Oh, sir, I only wanted to see if you didn't need somethin' more.'

"'No, no,' says he, 'I've made a rale good supper.'

"'I loves my flowers,' Aunt Patty says, 'an' likes to hoe 'em at sundown so they can sleep nice an' soft.'

"'Do you?' says he. 'I reckon you're a kind woman.'

"He turned around agin an' begin to look over his pocketbook. She hoed an' hoed an' hummed a little tune. All at once she slipped up, an' I heerd her say, 'Boys, I give it to him good, right in the back of the head. He fell onto the table, an' the water he had been drinkin' was red as currant wine.'"

"James Moore, I'll swear you next," the magistrate said to the new tenant of the farm. This man proceeded to testify concerning the finding of the chest as he was plowing in a wet spot where he had removed some brush.

Cy James was recalled and gave testimony about other buried bodies, chiefly of children slaughtered in wantonness or jealousy or to avoid pursuit.

"Take this boy," Constable Hicks said to Joe Neal, "and hold him fast."

"Goy!" said Clayton with a terrible frown at Cy James. "We may have to hang him yet! Guilty knowledge of these crimes for so many years constitutes an accessory. It would have been well for you, depraved young man, if you had possessed the principle of *this* young gentleman."

The senator placed his hand upon a sitting figure, and there arose in Hulda's sight the image of her lover, Levin Dennis.

"Constables," said Dr. Gibbons, the magistrate, "I shall give you your warrants now. The Maryland authorities propose to deliver your prisoners at the state line without waiting for extradition proceedings."

"Goy," said Clayton. "They may have friends in the executive chambers at Annapolis. No, boys, act together like patriots, as the Maryland and Delaware lads served in the same revolutionary brigade. Joe Johnson is due here at noon tomorrow. Be careful not to disturb old Patty nor awaken her suspicions till he arrives. She is almost past doing evil, but he has a lifetime left to do it in."

"Constable Neal, I'll shove them over the line to you," said the Maryland officer.

"Look out when you lay on to old Patty, Constable Wilson; she may be loaded and go off," exclaimed the Delaware officer.

"Doctor Gibbons," said Clayton, "waste no time with them at the hearing in Seaford. Get horses and send them right to Georgetown jail. They are slippery as eels. Goy!"

As Cy James was being taken to a secure place in the garret, he turned to Levin Dennis, wilted and crestfallen. "Oh, Levin," he said, "Huldy won't have me now, I know. Won't you stand by me, Levin? She's goin' to marry you, and I'll give ye all I've found."

"Huldy!" Levin exclaimed. "Must I leave her yonder in the tavern another night?"

"No," answered Hulda, coming forward. "We are both preserved, my friend. But I must have made my bed in the forest this night if God had not directed me to you."

As they clasped each other fondly, Senator Clayton exclaimed, "What? Doves among the rattlesnakes. Goy!"

Pleasure Drained

Chapter 43

The dawn had not broken when that fleet traveler Joseph Johnson, anticipating his enemies by hours, noiselessly tied his horses at the tavern and nearly fell into the arms of Owen Daw.

"Thar's queer people hangin' round yer, Joe," the scapegrace said. "They say a blue chist has been dug outen the field yonder, an' bones in it. I 'spect they're a-lookin' fur you, Joe."

"I'll give you a job, Owen," said Johnson. "Run these horses into my wagon thar, while I git some duds together before I hop the twig."

Slipping to the rear of the house, he entered and looked in Patty's room. She was not there. A slight smell of gunpowder seemed to be in the hall. Passing rapidly up the stairs, Johnson saw a light shine in McLane's room and kicked the door open, exclaiming, "Bad luck everywhere. The gal's stone dead, and the beaks are round us. Wake up, McLane!"

"Joe!" said a voice, and Patty Cannon threw her arms around him.

"To burning fire with you!" bellowed the filial son. "Take your arms away!"

"Let us make up, Joe. Everybody has run away from us. Huldy is gone, too. McLane is dead."

"Dead? Dead where?"

"There!" She pointed to a featherbed lying upon the floor, the outlines of which were unusually pointed and stiff for feathers.

Joe touched it with his foot and bounded back. "Hellcat!" he cried. "Is this one of your tricks?"

"I did it fur you, Josie. He brought it on hisself. There's his portmanteau full of money to pay our traveling expenses. He's sewed up beautiful, an' in the bay you can drop him to the bottom."

Joe Johnson's face became livid and pale. He rushed upon Patty Cannon with both hands raised, struck her to the floor, and put his boot upon her. "If I had time, I'd have your life," he hissed, "but it would lose the uptucker a job. Tonight I leave forever. Your daughter Margaretta wishes never to see you again. Take this crib and the blood you still must shed to keep your old heart warm, and take my curse to choke you on the gallows!"

He rushed away and gave a low whistle at the window. Daw and Joe's brother, Ebenezer, bounded up the stairs to the garret and drove the captives out.

"One word from you today, white nigger, will scatter your brains in the woods!" Joe Johnson drew a pistol as he spoke, and Jimmy Phoebus saw his nervous determination too clearly to provoke it.

"Put this dab on the wagon," Johnson said, referring to the featherbed.

"Joe!" came the voice of Patty Cannon from the guest's room, "take the poor old woman that's raised you along."

"Stow yer wid!" he answered. "We go to be gentlemen in a land where you would spot us black. Cross cove and mollisher no more. Raise another Joe Johnson, if you can, to make this old hulk lush with business. I give it to you."

He was gone in the vague dawn. She fell upon her face across the little bar and moaned, "A pore, pore old woman."

How long she had been leaning there, she did not know, when a familiar sound fell on her ears. She looked up with a cry of recognition: "Van Dorn! God bless you, Van Dorn! Is you alive again?"

The captain was supported in the arms of another man, who took him into the bar and laid him upon her pallet, muttering, "I loved him as I never loved a male."

∞

The morning was well advanced, and the sun made the gaunt and steep old tavern rise like a mammoth from the level lands, filling its upper front rooms with golden light. Patty Cannon sat in one of them by a window and talked to Van Dorn. She had tenderly washed and redressed him and placed him in her own comfortable rocking chair of rushes with his feet raised and blanketed upon a second chair.

"Oh, Captain," she said fondly, "how clean and sweet you look—like my good man again. Don't be cross to me; my heart is sad."

"*Chito*, Patty, *chito! You* sad? I like to see you saucy and defiant. Let us not repent. So, Joe has left you?"

"With cruel curses. My daughter hates me, he says, an' means to be a lady where I can't disgrace her. Oh, honey, to raise a child an' have it hate an' despise you goes hard, even if I have been bad. There's nothing left me now but you, Van Dorn. Do not die!"

He coughed carefully, as if coughing was a luxury to be very mildly exerted, and wiped a little blood from his tongue and lip.

"I'll try not to die till I comfort you some, *Marta delicioso*. The ball is at my windpipe, and when the blood trickles in, it makes me cough. I must beware of emotions, the surgeon says, lest it drop into my lung and break a blood vessel by some very spasmodic cough. So do not be too beautiful, or I might perish."

He stroked his long mustache with the diamond-fingered hand and drew his velvet smoking cap tight upon his silken curls, but he was too pale to blush as formerly.

"Captain," the woman said, "you are so much smarter than me, that I'm afeard of you. Am I beautiful a little yet? Do I please you? I know you mock me."

"*O hala hala!*" sighed Van Dorn. "You are the star of my life. All that I am, you have made me. I worship you. When you are gone, human nature will breathe and wonder. Do you remember when first we met?"

"A little, Captain. Tell it to me again. Praise me if you kin. I'm almost desolate."

Her lip trembled, and she glanced at the fields across the way. There seemed to be more life than usual there, but she did not look carefully.

"How many years it has been, Patty, we will not tell. I was coming home from Africa with an emigrant—a Briton. He was the officer in the blockading squadron who seized my privateer with all her complement of Guinea slaves. His name was all I took from him—Van Dorn. You got all the rest."

She stole a startled look at him out of her listening eyes, as if this might be unpleasant talk, but he parried it with a compliment.

"*Chis! Dios!* What a family of beauties you were—Betty, with her hoyden air, Jane, with her wealth of charms, and Patty, with her bold, rich eyes and conquering will. We sailed into the Nanticoke, mistaking it for the Manokin. When my friend broke me up as a slaver, he pitied my misfortunes and learned to like my company. 'Dennis,' he said, 'that country you praise so well has infatuated me. I'll resign my commission and buy a little vessel and settle in America with you for the sake of my daughter.' *Ayme*, that poor little wildflower. Where did she spend the chill night yesterday, Patty, can you tell?"

He coughed again, very carefully, and his eye never left his hostess, as though he feared she might miss some pleasing feature of his story.

She trotted her foot and muttered, "You made me jealous of her. I got to hate an' fear her, lovey."

"Voluptuous as two young widowers were after a long cruise, we tarried among you sirens, and I, almost at the threshold of my home, where my wife believed me dead, yet waited longingly. My friend, entasselled with bright Betty, sooner felt remorse at the spectacle of his little child so ill caressed. He beckoned me away, but he had shown his gold and could better be spared than reckless I. You know the cool, deep game, dear Pat. *Hala ha!* I was made to buy the poison you sisters gave Van Dorn and thereby appear an accomplice in his death. Never till this week has that murder given up a testimony—the portion of the dead man's coin your mother stole and hid, which Hulda has now inherited at last. *Verdad es verde!* I became afraid to leave you. I am here at the death with you, my old enchantress."

A crack ran through the empty wooden house, which made Patty rise. Van Dorn, as he was called, enjoyed her uneasiness like a pallid mask painted with a smile.

"Captain," she said, "how many people I see out yonder in the fields. Maybe thar's to be a fox chase."

"Sit, Patty. In my last days of life let me drink the wine lees of your memory. You are so dear to me. Turn in the golden sun, that I may linger on that face which autumn's ashes fall upon, though through the dead leaves I see the russet colors smolder yet. How daring was your girlhood. The poor blacksmith farmer, whose name you will transmit forever, fretted you with his sickness and his scruples, so you stilled him with the same cup you mixed for Betty's husband. You gave his daughter as wife to his apprentice, a strong, stolid man, capable of heroism. He died for you on the shameful scaffold. He died like a man and never told, though all the crowd knew who his instigator was."

"Van Dorn, you hurt me," Patty interrupted. "I cannot laugh today, an' these tales depress me. Where shall we go when you are well?"

"*La gente pone, y Dios dispone!* Stay and chat awhile. I would not see you discouraged for the world, you unfathomable angel. In this mangy corner of the globe you looked over the land like Catherine from her sterile throne over the mighty steppes and levied war upon the hopes of man. How you did trouble Uncle Sam, great Patty, robbing his mails between Baltimore and the Brandywine. Young Nichols still serves his term for that shrewd trick you taught him of cutting the mailbags open, as he sat with the corrupted drivers on the crowded stage, and stealthily throwing the valuable letters in the road to be gathered by a following horseman. *Es admirable!* Young Perry Hutton, reared by you to kidnap, then to drive the mail and filch its letters, perished on the gallows for killing a mail driver who detected him under his mask. Young Moore—was he your connection, darling?—fell under the driver's buckshot while stopping the mail stage at Gunpowder Forge. And Hare. . . ."

"Captain," Patty interrupted, "I see men an' boys all over the fields yonder, runnin' an' diggin' an' draggin' away the bresh. Is them ole buryin's of mine suspected?"

"Pshaw, darling, 'tis your warm imagination and Joe's unkindness. I would make you happy with the memory of your daring acts. *Que maravilla!* In your little pets you stamped out a life when another woman would only stamp her foot. There was that morning when your fire would not burn, and a little black child bawled with the cold and angered you. If its body is ever dug up, where it was laid, the skull cracked with the billet of wood will tell the tale. You once suspected me of truancy from your charms—*Quedo, quedo!* exacting dame—and the pale offspring of poor Hagar you threw upon the blazing backlog and grimly watched it burn. Not even you can number the children whose cries you could not still, that yet are stilled till hell shall have a voice. Evangelists, Patty, dipping their pens in the blood of saints to write your crimes, would make the next age infidel, where you will seem impossible and all of us mythology."

"Be still," the woman cried, rising and walking in her rolling gait to watch things without that stirred her mind more than her lover's recitation. "What good kin these tales do you, Captain? My God, the roads is full of people, an' they are all lookin' yer. Is it at me, Van Dorn?"

He coughed painfully and answered, "Only a quarter race, I'd guess, dear Pat. What are you fearing at your time of life?"

"No," cried Patty Cannon defiantly, taking something from her bosom. "If the worst comes, here is the same dose I gave my husband."

"Bravo, Patty! You only tarnish into age, like an old bronze that is made harder by time and oxidizing. I was a gentleman and yet you mastered me. How strange to see us beleaguered here together, myself by death and you by the law. Why, we have defied them both. Let them come on! Do you believe in everlasting fire—that every injury is a live coal to roast the soul? I know you do. And if you do, how beautiful your rosy grate will be, tough charmer, with boys spoiled in the bud, husbands in the blossom, families of free men torn apart, and children, born free as the flag of their country, sent to perpetual bondage and the whip. *Poca barba, poca verguenza!*[1] Who but a woman could have put it into William Bouser's head—when she had kidnapped him and thirty Negroes more and sold them all to Austin Woolfolk in Baltimore—to rise at sea on Woolfolk's vessel and massacre the officers, only to be hanged at last—and all to make Woolfolk a better customer."

"There are people all round the house, Van Dorn. I hear 'em on the stairs an' in the rooms. Have mercy!"

"Devils, Patty, or men? Both are your courtiers, remember, and perhaps they crowd each other. What do we care? *Que contento estoy!* Perhaps I am indifferent because no blood is on my hands, vile slaver though I am. You could teach Joe Johnson and his low-browed brother to kill—me, nothing worse than to steal and fondle you. You believe in hell, Patty. I am a believer, too, but I believe in heaven."

"Oh, Van Dorn, how you do talk!"

"Since you entrapped my young son Levin, fair fiend, do not start to have his father make another Johnson of him. I discovered the sin you meant to spot me with through the little girl—the beauteous damsel now—Hulda Van Dorn. Listen, Patty. It was my son, rich with his mother's loyalty and love, that shall never learn of my ruin here nor see me more—it was my Levin, set free by me, who gave the news at Dover and beat us back."

He had partly risen as he spoke, and the exertion seemed to choke him. The woman sat in dreadful silence, watching the veins rise upon his pale and willful face. He caught at his throat, and for a time could

---

[1] *Spanish proverb: "Little beard, little shame."*

speak no more.

"Patty," he said at last between his coughing spells, "I believe again. I have seen my wife, true as an angel, beauteous as a child in prayer for me. An honest man waits my death to love her better and be the father of my son. *Hala o hala!* I have had the daughter of my murdered friend to kiss and bless me and to love my son. My son has given me his confidence, unknowing whom I was, and shown to me a brave, pure heart. *Yo soy amado!* Their prayers may knock for me at the eternal door, but thou, murderer of my youth, no heart will pray for. Believe in hell and die! *Ha! hala! ho!*"

With a mocking smile in his blue eyes, like fading stars at dawn, he pointed a white finger at her, and the rosy morning flowed all around his mouth as the bullet, detached in his emotion, fell towards the lung and awakened hemorrhage. To the last of his strength he pointed at her, then fell back in crimson linen, smiling yet in death.

Terrified, the mistress sat, the image of paralysis, till her door slowly opened, and there entered, hand in hand, young Levin Dennis and Hulda Van Dorn.

"Levin," the young girl said, composed as one to whom reputable life and obsequies were familiar, "I have heard the dying sentences of this strong, misled, disappointed man. Let us kneel down, dear friend, and say a prayer. He was our father, Levin; he was not Van Dorn. That is my name, the daughter of his friend. He was Captain Oden Dennis of the privateer *Ida.*"

As they knelt with closed eyes, the room slowly filled. Patty Cannon's arms were seized by two constables, and the warrant was read to her. She heard it with humility, making no answer but this: "Once I had money an' friends a-plenty. My money is gone an' so is my friends. There's no fight now in pore ole Patty Cannon."

The Death of Patty Cannon

Chapter 44

As Patty Cannon left the tavern, the crossroads were full of people taking their last look at the spot where she had triumphed for nearly twenty years.

None thought to look for Van Dorn nor ask what had become of him. Sorden removed his body to a spot in the pine woods, where he dug an unmarked grave. Only three mourners stood around it, and Sorden said the final words with homely tears: "I loved him as I never loved a male."

The Maryland constable marched Patty Cannon to a plank bridge which crossed a ditch running nearly on the state line, and tradition still believes that Joe Johnson was hiding beneath it at that moment. There, driven across the boundary like some borderer's cow, the queen of kidnappers was seized by the Delaware constable and placed in a small country gig wagon. Followed by a large, mounted posse, they took the road to Seaford, five miles distant.

Patty watched the small funereal cedars and the monumental poplar trees rising from the underbrush, the dark streams flowing into inky millponds, the close, small pines, scarcely large enough to moan, but trying to do so in a baby tone, and her eyes turned to the sand, where she would soon be.

Not agony nor repentance nor hope of escape fluttered her cold heart, but only a feeling of being ill treated and ungratefully deserted by her friends. No preacher had come to tell her the naked gospel, though some had bowed to her respectfully and even begged her oats and made subscriptions from her ill-gotten silver.

Seaford was a sandy place on a bluff of the Nanticoke, and as the procession came in, a party of surveyors working for Milburn's railroad paused to jeer the old kidnapper. She had grown suddenly old, and the voice that had always been so forward did not reply.

John Gibbon, an educated young Irishman who had landed at Lewes and married a lady from Maryland, was the legal spirit of the little town. As his office was too small for the purpose, a hearing was conducted in the tavern at the foot of the hill, near where a millpond brook dug its way to the Nanticoke. Boxbush walks surrounded the tavern, and willow trees bordered the cold riverside. At pauses in the examination, wildfowl could be heard playing and piping in the falling tide.

The evidence of Cy James and other cowardly companions was quickly given, and the procession started through the woods and sands to Georgetown, twelve miles to the east. All the town was waiting for Patty Cannon, and the jail immediately closed her in.

∞

"I didn't ezackly make out what that cymlin-headed feller did it fur," Jimmy Phoebus remarked in the hold of an old oyster pungy, where he and the other captives had been placed, "but the file he fetched me has done its work at last. Yer, Whatcoat, take this knife he also slipped me an' cut these cords."

Standing up, Phoebus took stock of the situation. "Thar's two of us yer, Whatcoat—no, by smoke, thar's three."

The docile colored man opened his eyes. "Him!" he exclaimed, indicating the featherbed with its stiff, invisible contents. "Joe'll chuck him overboard down yer about deep water somewhere."

"Now for a little hokey-pokey," said Phoebus. "I think I'll git in thar myself an' let Joe sell t'other feller fur a nigger."

He began to explore the rotten old hold, which contained oyster rakes, fish lines, and the usual utensils of a dredging vessel, and soon discovered that a passage could be cleared to crawl from forecastle to cabin by the removal of a few boards.

"Yer, Hominy," he said, "get to work with your needle, old gal. I'm goin' to take you home."

∞

With a good start and fair wind, Johnson was off Vienna at eight o'clock. "Ten mile to go," he said. "After I pass Chicacomico Wharf an' git abaft the marshes, they can't catch me with a racehorse. I'm boozy fur sleep. Thar's two in this crew I don't know, an' I must be helmsman. Bingavast! I'll make my nigger work his passage."

He walked to the hatchway over the hold and slid it back. Dropping in, he set Whatcoat free with a few expert blows of the professional smithy, merely glancing where Phoebus lay upon his face. "Cool cucumber of a bloke," Johnson said. "He'll be too much fur me in a trade. I'll have to stifle him."

Ordering the mulatto man astern, Johnson gave him the tiller and sat nearby, nodding till the second wharf on the starboard was passed.

"Even Gabriel can't overhaul me now," said Johnson. "Thar's no more road on the Dorchester side, an' Somerset roads is gashed by creeks an' barred by farm gates. I'll sink that dab an' stiffy."

He called the two deck hands and lifted the body out of the hold. Phoebus still placidly slept upon his face, and Johnson looked at him with envy.

Ropes were put around the bed and drag irons attached to them, and the whole weight was unceremoniously thrown overboard at Hungry Neck Point. "There goes a great hypocrite, gentlemen," the dealer remarked. "He wasn't above piracy ef he could git another man to fly the black flag for him. I reckon he'll be conservative enough after this. An' now I'll snooze. Steer her for Ragged Point, yonder," he said to Whatcoat, "an' when you git thar, wake me. It's clear broad inlet all the way. An' remember, nigger, I sleep and shoot on hair triggers."

With his pistols in his hands, Johnson lay down in the cabin a few feet from the helmsman. He had been without rest for many nights, and sleep soon bound him in its own clevis an manacles.

When he awoke, he could not recall for a moment where he was. The tiller was unmanned, and stars shone in the hatchway. A cold draft blew through the old hulk, and as he dragged himself up the steps, he saw woods nearby and heard the voices of solemn pines. The vessel was aground, and wild geese were making jubilant shrieks as they cut the water with their fleecy wings. The outlaw gazed and gazed and finally muttered, "Deil's Island, or I'm a billy noodle. I run from it the last time I was yer, an' my blood runs cold to be yer agin. My daddy got his curse from this camp meetin'."

Johnson slid back the hatchway and leaped into the hold. Starlight and moonlight followed him and revealed nothing except a man peacefully sleeping upon his face, as Phoebus had last been seen. The kidnapper shook his captive but could not awaken him. He turned the man over, and his eyes met the cold, blue stare, the Roman nose, and the bloody lips of Allan McLane. With a shriek the outlaw bounded upon the deck and ran to the bow of the pungy.

"Help me," came a faint cry from the forecastle.

Peeping in, Johnson recognized one of his crew, gagged and tied fast with his companion.

"Now, spiflicate me!" said the skipper, relieving the man. "The ruffian cly you! Who did this?"

"The white nigger did it, Joe. He crawled through the stays to the cabin and got your pistols. Him an' the yaller feller at the helm come up the fo'castle on top of us, and next, two other men jined 'em. They said ole Samson had give 'em the wink. Ef you had awaked, thar was a man sot over you to stab you to the heart."

"The portmanteau?" cried Johnson.

"That's gone, I reckon. They sowed up a feather an' oyster-shell man on a plank for you to heave overboard. That's what they said. They steered for Deil's Island an' sot the Island Parson to watch that you don't git the pungy off. I reckon they're halfway to Princess Anne."

Joe Johnson heard no more. He released his creatures from their bonds, took the pungy's canoe, and gave the command: "Row fur the open bay. We'll strike St. Mary's County or Virginny. Bingavast! Hike! Never agin will I put foot on this Eastern Shore."

∞

Jimmy Phoebus, Samson, and Levin Dennis met again at Georgetown, and Levin told the mystery of his father's disappearance.

"Never tell your mother, Levin, that Captain Dennis died in that Pangymonum. It would break her heart."

"Let her understand," Samson said, "that he got wrecked on the *Ida*. It looks a little bad, but the slave trade sounds better than kidnappin'."

"They say that Allan McLane owned that vessel," Phoebus put in, "but he didn't live to know his loss. He'll meet his heathens at the judgment seat."

"Who fed mother?" Levin asked. "Hulda can't explain that."

"I kin, Levin," Samson said bashfully. "It was me. Good ole Meshach Milburn, that everybody's down on, pitied that pore woman an' made me set things she needed in her window. He said if I ever told it, he'd discharge me."

"Dog my skin," Jimmy Phoebus exclaimed. "The next man that calls 'steeple-top' after ole Meshach, I'll mash him flat! But come, son, I've buried Huldy's family relics at Broad Creek. We'll hire a wagon an' stop on the way at ole Broad Creek 'Piscopal Church. There I'll have you married to Huldy."

The sword hilt and coins were disinterred, and in that ancient edifice of hard pine, where the worship of her English race had long been celebrated, the naval officer's daughter became the wife of the son of his voluptuous and perverted friend.

As Jimmy Phoebus kissed them, he said, "Levin, when your mother says 'Yes,' all four of us will settle in the West. Illinois has become a free state, an' I reckon that'll suit us."

∞

By her affability and sorrow, Patty Cannon had easy times for a while and was allowed to eat with the jailer's family, but as the examination proceeded before the grand jury, and her menials hastened to throw their responsibility in the crimes upon her alone, all outer opinion demanded that she be treated more harshly, and some of the irons she had manacled upon her captives were riveted upon her own ankles. Dropsy soon began to appear in her legs and feet, and after it became evident to her that neither money nor friends were forthcoming in her defense, she fell into a passive despair.

Conferences between Jimmy Phoebus and Cy James led to the recovery of portions of Hulda's father's money and valuables, which Patty had hidden in flowerpots and bee hives, and it was agreed that Hulda was to have whatever remained of it after Phoebus procured Cy's release.

Many people in the region who were considered to be respectable feared that Patty Cannon would make a minute confession and implicate all who had dealt with her band. Among these was Judge Custis, who opened his skeleton-in-the-closet to John M. Clayton one spring-like day. They were sitting in the parlor of the Methodist parsonage, where they had gone to ask the pastor to wait on the aged chancellor, who had been taken ill in the courtroom and lay in the hotel.

"Clayton," Judge Custis said in a low tone of voice, "what this woman may do or tell, you would not think concerned me, but I will show you how deep her influence has reached and explain why I would not pursue my own servants to her den. In this I humiliate myself before you."

"You had been trading with her; I guessed that much."

"Such was the case. When I was a collegian at Yale, I returned home one holiday and fell in love with a beautiful quadroon, the property of my uncle in Northampton County. She was an elegant woman with a good education and had been my playmate. I was ardent and good looking and easily found lodgment in her heart, but the conquest of her charms was long and agonizing. You must believe me when I declare that I fell dangerously ill because she refused me. I made a confidant of my doctor, and he told the girl that she must choose between my death and her surrender. Pity then prevailed, even over religion. I was happy in every point but one—the injury which concealment worked upon her self-respect. For my mistress was my own cousin."

"Goy!"

"I never desired to marry, and no children had been born in my patriarchal relation, but in the course of years my uncle became pressed for debts and appealed to me to save my beautiful handmaiden from sale. He was in full sympathy with my relation to her because she was his daughter."

"Goy!"

"The case was urgent. I possessed some Negroes, the legacy of my mother, but to sell them publicly would be a stigma both upon my humanity and my credit. I adopted the cowardly device of letting a kidnapper slip them away and take a large commission for his trouble. I saved my lady but at the expense of a secret."

"And Joe Johnson depended on that secret when he was suddenly driven into your house and found your old servant demoralized by the announcement of your son-in-law," Clayton observed.

"Yes, and the scoundrel pressed his advantage. He saw my daughter—not Vesta, but her half sister, Virgie—and between his persecution of her and my brother-in-law's vindictiveness, poor Virgie was literally run to the ground and into it. She is in her grave."

Judge Custis broke into a fit of sobbing, and Clayton passed an arm around him, saying, "Never mind now. Never mind, old friend. Johnson is fled, and McLane, they whisper, has never been seen since he entered Johnson's tavern. His will was found there, and your daughter gets her mother's property and servants back."

"I must finish my story," Judge Custis said, stanching his tears. "We also became poor, and to save others it became necessary that I marry and get money by my own prostitution. My God, how we are repaid! A bride was found for me in Baltimore, the sister of Allan McLane, and a beauty. I began married life with the best intentions. My poor mistress advised me to turn to my wife and become a true man. She told me so with her heart breaking. In heaven, where she dwells with our poor child, she hears me now and knows I speak the truth."

Custis broke again and leaned his convulsed head on Clayton's breast, whose own widower's grief gushed forth responsively.

"Children were born in Teackle Hall. I was becoming adjusted to my servitude when Allan McLane, in his love of vindictiveness and low, formal respectability, conceived that my poor quadroon required some chastisement for having been his sister's rival, and he set a trap to buy her. In order to protect her, I was forced to have her bought and to bring her again to my care. Thus our passion was revived, and giving birth to Virgie, she died. Reared together, but unconscious of their kindred, my daughters loved each other dearly, and when in heaven, they shall hide in the radiance of each other and cover my sins with their angelic wings."

"Rise up, friend," said Clayton. "At least your transgressions are washed in sincere tears. Hear the birds all around us, loving and filling the air with praise. Come out!"

As they stepped upon Georgetown Square, they saw John Randel, Jr., who was now leading a party of surveyors to locate an opposition railroad to Meshach Milburn's. These and many others were pressing towards the whipping post and pillory, where the mulatto woman who had entertained Virgie in Snow Hill the first night of her flight stood exposed by the sheriff.

"This free woman, Priscilla Hudson," cried the sheriff, "is to stand one hour in the pillory for the crime of lending her pass to a slave. The governor has graciously taken off the thirty lashes she was sentenced to. At the end of one hour she is to be sold out of the state to the highest bidder for the term of her natural life."

The poor woman stood there, bare almost to the bosom, her clothing having been partly removed before the pardon of the stripes was announced. She was delicate and lovely to see and the mother of free children. Her head and arms were thrust through the holes in one leaf of the pillory, and thus thrown forward, her modesty was exposed to the wanton gaze of the crowd. On the other side of the same platform, pilloried in like manner, stood a female chicken thief, impudent, indifferent, chewing tobacco and spitting it upon the pillory floor.

As Clayton and Custis observed this scene on their way to the tavern, an egg, thrown from a window of the jail, struck Mrs. Hudson in the face, and its contents streamed down her white and shivering breast.

"Shame! Shame!" cried the people, as they saw the woman weep. Then the female face in the jail window turned their cries to curses: "Hang her! Hang her!"

For the last time in her life, Patty Cannon's bold and comely face swelled with passion to the roots of her glossy black hair, and the few who saw her rich, dark eyes inflamed with anger say their pupils were dilated like the wildcat's. She was gone in a moment, and the sheriff wiped Mrs. Hudson's face and breast with a handkerchief passed up by a colored woman.

Two men began to circulate in the crowd, hat in hand, soliciting contributions to buy the woman. One was a blind man whose eyes were bandaged, and a white man led him, calling loudly, "The abolitionists have raised three hundred dollars to buy this woman's freedom. As some mean people may bid her up high, we need a hundred more. This man, her husband, stole her pass to slip a friend away. We couldn't git the evidence in, but it's God's truth, gentlemen. The woman's nursed my wife an' done a heap of good, and she come here of her own free will out of Maryland to nurse the chancellor."

Little money was raised in the crowd, as there was little to give. Sorden turned to the two distinguished strangers. "Gentlemen, will you let the Hunn brothers and Tommy Garrett and the Motts give three hundred dollars for a woman they never saw, and we, who see her always doing good, give nothing?"

"Pity!" sobbed the blind man. "I'm burned so bad nobody will buy *me*, but I stole her pass to help a slave that I fell in love with."

Judge Custis left Clayton's side and waited till the hour in the pillory was done. After a fierce contest, Sorden came off victorious at the sale, though it took every dollar the judge could raise in Georgetown on his private credit.

"What is the name of the girl you gave her pass to?" the judge asked the blind mulatto.

"Virgie, marster."

"My heart told me so," exclaimed the judge. "Your crime has been punished enough. I will send you to your wife."

∞

That evening John Randel, Jr., observed, "Devil Jim Clark has squared the circle."

"Not dead?" asked Clayton.

"Yes, dead and buried. He was cleaning up his contract on the canal and mistook the white Irish laborers there for kidnapped niggers. They set on him and beat him so that he never recovered. They say he was 'converted' on his death bed. As the saying is, 'he died triumphantly,' but the darkeys report that the devil came straight down with a chariot and drove him off."

"I'm reserving that fellow Whitecar," Clayton said, "to punish when I can use him to sustain an argument in favor of admitting Negro testimony in kidnapping cases. Without that admission these kidnappers cannot be convicted. Even Patty Cannon may escape us, though she has killed white men."

"A disease called leprosy," another interjected, "has broke out in Derrick Molleston's cabin. Sam Ogg has got it too. They say he fetched it up from the breakwater. Nobody will go near them. Black Dave is dead. He said he killed a man at Princess Anne. The young wife of Levin Dennis stayed and prayed with him to the last, and he went off humble and happy. But, my skin, another kidnapper has rented Johnson's tavern a'ready."

"The railroad will clear all these evils out," exclaimed Randel. "I've put it into poetry," and he began to recite:

>To dark Naswaddox forest fled
>   The murderer from the main,
>And with the otter laid his head
>   Amid the swamp and cane:
>"Here nothing can pursue my ear,

> From traveled paths astray;
> I shall forget, from year to year,
> The world beyond the bay!"
>
> The hunted man one morning heard
> A whistle near and strong,
> And in the night a fiery light
> The thickets flashed among:
> The demon of the engine rushed
> Along on blazing beams—
> The hound the murderer had flushed,
> The outlaw's path was Steam's!

∞

The cry of hate from the crowd around the whipping post, as it awoke Patty Cannon's last anger, also determined her last crime.

Fear was relative in her. She had neither the fear of men nor of shame, and only of death as it involved a hereafter. Whether that hereafter was a latent conviction in her mind or the vivid admonition of guilt and dead men's eyes peering over her dreams and into the silent, lonely watches of haunted midnights, who shall tell. There is no analysis of a native and ancient depravity. It is sown in the marrow; it strengthens in the bone; and with a cunning, daring self-assertion, gambles upon the faith of living and not of dying. Its very fears push it onward and make it cruelly tantalize its own fate, as cowards lean over graveyard walls and shout with an inner trembling, "Come forth— I dare you!"

So had this woman, conscious of her desserts, bullied eternal justice through long postponements, never doubting, while never vexing the spirit of God, until the number of her crimes crowded the tablet of her memory. Faces without names and deeds without memoranda gazed out of the hideous gulf of her past life, a procession the longer that strangers were in it. Shrinking from her, yet pressing on, they exclaimed her name or only shrieked, "'Tis she!" as if her name was nothing to her curse.

As she slept in her chains, children's eyes watched from faroff corners as if to say, "Give us the whole life we would have lived but for you."

The Death of Patty Cannon   425

As Patty's swollen limbs festered to the irons, the cries of babies' floated in the air and seemed to draw near her breasts as if for food, only to convulse there in screams of pain and move away with the sounds of suffocation she had heard as they expired.

All night there were callers on her, and whom they were, no one could tell. The jailer's family saw her lips move and her eyes consult the air as if trying bravado upon ghosts who had come, demanding payment on bills long overdue. Some of these mystic visitors she jeered and defied, and she stamped her feet as if they had no rights in equity against her soul.

Then suddenly a helpless something would appear and paralyze her with its wail, like a babeless mother or a motherless babe, and with her forehead wet with the sweat of agony, she would chuckle, "Nothin' but niggers. Nothin' more."

Day brought some relief to her but also other cares, and of these the chief was money. She had always been a spendthrift, robbing people of their riches or taking their liberty or life for her own selfish dissipation. And what had she bought with it? Nothing! She had wrecked her soul to spend for such trifles as children want—candy and common ornaments, a dance and a treat, a gift for some boor or forester or Negro she was misleading, or to establish a silly reputation for generosity.

Now she had no money to appease the greed of habit nor even to satisfy necessity, none to buy dainties or liquor, none to spend on the jailer's family to keep the reputation of kindness alive, none for decent apparel to appear in court, none to corrupt the law or to hire witnesses and attorneys.

The demons she had created alternately seized the day and the night—the demon of money plagued her by day; the demon of murder pursued her by night. Each morning she had insatiate wants, all night, remorseless visitors. And close before, the gallows filled her view, with the devil tying the noose.

That devil she plainly saw. Whenever she looked, he was always in the jail yard fixing his ropes, sliding the nooses, examining the gallows like a conscientious carpenter. In his complacent smile was an awful terror that froze her dumb. He seemed so impersonal, so joyous, so industrious, as if he had waited for her like a long creditor and compounded the interest on her sins till the infernal sum made him a millionaire in torments. A devil it was, real as a man—a man whose unscarred age, old as the rising sun, still came and went in immortal youthfulness and satisfaction. He looked like a storekeeper, a man of accounts, a cosmopolitan kidnapper who knew a good article and had it now. She was so terrified that she wanted to cry to him and see if he would not become more human and sauce her back. But the longer she watched, the less he looked towards her, though she knew his smile was meant for no one else. To hang upon his cord was very little. To go with him after it was stretched, down the burning grates of hell and see him all so cool and busy in her misery, was the gnawing vulture at her heart.

She tried to throw responsibility for her sins upon a vague, false parentage and say that she was bred to robbery and vice, but something in her heart responded, "No, you had beauty and health and chaste lovers, whom you rejected or tempted, and a mind that was ever clear and knew right from wrong. Though drenched in innocent blood, conscience never gave you up. The often-murdered monitor revived and cried aloud like the striking of a clock, but never was obeyed."

Thus haunted, deserted, peeped in upon from the hereafter, racked with vain needs, her outlets closed to every escape or subterfuge, revenge itself dead, and disease assisting conscience to banish sleep, the wretched woman crawled to her window one day and saw the helpless effigy of her sex exposed there for doing an act of humanity. An instinct she immediately obeyed exacted from her one last, familiar, heartless deed—to show the crowd that even she, Patty Cannon the murderess, had no respect for a nigger. That doctrine long survived her, though she found it old when she came among them.

She aimed an egg at the breast of her sex, and with a barefaced grin she saw it strike and burst. The next moment the crowd had recognized and defied her.

In the exasperation of their shout, a convulsion of desperate rage overcame the murderess. In uncontrollable recklessness, too helpless to retort in any other way, she exclaimed, "They never shall see me hang, then," and swallowed the arsenic she had concealed in her bosom.

That night she died in awful torments.

∞

*Sussex County Courthouse in Georgetown, Delaware
The jail stood behind the courthouse. Patty Cannon was originally buried on its grounds and moved shortly after 1900 to an unmarked grave in Potters Field at the new jail.*

The venerable chancellor, lying in the hotel near the whipping post and watched by the released Mrs. Hudson, heard the night voices on the square say, "Patty Cannon's dead. She's took poison."

A mighty pain seized the chancellor's heart, and his groans called a stranger into the room.

"Is that dreadful woman dead?" asked the chancellor.

"Yes. She will never plague Delaware again, marster."

"God be thanked," the old man groaned. "Justice and murder are kin no more."

They say he died that instant of heart disease.

Chancellor Ridgely lies in a brick vault, center, right, in Old Christ Churchyard, a block from his home on Dover Square. His wife, Mary Brereton, lies center, left.

The Judge Remarried

Chapter 45

Vesta found her circle reunited, though with many absentees at Princess Anne.

Aunt Hominy took her place in the kitchen and cooked with all her former art, but her voice and understanding were gone. She never would go past the Entailed Hat, still regarding it as the cause of all her errors and dangers, though she seemed to admit its unevadable dominion.

Finding Samson Hat desirous of having a partner, the poor woman Mary had faith enough left to make her third marriage with him. His means not only made good the property she had lost, but the hale old man presented her with a baby boy, who took the name of Meshach Phoebus, and on whom Judge Custis remarked that it ought to have been a red-headed nigger, having both the fiery furnace and the blazing sun in its name.

On Samson's death, which resulted from rheumatism, his widow joined James Phoebus in the West, where he lived happily with his bride and stepson and often wrote home of a friend he had there named Abe Lincoln, who made flatboat voyages with him down the Mississippi. Both Ellenora Phoebus and Hulda Dennis reared Western families, which played effective parts in the drama of civilization.

With the approval of her father and husband, Vesta lost no time in setting free every slave about Teackle Hall and on the farms. Roxy became the wife of Whatcoat, the rescued freedman, and replaced poor Virgie, whose body was brought home and interred by the church where she had been her sister's bridesmaid. Vesta's grief for Virgie was quiet but long, and that of an equal, though she never knew how equal.

In the fatalities thronging about her marriage, Vesta observed one signal blessing—the complete reform of her father's habits. He drank nothing, replacing the pleasures of wine with fruit, while exercise and business on her husband's behests supplanted his former vagrant visits to the forest for politics and amours. Aware of his sociable and voluptuous nature, Vesta desired to see him married again to complete and secure his reformation. While she was yet puzzling to think of a wife to suit him, he solved the problem himself by cleanly cutting Rhoda Holland out from under the attentions of William Tilghman.

Rhoda had rapidly learned and had corrected her grammar without losing her humor. Her free, warm spirit soon made her an elegant woman in whom a worldly ambition germinated. She may have patterned it upon her uncle, or it may have emanated from his ambitious family stock. Possessing a higher vitality than Vesta, Rhoda Holland soon showed more insight, quicker intuitions, more self-love—though not selfishness, less scruples, perhaps, in dealing with her lovers, and a pushing spirit that Vesta only mildly reproved, since she made the allowance that it was in part inspired by herself.

"Take care, dear," Vesta said one day, "that you do not grow away from your heart. Do you love William Tilghman? He is too true a man to be hurt in his feelings. Nothing in this world, Rhoda, is a substitute for principle in woman."

"I don't want to lose principle," Rhoda said, "but I am afraid I love life too much to be a pastor's wife. I haven't seen the world for very long, and I'm wild in it. I want to go and look and see everywhere. I feel my heart is in my wings. Must I sit on a nest?"

"The question is, dear, do you love him?"

"Auntie, I reckon I love William as much as he does me."

"But he is devoted, Rhoda."

"If I thought I had the whole, full heart of William, Aunt Vesta, and it would give him real pain to disappoint him, I would marry him. But I have watched him like a cat watches a mouse. He wants to marry me to make other people than himself happy: to reconcile you and uncle more; to take uncle more into your family by marrying his niece. William is trying to love Uncle Meshach like a good Christian, Aunt Vesta, but he thinks more of your little toe than of my whole body."

The crimson color came to Vesta's cheeks so quickly that she felt ashamed of it, but in place of the anger that many wives would have shown, she shed some quiet tears.

"Rhoda, don't you know I am your uncle's wife?"

Rhoda threw her arms around Vesta. "Forgive me! When you tell me, Aunt Vesta, that William loves me dearly, I'll gladly marry him. I don't want to make happiness impossible, when to wait would be better." She kissed Vesta tenderly and whispered, "It's not selfishness that makes me behave so. I do love William. It's a sacrifice to let him go."

Vesta looked up and found Rhoda's eyes filled with tears. "Strange, tender girl," she said, "what makes you cry?" Then together they shed tears of respect for each other.

Soon afterwards, Judge Custis was sent to Annapolis by Milburn and requested that Rhoda accompany him as part of her education. Vesta also went at her husband's desire.

They were taken to the landing by Milburn and the young rector. As the steamboat approached, Tilghman said, "Rhoda, your uncle has given his approval and wishes us to marry. I ask you to consider my proposal while you are gone and come home with your reply."

The impetuous girl threw her arms around him and kissed him in silence, then covered her face with her veil and waited in tears for the steamboat to carry her to the world she had never seen beyond the bay. Her stillness and grief continued, and going to bed that night, she turned up her face, discolored by tears, for Vesta to kiss her. "Auntie," she said, "don't think I have no principle. Indeed, I have some."

∞

Annapolis, half a century the senior of Baltimore, was now almost one hundred and fifty years old. It had been the first town to take root in all the Chesapeake land and was the stern monument of Cromwell's protectorate. Its handful of expelled Puritans from Virginia, compelled to organize their county under the name of the Romanist Anne Arundel, unfurled the standard of the Commonwealth, reddened with a tyrant king's blood, against the invading army of Lord Baltimore, shouting, "God is our strength; fall on, men!" and annihilated feudal Maryland. And after King William's similar revolution in England, "Providence Town" took his queen sister's name, Annapolis, as did Princess Anne across the bay.

Annapolis became a place of fashion and court with horse races, stage playing, a press, a club, fox-hunting clergymen, a grand state house, the town residences of planters, the belles of Maryland, and the seat of war against the French, the British crown, and the slave-holders' insurrection.

It was now in a state of comfortable decline, having yielded its once superior influence and society to Baltimore and Washington, but a lobby, the first in magnitude ever seen in this province, had assembled here in the name of canals and railroads to compete for the bonded aid of the legislature. Judge Custis led the forlorn hope of the Eastern Shore for some of the subsidy so liberally showered upon the cormorant Baltimore.

The judge was instructed to lobby at Annapolis for one million dollars, one-eighth of the grants being made by the state. He was supported by Meshach Milburn's funds, while Milburn, meantime, continued to buy and grade right of way for one hundred and thirty miles of railroad out of his private resources. The adventure was gigantic for the private capital of that day, and the unpopularity of the adventurer at home was soon testified to at the state capital.

Vesta, being herself of divided Maryland and Virginia sympathies, looked with a gentle patriotism upon the little capital with its old, roomy houses of colonial brick, its circles and triangles in the public ways, and the unchanged names of such streets as King George, Prince George, and Duke of Gloucester.

Rhoda, on the other hand, was excited in everything she saw. She seized on the historical and political relations of Annapolis with a strong faculty till Judge Custis said, "Vesta, that girl is of the old rebel Milburne stock. She takes it all in like a wild duck diving for the bay celery."

With two such beautiful women to speak for it, the Eastern Shore Railroad seemed at first to have many friends, but it was not in the nature of the enterprising elements about Baltimore to yield a point, however complaisant they might appear.

Vesta did not go into general company, but her influence was mildly exercised in her rooms at the old hotel and in her carriage as she made excursions in pleasant weather to the South and West Rivers, to the forest of Prince George, and to the thrifty Quakers of Montgomery. She wrote and received a daily letter, her husband being attentive and tender as he had promised, despite his growing cares.

But the story of her sacrifice, shamefully exaggerated with all the intensity of expression habitual in a pro-slavery society whenever money is the stake and denunciation the game, was used to injure her husband's interests. Mr. Milburn was described as a vile Yankee type of miser and over-reacher, who had plotted against the fortune of a gentleman and the virtue of his daughter for a long series of remorseless years. Local opposition affirmed that he would use the railroad to ruin other gentry and oppress his native region, and that he was a Philadelphia emissary and an abolitionist, scheming to create a new state of the three jurisdictions across the bay.

Judge Custis, in spite of his popularity, did not escape censure. He was said to have winked at the surrender of his child for money and ambition and to have broken the heart of his estimable wife after he had lost her fortune in an iron furnace.

Senator Clayton, whose mother had originated near Annapolis, made a visit there from Washington and was entrapped into saying that Delaware would furnish all needed railway facilities for the Eastern Shore and that two railways there would never pay.

Finally, Judge Custis wrote to his son-in-law to come to Annapolis and meet these misstatements in person. Milburn came, and his pride being irritated by the nature of the opposition, he wore his ancestral hat to the scene of combat. He became at once the most marked figure in Maryland.

In one end of the state he was caricatured in drawings and verses as the generic Eastern-Shore man, wearing such a hat because he had not heard of any later styles. The connection of a man of last century's hat with such a progressive thing as a railroad seemed to excite everybody's animosity. His railroad was called the "Hat Line," even in debates, and coarse people were hired by wits in the lobby to attend the legislature with petitions for the Eastern Shore Railroad, the whole delegation wearing preposterous hats gathered from all the old counties and from the slop shops of Baltimore.

Word was sent from Somerset that Milburn retained his hat from no amiable weakness or eccentricity, but because he had entered a vow never to abandon it till he had put every former superior under his feet. He was also represented as a victim of gross forest superstition, who had bargained with the devil and was allowed to prosper as long as he braved society with his tile.

The hotel servants chuckled as he went in and out. The oystermen and woodcutters called mockingly to each other as he passed by. Respectable people said he could have no consideration for his wife, to degrade her so by raising the derision of the town. Judge Custis finally remarked, "Milburn, I resolved many years ago never to address you again on the subject of your dress, but my duty makes me break the resolve. Your hat is the worst enemy of your railroad."

Vesta, however, was the hat's greatest victim. It lay upon her spirits like a shroud. The perpetual admonition and friction of this article drove her into silence and gloom, poisoned the air, and blocked the sunlight. It made going out a constant running of the gauntlet, hospitality a comedy, and human observation a wondering stare. The hat was the silent, unindicated thing that stood between her and her husband and the rest of the world. She never mentioned it, for she understood that it was forbidden ground. As kind and liberal as Milburn was in every other thing, she dared not allude to a matter which had become, like a callused sore, the center of his nervous organization; yet she saw, from other than selfish considerations, that this hat was his own worst foe.

Some positive vice, and he had none, some calculating conspiracy, and he was direct as the day, some base amusement, hidden habit, or acrid disease would hold him captive less than this aberration of behavior. Had he been a hunchback, men would have overlooked it. They would not have resented a hideous goiter or tumor, but extreme gentility and highbred courtesy could not refrain from turning to look a second time at a man with a beautiful lady on his arm and a steeple hat upon his head.

The existence of any subject which man and wife cannot discuss, yet which is a daily ingredient in their lives, becomes the chronic intruder in their household, and when a trifle, it is all the more an obstacle, as there is no reasoning about it.

This hat had long ceased to be external. It was worn on Milburn's heart and stifled the healthy throbbing there. It made two men of him—the outer and the household man—and, like the Corsican brothers, they were ever conscious of each other, and a word to one aroused the other's sensibility.

"If people would ignore him," Vesta observed, "I think he would lay his hat aside, but that is impossible. We do not know who sets a fashion, but a man who dares to set one that is obsolete must be a martyr. No one can practice independence but a lunatic. Oh, what tyranny exists that no law can reach, and how much of society is mere formality."

Vesta pitied her husband, but the disease was beyond her cure. She had anticipated compensation for her marriage in a larger life and society and in the exercise of her mind, especially in art and music, but the baneful hat not only darkened her threshold but closed the vista of every other one. She considered escaping by a visit to Europe. Her father had promised a trip before his embarrassments, and her husband had spoken of it as due her in the way of musical perfection.

"Uncle," Rhoda said one day, "do put off that old hat. Aunt Vesta could love you so much better. People think it is cruel. Listen to your wife's heart and not to your pride."

"Stop!" said Milburn. "One more reference to my honest hat and you shall be sent back to Mrs. Somers."

Perhaps it was this dreadful threat, or only the fascination of Judge Custis's position and attentions and remarkable gallantry, that disposed Rhoda to turn her worldly sagacity upon the father of her friend.

The visit to Annapolis occupied the whole winter. As it proceeded, Judge Custis, desirous of a fixed settlement in a home again, began to feel a powerful passion to possess Rhoda Holland. He contended against it in vain. Her beauty, coquetry, and ambition seized his fancy and worked upon his imagination. He had seen her grow from a forest rose into the noblest flower of the garden, superb in health, rich in colors, tall and bright and warm. She began to lead him on from mere mischief. He was wise and observant of women, and he threw himself in the place of her instructor and courtier. She became his pupil, and an exacting one, driving his energies onward, demanding his full attention, stimulating his mind.

Vesta soon saw that her father was a blind captive. "Is there any law, husband," she asked, "to prevent Rhoda from marrying Judge Custis?"

"I think not. In a society where every degree of cousins marry together, it would be as gratuitous to interfere in such a marriage as to forbid my hat by law."

"He is so enamored of her," Vesta said, "that I fear the results of her refusing him. Father is a better man than he ever was. A wife that can retain his interest will now keep him steady all his life."

The adjournment of the legislature was at hand, and it became clear that another year, perhaps years unforeseen in number, would have to be occupied in the slow, illusive quest.

Early one morning Judge Custis found himself above the dome of the old State House, where he frequently went with Rhoda at that hour to look out upon the bay and town. He turned to her with a sparkle of humor, yet a flush of the cheek, and said, "My girl, what is to be your answer to Pastor Tilghman's marriage offer?"

"It cannot be," she replied.

"Then I am free to ask for another. You have seen that I am foolish for you, Rhoda. I was your admirer when you were a poor forest girl."

"And when you were a married man," Rhoda interrupted. "How splendid and sly you were. Even then I was delighted that a great man like you could even flirt with me. Perhaps you will cut up the same way again?"

"No, Rhoda. This is my last opportunity. I will devote my remaining life to you. I am fifty-five, but it is the best fifty-five in Maryland. You shall have the devotion of twenty-five."

"I want to be taken to Washington," Rhoda said. "I think I could marry an old man if he took me there."

"I will run for Congress, then, and you will make a great woman in public life. I do not ask you to love me, but to let me love you. Marriage has been a tragedy with me. I will be a repentant and fond husband. Hear my selfishness and make the sacrifice."

"If I say yes," said Rhoda, "it is not to settle down and nurse you. You are to be what you have been this winter—a beau and an ever fond and gallant gentleman."

"Yes. As long as time will let me."

"Then say no more," Rhoda answered with a little pallor. "If the rest are willing, a poor girl like me will not refuse you. But say, like Ruth, 'Spread thy skirt over thine handmaid, for thou art a near kinsman.' I love your daughter."

Only half pleased with the turn affairs had taken, Meshach Milburn hastened to Princess Anne in advance of the party and sought William Tilghman. "Dear friend," he said, "I hope your heart was not committed to my wayward niece."

"Has she engaged herself to another, Cousin Meshach?"

"Yes. To Judge Custis. You know what a taking way he has with girls. It was not my match, William."

There was no disappointment on the young man's face—rather a flush of spirit. "Cousin Meshach," he said, "I thought I interpreted Rhoda right and could make her happy. Since I was mistaken, it is better that she has been sincere. My heart remains a bachelor's and a priest's, and the bishop has sent for me to take a larger field."

He united Rhoda and the judge, as he had married his first love to another. She was pale and in tears. He kissed her at the altar and gave his hand to the judge warmly. "I know you will be a better Christian, Cousin Daniel. God has given you much love. Our prayers for you have been answered."

Vesta was disappointed, having expected to see William made happy in a marriage with Rhoda.

The Curse of the Hat

Chapter 46

As spring burst upon Princess Anne in cherry blossoms and dogwood flowers, in herring and shad weighting the river seines, in broods of young chickens and early corn and cantaloupe, life in human veins also unfolded in infant fruit, and Vesta became a mother.

The forest and the court had harmonized in the offspring, and the young boy took the name of Custis Milburn. Healthy and comely, as if society had made the match for nature, the infant flourished without a day's ailing and grew like a miracle before its parents' eyes, having the symmetry and loveliness of the mother and the bold, challenging countenance of the father. To Meshach he brought the satisfaction of an improved posterity and an heir to his success. To his mother the son was compensation for the loss of worldly society.

Vesta found more joy in Teackle Hall with this wondrous product of her sacrifice and pain than with the admiration of all the good families in Maryland, and a sense of warmth and gratitude arose towards the father of this matchless gift. "I have not given him my whole loyalty," she reflected with piety. "I have let trifles stand before my vows."

Accordingly, when a conscience stricken Milburn came before his wife one day to make some restitution for exacting a marriage without love, Vesta surprised him by kissing him and saying, "I have been very proud and stubborn, Sir. Do forgive me."

He pressed her to his breast, while his tears ran over her face. "Honey," he said, "what a mockery my crime to you has been—to think that you could ever love me. I will give you freedom. Dear as your captivity is to me, your cage shall open and you shall fly."

Vesta stepped back at these strange words and waited for him to explain.

"I will send you to Italy with our child," he continued. "Your father shall also go, if you desire. Go from me and these unloved conditions, this hateful bondage and constraint. I hope you can find forgetfulness of this unworthy marriage in your music and your noble mind. I can live in the recollection of the blessing you have been to me."

"What?" said Vesta. "Do you command me to leave you?"

"Yes, let it be that. I know how conscientious you are, darling, but it is your duty to go. A hard struggle is before me. I am deeply embarked in an untried business. Go and find happiness in a happier land."

She put her arms around him. "Leave you?" she said. "What have I done to be driven away? How could I reconcile myself to let you live alone? 'For better or for worse,' I said. God has made it better and better every day."

He held her head between his palms and looked into her eyes to see if she spoke from the heart.

"Husband," she whispered, "I love you."

∞

After this reconciliation the minds of both husband and wife turned to the disturbing hat as the subject of their estrangement hitherto.

Milburn said to himself, "What a sinner I have been to distress that poor child with my miserable hat. At the first opportunity she gives me, I will lay it aside forever."

Vesta said to her father and his bride, "What a wicked heart I have kept, to oppose my husband in such a little thing as his old hat—the badge of his reverence to his family and his bravery to an impertinent age. I have let it discolor my married life and all the sunshine, but my baby has melted my obdurate heart. Come, unite with me, and let us show him that we will proudly adopt everything he wears."

When Milburn next went out, therefore, his wife came with a beaming face and elastic step and put his steeple hat on his head. He looked at her grimly, but she stopped his protest with a kiss.

He thought to introduce the subject to Judge Custis, but that fond bridegroom broke in with, "Milburn, you're a game fellow. It was impudent in me to say one word about your hat. I'll get one like it myself if I can find one. Tut, tut, man, it becomes you. Say no more about it."

Milburn undertook to make the explanation to his niece, but before he could well begin, she cried, "Uncle Meshach, Aunt Vesta is just in love with your hat. She won't hear of your wearing any other. We're all going to stand by it, Uncle."

A man chooses his own verdict by a long course of behavior. Austerity in the family begets fear. An affectation, whether of folly or resentment, is at last credited to nature. Man is seldom allowed to escape from the trap of his own temperament.

So Meshach Milburn never obtained the opportunity to relieve himself of the affliction with which he had afflicted others. Like an impostor who has established the claim of deafness, to have mankind bawl in his ear, the hatted specter was made to feel uncomfortable when he put off his tile. He was like a boy who had pricked a cross upon his hand in India ink, and growing to be a man with taste and position, must see the indelible advertisement of his vulgarity whenever he takes a human hand.

To have put on any other hat would have subjected him to new hoots and comments. He must have climbed as high as the pillory to explain the change and make apology. The society he had faced in defiance seemed all at once united to refuse him a status without his Entailed Hat. To appear in Princess Anne in a new, contemporary headdress, would have taken the courage of throwing off a lifelong alias and living under a forgotten name. Milburn saw that he must wear his old hat for life. He bent under the servitude and was alone the victim of it now.

Failure and Restitution

Chapter 47

The railroad struggle was renewed from year to year. The legislature was annually beset by strong lobby forces, and an embittered contest between the Potomac Canal and the greater railway company left the Eastern Shore Railroad out of notice.

Locomotive engines of native invention began to appear. As Vesta's son became a young horseman and learned to read, the railroad to Washington was finally opened and then extended to Harper's Ferry.

The venerable courthouse at Princess Anne with its eighty-seven years of memories burned down during these proceedings. A panic swept over Patty Cannon's old region at the whisper of another Nat Turner rebellion among the slaves, but no mention of the thousands of abductions there was made in the anti-Masonic convention at Baltimore. Because one white man had been stolen, Samuel S. Seward and Thaddeus Stevens nominated Mr. Wirt for president.

The murder of Jacob Cannon by Owen Daw did produce some distant comment a little later, chiefly because of the apathy of the Delaware society to pursue the murderer. The Cannon brothers had become detested in their own community, and when they sued Daw for cutting down a bee tree on one of their farms and enforced a judgment of ten dollars, Daw loaded his gun and started for Cannon's Ferry. He waylaid Jacob as he was leading his horse off the ferry scow.

"Are you going to give me back that ten dollars, you old scoundrel?" Daw shouted.

"Stand back!" answered Jacob. "The quotient was correct. The *lex loci* and the *lex terrae* were argued. The *lex talionis*...."

"Take it!" cried the villain, firing his shotgun into the merchant's breast.

Jacob Cannon staggered to the fence at the head of the wharf, caught there a moment, and fell dead.

"You scoundrel," screamed Isaac Cannon from his window, "to kill my brother, my executive comfort."

"Yes," answered O'Day, "and I'll give the other barrel to you!"

As Isaac Cannon barricaded himself, Owen O'Day collected his effects and betook himself to the wilds of Missouri.

Cannon's Ferry fell into decay when the railroad at Seaford carried off its trading importance, but there are yet to be seen the never-tenanted mansion of the disappointed bridegroom and the gravestones which show how Jacob's fate frightened his brother Isaac to a speedy tomb.

The Cannon Graves

In the meantime, John M. Clayton had made use of the fears of Calhoun and his nullifiers, who were menaced by the president with the penalties of treason to assist in passing a great protective tariff bill, thus establishing manufacturing in the same period with the railways. This triumph in the senate left Clayton free to conduct Randel's suit against the canal company, which occupied as many years as the railroad enterprise of Meshach Milburn.

Though soon to be weeded out even in its parent England, the barbarous system of "pleadings" was then in full vogue—trials of traverses, demurrers, avoidances, rebutters and surrebutters, rather than a trial of facts.

Clayton's pleadings require a bold, dull mind to read them now, but he tired his adversaries out, and his cousin, Chief Justice Clayton, who was jealous of him, had yet to decide in his favor.

After a lapse of years the issue came to trial at the old Dutch-English town of New Castle. From the magnitude of the damages claimed, the weight and number of counsel, and the novelty of trying a great corporation, it was popularly supposed to belong to the class of squaring-the-circle problems—something that would be going on at the final end of the world.

"Never you mind, Bob Frame, Walter Jones is a great advocate, but goy, he don't know a Delaware jury. I'll get my country seat up here on the New Castle hills out of this case," Clayton said as he pitched quoits with his fellow lawyers from Washington and Philadelphia on the green battery where the Philadelphia steamer came in with southern passengers for the little stone-silled railroad.

John Randel, Jr., had ruined a fine engineer to become a litigious man. He had surveyed the great city of New York and planned its streets above the new city hall. Elevated railroads were his projection half a century before they came about. He now looked upon engineering with indifference and considered himself to have been born for the law. He sued his successor and fellow New Yorker, engineer Wright, and was nonsuited. He garnisheed the canal officers and beset the legislature for remedial legislation, even threatening Clayton with damages.

In the midst of many other duties, Clayton, in course of time, convicted Whitecar of kidnapping on Negro testimony, having obtained a ruling to that end from his cousin, the chief justice. In order to spite Clayton, a constituent named Sorden (not the personage of our tale) was prosecuted for kidnapping and cleared by Clayton after a marvelous exhibition of eloquence. Sorden repaid the obligation years after our story closes by breaking a party deadlock in the Delaware Legislature, where he had become a member, thereby sending Clayton to the American Senate for the fourth time.

∞

Judge Custis took the field for congress on the railroad issue and was elected through the forest vote, and his wife went through a Washington season with as much dignity as enjoyment, few suspecting that she was not the judge's social equal.

As Milburn pressed his bill for assistance year after year, the Entailed Hat became more common on the streets of Annapolis than it had been in Princess Anne. The ancestral hat defied all worldly hostility but became the iron helmet to bend its wearer's back. Milburn prayed in secret for some pitying angel to break the spell that bound him to it, but none conceived that he would let it go.

His boy grew strong and took his father's dress to be a matter of course. Vesta continued to press upon her husband the nauseous ornament he had so long affected. A wide conspiracy seemed to have been formed to drive his head into that hereditary wig-wam, and he could not escape it.

Even Grandmother Tilghman, who was now an inmate of Teackle Hall, forgot all about the queer hat and rejoiced to herself that Bill had not married "that political girl."

Milburn had maintained his financial solvency by turns and sorties that even his enemies admired, but a railroad built along one man's spine and terminated by a steeple depot on his head must wear out the unrelieved individual at last.

The banks in Baltimore began to break. Fierce riots ensued, and the state debt, through aid to public works, mounted up to fifteen million dollars. Too late, the Eastern Shore Railroad obtained the vote of the subsidy expected, and the state treasurer could not find funds to pay it. The gazettes announced the failure of Meshach Milburn, Esq., of the Eastern Shore.

Without an instant's hesitation Vesta surrendered her own property, and she and Rhoda Custis opened a select school in a part of Teackle Hall, renting the remainder for residences.

"Why do you make this sacrifice?" her husband asked. "Nobody expected it."

"They may say we were married to protect my parents," Vesta answered, "but not that it was to secure myself. My boy shall have a clear name."

His failure ended the active life of Meshach Milburn. Too considerate of his family to renew his former low endeavors, he became, through Judge Custis's influence, a clerk in the county offices and wore his hat to stipendiary labor with the regularity but not the rebellious instincts of old days.

Vesta saw that Milburn's misfortune extinguished the last remnant of animosity in her father's mind, and the two men went about together like two old boys who had both been prisoners of war and were cured of ambition.

Milburn resumed his forest walks and bird tamings. All traces of ambition left his countenance, and he was as dead to business things as if he had never risen above his forest origin.

He often talked of William Tilghman and seemed to wish to see him, though for no apparent purpose.

The Asiatic cholera, having begun to make annual visits to the United States, one day singled out the wearer of the obsolete hat and put the household at Teackle Hall to the sternest test of affection and humanity. Whether from the respect his steady purposes had given them or the natural devotion in a sequestered society, no soul left his side.

But it brought the final visitation of poverty upon Vesta. Her school was broken up. She dismissed it herself and calmly sat by her husband's bed to soothe his dying weakness and await the providence of God.

He rapidly passed through the stages of cramp and collapse, a nearly perished pulse, and the cadaverous look of one already dead; yet his intellect, by the law of the disease, lived unimpaired.

"The stream cannot rise above the fountain," he said huskily. "All we can get from life is love. You have showered it on me, my darling, and been thirsty all your days."

"I have been happy in my duty," Vesta said. "You have been kind to me always. We have nothing to regret."

Though he looked at her, he wandered and seemed to be thinking of his mother. "Where can we go?" he muttered pitifully. "I burned the dear old hut. It would have been a roof for my boy."

His chin trembled, as if he were about to cry, and he sighed, "Fader an' Mammy's quarreled. The mockingbird won't sing. Ride for the doctor! Ride hard! Oh, too late, little chillen, they's both dead!"

He returned to perfect knowledge in a moment and fixed his eyes on Vesta, saying, "I leave you poor. I tried hard. Perhaps. . . ."

His eye was here arrested by some conflict at the door, where, not withstanding her imperfect wits, Aunt Hominy was striving to keep guard.

"De debbil's measurin' him in at las'," the old woman said. "Miss Vessy's 'mos' free."

"Admit me," commanded a clear, familiar voice; "I must see him. Mr. Clayton has won the lawsuit and two hundred and twenty-six thousand dollars damages. Cousin Meshach is rich again."

"That friendly voice," said Meshach with a happy light in his eyes, "I wanted to hear it again." But with his little strength he raised his hand to push away the intruder, who would have kissed him. "No! The cholera," he whispered.

"It's the bishop, uncle," cried Mrs. Custis. "Bishop Tilghman is here from the West!"

"Don't I know him," Milburn whispered with sinking voice and powers. "Honest man. Bishop of our church. Bishop in the free West. God bless him."

He was lost again for some time, and with all kneeling, the young bishop made a prayer.

After they arose, Milburn seemed speechless, yet he tried to raise his hand. When Vesta came to his aid, his long, lean fingers closed around hers, and he signaled to William Tilghman with his eyes. The bishop came near, and, by a painful effort, Milburn put his wife's hand in her cousin's, and his lips framed a word without a sound: "*Restitution.*"

"Glory be to God!" exclaimed Grandmother Tilghman, who seemed to see without sight all that was going on.

"I knew that if both would wait, it would be so," a tearful Rhoda sighed to her husband.

Though he was unable to explain it, there was still something on Milburn's mind. Every attempt was made, though in vain, to interpret his want, till Aunt Hominy broke the silence by mumbling, "He want dat debbil's hat."

Vesta saw her husband's eyes twinkle. She left the room and returned with her fine young son, and in his hand was his father's hat.

"What will you do if Papa leaves us, Custis?" Vesta said loudly, so the dying man could hear.

"I will wear my forefather's hat, Papa," said the child.

Failure and Restitution 447

The dying man drooped his eyes as if to say, "No," and looked fervently at his son and wearily at the old headpiece.

Vesta placed it on his pillow and waited to know his next wish.

He made a sign, which they interpreted to mean, "Lift me."

He was lifted up, livid as the dead, and raised his eyes towards his forehead.

His wife set the Entailed Hat upon his temples.

"Bury it," he said in a distinct whisper and passed away.

It has been said that she had a handsome, fascinating face, but if we can believe her biographers, no greater monster ever lived.

She has been called:

> The most celebrated woman criminal in the history of Maryland and Delaware;

> A degenerate creature;

> A woman void of all human emotions and sympathies;

> The queen of kidnappers and murderers;

> The wickedest woman ever to walk on American soil.

Turn the page for the largest collection of material ever published about Patty Cannon.

The Monster's Handsome Face

Patty Cannon in Fiction and Fact

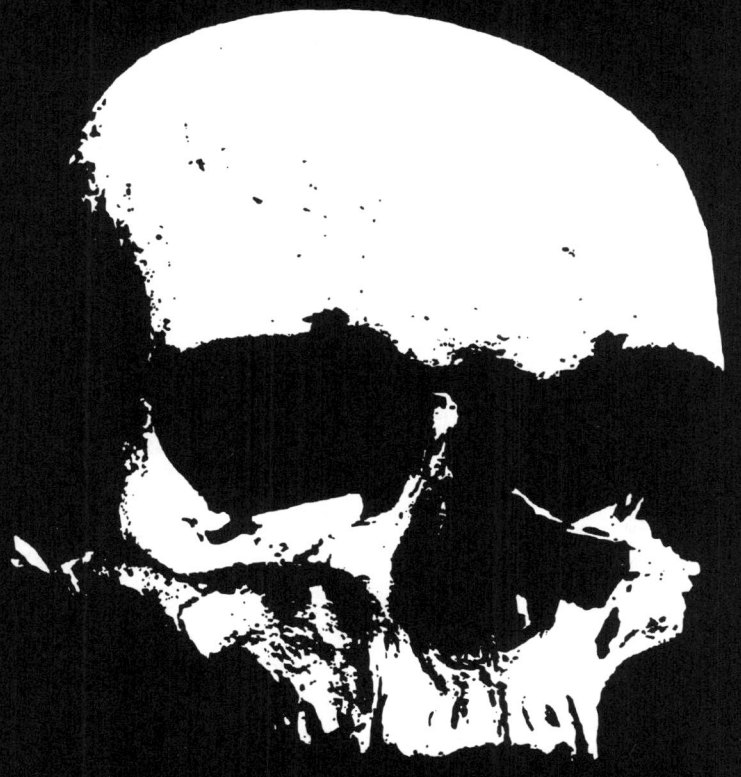

Hal Roth

According to newspaper reports and private diaries, Patty Cannon died in the Sussex County Jail in Georgetown, Delaware, on May 11, 1829, while under indictment for four murders. More than one hundred and seventy years later, few particulars about her life are known, and nearly every reported circumstance, including the account of her death, is controversial.

Patty is usually described as having been robust and handsome, with dark hair and eyes and a Gypsy-like appearance. She is reputed to have been fond of music and dance and apparently was a witty and engaging conversationalist. A woman of great strength, Patty is credited with having been capable of lifting as much weight as any man on Delmarva. In her final years, one writer claimed, she visited with prominent Dorchester and Caroline County families, telling fortunes and entertaining her hosts with amusing tales.

But at the time when abolitionists were expanding efforts to liberate slaves by secreting them north via the Underground Railroad, Patty Cannon, her husband Jesse, Joseph and Ebenezer Johnson, and a gang composed of as many as thirty outlaws were engaged in kidnapping blacks, both freemen and slaves, from Pennsylvania, Maryland, Delaware, and Virginia and selling them to slave dealers and plantation owners from the Carolinas through Georgia, Alabama, Mississippi, and Louisiana.

The identity of the individual who initiated the Cannon-Johnson traffic in human life is not recorded, but in that enterprise the principals gained a reputation surpassed by no one else. General robbery also appears to have been a common sideline for the gang—perhaps even river piracy—and murder was a casual act when deemed necessary or when emotions exploded.

During Patty's time the Delmarva Peninsula had many large plantations. Homes were scattered, and their residents were mostly self-reliant. Contact with neighbors was infrequent, transportation was slow, and the tavern played an important role by providing food, drink, lodging, and often entertainment to weary travelers.

Joseph Johnson's Tavern, usually described as the center of operations for Patty Cannon's gang, was located at the intersection of two narrow, unpaved roads on the state line between Maryland and Delaware, several miles west of Seaford. Today, the quiet, tidy community surrounding the heavily remodeled structure is named Reliance; then it was known as Johnson's Corners or Johnson's Cross Roads. It was a relatively remote, sparsely settled area with large tracts of timber.

Less than an hour distant, however, lay a highway by which a horseman or coach could travel to Dover, Delaware's Capitol, or north to Philadelphia, New Jersey, or New York. Several ferries and wharves were situated on the Nanticoke River only a few miles from the crossroads, and this navigable Chesapeake tributary was a convenient artery for reaching northern ports or for moving human contraband south.

In 1808 Congress made the further importation of slaves illegal, and the British Parliament, in 1811, also ended slave trade to its colonies, but because of the annexation of Louisiana in 1803 and the expansion of the plantation system in southern states, the demand for labor increased. Slavers continued for a while to land their smuggled cargo on American shores—as many as 250,000 additional Africans—but the trade decreased as risks intensified. The price for a strong, healthy, male bondsman sometimes rose to as much as a thousand dollars and more, a fortune in the early nineteenth century.

While the importation of Africans became a criminal offense, slave dealing within the borders of the nation remained a legal and lucrative enterprise almost everywhere except Delaware. Laws in the First State forbade exportation of human property for sale. In the neighboring Chesapeake region, however, as profits from the plantation system there began to decline, a brisk trade in Negro lives was inaugurated between Maryland, Virginia, the District of Columbia, and the Deep South.

Then, as the number of available slaves dwindled, the population of free blacks within our boundaries became an ever-widening attraction for kidnappers. Easily accessible from the gang's headquarters, the Maryland counties of Dorchester, Caroline, and Talbot alone, in 1820, were home to nearly six thousand African Americans who had been born outside the bonds of slavery or had labored for or purchased their liberty.

But even in states where laws prohibited slavery, freedom and independence for these individuals were tenuous at best. They had little education, few rights, and the white majority, through economic and political control, dictated where they would live, work, and even travel.

While the movement against slavery had begun in the North a century before Lincoln issued the Emancipation Proclamation, there was little affection for free blacks on most of the Delmarva Peninsula, and few whites demonstrated any concern for their welfare. Kidnappers raided their cabins and fields or lay in wait to ambush them on country lanes. Some poor blacks were enticed with the offer of jobs, shelter, or assistance. Then, often beaten senseless, chained, and shipped hundreds of miles from home, they found little opportunity for recourse.

With its strong Quaker influence, Delaware had passed a law in 1793, which imposed a penalty on kidnappers of thirty-nine lashes to the bare back, well laid on. After an additional hour in the pillory, with the offender's ears nailed to it, the soft portions of the ears were cut off. This last forfeiture was generally suspended by the governor.

Except for the efforts of Delaware's Attorney General and the courts of that state, the Cannon-Johnson gang experienced little challenge on the peninsula. Even then it took years, chance, and the personal crusade of a Philadelphia mayor to bring an end to the operation.

Patty Cannon's primary biographers have been novelists, and perhaps that is the only direction the literature could have taken. Because of the remote vicinity she frequented and the nature of her business, she lived a secret life and left a mostly-hidden and well-swept trail.

The Monster's Handsome Face is a collection of the oral tradition along with documents and selections from the most influential literature addressing the subject of this notorious woman and her associates. It is the most complete review of Patty Cannon's life and legend that has been published to date.

∞

The Monster's Handsome Face by Hal Roth—ISBN 0-9647694-2-5

Inquire at your favorite bookstore or order an autographed, hardcover copy from the publisher:

Nanticoke Books
Box 333
Vienna, MD 21869

$19.95 plus $2.00 shipping